CLICK TO PLAY

CLICK TO PLAY

David Handler

severn
House

This first world edition published 2009
in Great Britain and in the USA by
SEVERN HOUSE PUBLISHERS LTD of
9–15 High Street, Sutton, Surrey, England, SM1 1DF.
Trade paperback edition published
in Great Britain and the USA 2010 by
SEVERN HOUSE PUBLISHERS LTD

British Library Cataloguing in Publication Data

Handler, David, 1952-
  Click to Play.
  1. Murder–Investigation–Fiction. 2. Investigative
  reporting–Fiction. 3. Presidential candidates–California–
  Fiction. 4. Detective and mystery stories.
  I. Title
  813.5'4-dc22

ISBN-13: 978-0-7278-6811-4   (cased)
ISBN-13: 978-1-84751-175-1   (trade paper)

All Severn House titles are printed on acid-free paper.

Typeset by Palimpsest Book Production Ltd.,
Grangemouth, Stirlingshire, Scotland.
Printed and bound in Great Britain by
MPG Books Ltd., Bodmin, Cornwall.

This one is a shout out to the great
Billy Persky, who was nice enough to
offer me a seat at the table

ONE

Dear Mr Thayer – I apologize for reaching out to you this way but I must be so careful that no one finds out. I know you to be the single most trusted and influential journalist in America, and I need your help. I've just produced my memoir, you see. This is no standard showbiz memoir. It's much, much more explosive. A matter of life and death, actually. Not that I mean to sound melodramatic.

Mr Thayer, I know the real truth behind the most famous murder spree in Hollywood history. You may think you know everything there is to know about the Bagley Bunch murders. Trust me, you don't. You may think that I'm the hero of the story. Trust me, I'm not. Only a handful of people know what really happened to the cast of America's most beloved TV sitcom family during that awful week in the summer of 1972. I'm one of them. I was there. And now I'm ready to tell the whole world the truth. If I don't then next month's presidential election will seal the deal on an utterly ruthless political takeover by Herbie Landau, our creator, our lord and master, our father who are in prime-time heaven.

Herbie must be stopped. His puppet, Senator Gary Dixon, must be stopped. I know Gary Dixon. I was his co-star on The Big Happy Family for fourteen straight seasons. Believe me, Gary is not who he seems to be. His entire career is built on a lie. The public must know the truth before it is too late.

Everyone thinks they know what happened to the Bagley Bunch. They don't. I do. I participated in the cover-up. And now I must end my silence. Not that I flatter myself into thinking I can actually change the course of history, but if I don't try I'll never forgive myself.

Sir, I desperately need your help. Don't try to call me. I won't answer. Don't try to reach me by email or fax. I won't respond. Above all, tell no one about this. Just come. American Airlines has a daily non-stop flight to Los Angeles that leaves Dulles International at seven fifty-five a.m. There are seats available on Thursday's flight. Book one. A driver from Yslas

Security will be waiting at LAX to meet a Mr Lesh of Warner Bros Records. That's you. Don't share your real identity with him. Don't trust him. Don't trust anyone.

I repeat, tell no one about this. And destroy this letter immediately. I'll explain everything when you get here.

Sincerely,

Tim Ferris

PS. This is not a joke.

The world's oldest living Pulitzer Prize winner woke slowly that morning. As always, Ernest Ludington Thayer was amazed to be waking up at all.

His mind stirred first as he lay there in his eighteenth-floor apartment on Riverside Drive and West 114th Street, walking distance from Columbia. He and Elly had bought it when he started teaching at the School of Journalism back in seventy-six. Lying there, eyes shut, Thayer could picture her putting the coffee on in their big eat-in kitchen overlooking the Hudson River. See her standing there in her shawl-collared silk robe and mules, a long, lean Boston Brahmin who'd never lost her shape or her spirit. Truly the greatest of dames. Gone twelve years now. Part of him, a huge part, was ready to give up his daily struggle and join her. And yet he had to soldier on. Elly would want him to.

He heard the phone ring in a distant room. Little Mike answered it.

As Thayer lay there, waiting for his calcified body to awaken, he could recall every single word of a dumb-assed cream-puff question about the Smoot-Hawley Tariff he'd once asked Franklin Roosevelt. Yet his memory of last night was blurry. As was his bedroom, he observed, squinting at his surroundings. He could barely see without his eyeglasses any more. Although his eye doctor had assured him that his vision was phenomenal for a man of ninety-four. 'My Energizer bunny,' he'd called Thayer. To which Thayer had responded, 'Sir, I am not a rabbit. Yours or anyone else's.'

Ernest Ludington Thayer was a journalistic giant, the courageous muckraker who'd toppled Joe McCarthy. He had covered and known eight US presidents and three major wars. He had also outlived his era. Lippmann was long dead. So was Scotty Reston. And Red Smith, whom Thayer had idolized both as a writer and a man. They had all passed on. Thayer was the last man standing. Or lying down, to be more accurate, clad in his red flannel nightshirt and the thick wool socks he wore because his long, bony feet were always cold. The left one was completely numb, actually. His right ankle ached, as did his right hip, left shoulder and both hands. His neck was so stiff he could neither turn nor lift his head.

He heard heavy footsteps now and in lumbered Little Mike O'Brien, the pride of Far Rockaway, Queens, who was sixty-eight years old but would always be Little Mike out of respect for his late father, Big Mike, the much-beloved bartender at Toots Shor's. Little Mike was thickly muscled, with scar tissue over his eyebrows and a battered nose that zigzagged in three different directions. He'd fought forty-two heavyweight bouts as Irish Mike O'Brien. Battled Jerry Quarry to a draw but lost to him in a rematch. After he retired he became Thayer's regular driver. A lifelong bachelor, he'd moved in with Thayer three years ago. Cooked and did his marketing for him. And walked him to and from the journalism building for the weekly investigative reporting class Thayer still taught.

'Rise and shine, Ernie,' he hollered, standing there by Thayer's bedside in his knit shirt and slacks.

'Go to hell,' Thayer snapped.

'That's what I like about you. Always a kind word to start the day. Come on, let's move it. You summoned young Liebling up from Washington to see you this morning, remember? That was him on the phone just now. He caught the Acela. He'll be here in less than an hour.'

'Ah, excellent.'

Little Mike handed him his glasses. Instantly, the world around Thayer became much clearer. Which may or may not have been a good thing. Then Little Mike pulled back the bedcovers and went to work massaging Thayer's skinny, hairless legs, rotating each ankle, bending each knee and pushing it toward Thayer's chest. After several minutes of such torture Thayer swung his feet around, stepped into his slippers and rose slowly to his feet, wavering in mid-air as Little Mike helped him on with his robe.

'Can you make it to the john by yourself, Ernie?'

'Kindly allow me to piss with what little is left of my dignity.'

Thayer stepped creakily into the bath and emptied his bladder, clutching for dear life on to the handrail Little Mike had bolted to the wall. As he washed up he stared at the liver spots on his trembling arthritic claws and thought: *These are my grandfather's hands, not mine.* That sagging, hawklike face in the mirror wasn't his either. It belonged to a horribly disfigured villain in an old Dick Tracy comic strip.

He drew himself up to his full height, which had once been an imposing six-feet four, and hobbled down the hall to the kitchen. The apartment had twelve rooms crammed with books and framed, signed originals by Thurber, Hirschfeld and countless others. His favorite room was his office, with its wood-burning fireplace, antique pool table and the mammoth roll-top desk that once belonged to his father, the editor of the old *St. Louis Star*. Parked on the desk was the same Underwood that he'd been writing on since the fifties. He refused to use a computer.

The latest presidential campaign news was blaring away on the television in the kitchen. Senator Gary Dixon, the California Christian conservative, was leading Ohio Democrat Don Oakley by twelve percentage points in the latest Gallup and Associated Press polls. Last evening, the exultant one-time TV actor had delivered an impassioned speech on abstinence-only sex education to an overflowing crowd of true believers at the New Orleans Superdome. Flanking him up on the stage were his talk-show hostess wife, Veronica, the former Miss America who'd been his co-star on *The Big Happy Family*, and Jeremiah Staunton, the insipid tele-vangelist who was his so-called spiritual guide. 'With less than three weeks remaining until Election Day,' gushed the campaign correspondent, a young fashion model with Barbara Walters hair, 'it appears that absolutely nothing can derail the Dixon Express.'

'Kindly turn that shit off.'

Little Mike promptly did. 'Ernie, is it the presentation of the news that bothers you or the news itself?'

'It's the fact that it *isn't* news,' Thayer responded as he sat slowly at the table. 'It's spin. It's mo. It's whatever the hell they're calling it this week. That's not reporting. It's a weather forecast. What's hot. What's cold. Which way the wind is blowing.'

He'd rail away at his students for hours on the reporter's sacred duty never to accept what he or she is told by those in power. To seek out the full truth independently and then tell it straight. 'You are the only hope the public has,' he'd thunder at them. 'If you don't hold the government accountable then who will?' That was why the J-school still kept him around. That and because it would be too embarrassing to ask him to retire.

There was orange juice and coffee, a soft-boiled egg, buttered wheat toast. Thayer tapped at the egg, carefully peeling back its shell with his talon-like fingers. He scooped out a steaming spoonful and sampled it, his tongue finding the roughness of the temporary crown his annoying young dentist had put in last week. 'Excellent egg, Mike. You have a genuine gift.' He sniffed at the air with his long nose. 'And what's that delicious aroma?'

'My navy bean soup,' the old fighter replied, beaming at him. 'It'll be good to see Hunt again, won't it?' Hunt was a favorite of Mike's due to the young man's championship prowess as an Ivy League middleweight when he'd been an undergraduate at Columbia.

Thayer allowed himself a smile. 'It will be a distinct pleasure.'

Hunt Liebling, no relation to A.J., was the best pupil Thayer had ever taught. That kid would run right through a brick wall for a story. He had Halberstam's guts, Sy Hersh's vision, Izzy Stone's bullshit detector and Johnny Apple's way with a phrase. For his master's project he'd exposed an illegal high-stakes dogfighting ring in the South Bronx. Burrowed so deep into their operation that he got himself thrown in jail *and* stabbed in the chest. But the *Village Voice* bought the story and he was on his way. After 9/11 he'd anticipated the Iraqi invasion by more than a year. Flew over there on his own, learned the language and cultivated sources on the street. No one had filed eyewitness dispatches like his on the bloody, chaotic aftermath of Operation Shock and Awe. Soon he was taken on by a New York newspaper. He stayed in Baghdad for two more years, then reported from Tehran and Moscow before they brought him home as a national correspondent. He went underground as an illegal migrant worker for six months and won a Pulitzer for his series of articles on the appalling working conditions in America's meat processing plants. After that, they sent Hunt to Washington to spice up their White House coverage.

And that had been Hunt Liebling's downfall. He didn't play the Washington game. Wasn't deferential or tactful. And when Herbie Landau's Panorama Communications bought out the newspaper Hunt found himself constantly at odds with the new editorial regime. He left the paper after an unusually rancorous public battle. Ran his own Internet blog now, producing a torrent of political muckraking and commentary that was an indispensable – and often uncredited – source for the drones of the mainstream media. There wasn't a reporter in Washington or New York who didn't read *huntandpeck.com*.

Thayer could no longer shave himself. His hands shook too much. Little Mike shaved him every morning in the barber's chair they'd installed in Elly's dressing room. He sat back in the chair while Little Mike ran the badger shaving brush under hot water and got some lather started in the old pewter mug. He lathered Thayer's face and neck, wheezing through his broken nose.

'When are you going to get that deviated septum fixed?'

'I'm fine,' Little Mike grunted.

'You're not fine. You can barely breathe through that thing. And God knows how loud you must snore at night. If you had a woman in bed with you she'd need earplugs.' Thayer raised a tufty white eyebrow at him. 'Do you?'

'My sex life is my own business, Ernie.'

'I'll take that as a definitive no.'

In fact, Little Mike was so hungry for female company that he'd joined up with *secondchances.com*, an Internet dating service for older singles. Lately, he'd been pinning his hopes on Marie, a Long Island widow whom he'd escorted to a Wednesday matinee of *Phantom of the Opera*.

The old prizefighter had laid Thayer's clothes out on the bed for him just the way Thayer's mother once had. Starched white broadcloth shirt. Striped tie already loosely knotted. The gray flannel suit from Brooks. A navy blue cashmere sweater vest. Black wool socks. Polished cordovan loafers.

When he was dressed Thayer made his way into his study, settled his achy bones into his desk chair and lit his first Gauloise of the day. He allowed himself one cigarette after each meal and a fourth with the generous slug of twenty-one-year-old Balvenie single-malt Scotch that he sipped every evening before dinner.

Little Mike built a new fire atop the glowing embers from last night's fire and got it going. 'I can't believe you still smoke those damned things.'

'They make me look sexy.'

Young Liebling arrived ten minutes early. Little Mike let him in. Thayer could hear their voices out in the hall. After a brief stop in the powder room Hunt joined them in the study.

Hunt Liebling didn't enter a room – he charged in head first, bristling with intensity. 'Dude, your powder room toilet keeps running,' he informed Little Mike, his jaw working on a wad of Bazooka bubble gum. 'I'll fix it for you before I split but you really ought to yank out that old tank and put in a Toto low-flow. They use one-third the water per flush. Green is good.'

'I'm all for that,' Little Mike said. 'Still doing your road work?'

'Got to. If I don't my head will blow clean off.'

At age thirty-two Hunt Liebling remained blessed – some might say cursed – with a surfeit of energy that he quelled with a manic workload and hours of punishing exercise. With his olive complexion and Roman beak of a nose he'd always reminded Thayer of Carl Furillo of the old Brooklyn Dodgers, the greatest right fielder Thayer ever saw until he saw Clemente. Hunt was a compactly built five-feet nine, no more than 165 pounds. But he had the alert, smoldering gaze of a fighter. And there was something about his wrists and shoulders and the way he stood there coiled on the balls of his feet that left no doubt that he could take care of himself. He'd never acquired the polished look of an Ivy League-trained professional. His curly black hair was uncombed, his growth of beard at least three days old. He wore a rumpled V-neck sweater over a sprung T-shirt, beat-up leather jacket, jeans and running shoes. A knapsack was thrown carelessly over one shoulder. Hunt was who he was, a Swamp Yankee from Brattleboro, Vermont – and proud of it. Paid his way through Columbia working summers for his father, who'd been a plumbing contractor. Hence the preoccupation with low-flow toilets.

'How have you been, sir?'

'Never ask a man my age how he feels. He just may tell you and it'll cost you an entire morning.'

'I made a fresh pot of coffee, Hunt. Did you eat breakfast?'

'I'm good.'

'Young man, he didn't ask you how you were. He asked if you wanted breakfast.'

Hunt let out a laugh. 'Still busting balls.'

'Evidently they still require busting.'

'I'll just have some coffee, Mikey,' he said, jaw continuing to work his gum until he became aware of Thayer's icy gaze. 'Shit, I forgot.'

Little Mike fetched him a tissue before Hunt could deposit it on or under a piece of furniture, which was his usual habit. Then the old boxer retreated to the kitchen.

'How is Miss Reiter working out?'

'She's awesome. I can barely keep up with her.'

'And your web site? Are you turning a profit?'

'Breaking even,' Hunt answered with a shrug. 'Almost.' He was a reporter, not an entrepreneur. The strain of keeping afloat was getting to him, Thayer observed. There were dark worry circles under his eyes. And he seemed agitated, even by his usual high-strung standards.

Little Mike returned with Hunt's coffee, then slid the study's pocket doors shut and left them alone in there.

Thayer promptly pulled open the middle drawer of his desk, removed an envelope and set it before Hunt. It was a cheap white business-sized envelope, the sort sold in packs of forty at any drugstore or supermarket. It had a 44-cent stamp on it. Thayer's name and Riverside Drive address were hand-lettered in neat, careful handwriting. There was no return address, though it bore the postmark of Balltown, Iowa, 52073.

'There's actually such a place?' Hunt wondered.

'Population seventy-three, according to the 2000 census. It's a farming community outside of Dubuque.'

The letter inside was handwritten on plain white copier paper. Young Liebling stood by the brass desk lamp and read through it twice – first quickly, then slowly and carefully. Then he put it down on the desk and said, 'You're going, I hope.'

'No, *you* are. I'm too fucking old to go. I've written a letter

of introduction for you. I trust that Mr Ferris will be OK with
it. He'll have to be. He has no other choice.'

Hunt studied the letter once again. 'He's written you from
Los Angeles?'

Thayer nodded. 'That's where he lives.'

'So what's with this Balltown postmark?'

'A cutaway, I imagine. Afraid someone would intercept it.'

'Thursday is tomorrow. When did you get this?'

'Yesterday. He's cutting it rather close, admittedly.'

'That should be the least of our concerns about him.'

'Meaning . . .?'

'That he might just be a paranoid, delusional whack job.
Tim Ferris was a huge child star back in TV's golden age.
They're all crazy, aren't they?'

'Kindly avoid sweeping generalizations. I did some home-
work on our Mr Ferris last night. He's not living out of the
trunk of his car. He's president of this Yslas Security that he
refers to. It's the largest home security outfit in Southern
California. Furthermore, seven people – six of them famous
– did die during that week in seventy-two. The Bagley Bunch
killings were for real. And, at this point, there's no reason to
believe he is not for real.'

'Well, if that's the case then you've already made your first
mistake.'

'Which is . . .?'

'You've told someone else about it – me. Little Mike, too,
I'm guessing. Not that *I* mean to sound melodramatic.'

Thayer glowered at his one-time pupil before he said, 'I
don't suppose you feel like a Scotch, do you?'

Hunt went over to the oak bar, removed a pair of heavy
Ashburton glasses and poured each of them two fingers of
the Balvenie.

Thayer sipped the good Scotch, feeling it warm his old
bones. Feeling something else as well – the heady thrill of a
huge story. Hunt felt it, too. He could see it in the young
man's eyes.

'He says that Dixon's career is built on a lie.'

Thayer nodded. 'Yes, a thoroughly bedrock American
political tradition.'

'What *kind* of a lie? The Bagley Bunch case was solved,
wasn't it?'

'The killer was killed – shot dead on Stage Four of Panorama Studios. Never brought to justice in a court of law. But I do take your point. It's hard to imagine what remains to be said.'

Indeed, book upon book had been written about that terrifying week when someone had systematically stalked and murdered the former cast members of America's all-time favorite TV sitcom, *The Big Happy Family*, a Herbie Landau creation that was the No. 1 rated show on network television from 1954 until its triumphant run ended in 1968. Coming right on the heels of the Tate-LaBianco killings, the Bagley Bunch spree had set off a frenzy of panic in Los Angeles, its residents convinced they were in the grip of another marauding Manson family. But the truth about the killer's identity had proven even more horrifying.

'Ferris was there that night on Stage Four. That much we know.' Thayer gazed broodingly into the fire before he added, 'Mind you, there's a chance that he's fronting for the Dixon camp. Whatever he hands us may be designed to blow up in my face, à la the Dan Rather debacle back in 2004. If they can take me down it would certainly stifle the media's enthusiasm for going after Dixon.'

'Why would they bother? The election's already in the bag. Besides, *what* enthusiasm? I know bloggers who are trying to dig up dirt on Dixon, but the mainstream press? Forget it. They all work for Herbie. And Dixon's his boy.'

'That being said,' Thayer stated slowly, 'will you go?'

'Are you kidding me? I'm already gone.'

'Not so fast, young man,' Thayer cautioned him. 'I need your assurance that you'll be heading out there in search of a story – not revenge.'

'Sorry, I can't give it to you. I'd be lying if I did. And, Mr Thayer, I don't know how to lie to you.'

Or how to let go of a grudge. Not that Hunt didn't have just cause. It was Herbie Landau's ruthless quest for empire that had cost him his job on the newspaper. Hunt had ferreted out a major scoop about how the Pentagon was deliberately under-reporting American troop casualties in Iraq in 2005 and 2006. His story set off such a political firestorm that his main Pentagon source panicked and insisted that Hunt had misrepresented his remarks. The White House demanded the paper issue a retraction. Meanwhile, Panorama Communications was in the process of buying up Peck Broadcasting, owner of eighteen television and forty-four radio stations in the Southwest, an acquisition that required FCC approval. Thayer had heard from several people he trusted that the White House told Herbie if he ever wanted his FCC approval then he would see to it that his paper retracted its story. He had. Bailed on Hunt even though Hunt had excellent notes – and was vindicated a few weeks later when the *Baltimore Sun* confirmed his story. Hunt responded by publicly blasting not only the White House but Herbie Landau personally, for which he was promptly fired. Then Herbie launched a whispering campaign that Hunt was mentally unstable. No other major newspaper would touch him after that. And so Hunt Liebling had said hello to the brave new world of online journalism.

'Never let your editorial judgment be clouded by personal feelings,' Thayer lectured him sternly. 'Slay them with cold, hard facts.'

'Don't I always?' Hunt paced the study, his fists clenching. 'Sure, I'd love to stick it to Herbie. But I'm totally neutral about Dixon. Aside from the fact that he wants to tear down the wall between church and state, ban the teaching of evolution in our public schools, kick twelve million brown people out of the country and kill all Muslims, I think he'd make a heck of a president.'

'Kindly sit down. You're giving me a stiff neck.'

Hunt threw himself into a leather chair and tossed back the rest of his drink. Then he was back up on his feet again, pacing. 'Will you destroy that letter like Ferris says?'

'I will not. It's documentary evidence that he contacted me.' Thayer tucked it back into the middle drawer of his roll top with his collection of fountain pens, all of which were in perfect working order. 'Let's discuss expenses, shall we? Because I don't intend to stick you with the air fare.'

'I can handle it,' Hunt said, waving him off.

'You don't need traveling money?'

'I've got money,' he insisted, hoisting his knapsack back over his shoulder.

'Of course you have.' Nonetheless, Thayer had made out a $5,000 check to *huntandpeck.com*. He didn't consider it a donation. It was an investment in the future of independent American journalism. Little Mike had it waiting for Hunt on the hall table along with his letter of introduction. 'Have a safe trip, son. Come back with a page-one story.'

'Count on it,' Hunt Liebling said, grinning at him. Then he slid open the pocket doors and went barging out the same way he'd barreled in.

It was the last time that Ernest Ludington Thayer would ever see his talented young protégé.

TWO

Hunt almost tore up the old man's check three times. Once as he was riding the No. 1 subway train downtown, his jaw working on a fresh piece of Bazooka. Once more while he was waiting for the Acela in Penn Station's non-luxurious seating area, which bore a remarkable resemblance to a holding pen for steers soon to be converted into McPatties. And yet again as the Acela hurtled him back to Washington and he sat there, check in hand, staring at Thayer's shaky signature. His mentor used a fountain pen. Did anyone else in the world still use a fountain pen?

Hunt fully intended to tear it up, but he couldn't. He owed his landlord two months' back rent. His credit cards were maxed out. And now he had to scrape together plane fare to Los Angeles *and* cover his living expenses while he was out there. The painful reality was that Hunt couldn't afford to chase after the Tim Ferris story. Thayer knew that. The old man knew everything. So Hunt slid the check carefully back in its envelope, even though accepting it didn't sit right.

I'm a journalist, not a faith-based charity.

He reached into his knapsack for his laptop and downloaded the Toto low-flow specs for Little Mike:

Mikey – I'm attaching the info on the toilet I was telling you about. Just order one and I'll install it for you next time I'm there. Hell, it's the least I can do.

It was great to see you and Thayer again. Between us, I'm thrilled he's chosen me to be his legman on such a mondo story. But don't tell him that. His head might swell. Keep your left hand up. You always drop it when you're tired. That's how Wepner nailed you in the ninth.

Best regards, Hunt

Hunt also sent off a quick email to his kid brother, Brink, an actor who lived in New York. Ordinarily, Hunt would have stopped by to see his closest living relative while he was in the city. But today that just wasn't possible.

It still felt like summer back in Washington. The sun was warm, the afternoon breeze balmy. She was waiting out in front of Union Station for him with her top down, honking her horn as if he wouldn't notice that red '87 Alfa Romeo Spider Veloce five-speed convertible. Or her standing there beside it, waving both arms at him.

Clarissa Colette Reiter – known to one and all as C.C. Reiter – was Thai on her mother's side, Russian Jewish on her father's, and all gorgeous. Tall and willowy with shiny black hair down to her butt, skin like silk, eyes the color of jade and truly amazing cheekbones. She wore a cropped T-shirt, skin-tight jeans and an interesting assortment of toe rings. Driving barefoot, she insisted, gave her a better feel for the car.

'Thayer kicked in a donation of five large,' he informed her as she tore out of there on to Massachusetts Avenue, Steve Earle's *The Revolution Starts Now* blaring from her customized sound system.

'Cool. We can pay off our server.' C.C. had a clipped, ironic way of speaking. Hardly moved her mouth at all. 'They're threatening to cut us off.'

'Pay yourself while you're at it.'

'Right, chief.'

'Don't call me chief. I'm not Perry White and you aren't Clark Kent.'

'Want to hear *my* good news? The Justice Department subpoenaed our favorite Miami Congressman's credit card records. And found *six* charges to the Starz Escort Service when he was home during the August recess taking the pulse of the voters. Either a lot of the voters in his district are hookers with irregular heartbeats *or* he's just a horny fur ball.'

'My money's on the fur ball angle. Great stuff, C.C. How'd you get it?'

'I have a guy at DOJ.'

'I'll just bet you do, you bad girl.'

'Ow, Daddy, don't hurt me,' she pleaded, maneuvering through the late day crawl of government wage slaves with the total self-assurance of someone to whom nothing bad has ever happened. It was the same way C.C. Reiter chased after a story, ate an ice cone and made love. As she worked her way on to K Street, lobbying capital of the un-free world, Hunt found himself recalling the rainy night when she'd first shown up on his doorstep.

Hunt had the ground-floor apartment – or English basement, as the Georgetown realtor affectedly called it – in a chic Federal row house on Dumbarton Street that belonged to Wolf Blitzer's urologist. Hunt's place was decidedly un-chic. The dark, heavy furniture was from the 1940s. The wallpaper was floral, the carpeting musty. And the entire apartment smelled of moth-balls and chicken soup. You'd have sworn that someone's grandmother lived there. Actually, the urologist's had until her recent death. Hunt took it, furniture and all. Turned the dining room into his office, installed a speed bag in the living room and he was home – his only other contribution to the decor being the dirty clothes, empty pizza boxes and beer bottles that were strewn everywhere.

That night, he'd been at his computer finishing off a 3,000-word open letter to Will Shortz in which he blasted the *New York Times* crossword puzzle editor for using 'Govt. clean air watchdog' as the clue for the three-letter answer 'EPA' in that morning's puzzle. Hunt's argument: Shortz ought to call the Environmental Protection Agency the '*Former* Govt. clean air watchdog' since it had devolved into little more than the lobbying arm of the extraction industry. Hunt was citing example upon example of how the EPA had caved to big oil when suddenly his worst techno-nightmare happened – the screen just went blank. His posting, for which he had no back up, was gone. Didn't exist. Never had. Which sent him into such a frenzy of frustration that he tore off his beloved No. 14 Steve Grogan Patriots jersey and attacked his speed bag. *Whacketa-whacketa-whacketa.* His hands quick, muscles popping, sweat pouring down his bare chest. *Whacketa-whacketa-whacketa . . .*

He almost didn't hear someone banging on his door. Cursing, he went and opened it. Standing there in a trench coat was one of the most beautiful young women he'd ever seen in his life. He stared at her, speechless, his bare chest heaving. She stared back at him. Specifically at the jagged three-inch knife scar that slanted across his left pec.

The first words he said to her were, 'Wow, it's raining.'

The first words she said to him were, 'Wow, Professor
Thayer was right. Nothing gets past you.'

'And you are . . .?'

'That C.C. Reiter person who's been emailing you endlessly.
You told me to stop by.'

'Oh, right.' She'd just graduated from the J-school. Did her
undergraduate at Princeton. Father and mother were both
surgeons in the Philadelphia area. 'Sorry, but now is not a
good time. My computer just ate a whole evening's work.'

He was closing the door in her face when C.C. said, 'Did
you undertake a hard-drive recovery search?'

'Of course I did,' he assured her. 'Um, that is what exactly?'

'Here, read this.' She handed Hunt an envelope and charged
past him into the apartment. 'What's the file named?' she
called to him as he fetched his Grogan jersey.

'Shortz – with a Z.'

She got busy at his keyboard, her slender fingers flying,
her focus so intense she barely seemed to notice the wads of
Bazooka that were stuck to his monitor like talismans. All
sorts of unfamiliar menus and tool bars raced rapid fire across
the screen until . . .

'Here's something,' she murmured. 'It opens with "Dear
Will" and . . . blah-blah . . . closes with, "Kindly stick to
puzzles and stay out of politics, about which you obviously
know nothing. Sincerely, Hunt Liebling." Is that it?'

'My God, can you save it?'

'Just did.'

'What are you, a geek?'

'I prefer to think of myself as technically adroit. It's less
pejorative.'

'And you say you know Thayer?'

'You didn't read his note yet, did you?' she said reproach-
fully.

He hadn't. He'd been too busy looking at her gleaming
black hair and flawless skin. Couldn't help himself. He hadn't
slept with a woman for three months, seventeen days and six
hours, not that he was counting.

She glanced around at the clutter, wrinkling her tiny nose.
'This place is just like my freshman dorm. I didn't know
grown-ups could live like this.'

'OK, try to find the key flaw in your premise.'

'You're not, in fact, a grown-up.'

'Bingo.' He opened the envelope and read Thayer's note:

Dear Hunt – This will introduce you to Miss Clarissa Colette Reiter. She is my best pupil, and has expressed an interest in doing the sort of Washington-based independent insurgent work you are presently doing. You may be able to help each other. Warmest regards, Ernest

'I've been dying to meet you,' she explained, coloring slightly. 'You're kind of my idol. Seriously, is there anyone in this town who you trust?'

'Sure,' he replied. 'Myself. Tell me why you want to be a journalist.'

'Because somebody has to keep the fuckers honest.'

'It isn't easy. They'll try to co-opt you. And they're very good at it. They'll flatter you. Feed you little morsels to make you feel special. Not many people are strong enough to stand up to power. Are you?'

'I can stand up to anyone. How did *you* get into it? Your father a journalist?'

'No, but he respected them. That's how I got my name. My brother and me both.'

She frowned at him. 'Hunt is . . .?'

'Short for Huntley. As in Chet Huntley. My brother Brink is named for David Brinkley. Huntley and Brinkley anchored the evening news for NBC way back in the old days. Had this famous sign-off where they said, "Good night, Chet" and "Good night, David." They were Pop's idea of the kind of smart, classy guys he wanted us to be.'

'OK, but why didn't he name you Chet and David?'

'You'd have to ask him that. Except he's dead. He and my mother both. Next question.'

'Would you take me on as your intern for a few months?'

Hunt didn't play well with others. But C.C. Reiter had two huge things going for her. She was a techie. He'd been looking to upgrade so that the blog could handle streaming video. Second, she was willing to work cheap. And, OK, three things – he was ga-ga over her from the second he saw her standing out there in the rain.

They were in bed together by the end of her first week,

which they agreed was incredibly unprofessional, but the attraction was too strong to resist. They just looked at each other and they knew. Same as they knew she'd move in with him. For those first few weeks they were thermonuclear together. C.C. hooked him up with a turbocharged server that gave him the uploading capacity he wanted. Set up a direct link so that his loyal readers could make electronic donations. Took control of his finances. Paid his bills. Kept him afloat – or at least tried. At first, Hunt supervised her reporting closely. C.C. took editing well. She wanted to learn, had a keen bullshit detector and was fearless. Soon she was working her sources over the phone like an old pro, coaxing, flirting, never taking 'no' for an answer. Within a month she'd taken over the blog's weekend postings. Her reporting was thorough and careful, her writing forceful. She was even easy to live with. Had no rules.

Well, one rule: no wads of bubble gum on the monitor ever again. Ever.

But by the end of the summer Hunt sensed that something was changing between them. Maybe it was being together twenty-four hours a day. Maybe it was his own well-proven limitations as a boyfriend: every relationship he'd been in had ended with a woman telling him that he wouldn't make emotional room in his life for someone else. Not that C.C. said any such thing. She just turned chilly on him. Labor Day weekend she went home to see her folks for a few days. When she returned they were done as a couple – he knew it as soon as she walked in the door. She told him she'd be honored to continue interning for him but that was she was moving in with a college classmate a few blocks away.

To his surprise, their new arrangement worked out fine. C.C. was still at his place eighteen hours a day. Still an enthusiastic, invaluable worker. And they were still friends. Just friends without privileges.

And now they were stopped at a red light on Pennsylvania Avenue with Warren Zevon blasting out of her stereo. C.C. reached around behind her seat for a gift-wrapped box. 'For you.'

He tore open the wrapping paper, peering at his gift suspiciously. 'A *new* smart phone? The one I've got is only six months old. Did it already get dumb?'

'No, but this one's totally boss. Here, look, you can Twitter . . .'

'I report the news. I *don't* tweet.'

'And you can file voice messages directly on to the blog. Won't even need your laptop any more. Just enter your password and you're in. I've already programmed it for you.'

'But I like having a keyboard.'

'It has a touchpad right here, see?'

'I'm not a thumb troll. I need a real keyboard that I can pound.'

'It's a cell phone, not a heavy bag. And this is a wireless world, Hunt. You've got to learn how to live in it.'

The light turned green. She floored it onto M Street.

'Who'd you get the offer from?'

'The *Post*.' Her mouth tightened slightly. 'They want me to cover Capitol Hill.'

His heart sank, but he forced a big smile on to his face and said, 'Congratulations, Reiter. It's about time they noticed you.'

'You're not going to talk me out of it?'

'No way. I'd just be holding you back. We both know that. But could you stick around for a week or two? I have to leave town.'

'No prob. I told them I'd need a little time. Where are you . . .?'

'Los Angeles. I need a seat on the seven fifty-five a.m. flight out of Dulles tomorrow. Also some cash from the ATM if there's any left in the account.'

'What's in LA?'

'Maybe nothing, maybe the Holy Grail. Don't ask me what it is.'

'Because I'm leaving?'

'Because that's how the source wants it.'

'You've never shut me out of a story before.'

'I've never had a story like this before.'

'Does Thayer know? Is that why you went to see him?'

'I have no idea when I'm coming back, but I'll continue posting. I can take my laptop and this . . . thing. And, hey, thanks for putting up with me, Reiter. I know I'm not easy to get along with.'

C.C. let out a laugh. 'Get out! This has been nothing but a party. Want me to find you another intern?'

'No, that's OK. I was never really looking for one in the
first place, remember?'

His flight to Los Angeles left two hours and forty minutes
late. No one bothered to explain why. They lost another half-
hour sitting on the tarmac after they touched down at LAX.
All of which gave Hunt time to power his way through *This
Is Not The End*, the authoritative 823-page history of the Bagley
Bunch murders that had been written by the reporter for the
Los Angeles Times who'd covered the murders. Hunt needed
to brush up. He wasn't alive in the summer of 1972. Plus he
was no fan of *The Big Happy Family* – the heart-warming,
much beloved TV oldie was strictly his idea of saccharine
goo. Hunt couldn't relate to the plastic-fantastic Bagley Bunch
that gathered around that same dining table every week in that
solid colonial home at 271 Maple Lane in Smithfield, USA.
Kindly, beautiful mom Jane, in her chiffon dress, high heels
and pearls. Wise and patient dad Walter, in his corduroy sport
jacket with the leather elbow patches, the one he changed into
when he got home from the office where he went and did
who the hell knew what. There had been five Bagley kids.
Gary Dixon played Walt Jr, the straight-arrow big brother.
Tina Shea was blonde, popular Laurie. Kelly Graham was
Barbara, the smart one. Kip McManus played Eddie, the wise
guy. And Tim Ferris – known back then as Timmy – was the
adorably freckle-faced baby brother with the pumpkin head
and squeaky voice known to one and all as Beanie. An entire
generation of Baby Boomers had grown up identifying with
the Bagley kids (who were no longer kids by that summer of
seventy-two – Gary Dixon was thirty-three and Tim, the
youngest, twenty-five). Even now, a half-century later, young
viewers by the millions continued to be enthralled by the feel-
good white middle-class mythology of *The Big Happy Family*.
The reruns ran day and night on nostalgia-oriented cable
TV channels.

Hunt didn't think of Herbie Landau's sitcom creation as
entertainment. He considered it a drug. But he wasn't flying
out to LA because of any old-timey sitcom. This was about
the presidential election. It was about the future.

There was a driver waiting for him outside of the baggage
claim area with the words *Yslas Security* stitched in gold over

the breast pocket of his shiny black suit. The placard he held read: *Lesh – Warner Bros. Records.*

'Is that all of your luggage, Mr Lesh?' he asked Hunt politely.

'I'm good,' answered Hunt, who was accustomed to traveling light after working overseas. Everything he'd need for a couple of weeks in LA was crammed either in his knapsack or his shoulder bag. In his wallet he had $450 in cash – every penny in his account until Thayer's check cleared.

It was hot in the bright October sun. Hunt stripped off his leather jacket before he jumped in the back seat of the black Lincoln town car. His driver steered them out of the airport and on to the San Diego Freeway heading toward the West Side.

'Can you tell me where we're headed?'

'Make yourself comfortable, sir. We have a ways to go.'

Hunt knew his way around LA. Knew that when they didn't get off the freeway at either Santa Monica or Wilshire that they were not heading for Century City or Beverly Hills. Instead, they cruised past Sunset and climbed over the hills into the San Fernando Valley, where the ochre-colored smog hung heavy and low. They didn't get off at Ventura Boulevard, gateway to Studio City. Just kept on going out into the sun-baked flatlands of Van Nuys until they got off at Devonshire, which took them past several shopping centers before they turned into the parking lot of the Pacoima Grand Prix, a go-kart raceway. The lot was deserted, the raceway no longer in business.

Hunt's driver stopped in front of the padlocked entrance, hopped out and opened Hunt's door for him. 'Someone will be along to pick you up, sir.' Then he drove off and left Hunt there.

Hunt stood with his gear in the broiling sun, smelling the hot tar of the trash-strewn parking lot and wondering what the fuck – until a black Ford Explorer pulled in ten minutes later and approached him.

The driver who got out was in his sixties but very fit looking. He had a bristly gray crew cut, wide-set blue eyes under a bony shelf of a brow and ears that folded forward like a bobcat's. He had on a short-sleeved blue button-down shirt, tan slacks and hiking shoes. On his left wrist he wore a huge skin-diver's watch. On his face a very pissed expression. 'I don't know you,' he snapped.

'That makes us even, dude. I don't know you either.'

'Where's Ernest Thayer?'

'He can't travel, so he sent me.' Hunt handed him Thayer's letter of introduction.

He tore it open and read it. 'It says here that you have his complete trust.' Glanced up at Hunt, frowning. 'Your name's familiar to me. Why is that?'

'Couldn't say.'

He pocketed the letter, shaking his head. 'I'm not sure how Tim is going to feel about this.'

'Well, get sure. Or take me back to the airport. Because if I stand here five more minutes I'm going to melt into the pavement.'

'Very well,' he said reluctantly. 'Get in.'

By the time Hunt climbed in next to him the man had warmed a bit. 'Sorry for this cloak and dagger business, Hunt. I had to make sure you weren't being tailed. I'm Duane Larue,' he said, sticking out his hand.

Hunt gripped it. '*The* Duane Larue?'

Detective Lieutenant Duane Larue had been front and center for every horrifying moment of the Bagley Bunch killing spree. Before that, he was one of the detectives who cracked the Manson case. A decorated hero.

'That was a lifetime ago,' he said quietly. 'I'm Tim's business partner now. And his friend. I look out for the guy.' Duane's alert blue eyes bored into Hunt's. 'I hope you're as good as Ernest Thayer says.'

'Dude, so do I.'

Duane took the Golden State Freeway back to the Ventura Freeway and headed north past Encino and Tarzana to Woodland Hills, where he picked up Topanga Canyon Boulevard and started climbing into the Santa Monica Mountains. He observed all speed limits, his eyes making regular sweeps of the rear and side-view mirrors for a tail. Topanga Canyon twisted and turned its way through hill country where there wasn't much of anything besides bone-dry brush waiting to catch fire the next time the Santa Ana winds blew. The mountains crested at a couple of thousand feet. There was a state park up there. Then they began their snaky descent into the remote colony of Topanga.

'They used to hang the freak flag high around these parts,' Duane recalled. 'Hippies of all shapes and sizes. These days, it's full of movie people.'

Hunt could practically smell the money as they cruised through the shopping district, where funky organic farm markets sat shoulder to shoulder with chic restaurants and boutiques.

Duane turned off at Topanga Canyon and steered them through a maze of steep, narrow canyon roads until they were way up high looking out over the sparkling blue Pacific. Huge trophy mansions clung to the hillsides there. Up ahead of them, at the very top of Saddle Peak Road, a walled hilltop estate sat behind a security gate.

'Hunt, I need you to duck down below the dashboard until we're inside.'

'You what?'

'We believe the front entrance is being watched.' Duane hit the brakes and stopped there in the middle of the road. 'Please duck down *now*.'

Hunt complied. The ex-detective triggered the front gate with a remote control and they passed on through, the gate slamming shut after them.

'OK, you can sit up now.'

They were in a forest of sycamores, oaks and laurels. There were twenty acres in all, he later learned.

'Our security system is state-of-the-art,' Duane said as they started up the steep private drive. 'Motion detectors on all of the walls. No one gets in or out.'

There was a panoramic view of the ocean and a swimming pool fed by a twenty-foot waterfall. And, perched at the very top of the hill, there was a house unlike any Hunt had ever seen. Its walls were entirely of glass with support beams of steel. The roof was corrugated iron. It resembled, Hunt decided, a really big glass tool shed.

Duane parked by the front door. A steel front door more common to a factory than to someone's home. It swung open and out came a black woman in her sixties. She was a massive woman, particularly in the chest. She was also an inch or two under five feet tall. She examined Hunt with an intensely suspicious look on her face, then led them inside without a word.

The living room and dining area were one airy open space. The flooring was polished bamboo. The furniture sleek and modern. No cushions or rugs anywhere. Nothing but hard surfaces that gave the place a decidedly monastic feel. There was an open doorway to the kitchen. A hallway to the bedrooms. And there were observation decks. One looked out over the bone-dry canyons to the east. The other faced the Pacific. That was where Duane escorted Hunt.

Tim Ferris sat naked out there in the hot sun on a yoga mat. He was in the lotus position, backs of hands on his knees, gaze focused out at his amazing view, which ranged from Palos Verdes all the way to Point Dune. 'Remember to breathe,' he told Hunt softly. 'I've had visitors faint dead away out here.'

'I can believe that,' said Hunt, his jaw working on a fresh piece of gum.

The former child star had once been ruddy and handsome. Now he looked like a cross between a Gila monster and the late Roy Cohn. He was deeply tanned but not in a good way. His flesh had a yellowish cast, as if he'd been dipped in tobacco juice. His cheeks were sunken. And he was incredibly gaunt – spine, ribs, hip bones poking right out of his skin. Tim's head was shaved, his fingernails and toenails long, yellow and unsightly.

Before him on the deck sat a mug of what looked to be green tea. Also a little ceramic pitcher and saucer and a miniature brass gong. There was a bench alongside of the railing where Duane took a seat. A Kerry Blue Terrier lay in the shade beneath it watching Hunt through its long, floppy eyebrows. The dog bore an astounding resemblance to Casey, the Bagleys' dog on *The Big Happy Family*.

'Tim, Ernest Thayer's too frail to fly,' Duane informed him. 'He sent us a trusted associate named Hunt Liebling. Hunt has his own web site.'

'Hunt Liebling?' Tim looked up at him now, the whites of his eyes a ghastly yellow. 'You're the reporter who said that Herbie cared more about corporate profits than he did the lives of our soldiers.' His voice was weak. An old man's voice. 'You told the truth and he fired you. Remember, Duane? It was incredibly cool. *You're* incredibly cool.'

'Glad you thought so. Not many editors did.'

'In answer to your first question, Hunt, I have pancreatic cancer. They call it the silent killer. By the time they detect it you're already gone. It's eating my liver now. I have only a few weeks left. I've refused chemotherapy. I wish to die cleansed.' He paused to sip his tea. 'In answer to your second question, yes, that's Casey. Although he goes by Rudy. He's the sixth in a long line of Caseys. Still does occasional promo appearances for that overpriced dog chow of his but he's mostly retired. His trainer, Flynn Leverett, brought him to me from Santa Barbara when I got ill. Flynn inherited the Casey franchise from the old man, Perc. We're kindred souls. And Rudy's been a real comfort to me. Come say hello to our guest, Rudy.'

The Kerry Blue got up and approached Hunt, his pointy ears on alert. He was not a big dog, thirty-five pounds tops. And his coat wasn't so much blue as it was charcoal. Hunt held a hand out to him. Rudy growled and retreated to his spot under the bench.

Tim frowned at Hunt. 'Don't you get along with dogs?'

'I don't get along with anyone.'

'Maybe you'll do better with Lola.' He reached down and pinged the brass gong with a Fu Manchu fingernail. The short, massive black woman joined them. 'Lola, this is Hunt Liebling. He's a very distinguished journalist from Washington, DC.'

She nodded and said, 'Pleased to meet you, sir.'

'If you'd like anything to eat or drink Lola can get it for you,' Duane said.

'Actually, I could handle some lunch.'

Lola headed back inside to take care of it.

'Have a seat, Hunt,' Tim said. 'Relax.'

'I'm relaxed.'

'Then why are your fists clenched?'

'Force of habit. I spent a lot of time in the ring.'

'Were you any good?' asked Duane, muscular arms crossed before his chest.

'I held my own.' Hunt flopped down on the bench, his eyes falling on the little ceramic pitcher next to Tim's tea mug.

'My neti pot,' Tim explained, following his gaze. 'I use it to cleanse my sinuses with sea water. I'm purified by every breath I take, just as I'm purified by that glorious sun up there. They're keeping me alive. Not that I'm afraid of what's ahead. I accept that I'm on a journey. Soon, I'll be embarking on the next phase of it. That's what death is. That's all.' Tim spoke the words with Zen-like calm, yet his jaundiced eyes were those of a terrified animal.

Lola returned with a ham and cheese sandwich and a glass of milk. Hunt thanked her. She went back inside.

He parked his bubble gum on his plate and went to work on the sandwich. 'Want to tell me what you've got on Gary Dixon?' he asked, munching.

'A man in a hurry,' Tim observed, nodding his shaved head. 'That's cool. I'm one myself, sad to say. I reached out to Ernest Thayer because the public needs to know the truth. There will be fallout, Hunt. And it will be huge. You don't ever want to mess with people who believe they have God on their side. But I have to. I can't leave this phase of my life with what I've done hanging over me. My karma won't be clean. I need to tell people my story. Gary has played a huge role in it, but this isn't just about Gary. Or that week in the summer of seventy-two. Or *The Big Happy*, as we not so fondly called it. It's so much more than that. Child stars like us, we were tender young meat that got thrown to the lions. Not one of us got out unscathed. I mean, God, there's *so* much you don't know.'

'Such as . . .?'

He stared at Hunt for a second before he said, 'You don't know that my dear sweet Tina once told me she'd slept with fifty-six men by the time she turned twenty-one. Her first was our own loveable Herbie. He started banging her in her trailer back when she was a juicy fifteen.'

'Tina Shea was the first victim. She was staying in your bungalow in Laurel Canyon. That's where she was found.'

'With a needle stuck in her arm. She was supposed to be meeting the rest of us for dinner at the Du-Pars in Studio City. We met there every Friday, all except for the California GOP's poster couple – State Senator Dixon and his stuck-up wife, Veronica, were much too important to hang with us. Herbie always had big plans for him. Shot around him while Gary went to law school. Even wrote it into the show. Herbie wrote and directed Gary's political rise just like it was a spin-off of *The Big Happy*. I called it *Walt Jr Goes to Sacramento*. Anyway, yeah, we were at Du-Pars when Herbie . . .' Tim's thin voice faltered. 'He came and told us the news. The police were saying Tina ODed. I told them no way. Tina had gotten her life back together. She was clean. You'd have to hold a gun to her head to make her shoot dope again. But the fools didn't believe me. Except for Duane. He'd stopped by for a look because he said her overdose was . . . what was it you called it?'

'An untimely death,' Duane said quietly.

Tim leveled his gaze at Hunt. 'You don't know that my other sister, Kelly, with her goody-goody image and her goody-goody variety show, was actually seven-weeks pregnant the night *she* was murdered. No one knows that. It was covered up.'

'Oh, yeah? Who was the father?'

'Well, it wasn't her storybook fiancé. You do remember that Kelly was engaged to marry her handsome young minister, don't you? The one who'd served time in Oklahoma for assault, robbery and fraud under the name Joseph Wayne Timmons before he came west, opened a storefront ministry in Downey and started calling himself the Reverend Jeremiah Staunton.'

The very same Reverend Jeremiah Staunton who was now Senator Gary Dixon's spiritual adviser. The televangelist's checkered past was no secret. He spoke proudly, and often, of how the Lord had helped him overcome his youthful transgressions.

'Dude, who *was* the father?'

Tim wouldn't say. Just sipped his tea and kept going: 'You don't know that after we went off the air Kip became the number-one dope dealer in Hollywood. Herbie banned him from the Panorama lot when he found out Kip was peddling weed, hash and acid out of the commissary. You don't know the real Herbie. He was a bully and a screamer. Also a non-stop pussy hound who had three very bitter ex-wives scattered around the globe.' Tim's face darkened. 'His relationship with his own son, Errol, was utterly poisonous. They couldn't even be in the same room together.'

'Errol was a writer himself, wasn't he?'

'A very gifted one, funny as hell. Always chewed Beeman's Black Jack gum,' Tim recalled. 'Errol wrote for the Lampoon while he was at Harvard, then went right to work for the *Smothers Brothers Comedy Hour*. After CBS courageously yanked them for *Hee-Haw* he launched *Tricky Dicky*, his own radio show on KRLA. He used to do a drop-dead take-off of us – *The Big Sappy Family*. Remember, Duane?'

Duane just sat there, arms folded.

'You don't know about my on-screen father, Darren Beck,' Tim went on. 'Or about Glory Wills, who played my mother. And you for damned sure don't know about me. I was once a normal, happy six-year-old, Hunt. I never wanted to be a kid performer. But *Mother* was convinced that I was born to play Beanie. She *made* me audition. She *made* me . . . I'd get so overwhelmed by stage fright I couldn't leave my trailer. Mother would beat me with a hairbrush until I had welts up and down my backside. Then I'd throw up. But I went out there. And I was adorable. A star. A great big fucking . . .' He breathed in and out, struggling to calm himself. 'I even had my own talking Beanie doll. You pulled on a string and it said, "Talk to the Big Cheese – that's me." That stupid line of mine was so famous that Ike adopted it. Can you imagine what it's like being eight years old and having the President of the United States imitating you?'

'No,' Hunt said. 'No, I can't.'

'That doll freaked me out,' Tim recalled, shuddering. 'All of it did. I lived in a state of sheer terror for years – until Kip turned me on, God bless him. That's how I survived. By being stoned on weed and acid. The last five seasons of *The Big Happy* I was stoned every single day. And I was stoned when I recorded "Sugar on Top", my bubble gum hit.' He sang Hunt the refrain in a trembling falsetto: '"*You're sugar, sugar, sugar on top. Candy, candy lollipop. If looks could kill. Ooh what a thrill. You're my sugar . . .*" Remember it, Hunt?'

'Who could forget it?' Hunt sure as hell had. But the ex-child star was rolling. He didn't want to slow him down.

'I was stoned when I lip-synced it on *American Bandstand*. Stoned every time I went out and sang it on that bus and truck tour with Chuck Berry, Ronny and the Daytonas and Ike and Tina Turner. I stayed stoned until I flipped out but good on orange sunshine. It was the tumbleweed in the cul-de-sac,' he explained.

Hunt glanced uncertainly over at the impassive Duane before he said, 'The tumbleweed in the what?'

Tim said, 'My father left us when I was four. Which, trust me, is very disorienting. If you don't have a father when you're growing up then you don't know who to hate. Although I made out well enough. We lived in a little tract house on a cul-de-sac in Sepulveda, the outer reaches of the Valley in those days. The morning after a furious Santa Ana wind blew I went out early to play and found the hugest tumbleweed in the world sitting right there in the street. My father, whose face I couldn't remember, got a can of lighter fluid from the garage and told me to stand back. Then he squirted fluid on the tumbleweed and set fire to it with his cigarette lighter. Instantly, it flared two stories high. And just as instantly it disappeared into thin air. Years later, when I started flipping out, I couldn't look at a lit match without it turning into that fucking tumbleweed. It'd keep flaring, hotter and hotter. And there'd be sirens and the rumble of fire trucks and I'd get so overcome by terror that I couldn't come back from it. By seventy-two, hell, I'd already made three visits to the funny farm, where life is beautiful all of the time. I was out of the business by then. Chauffeuring talent around town for Steve Yslas, who was nice enough to give me a job. Steve was chief of security at Panorama when we were kids. Just a great, great guy. His daughter, Elvia, became my wife. I'd loved her since we were little kids. Not that I ever deserved her. Not the way I'd lived. She . . . Elvia had these huge, dark eyes that could always see right inside of me.' Tim's own eyes had filled with tears. He swiped at them, sniffling. 'I never could shake that damned tumbleweed. My shrink used to tell me to focus on something else within the picture frame of my memory. So I focused on the cigarette lighter in my father's hand. It was shaped like a small pocketknife. Had a painting of a pin-up girl on it, one of her tits exposed. But no matter how hard I tried I couldn't remember anything about the man who was holding it in his hand.'

It fell silent up there on Tim's mountain top. Hunt became aware of a rotten odor in the air, the smell of carrion that had been baking out in the hot sun. An odor, he realized, that was emanating from Tim.

He studied him, this dying man who'd just admitted to multiple mental breakdowns, and wondered if he'd been sent out here on a fool's errand. How reliable a source could Tim Ferris possibly be? True, he had a lot to say. But was any of it connected to reality? Why was he harping on a fifty-year-old story about a cigarette lighter and the father he never knew? 'Please don't take this the wrong way,' Hunt said, 'but did you reach out to Mr Thayer because *you* wish to confess to the Bagley Bunch killings?'

Tim let out a hoarse laugh. 'God, I wish it was that simple.'

'You wrote him that you're not the hero of the Bagley Bunch murders.'

'I'm not even close.'

'So who is?'

'You'll have to decide that for yourself.'

Hunt finished his sandwich, munching on it slowly. 'And how will I know if your story's true?'

'You'll have to decide that for yourself, too.'

'You've kept quiet for an awfully long time.'

'Because I wanted to stay alive. And that part wasn't easy. I'm only here because I had major, major leverage. Plus I was bought off. I became a rich man for my silence. Are you surprised?'

'I don't know you well enough to be surprised.'

A vulture circled lazily overhead. Tim watched it, clearly unnerved by its presence, before his frightened gaze returned to Hunt. 'Have you told anyone you're out here?'

'You've got nothing to worry about, dude.'

'I have *everything* to worry about. My phone's being tapped. My computer's been hacked into. Herbie has a warehouse in La Mirada filled with Cal Tech wonks who do nothing day and night but comb through peoples' phone records and credit card statements.'

'OK, then maybe they do know I'm here. I used a credit card to buy the plane ticket.'

Duane said, 'It's conceivable that you'd have other journalistic business in LA, isn't it? Nothing to do with Tim?'

'Sure. Why not?'

Still, Tim seemed panicky now. His fear was real. Hunt didn't doubt that. But was the cause of it real or was he simply out of his fucking mind?

'A crime was committed, Hunt,' he said in a low, insistent voice. 'I want to see some justice carried out before I die. I want to keep some very, very dangerous people out of the White House. I want . . .' Tim's eyes puddled with tears again. 'I want my daughter, Alicia, to be proud of me.'

'And where is she?'

'We don't speak any more.'

'Dude, that isn't what I asked.'

'I've produced a detailed, factual account of that week. The real story of what happened. There are two copies in existence. One is elsewhere for safe keeping. It's better for you if you don't know where. The other copy's right here in my wall safe. Although part of *it* is elsewhere, too. I'll explain why when the time comes.'

'Why can't you tell me now?'

'Believe me, I have my reasons.'

Hunt puffed out his cheeks, not liking this game at all. 'How many people have seen it so far?'

'No one has seen it. No one besides the three of us even knows it exists. Not even Lola. She doesn't know the combination to the safe either. Only Duane and I do.'

'She lives here with you?'

'In Van Nuys with her husband,' Duane answered. 'Tyrone will be by later to pick her up. Lola can't drive these roads after dark any more because of her cataracts.'

Hunt unwrapped a fresh piece of Bazooka and popped it in his mouth. 'Why don't you just hand this memoir of yours over to someone like the *LA Times* or *60 Minutes*?'

'Institutions are much too fearful. An individual has ten times more courage. The right individual, that is.'

'Have you already reached out to someone besides Mr Thayer?'

'No.'

'Do you have any kind of affiliation with the Oakley campaign?'

'I have zero interest in partisan politics.'

Hunt sat there, jaw working on his gum. 'OK, then let's roll. I can start reading it right now.'

Tim shook his head. 'It's not written down. I'm a performer, not an author. Duane bought us a Sony Digital Handycam and filmed me right here in the den telling my story to the camera. It took us a number of evenings. A few hours at a stretch was the most I could manage. At times, I found it necessary to leaf through my notes. What I mean is, you won't mistake it for a Ken Burns documentary.'

'I downloaded the mini-DVDs on to a computer so I could edit them,' Duane said. 'Then I burned them on to two sets of DVDs – five DVDs to a set. When I was done I destroyed the mini-DVDs and the camera. Also Tim's notes.'

'What about the computer? You said you were worried about hackers.'

'I used one that belonged to an innocent third party – a residential client of Yslas Security who didn't know they were loaning it to me.'

'You stole a computer from someone's house?'

'It was reported missing,' he allowed. 'And, yes, I destroyed it, too.'

'Sneaky,' Hunt said admiringly. Though he did wonder just how far Duane could be trusted. Clearly, the ex-detective had some larceny in his soul.

'You can watch the DVDs right here on the TV in my den,' Tim said. 'Each is between sixty and ninety minutes long. It'll take you a couple of days to digest them – I imagine you'll want to go through them more than once. If you have any questions when you're done . . .'

'Oh, I'll have questions,' Hunt promised him.

'I'll be happy to answer them until you and Mr Thayer are satisfied. When you are I'd like you to post them on that web site of yours for the whole world to see. You can do that, right? Because it's vital that we bypass Herbie's media machine. We have to get my story directly to the public.'

'Why don't you just post it yourself?'

'Because I'd be dismissed as a wild-eyed crazy, that's why. I need the endorsement of someone who has a reputation for integrity.'

'Which Mr Thayer and I both work very hard to protect.'

'I can respect that.'

'Fair enough. Is there a really cheap motel somewhere nearby?'

'I'd rather you not leave the property until we're done.'

'You'll be very comfortable in the pool house,' Duane added.

'No, no. I like to come and go as I please.'

'Too risky,' Duane said. 'If we book you a room anywhere nearby there's a chance Herbie's hackers will flag it. And we'd have to keep sneaking you in and out of the estate. Changing vehicles, taking different routes.'

'Dude, I can't just disappear off the face of the earth for two days.'

'Sure you can,' Tim said. 'That's nothing. I'm about to disappear forever. Right now, I need to lie down. I'm *so* tired . . .' He climbed slowly to his feet, a shriveled bag of bones. Duane led him inside.

Rudy stayed out on the deck with Hunt, studying him through his floppy eyebrows. Then Lola appeared with Hunt's overnight bag and led him down the stone steps to the pool house, Rudy tagging right along with them.

'Does he want to be friends?' Hunt asked her, glancing back at the dog. 'Or is he just afraid I'll steal the silver?'

'Mr Tim don't own no silver,' she responded, puffing slightly.

The pool house was a miniature version of the main house. All glass, with spare, modern furnishings. There was a flat-screen TV on the dresser. There were shutters for privacy.

'He'll stay in bed for most of the day,' Lola confided as she bustled around opening the shutters. 'Mr Duane stays right there with him. Hasn't spent a night in his own home for months. Just sits up with Mr Tim. Mr Tim has no one else. He don't even know where Alicia is no more.'

'Have you been with Tim a long time, Lola?'

'Longer than you been around. I took care of his mother in Sepulveda back when my Tyrone was in Nam. Miss Ina was left paralysed by a stroke. She and Mr Tim fought like crazy but he moved right back in so he could help take care of her. Well, not *in*. He slept out in the driveway in his old trailer. Bought it from the studio. It was shaped just like a Hormel tin. His canned ham, he called it. Mr Tim had his demons but he lifted himself up. Stayed positive right up until Elvia died of heart trouble four years back. He's never been the same since then. Mind you, Elvia had divorced him long before she passed. But he never stopped loving her. Didn't know how to.' Lola glanced around at the place. 'There are clean linens in the bathroom, toiletries if you need them. I'll leave your dinner in the kitchen. Anything else I can get you?'

'A length of rope.'

She frowned at him. 'What you be needing that for?'

'I want to jump rope.'

Lola's face broke into a smile. 'You mean like a little girl with pigtails?'

'I mean like a fighter who's in training for mortal combat. Why, do you have a problem with a man who jumps rope?'

'Sir, I've been dealing with show-business juveniles for some thirty-five years now. Not only Mr Tim but Mr Kip, whose eccentricities could make your hair stand right on end. You want to skip rope, you skip rope.' Lola went and fetched him a coiled rope from a garden shed next to the pool. 'Just don't break any of my lamps.'

Hunt was boiling over with pent-up energy. But a good, long run wasn't doable if he was confined to the property. He climbed into his nylon gym shorts and jumped rope by the pool. Followed that up with a half-dozen sets of one hundred push-ups and sit-ups. Then dove into the pool and swam laps, Rudy running alongside of him lap after lap, barking at him. Hunt took a shower after that and didn't much care for the way it drained. Cleaned out the trap and dug an earring stud out of there.

While he toweled off he flicked on the Panorama News Channel. The biggest campaign story of the day seemed to be that Don Oakley, whose beleaguered campaign kept selling him as a Man of the People, wore custom-tailored suits that ran him $2,800 apiece. It didn't seem to bother Panorama that Gary Dixon, noted paragon of prudent Christian virtue, paid a reported $4,000 to a Beverly Hills tailor every time *he* needed a new suit. *That* wasn't news. Hunt flicked around and found the story dominating all of the news channels. Outraged, he powered up his laptop and posted a stinging rant on the trivialization of modern American politics. 'We are deciding who will be our next president,' he wrote. 'Not the winner of *Project Runway*.'

Lola's husband, Tyrone, arrived at six in a green Buick Le Sabre to pick her up. Soon after that Hunt moseyed up to the house with Rudy on his heel. The dining table was set for one. In the kitchen Lola had left him a mountain of fried chicken, coleslaw, mashed potatoes, corn and biscuits. Also a chilled six-pack of Sam Adams. Hunt popped open a bottle and ate at the dining table, watching the sun drop into the Pacific as a cool evening breeze blew through the open house. He had just finished cleaning his plate when Duane joined him.

'Tim will sleep for a while now. I took the liberty of removing these from the safe . . .' In Duane's hand were the DVDs they'd made – boxed up in a set just like a season of *Seinfeld* or, more to the point, *The Big Happy Family.*

The words *Tim's Story One–Five* were scrawled on the side of the box.

Hunt counted four DVDs nestled in there. 'So there's a volume missing?'

'Not missing. Just somewhere else, like Tim said.'

'Where, dude?'

Duane settled into a chair across the table from him. 'He'll tell you when the time comes.'

'Why can't you?'

'Tim has a very fixed idea about how he wants to do things. And it's going to be his way all of the way. He . . . hasn't much time left.'

'This must be real hard for you.'

'I've known the guy my whole life.' Duane ran a hand over his gray crew cut, swallowing. 'I still can't believe he'll be gone soon.'

'You two grew up together?'

'I grew up with Beanie. Identified like crazy with that fool character of his. We were the same age. Always confused. Always screwing up big time.'

'So you were a fan.'

'His biggest. It was a genuine thrill to meet him and become his friend.'

'I have to ask you a rude question – how together is he?'

The ex-detective's jaw tightened. 'Do you mean is he nuts? He has his good days and his bad days. But his story's the real deal, if that's what you're wondering. Couldn't be more real. Trust me, I was there.' Duane poked at the boxed DVDs with a finger. 'We can get you set up in the den right now, unless you're tired from your flight and would rather wait until the morning.'

'OK, there's something you need to know about me.'

'And that is . . .?'

'I never get tired.'

THREE

Mr Gillis was late. But Ross the bartender told Tyrone to relax; the man would be there by eight thirty at the latest. So Tyrone Gilliam nursed a Coors at the bar and waited, wondering how he'd gotten himself into such a mess. Lola would kill him if she found out. Positively fry his big black ass. How in the hell did this happen?

Who was he fooling? He knew exactly how.

It started one night four months ago, right here in the Jack of Diamonds, a neighborhood place on Lankershim and Vanowen. The Jack got by on its after-work crowd, a mixed Valley crowd. Nobody getting too out of hand. Ross was into a bit of bookmaking. Nothing major, but he knew people.

Tyrone and his poker night buddies often met there for a beer before heading off to somebody's house to play. On that evening four months back Lola had been in a foul mood. Fussing at him for no reason. When the fellows took off for Encino to play nickel-ante Tyrone decided he'd rather just stay put and have another beer in peace.

That was when she walked in. She was a tall, slender black woman in her late thirties or early forties, elegantly dressed in a dark blue gaberdine suit. A very subdued and proper sort. Not much make-up or bling. No wedding ring, which was a bit surprising since she was a real looker with smooth skin and good long legs. Definitely a professional woman. Tyrone could tell by the way she carried herself.

He could also tell she wasn't accustomed to showing up in a bar by herself. She seemed very uncomfortable as she stood there glancing around. Reluctantly, she made her way to the bar and perched two stools over from Tyrone. When Ross moseyed over she told him she was waiting for someone. Ross nodded and left her alone.

'Don't you worry, miss,' Tyrone spoke up. 'He'll get here.'

'*Excuse* me?' she responded stiffly.

'Your date. He won't leave you hanging here all by yourself. Wouldn't dare.'

'Oh, I see.' She thawed perhaps one degree. Tyrone was no leering lounge lizard in tight pants, after all. He was a stocky, balding man of fifty-eight. 'I'm supposed to be meeting my friend Sheila here for a celebratory glass of wine. She's just been named vice principal of her school.' She looked down at her slim, plain wristwatch. 'I'm nearly a half-hour late. I hope she hasn't been here and gone.'

'If she has I would have seen her. She a black girl, miss?'

'No, a blonde. A big girl in her early thirties.'

'Don't believe she's been in.'

'Maybe I'll just wait here for another minute.'

'You go right ahead. I'll make sure no one bothers you. Fine-looking young lady such as you must be used to a lot of attention. I hope you don't have a jealous husband.'

She didn't go near that. Just checked her watch again and said, 'I wonder if Sheila forgot.'

'My name's Tyrone Gilliam. I'm a happily married man going on thirty-seven years. How about if *I* buy you that glass of wine?'

Her name was Saundra James. Saundra taught fifth grade at Fairburn Elementary on the West Side and owned a two-bedroom condo in Reseda that until very recently she'd shared with her elderly mother, an Alzheimer's patient who was now in a managed care facility. Saundra had been divorced from her husband, Ron, for five years.

The wine loosened her up a little. She grew quite animated when she started telling him about her fifth graders and how smart they were.

And he told her a little about his own job at the Department of Motor Vehicles right down Vanowen. Like the time this terrified little sixteen-year-old named Brandi flunked her parallel parking test and threw up all over the front seat of her mama's Acura. 'So *what* does she do?' Tyrone said, warming to the telling. 'Comes right back in one of those new models that parallel park themselves!'

Saundra laughed. He liked her laugh. Liked that she listened when he talked about his work. Lola no longer did. Not that Tyrone blamed Lola. His job was steady, but pretty much all he had to look forward to until his retirement was a thousand more Brandis. Or a stool behind the counter issuing plates to impatient, snarling people.

The two of them left the Jack together. Out in the parking they discovered that Saundra's Accord had a flat tire. Sighing, she reached for her cell phone to call AAA.

'Don't bother,' Tyrone told her. 'If you've got a spare I can change it for you in half the time it'll take for that truck to get here.'

While he was doing that Saundra confessed that being on her own could get awfully demanding sometimes. 'I'm absolutely thrilled to own my own condo. But I'm responsible for the upkeep, and there's no one around to take care of those little things.'

'What kind of little things, Saundra?'

'Like the exhaust fan in my powder room. It sounds as if it has rocks inside of it. I can't even use the thing any more. Now I have to call an electrician and he'll charge me at least sixty-five dollars just to come out and tell me—'

'I can stop by on Saturday morning and have a look.'

'I couldn't ask you to do that,' she said shyly.

'Believe me, it's no trouble at all.'

That's how it started. Him skipping his regular golf game to check out the recessed ceiling fan in Saundra's powder room. Her condo was furnished in pastel colors. Very sophisticated. Very Saundra, who looked exceptional in jeans and a polo shirt.

And the fan really did sound like it had a load of gravel inside.

'That motor's on its way out, Saundra. Needs replacing.'

She showed him where the circuit breakers were and fetched him a step stool. He disconnected the motor, unscrewed the assembly from its housing and pulled it free. The manufacturer's name and the part number were stamped on it. That night, he ordered Saundra a new one online from the factory in Akron, Ohio, and had it sent to his workplace. When it arrived he installed it for her and flicked it on. Purred like new.

As thanks, Saundra insisted upon cooking osso buco for him on his poker night. She was a very good cook. Had impeccable table manners. This was a real lady.

There were other little jobs that Tyrone helped Saundra with in the weeks ahead. Her leaky kitchen faucet. Her warped front door that stuck. He also went with her to make sure she got a good deal on a new set of tires for her Honda. Tyrone saw nothing wrong with helping Saundra out. He felt real easy and relaxed when he was with her. They'd talk about all kinds of things. He and Lola almost never talked any more.

It was all perfectly innocent – until the evening he stopped by to help her hang some Haitian folk art she'd bought at a flea market in Gardena. Right away, she was all tense and upset.

'Something wrong, Saundra?' he asked.

'Very wrong,' she confessed, her eyes shining at him. 'You'll have to stop coming by, Tyrone. I–I'm afraid I'm falling in love with you,'

She trembled when he touched her. She'd only been with three other men in her life. None in the past several years. She was starved for affection. And so grateful for his gentle patience. Afterward, she whispered, 'I feel safe with you, Ty.'

No one else had ever called him Ty. He loved it. Loved how silky smooth she was from head to toe. Loved the soft little cry she made when he entered her.

He loved how young he felt again.

From then on, Tyrone's entire life revolved around the two times a week he and Saundra made love. He gave up poker and golf – not that Lola knew, mustn't know – and started taking the little blue pills. Saundra would cook them gourmet meals at her place. They'd drink wine and dance to Al Green. They'd kiss and kiss and kiss.

He had never cheated on Lola before. But he was fifty-eight years old and he knew this was it for him – the very last chance he'd ever have to be with a lovely, classy young lady such as Saundra James. And so he took it. And he thanked God for it.

Their love affair had been going on for nearly a month when she informed him one night over Sole Meunière that she was putting her condo on the market.

Tyrone's eyes widened. 'Why, honey? Where are you going?'

'Someplace I can afford. The real estate market's very poor right now. I may have to sell at a loss. But if I don't sell then I'm staring at personal bankruptcy.'

'Saundra, why didn't you say anything before? If you're in trouble, I'm here to help. Tell me what's going on.'

Her adjustable rate mortgage had shot up $1,800 per month just as her mother's neurologist had recommended a new treatment that wasn't covered by Medicare. Before Saundra knew it she'd fallen three mortgage payments behind. Her lender was threatening to foreclose unless she sent them a certified check for $11,560 within the next ten days.

Tyrone hadn't hesitated to withdraw $12,000 from his retirement nest egg so Saundra could square herself. Lola kept close tabs of their finances so he had to put it back fast. Did so by borrowing it from his credit union without telling her. All this bought him and Saundra some time – until the transmission blew on Saundra's Honda. Now she was talking about moving in with her married sister in San Diego. Desperate at the prospect of losing her, Tyrone gave her another $6,000 right out of his checking account, then asked Ross to get him into the nightly poker game that ran next door to the Jack in a room at the Rodeway Inn. Tyrone considered himself a top-flight poker player.

'Can you handle the table stakes?' Ross asked him.

'I can handle them.'

Tyrone borrowed another $10,000 from his credit union just to make sure. Only he lost that $10,000 and another $10,000 he didn't have, putting him in such a deep hole he didn't know how he'd get out. It was Ross who put him in touch with Mr Siner, the pale, jiggly loan shark with the perpetual sheen of perspiration on his soft face. Tyrone borrowed $20,000 from him at 10 per cent interest per week so he could square his gambling debt and make his mortgage and credit union payments. When he fell two weeks behind on his interest Mr Siner advanced him another $10,000. Soon, Tyrone was into him for $40,000, which translated to $4,000 a week just on the interest alone.

That was when Mr Siner introduced him to young Mr Gillis, who was sitting there next to the loan shark in a booth one night, sipping a beer. Mr Gillis was a huge white man with a shaved head, a goatee and a menacing glower. Tyrone immediately felt sure that this goon was going to take him out in the alley and break his thumbs.

Except Mr Gillis turned out to be just as friendly as could be. 'My man,' he exclaimed warmly. 'It seems you've got yourself a small problem.'

'Yessir, I do. And I don't usually end up in this sort of situation, believe me.'

'No need to tell me that. I know you're a stand-up guy. But shit happens, right?' Mr Gillis leaned over the table toward him. 'Maybe we can do each other a good turn. I have a little problem myself. You help me out with mine and I can help you with yours. How does that sound?'

'Are you saying you'd pay off the debt?'

'Already have, Tyrone. I've taken it over from Mr Siner. You owe that money to me now.' Mr Gillis handed him a business card. 'I want you to call to this number for me now and then. A simple phone call, OK?'

Tyrone studied the card, which had nothing printed on it except a phone number with a 213 area code. No name or address. 'A phone call concerning . . .?'

'What goes on at the Tim Ferris estate on Saddle Peak Road – where your wife, Lola, spends each and every day.'

'How do you know where my Lola works?'

Mr Gillis shrugged his big shoulders. 'Common practice when we put money out there. Banks require collateral. So do we.'

Tyrone wondered just exactly who *we* was. The mob? What had Mr Tim done to piss *them* off? 'Why is that information worth money to someone?'

'Don't worry about stuff that don't concern you, Tyrone. You've already got enough on your plate. And I don't just mean the forty large. If Lola ever finds out about your teacher lady she will *kill* you. We don't want that to happen, do we?'

'No, we do not,' Tyrone murmured.

'So start taking an active interest in Lola's work,' Mr Gillis said easily. 'Report in on how Ferris spends his time. Who stops by to visit him. Who he talks to on the phone. You do this for me and we're square, word of honor. Is it a deal?'

'Can I think it over, Mr Gillis?'

'Of course. Take as much time as you need.'

That very same night a man who said he was a friend of Lola's phoned Saundra and threatened to throw acid in her face if she didn't stay away from Tyrone. Saundra told him about it the next day, sobbing.

And so Tyrone did as the man asked. He couldn't suddenly start pumping Lola about every little thing that went on up there. Dumb Lola wasn't. But as the weeks went by he did find out that Mr Tim's estranged daughter, Alicia, had somehow managed to change her identity – the dying man could no longer find her. Tyrone also learned the combination to the wall safe in his den. A feverish, delirious Mr Tim had insisted that Lola memorize it one morning. Any time Tyrone had information he would dutifully phone the number on that card and leave word. Mr Gillis would meet him at the Jack.

Tonight, Tyrone had something really big that Lola had just fed him on the way home. Only Mr Gillis was very late and Tyrone was getting antsy waiting for him. He had a date with Saundra and his little blue pill was kicking in. Felt as if he had a live ferret jumping around in his boxers.

It was nearly nine when the big man plopped down in the stool next to him. 'Sorry I'm late, my man. Kind of busy tonight.'

'Same here. I've got to be heading out real soon myself.'

'You have something for me?'

'Yessir, I do. And I thought this might be a good time to . . . that is, I was wondering if this would maybe square my tab.'

'We'll see, Tyrone,' Mr Gillis said in a tone that made it painfully clear that Tyrone would never, ever be square with him. 'What have you got for me?'

Tyrone told him: 'Mr Tim has company.'

FOUR

Herbie sat back in the recliner and sipped his hot cocoa, enjoying the late show in the plush, carpeted master bedroom suite of Ronald Colman's house. It was white carpeting, wall to wall. The whole house had it – every room except for the kitchen. The new Hollywood crowd, the kids, all wanted floors of imported tile or some exotic eco-friendly hardwood. Not Herbie Landau. He went for spotless white carpeting. And central air that kept the place at a cool, clean 70 degrees no matter whether it was winter or summer outside.

Herbie loved this rambling English manor house off Benedict Canyon. He'd bought it in the early Sixties for $99,500, which was a lot of money then. It had belonged to numerous others after Ronald Coleman lived there, but to Herbie it was the great star's house and always would be. Although he hadn't been aware of it until his second wife, Piper, found a file in the butler's pantry crammed with delivery slips and owner's manuals for every hot-water heater and kitchen appliance going back forever. And there it was from 1947 – the slip for a new Frigidaire to one Mr Ronald Coleman, 1003 Summit Drive, Beverly Hills. His phone number had been Crestview 5-7325.

These days, the place was worth north of $8 million. Partly that was inflation. It was also because Herbie had bought the house next door in 1982 and tore it down to make way for an Olympic-sized pool and his own personal two-acre orange grove. Herbie had always wanted his own orange trees. It had been a fantasy of his growing up in the slums of Bed-Stuy during the Great Depression. The balcony of the master suite looked right out over his grove. It was a satiny, elegant suite designed by Babette, an interior decorator who he'd dated for a while. The damned woman knew eleven different ways to say off-white, including soft white, winter white, antique white, colonial white, bone, ivory, eggshell and white linen. The relationship ended but the decor stayed. The only change he'd made was the addition of the black leather recliner that faced the bed.

He sipped his cocoa contentedly as he relaxed there in it and watched the late show. It was Herbie's favorite kind of late show – a live-action one for him and him alone. Two naked women, both top-flight porn performers, licking and sucking each other senseless on his king-sized bed. One a blonde, the other Asian. And if that Asian girl was a day over sixteen then his name was Bob Stack. He'd rented them from Eva, the same Hollywood madam who'd supplied Saundra James, a $1,000-a-night call girl back in her succulent heyday. And still a consummate pro. Saundra was getting $1,500 a week to play Tyrone Gilliam's lonely schoolteacher, not counting whatever else she conned out of the horny bastard.

The girls on the bed were talking dirty to each other now. Herbie had never cared for foul-mouthed women. He barked at them to stop it. They obeyed, happy to oblige. Hell, they'd have let him join in if he wanted. And ten years ago, maybe he would have. But at age eighty-one Herbie was happy just to watch.

Not that he was out of bullets. Hell no. He was on the verge of his greatest conquest of them all – the White House. He wasn't the candidate himself. Couldn't be. No one would elect a googly-eyed, frizzy-haired Jew from Brooklyn president of the United States. But he could *create* a president. *Own* a president. Same as he'd created and owned *The Big Happy Family*, then used that as leverage to take over Panorama Studios and build it into a multinational media empire. Running the table just like when he was hustling pigeons back at Sal's pool hall on Nostrand Avenue. Hustling, always hustling, so that no one could treat him the way they'd treated Harry Landau.

Herbie could never get enough of the two things that were denied him when he was growing up: power and pussy. He'd spent his entire adult life going after both. Never letting up. Never taking 'no' for an answer. Never feeling the slightest regret. Well, he did have the one regret: Errol. He would always feel bad about him. The rest? The frightened paper pushers who he'd shoved aside? The shallow, greedy bitches who he'd used and discarded? Not a chance.

I did what every other man alive would do if only he had the nerve.

The little Asian girl was going down on the blond now,

wiggling her smooth, perfect young ass at him. In a few short years it would sag and wattle just like every other woman's. Right now, it was like fine porcelain. *Get it while you can, honey.* And she was. Each girl was taking home $5,000 for a pleasant, safe two hours of work.

Which was, what, four years' pay for a working man back in the old neighborhood? Hell, Harry Landau never made more than $25 a week driving that produce truck of his through the streets of Brooklyn fourteen hours a day. They lived in a cold-water flat on Gates Avenue, smack dab in the heart of the Bedford-Stuyvesant section. Harry, Thelma and their little Herbie sharing a parlor, kitchen and two small bedrooms. The bathtub and sink were in the kitchen, toilet down the hall. During the summer the apartment was so stifling a person could barely breathe. Winters Herbie had to sleep with his coat and stocking cap on. He could see his own breath.

He was a sickly kid. Measles. Mumps. Pneumonia. Also painfully undersized. When he started Boys High he was four-feet eleven, weighed eighty-one pounds and had a dreadful stammer. The other boys would beat the snot out of him with appalling regularity. And if he stammered at the dinner table Harry would reach over and flick his ear with a fingernail the size of a clamshell.

Harry and Thelma snarled at each other constantly across that kitchen table. Harry in the sleeveless undershirt that showed off his big, hairy shoulders. The man was a gorilla. Thelma was a dour, snappish woman with milk-white skin and coal-black hair she combed straight back from a widow's peak. As she reached middle age Herbie's mother developed an uncanny resemblance to Bela Lugosi. Whenever she went down the block the neighborhood kids would taunt her, by crying, 'I vant to suck your blood!'

Herbie couldn't recall ever having a single pleasant conversation with his father. Harry Landau hated his life. The man got crapped on by everybody. As Herbie grew old enough to grasp this, he vowed that he would never be a loser like Harry Landau.

Herbie was a newspaperman before he was anything else. Worked nights as a copy boy at the *New York Daily News* while he was still in high school and dreamt of becoming a war correspondent. Instead he got drafted and spent the final months of the war on a flatulent old supply ship in the Pacific. To keep from going totally nuts he started a journal of those endless days and nights aboard the USS *Fairfax* with its crew of hapless oddballs. After the war, Herbie's comic diary became a best-selling book, *The Rub-a-Dub Tub*. By then he was studying drama at NYU on the GI Bill. Winchell hailed him as 'The Wunderful Wunderkind' when twenty-four-year-old Herbie transformed *The Rub-a-Dub Tub* into a Broadway hit. Soon he adapted it for the big screen, providing Tony Curtis with one of his first starring roles. After he'd turned it into a popular television series, too, Panorama approached him about creating a heart-warming family sitcom. Herbie agreed to do it if they'd also let him produce and direct. They said yes. And so *The Big Happy Family* was born.

By then, he had not spoken to his own parents for more than six years.

'Wrap your legs around her neck,' he ordered the writhing blonde now. Directing, always directing. '*Move* those hips . . . Atta girl . . .'

His private cell phone rang. It was Mort, who only called him this late if he had something important.

'What?' Herbie growled into the phone.

'I'm on my way over,' Mort responded.

Herbie's English butler, Milton, let him in downstairs. Herbie had always wanted a butler like Arthur Treacher, complete with the dead-trout face and bone-dry delivery. That was Milton.

'Mr Weingarten, sir,' he announced, tapping on the bedroom door.

Mort Weingarten wasn't fazed by the two naked girls on the bed. He'd spent a lot of years with Herbie. Took over his legal affairs back in the Fifties – and hadn't changed his look one bit since. Mort still wore a black suit, white shirt and black tie every single day. Herbie swore he hadn't aged a day either. When he was thirty the man looked fifty. And he still did, even though Mort was now in his late seventies. And he still had the same nickname – The Barracuda. Mort Weingarten was the most cold-blooded and efficient hatchet man Herbie had ever come across.

'Evening, Mort. Wanna fresh-squeezed glass of orange juice?'

'No, thank you.' Mort glanced over at the girls. 'Could we . . .?'

Herbie clapped his hands together. 'Nice job, girls. You can get dressed in the other room. Milton will show you out.'

They gathered up their clothes and padded out, smiling at Herbie uncertainly.

'We have a Gary problem,' Mort informed him after they'd gone. 'And you'd better brace yourself because it's bad. I've just heard from Baer.'

Joe Baer ran the top private investigative firm in the entertainment industry. Not many people knew this because he kept his name out of papers and had only one client – the law firm of Weingarten and Dewitt. Baer's job was to make certain that no one disturbed Herbie's world. Right now, that world revolved around Senator Gary Dixon.

'Spill it, Mort.'

'One of his operatives picked up something tonight from Tyrone Gilliam. It seems that Tim has a reporter staying in his pool house.'

'Are we sure it's a reporter and not a fucking swami or whatever?'

'Positive.' Mort cleared his throat, his pale, grayish tongue darting from his mouth. 'It's Hunt Liebling.'

The mere mention of that name was enough to make Herbie boil over instantly. 'Go and get him!' he roared at the lawyer. 'Bring him to me *right now* – before it's too late!'

FIVE

There were two of them and they came in quiet and quick soon after Hunt had turned off the nightstand light and closed his eyes, waiting for sleep to come. He hadn't locked the door to the pool house. Hadn't thought he'd needed to, the way Duane had bragged about the estate's security.

He'd thought wrong.

There were night lights on around the pool, so it wasn't totally dark inside the little glass house. As Hunt lay there, eyes open now, he could make out the one who was starting toward him – a no neck with a shaved head. Moving closer to the bed. Now he was right there next to Hunt, reaching for him with both hands and . . .

Hunt nailed him flush on the nose with a hard right. Then he sprang out of bed and slammed a left-right combination into the guy's midsection. By now the other one had flicked on a light. He was tall and rangy with stringy red hair. Hunt got low and drove him back against the bathroom door, kneed him in the groin and punched him in the left ear, which sent him to his knees. Now No Neck was on the move again – but before Hunt could turn around he felt a crack on the back of his head and everything went black.

When Hunt came to he was riding in the back seat of a Toyota Land Cruiser. His two visitors were in front. Red driving, No Neck riding shotgun. Hunt's head hurt and the flesh behind his right ear felt tender, but he wasn't bleeding. Or clothed. He was riding in the boxers he'd been sleeping in. His jeans and a T-shirt were folded on the seat next to him. According to his watch, it was nearly three a.m.

'What'd you hit me with?'

'A roll of quarters.' No Neck sounded as if he had a clothespin on his nose. He held a wadded-up tissue to it. 'I think you broke my fucking nose.'

'What'd you expect, dude? Who are you anyway? What do you want?'

'Just shut up until we get there, OK?'

They seemed to be heading downhill on Topanga Canyon. They stopped at a red light at Pacific Coast Highway. Ahead of them, across the highway, lay the inky blackness of the ocean. When the light turned green Big Red made a left and started in the direction of Santa Monica.

Hunt climbed into his jeans, pulled his T-shirt on over his head and gazed out the window, his head spinning – and not just from getting punched. He was still reeling from the three solid hours he'd spent watching Volumes One and Two of Tim's video memoir before bed. Still seeing Tim's gaunt, cancer ravaged face speaking directly, unflinchingly to the camera. Still hearing his thin, papery voice. A voice that had soared with righteous indignation when he spoke the incendiary words that Hunt would never forget as long he lived:

For three months, one week and four days, I was gay. And sexually active. And thirteen years old. The man who turned me out was that era's most famous closeted gay leading man in Hollywood not *named Rock Hudson – Darren Beck, the actor who played my kindly dad, Walt Bagley. Darren was gay. And, yes, I went down on him. Darren was my first. Gary Dixon, who played my big brother, was my second. It's true. America's next president is, and always has been, bisexual.*

Un-fucking-believable.

When he'd first met Tim out on his deck that afternoon, Hunt wasn't sure how coherent the dying child star's memoir would be. Turned out he was plenty with it. And what he had to say about Senator Gary Dixon, at least so far, was pure dynamite. The man went on at great length about Darren Beck's pool parties at his beach house in Trancas, parties that were attended by a gay mafia of studio execs, producers, directors and agents known throughout Hollywood as the Velvet Underground. According to Tim, a select handful of members were actors, too. Anthony Perkins was one, as was Montgomery Clift.

Darren always invited a bevy of boy toys who were anxious to chew their way to the top. Among them nineteen-year-old Gary. Gary was never forced to go to Darren's pool parties the way I was by Mother, who was convinced I'd come into close, personal contact with important people. Which, yeah, I did. Gary actually wanted to be there. He took to it. Took to me after *Darren passed me along. For several weeks, I was Gary's chief cuddle bud.*

When Tim's on-camera mother, Glory Wills, heard about how thirteen-year-old Timmy was spending his weekends she took it upon herself to round out his education at her own weekend retreat in Laguna – where, according to Tim, she climbed into his bed one night and bounced him off the headboard, ceiling and all four walls. After that, Tim's career as a gay boy toy was over. Except it wasn't. One of Darren's Trancas regulars, a sleazy B-movie director, had secretly filmed the Velvet Underground's exploits with a hand-held camera. He even spliced the footage together. Herbie Landau managed to get hold of the only print shortly before the guy died in 1965. Tim discovered this when, flush with his success as a bubble gum recording star, he marched into Herbie's office to announce he was leaving *The Big Happy Family.* In response, Herbie closed the drapes and screened the grainy, circa-1960 gay porn film that Tim took to calling *Monty and Me.* If Tim tried to leave, vowed Herbie, the film would surface on the Bel Air screening-room circuit.

He promised he'd turn me into an even bigger circus freak than I already was. And not just me. Gary was featured in that movie, too, don't forget. Herbie held it over him, too. Terrified that his fair-haired boy's sexual inclinations might jeopardize a bright political future, Herbie used it to muscle Gary into marrying Veronica Lane, the former Miss America who played his love interest, Sandy. And everyone lived happily ever after. Or so the public was led to believe.

But Tim knew better. Tina Shea's funeral was held at Hillside Memorial the Monday after her death. Herbie's son, Errol, showed up for it dressed in a top hat, tails and no pants. Father and son came to actual physical blows in the lobby of the chapel. At Tina's graveside, Tim's employer, Steve Yslas, told him that he had a job for him. The details of which were delivered to Tim that same day by a supremely ill-at-ease California State Senator Gary Dixon in the paneled study of Dixon's mansion in Pasadena's exclusive Oak Knoll section.

'Timmy, what would you say if I told you everything's about to come crashing right down on me?'

I listened to Gary's kids play Marco Polo out in the pool for a moment before I said, 'What's his name, Gary?'

'No, no. That stuff's strictly off-limits now. Herbie's orders. It's a woman. She's . . . pregnant.'

According to Tim, Dixon and their squeaky-clean on-screen sister, Kelly Graham, had been carrying on a secret love affair while she was busy preparing for her storybook wedding to the Reverend Jeremiah Staunton. Incredibly, the Reverend Jeremiah had been providing Dixon with religious counsel about the illicit affair – unaware that the other woman in the senator's life was, in fact, his own beloved fiancée. Gary had turned to the televangelist instead of his own minister out of sheer desperation.

'I'm searching, Timmy,' Gary told me. 'I'm always searching. The lord is testing me. Maybe he's punishing me, too. Jeremiah believes that He wants me to learn from my weakness. That this will make me a better, wiser leader. I've to got to deal with it, Timmy. If I don't then my political career is finished. I'm supposed to stand for everything that's decent and good. The voters can't know that I'm just another horny asshole with his dick in his hand.'

Kelly agreed to have an abortion even though she had profound qualms. Qualms she shared with Tim the next day when he chauffeured her up to the Santa Ynez horse country east of Santa Barbara in a Cadillac Fleetwood. Their destination was an ultra-exclusive so-called dude ranch where big stars went to have cosmetic facial surgery or an off-the-books abortion. Kelly did not go there to rest up from the grind of her variety show, *Thoroughly Modern Kelly*, as the world has been led to believe over the years. One more huge disclosure about that fateful trip: Kip McManus came along for the ride. Kelly wanted him along for moral support. Kip did not stay over at the ranch. He stayed at a motel called La Casa Del Mar a half-hour away in Santa Barbara under the name O. Nelson. But he was there.

'Timmy, I've been madly in love with Gary since I was thirteen,' Kelly confessed to me as I drove us north, Kip dozing in the back seat. 'He and Veronica have been so unhappy lately. I've tried to be a friend to him. We grew close. Too close. Jeremiah's a good man. I don't want to hurt him. That's why I had to break it off with Gary.'

'So it's over between you two?'

'It'll never be over. But it has to end. He won't divorce Veronica. I wouldn't want him to. They have the children to think of. Besides, I intend to marry Jeremiah and be a good wife. He and I are born again in our love for each other.

We've agreed not to sleep together until we're married. And here I am filming a weekly variety show while I'm seven weeks pregnant. I won't be able to hide it much longer. That's why I have to sneak out of town like this. Do you think I'm doing the right thing?'

'What I think doesn't matter. What do you *think?'*

'That I'm killing my baby to save all three of our careers, and that I'll regret it for the rest of my life.'

After they dropped Kip at his motel they drove on to the ranch, where Kelly underwent a physical exam by the doctor who'd be performing the procedure in the morning. She and Tim were served dinner before they settled into their cabins for the night.

I left my door open so I could enjoy the cool night air through the screen door. I also wanted to make sure nobody could drive up on us in the night without me hearing them. I flicked off my light and lay there listening to the coyotes howl. I found their calls strangely soothing. I dropped off quickly. Heard nothing else all night. Which was too damned bad. Because when I woke up I discovered that someone had gotten into Kelly's bungalow during the night and stabbed her in the neck four or five times. My Kelly was dead in a pool of blood. She and her unborn baby both. First Tina, now Kelly. Two of the Bagley Bunch were gone. And Kip? Kip had checked out of his motel less than an hour after we dropped him there. Kip was missing.

So concluded the second volume of Tim's memoir, which was proving to be even more morally depraved than Hunt could have imagined. One explosive insider revelation after another. A treasure trove of dirt. Not that this was Hunt's usual brand of muckraking. This was Hollywood Babylon, Revisited. But Hunt could not believe what this man had been sitting on for all of these years.

If it was true, that is.

Was it? Could Tim's story be substantiated in any way, shape or form? Because Hunt was going to need concrete corroboration. Something like, say, a first-hand look at that vintage snuff film he'd called *Monty and Me*. If it really existed. Being realistic, it was pretty damned unlikely that Gary Dixon could have kept his bisexuality under wraps for all of these years. Hell, that would rank as the mother of all cover-ups.

It couldn't be true, could it?

The traffic was very light on Pacific Coast Highway. They reached Santa Monica in no time. As they approached Will Rogers State Beach they slowed up and turned into the parking lot, which was deserted except for a black stretch limo. A chauffeur leaned against it smoking a cigarette.

Out on the wide swathe of beach a man sat by himself facing the water. He had a couple of lanterns lit and a small fire going.

'He wants to see you,' No Neck told Hunt. 'Don't keep him waiting.'

Hunt climbed out of the Land Cruiser and started across the soft sand, listening to the surf pound. As he drew closer he realized the small fire was a portable barbecue. A half-dozen garlic sausages were cooking away on it, the fat sizzling as it dripped down into the hot coals. Seated there on a plastic lawn chair, carefully turning the sausages with a long fork, was an old man in a loud Hawaiian shirt and baggy slacks. A paunchy, shriveled old man with buggy eyes, loose jowls and whorl of thinning white curls that made his head look way too much like a scrotum.

As Hunt stood there watching the great Herbie Landau turn the sausages he wondered if it was legal to have an open fire on this beach. Then again, people like Herbie didn't worry about such things.

'I didn't know a soul when I first moved out here from New York,' Herbie said, his eyes never leaving the sausages. 'My first wife thought this town was a cultural armpit and moved back right away. I'd drive down here by myself in the middle of the night and stay until the sun came up, wondering what the fuck I was doing here.' He peered up at Hunt with those googly eyes of his, studying him closely. 'What the fuck are *you* doing here, Liebling?'

'I got whacked on the head and dragged here, dude.'

'Don't call me dude. I'm too old and too rich.' There was an empty lawn chair next to Herbie's. Also an ice chest and a folding table laden with buns, mustard, paper plates. 'Have a knoblewurst. I get 'em flown in from the Lower East Side. I got Dr Brown's Cel-Ray tonic, too. Siddown, will ya?'

Hunt settled into the chair, which sank into the sand under his weight. Herbie forked a knoblewurst into a bun, smeared it with Gulden's mustard and passed it to him on a paper plate. Hunt took a bite. It was crisp on the outside, juicy inside, awesome good.

'Duane told me they had good security up there,' he said, munching.

'It's true, they do.' Herbie handed him a Cel-Ray tonic. 'But I'm a lot smarter than Duane Larue. Never forget that.'

Hunt took a swig of the tonic, wondering if Tim's good friend might be in Herbie's pocket. That would explain how Herbie's goons had slipped in and out so easily. It would also answer his next question: 'How'd you know I was here?'

'I have my ways.' Herbie chomped down on his knoblewurst, juice and spittle flying. He ate like a wild animal. 'I want to know why you are.'

'I'm working on a story.'

'*What* story?'

'That's my business.'

'See, that's where you're wrong. Anything to do with Tim Ferris is *my* business. He's one of my kids and always will be. I care about him, and right now he ain't doing so hot. I won't let some human blowtorch like you burn him. Why are you here, Liebling?' Herbie's voice was harder this time.

'I'm trying to dig up dirt on your boy. Tim agreed to talk to me.'

'Bullshit. Tim Ferris has turned down every single interview request for the past twenty years. Why would he suddenly say yes to you?'

'He likes my work – or so he led me to believe. By the time I got here he'd already changed his mind. All he's done is spout new age platitudes at me.'

Herbie's buggy eyes narrowed. 'He hasn't told you anything?'

'The man's just playing head games with me. I'm heading back to DC.'

'So why are you staying over in his pool house?'

'Couldn't get on a flight until later this morning.'

'Tim doesn't usually take in overnight guests.'

'I can be very persuasive.'

'Is that a fact? Then how come you haven't persuaded me to believe a single fucking word you've been saying?'

'That's your problem, not mine.'

'No, no. It's *all* your problem, Liebling. Tell me, has Tim shown you anything?'

'Like what?'

'Like a creaky old black and white movie that maybe appears to have some nasty stuff on it.'

Hunt's pulse quickened. It was real. *Monty and Me* was real.

'Because those things can be faked, you know. If I were you, I'd be extremely wary of a movie like that.'

'Why would Tim Ferris want to fake something?'

'To punish me.'

'So this is about you?'

'Damned right it is. Don't let his Brother Moonbeam act fool you. Tim Ferris is one bitter, vindictive son of a bitch. Also a pathological liar.'

'I thought you cared about him.'

'I do. And I'm trying to protect him – from himself. He's a fucking loon and has the papers to prove it.' Herbie took a long drink of his Cel-Ray tonic, studying Hunt thoughtfully. 'You probably won't believe this, given how we tussled before, but I like you. You've got moxie. You don't play by other people's rules. Neither do I. So I'll let you in on a little secret of mine. I have a dream . . .'

'Yeah, you and Martin Luther King.'

'Watch your mouth,' he snarled. 'And listen to me. I won't let you or anyone else get between me and my dream. Are we clear?'

Hunt polished off the last of the wurst, wiping his fingers on a paper napkin. 'Can I go now?'

'Siddown! Who do you think you're fooling, you little pisher? That blog of yours is a zero-revenue operation. Thayer just had to bail you out to the tune of five grand. You were so grateful you promised to install a new toilet for him, free of charge. Kind of touching, really.'

A shiver shot through Hunt's body. Duane and Tim weren't kidding. This man's geek squad had hacked right into his bank accounts and emails.

'Your career is toast and we both know it. Hell, your landlord would have evicted you three months ago if it hadn't been for your benefactress, Miss Reiter.'

'C.C.'s my intern. I pay her every two weeks.'

'She never deposits the checks, asshole. Just channels the money back into your so-called business. She went to Philadelphia over Labor Day, right?'

'Yeah, to visit her folks.'

Herbie smirked at him, a nasty smirk. 'That's all she told you?'

'Why, what else is there to tell?'

Herbie spelled it out for him in great detail.

'You're full of shit,' Hunt blustered in response.

'No, *you* are, my young friend. You're living in a dream world. You and your actor-slash-bum of a brother. You and Brink are very close. You didn't stop to see him while you were in New York and felt guilty about it. Told him you might be sending him something from out here.' Herbie shook his head. 'I didn't follow that whole business about the Alamo.'

'I have no idea what you're talking about.'

'Yeah, you do, but that's OK. It's not too late for us to straighten this out.' Herbie studied the surf, shoving his lower lip in and out. 'Can Brink act?'

'They thought so at Yale Drama School.'

'I could make a phone call tonight. By lunchtime he'll have a starring role in a prime-time network series we're shooting in New York.'

'Don't do me any favors.'

'Friends do favors for each other.'

'We're not friends.'

'I want us to be. That's how I like to handle things.' Herbie reached into the pocket of his Hawaiian shirt for a folded slip of paper. 'You accept donations, don't you? Here's a check for fifty grand. Take it. Go back to Washington and write your angry rants about how I'm trying to destroy free speech in America. Consider me one of your backers. I love irony. Always injected it into every week's episode. Irony and a nice little lesson. Know what the lesson of this episode is? That I will *not* let you crap all over my life's work.'

'You're not going to buy me off,' Hunt said, refusing to take the check.

'Thayer's money is good but mine isn't, is that it?'

'He doesn't expect anything in return. Just good reporting. Speaking of which, what's to stop me from posting this close encounter of ours?'

'Not a thing,' Herbie said easily. 'Aside from your life and the lives of everyone you hold dear. I can hurt you, Liebling. I *will* hurt you. Don't make me do it. Pack your bags and go back to Washington. I'll be monitoring the passenger manifests of the major airlines. I want you on a flight out of here within the next twelve hours.'

'Not a chance. You're not running me out of town.'

Herbie heaved a sigh of disappointment. 'Then I hope you're prepared to deal with what happens next.'

'Like a famous clown once said, bring it on.'

'Oh, I will,' he promised. 'This has been a friendly conversation. I admire journalists. Started out as one myself, you know. But next time, and I really hope there won't be a next time, our meeting won't be like this.'

'Oh, yeah? What'll it be like?'

Herbie Landau hocked and spat into the sand at Hunt's feet. 'I'll be the windshield and you'll be the bug.'

SIX

Marie lay in the center of the king-sized bed with her stomach churning. It was four in the morning and she couldn't sleep. Never could when she knew she had to hurt someone. Marie Farlese was very sensitive when it came to bruising other people's feelings. And so she lay there in her three-bedroom raised ranch in Mineola fretting as she watched an old rerun of *NYPD Blue* on the TV. Anything to fill the silence.

Marie had to break it off with Mike O'Brien. She knew that Mike liked her. But it wasn't going to work out between them and Marie didn't want to lead him on or invest any more time in their relationship. Mike was a nice man. But he wasn't for her. The online dating service, *secondchances.com*, did have a pain-free procedure for extricating yourself from a dead-end match. But she and Mike had gone beyond any such cold goodbye. They'd corresponded online for weeks. He'd taken her to see *Phantom of the Opera*, which had been perfectly pleasant except for the way his broken nose whistled in the silences. Marie just didn't see a romance happening. Mike was well into his sixties and he wasn't able to travel, which was very important to her. He was a care giver for his elderly friend, Ernie, who'd been a very distinguished journalist in his day. For Mike, life was all about Ernie right now.

And, being honest, Marie was looking for a man whose life would be about *her*. She was fifty-four years old and this was *her* turn to have fun again. Like she had back when she and her girlfriends would climb into their skintight Sergio Valentes and zip on down to Asbury Park to see Springsteen at the Stone Pony. They'd drink and dance and howl the night away. She was plenty hot in those days. A stacked, sassy blonde. One night, on a dare, she marched right up to Southside Johnny at the bar and made out with him. Jesus, that was thirty-five years ago. But Marie refused to believe it was all over for her. She'd signed up with *second chances.com* because she wanted to fall madly in love again.

Running through the park in the rain in love. Screwing your brains out on the kitchen floor in middle of the afternoon in love.

She couldn't see herself having sex on the kitchen floor with Mike.

Marie hadn't been with a man since she'd lost Dom twelve long years ago. He'd only been forty-six when he passed. Tall and muscular with wavy black hair. Dom had always taken good care of himself, too. Watched his weight, didn't smoke. He was a toy and hobby rep with an office in the Toy Center on Broadway and West 24th Street. Dropped dead of a massive coronary occlusion right there one day when he was talking to a buyer at Toy Fair. No warning, no nothing. He left her with the house, his life insurance policy and a modest stock portfolio. He left her alone, was what he did. Her parents were gone. Her sister Rose was gone. Her daughter, Suzanne, was out in Tucson with that husband of hers, Paul, who Marie couldn't stand. And she'd buried her baby, Dom Jr, back when he was only seven. The greatest heartbreak of her life. She could never forget those big, sad eyes of his in that tiny, yellowing body. 'Did you have a good day today, Dominick?' his pediatric oncologist would ask him. 'Every day is a good day,' he'd answer bravely as he lay there dying from the leukemia.

Marie gazed over at his picture on her nightstand. Her little angel. The sight of his tiny coffin still haunted her. No one should ever have to bury her own child. She hadn't thought she would make it. But she'd survived. Just as she'd survived when big Dom died. She was strong. Nobody was stronger.

Dear God, I am so tired of being strong.

Mostly, Marie worked. She was employed by an independent insurance agent who had three locations on the Island. Her desk was in his Carle Place office, where she handled mostly home and auto policies, some boat insurance. She got along well with everyone there. Didn't make a fortune but didn't have to dip into her nest egg either. She dressed stylishly. Wore her frosted blonde hair fresh and modern. Went to pilates three times a week. Was on a bowling team with several other young widows, the Living Dolls, who got together every Tuesday evening at Sheriden Lanes on East Jericho Turnpike. She took adult education classes at the high school in art appreciation and Chinese cooking. Took ballroom dancing. Volunteered Saturday mornings at the soup kitchen at her church, Corpus Christi on Garfield Avenue.

Marie did these things to keep busy. But she was also hoping that she'd meet Him. She'd dream about Him while she was pushing her grocery cart down the produce aisle at Waldbaum's. He'd bump into her and say, 'Excuse me, do you know how to tell if a pineapple is ripe?' Not that she did, but they'd have a laugh over it and go for coffee. Then for long walks on the beach, followed by sex on the kitchen floor. God, did she want to feel a man inside of her again. But Marie never seemed to encounter Him. Besides which, let's face it, desirable men her age were strictly interested in a leggy young babe – not a widow with a sagging caboose. Marie couldn't blame them. She didn't particularly want to be with some balding fat guy with a hairy ass and an enlarged prostate. But it wasn't fair, damn it.

On her good days, Marie never gave up hope that He was out there somewhere. But on her bad days she felt as if she would never experience romance again. She'd joined *secondchances.com* out of sheer desperation. Corresponded with two incredibly boring widowers before she agreed to go out with Mike. She wasn't sure why. Maybe because he'd seemed so open and genuine. He'd go on and on about Ernie. In his most recent email he'd told her about a young journalist who'd just taken the Acela up from Washington to talk to Ernie about a story that Mike said might change the outcome of the presidential election. It all sounded very interesting. But Marie didn't see much of a future for her and Mike. And if there was no future then why lead him on? That wasn't right, was it?

She lay there, awake and alone, her stomach in knots. *I like you as a friend, Mike. I just don't like you 'that way.'* It's what she used to tell the boys back in high school. Should she email him or phone him? Phone him, definitely. It wouldn't sting so much that way.

Sighing, Marie gazed at the commercial that had come on to the TV, wishing she could meet someone like the Flea-B-Gone Man. What was he, maybe thirty? Nice, thick blond hair. Bright blue eyes. Broad shoulders, slim hips, a washboard stomach. And no louse either – a friendly small-town veterinarian who loved animals and kids. Someone, Marie felt certain, who'd always be attentive to her personal needs. Not like Dom, who could sometimes get resistant. 'Not tonight, sugar,' he'd say. 'My stiff neck's bothering me.'

Marie was willing to bet her entire stock portfolio that the Flea-B-Gone Man had never had a stiff neck in his life.

SEVEN

The Flea-B-Gone Man, who happened to be an actor named Brink Liebling, was currently starring opposite Marlon Brando in a gritty black and white spy thriller that took place deep behind the Iron Curtain. Brink was interrogating Brando, who was being his usual brilliant, maddening self. And yet Brink was plenty crafty, too. And moving right in for the kill – until his fucking alarm went off.

It was only five a.m. but Luze had to get up that early if she wanted to put in her hour at the gym before school. Generally, she'd slip out the door of their apartment by five thirty and he'd go back to sleep, per chance to dream he was playing the lead role in another classic drawn from his pantheon of Movies That Never Were – like Hitchcock's splashy Technicolor screen adaptation of *The Da Vinci Code* in which Brink starred opposite the incandescent Grace Kelly. Brink totally loved his movie dreams. Never knew what would happen next yet he always seemed to know his lines. Truly, he was a Star.

But after Luze left this morning he found himself thrashing around in bed, unable to journey back to his dreamland. Instead, he got up and logged on to the computer so he could read his big brother's email again, searching for any nuance, however slight, that he might have missed the first eleven times around:

To: Brink Liebling
From: Hunt Liebling
Subject: Remember the Alamo
Dear Fuckface – I'm a total shmuck. I had to be in the city today to see Thayer but I'm already heading home to catch a plane at dawn. I didn't have time to get together so I didn't call you. Couldn't be helped. Sorry, dude.

I'm going out to LA to work on another one of those little stories that may change the history of mankind. Or at least the winner of next month's presidential election. To be honest, I have no idea what I'm getting into. But

my gut feeling tells me it'll be impactful – to use Thayer's
least favorite new word in the English language.

So say a prayer for me, little brother. I could really
use a divine boost right now. My blog is a charity case.
I owe the butcher, the baker and the candlestick maker.
I really, really need this story. Seriously, if this doesn't
turn things around I may be forced to look for dishonest
employment. You heard me, an illegit full-time newspaper job somewhere. And, dude, we both know how
heinous that would be.

Your pals, Nate and Strom Thurmond

P.S. Don't be surprised if you get something from me
for safe-keeping.

Brink stared at the computer, his brow furrowing. It was
unheard of for Hunt to be in the city and not so much as call
him. Just this rather cryptic email in which his fiercely independent brother sounded, well, desperate. Plus he'd invoked
the Alamo, which was what they'd called their fort out back
of the house when they were kids. The Alamo was where the
Liebling brothers had repelled all would-be neighborhood
attackers. The Alamo was where they smoked their first cigarettes and, later, their first joint. *Remember the Alamo* was their
private code. It meant that Hunt was about to go off and do
something slightly crazy and dangerous. It meant that no one
would be watching his back, which was why he'd added that
postscript about sending him material for safe keeping.

Remember the Alamo was Hunt's way of saying *I love you.*

Brink had nowhere to be this early, but the old man hadn't
raised him to be a lazy bum so he dusted and vacuumed the
entire two-bedroom apartment. Luze Herrera, as he was fond
of telling her, had the best-looking housekeeper in all of
Harlem. Which he thought was funny and she, OK, didn't.

Starved, he wolfed down a three-egg omelet with slab bacon
and fruit salad. Put on a turtleneck, jeans and his riding boots,
then rode the elevator down to the basement. He and Luze
lived on the eighth floor of a rent-stabilized building on
Madison and E. 123rd Street overlooking Marcus Garvey Park.
Her place originally. Luze, a dark-skinned Dominican, blended
right in. Brink, with his shaggy blond hair and wide-set blue
eyes, did not. His was the only white face in the building, in

the whole neighborhood. But nobody gave him a hard time. The guys mostly ignored him. The women just stared. Sometimes, the young ones whispered to each other and giggled, which Brink was used to no matter where he was. After all, he was that rarest of rare breeds.

Brink Liebling, age twenty-nine, was a leading-man type.

Down in the basement he strode past the laundry room and out into the locked service courtyard where he kept his bike. The super's skinny twelve-year-old son, Kareem, guarded it for him like it was his own. Brink and Kareem had been pals ever since Kareem saw one of his commercials on TV. Brink wheeled the bike out to the sidewalk, locking the gate behind him, and kick-started it in the street, where its throaty roar turned heads up and down the block. It was a sky-blue 1947 Indian Chief that he'd bought from an old stuntman up in Glens Falls, NY, when he was shooting an episode of *The Sopranos*. He'd played a small-town cop. Cool gig. Even cooler bike. Had its original 74-cubic-inch 1200cc engine, original front and rear fenders, fringed leather seat, saddlebags. Brink did most of the repair work on it himself. The old man had taught both Hunt and him how to do just about anything with their hands. It was pretty much all he'd left them with. That and their stupid first names.

He went tearing off up Madison to E. 124th Street, took that over to Lex and headed downtown, loving this beautiful fall day, loving life. Brink was one lucky son of a bitch and he knew it. He worked. As much theater as he could – a revival of *Glengarry Glen Ross* at the Yale Rep earlier in the year. Quality TV like *The Sopranos* and *Law and Order: Criminal Intent*. Movies, including a small but choice role in the latest Scorsese. And, yes, he did those Flea-B-Gone commercials, which were national and brought in real money. Not Geico Caveman money, but decent.

Unlike Hunt, who'd inherited the old man's dark coloring, Brink took after their fair-skinned Yugoslavian mother. Casting agents had him slotted as a Midwestern type. He was three inches taller than his brother, square-jawed and as movie-star handsome as any movie star could ever hope to be. But there were a thousand tall, blond leading-man types in New York. Another five thousand out in LA. And only two or three dozen jobs at any one time, most of them filled by the same two or three dozen name actors who got hired over and over again. But his time would come. Brink knew this. His big break was just a phone call away.

Meanwhile, he had Luze in his corner. They'd been class-mates at Yale Drama School. Luze was fiery, gifted and exotically gorgeous. She'd found stage work in New York right away. A Shakespeare in the Park production of *Measure for Measure* for which she earned raves. But more often than not – too often – casting agents called her when they were looking for someone to play a hooker or drug addict. Luze hated such demeaning stereotypes. She also couldn't stand the audition process. The insecurity. The waiting. The rejection. The simple truth was Luze loved acting too much to be an actress. So she enrolled in New York City's fast-track program for public school teachers. Thanks to her Yale Drama School degree she landed at the LaGuardia High School of Music and Art and Performing Arts – the fabled high school from the movie *Fame*. Her students, many of them inner-city kids, adored her. She adored them. Plus she drew a steady salary with health benefits, and that didn't hurt one bit.

Brink cut across to Park Avenue on E. 96th and hung a left on to Millionaires Row. When he arrived at E. 77th he pulled up in front of a luxury pre-war building and spent a few good minutes dumping on the New York Jets with Pat the doorman, who was a cousin of Hunt's pal Little Mike. It was thanks to Little Mike that Brink had landed this sweet cash gig. Brink got his New Balances out of his saddlebags and laced them on. Then he rode the elevator up to fetch his charges from their apartments. Currently, he had six – Odin, Kobe, Jack, Sam, Shotsie and Bailey. Odin was a bloodhound, Kobe and Jack were labs, Sam and Shotsie German shepherds, Bailey a German shorthair. All were well trained and raring to run as they squeezed into the elevator together, their noses quivering, tails wagging.

It wasn't unusual for Manhattanites to keep their large, healthy young dogs cooped up in an apartment all day. But hiring a dog runner such as Brink, a serious fiend who'd competed in six straight New York Marathons, was strictly a luxury for the uber-rich. He charged each owner $50 per day for an hour of his time. It was hard to think of the gig as work. It was his basic daily cardio routine – for which he got paid $300 each and every day, Monday through Friday, that he wasn't otherwise engaged, minus Pat's $150 weekly kick-back. Between dog running and his Flea-B-Gone residuals Brink could hold his head high at home.

The leaves in Central Park were at their peak fall color. It was a gorgeous spectacle to take in as he and his dog team plunged into the maze of twisting paths known as the Ramble, the dogs straining against their leashes. He picked up the pace, feeling his blood pumping. The walkers and slower joggers up ahead could hear Brink and his herd charging up on them and moved out of the way. When they caught sight of his six giddy charges they almost always smiled.

As he was running Brink's thoughts strayed back to that strangely forlorn email of Hunt's. Clearly, his big brother was going through a rough patch. Talking about maybe looking for a straight job was not a good sign. Brink knew Hunt. He'd go to any length to avoid having to work under someone else's thumb again. Brink wondered what this election-related story might be out in LA. He had no idea, but did have a funny feeling that Hunt had ducked him because he was afraid Brink might try to talk him out of going. Brink admired his brother more than anyone he'd ever known. Hunt was a fearless seeker of the truth. A mighty champion of the underdog. Not once had Brink ever feared for him. Not even when he was right there in downtown Baghdad as the bombs started raining down. Hunt was a battler, a survivor. He never lost. Never.

As Brink raced through Central Park on this fine autumn afternoon, the dogs galloping happily along ahead of him, it dawned on him that for the first time in his life he was genuinely worried about his hero.

That was when the phone on his belt rang. Brink's agent calling. He flicked on the Bluetooth in his ear and learned that the producers of a top-rated New York-based prime-time cop show, *By Any Means Necessary* – better known as *BAMN* – wanted him to come out to Silvercup Studios to read for a 'significant' role. Brink promised he'd set it up immediately.

After that, Brink didn't worry about Hunt any more. He was too busy dreaming.

EIGHT

It wasn't as if she kept a formal record but C.C. was fairly certain that she'd just endured her most pathetic and humiliating night ever.

She'd worked late at Hunt's place, lingering in his apartment like a lovesick teenager, hoping he might phone in or email her. Hating herself for being such a wuss. Hating Hunt for being *Hunt*. She could not believe the butthead hadn't tried to talk her out of taking that *Post* job. Hadn't said, 'You can't go. I'll be lost without you. I love you.' Hadn't taken her in his arms and kissed her and *made* her stay. All he'd said was, 'Thanks for putting up with me, Reiter.' Like she ran the quaint country inn where he'd been staying for the weekend.

This from the first great love of C.C. Reiter's entire twenty-three-year-old life.

There had been guys before Hunt Liebling. But never *the* guy. Not until that night C.C. first laid eyes on Hunt standing there in his doorway with his shirt off and the sweat pouring off him. For a while, it had been incredible between them. In her mind, it always would be incredible. It just hadn't worked out when it came to the day-to-day living thing. Hunt was a self-contained loner who cherished his independence. Fine, she got that loud and clear. And so theirs became strictly a business relationship. But that still didn't erase what they'd had together. Unless, that is, it had never meant much to him. This was the part that hurt. That she hadn't mattered to him.

When it drew past midnight and Hunt still hadn't checked in she closed up and went slinking home to her own place on Olive Street. Climbed into bed and spent the remainder of the night binging on Häagen-Dazs chocolate ice cream and sobbing uncontrollably. She never did sleep. Just dragged her sniffly, swollen-eyed self back there in the morning and reread his posting about the fuss Panorama News Channel was making over Don Oakley's wardrobe. It was good stuff. Typical Liebling. Also typical of him to post while he was on the road. Not that she had the slightest idea what the hell he was doing out there.

That was the other thing: him not telling her what he was doing in LA. How could he not trust her after everything they'd been through together?

Simple. Because she hadn't meant anything to him.

Her tears started flowing again. Too exhausted to fight them, C.C. dug his No. 14 Somebody Grogan Patriots jersey out of his closet and put it on because it smelled like him. Climbed into his bed and lay curled up there in a little fetal ball, berating herself for being such a pathetic crushed flower.

That was when he finally called her on her cell.

'Jesus, Hunt, where *are* you?' she demanded, sniffling.

'Don't speak. Someone may be listening in.'

'Someone may be *what*?'

'For all I know this whole pool house may be bugged.' He sounded very tense and weird. 'You would not *believe* the shit that's going on. I just got *abducted* in the middle of the night. Listen up, Reiter, this is mondo important. Where are you right now?'

'At the office. Where else would I be?'

'Then how come you don't sound like your usual self?'

She got up out of his bed and went and sat at her work station. 'What do you expect? I haven't heard from you since you left. Now you call up and go all Fox Mulder on me. *Who* abducted you? Did you find Samantha?'

'This isn't funny. I'm up against something really huge. Don't ask me what because I can't say anything more until I get home.'

'Then why did you call?'

'Because I can't believe what I just heard.'

'Which is . . .?'

'That when you were in Philadelphia you sold twenty thousand bucks worth of IBM stock and signed over the proceeds to *huntandpeck.com*.'

C.C.'s face suddenly felt very flushed. Her heart was pounding fast. 'How did . . . You talked to my parents?'

'Yeah, right.'

'Well, then how did you find that out?' she demanded.

'Hold on, there's more. You gave another eight thou to the blog back in July. Plus you haven't deposited a single paycheck. That adds up to something like thirty-four thousand dollars of your own money that you've plowed into my operation since you came to work for me. And you've never said one word.'

'Because I figured you'd go all he-guy and tell me not to.'

'You figured right. I want a complete accounting of every single penny you've spent. I'm paying you back.'

'There's nothing to pay back. They were donations.'

'I don't accept charity. Well, OK, I do. But not from you. I took you on as my intern, not my patroness. And if I'd had the slightest inkling that you—'

'Hunt, will you kindly shut the hell up and tell me how you found out?'

He paused for a moment before he said, 'I can't.'

'Oh, yes, you can! Who's been accessing my confidential financial records?'

'Trust me, *confidential* means shit to a warehouse full of Cal Tech-trained hackers.'

She breathed in and out slowly. 'Oh, man, my life's just getting better and better . . .'

'Why, what else has happened?'

'*Nothing*, OK?'

'You're worth millions, Reiter. I can't believe you never told me.'

Her father's family had operated a leather tannery in Lowell, Massachusetts. When the business was sold she'd inherited a share of the proceeds. Her wealth made C.C. uncomfortable. She hadn't done anything to deserve it. 'It's just money. It doesn't mean anything.'

'It does when you don't have any.'

'Look, I believe in what you do so I invested in you. It was strictly about the work. Not about us, if that's what you're worried about.'

He fell silent. Did not, repeat not, want to go there.

'My father was. Worried, I mean. He said I was throwing away my future on some Internet nutso who howls at the moon. He said you were just using me for my money. Which I set him straight about. I assured him that when it comes to money you're a total doofus.'

'Hey, thanks for sticking up for me.'

'Hey, no prob. But I did decide that it wasn't ethical for me to be sleeping with you if I was financing the site.'

'*That's* why you moved out?'

'Hunt, I need to know who's been hacking into my records.'

'I'll tell you as soon as I get back.'

'Which will be when?'

'I honestly don't know. And things may get skunky for a little while. Do you think you could stick around through the election? The sad truth is I'm pretty lost without you.'

'You're only saying that because I'm leaving. If I stay, you'll want me to go.'

'That's totally not true.'

'It totally is. You don't need anyone else in your life. You don't *want* anyone else. And that's fine. That works for you. But it doesn't work for me. So I'm leaving when I said I would. And I'll see you when I see you.' And with that C.C. hung up on the first great love of her life and sat there at her computer, shaking. Why was somebody hacking into her personal life? What else did they know about her? What did they intend to do with the information?

As she sat there, her mind racing, C.C. Reiter realized she was no longer feeling wussy. Now she was just pissed.

NINE

'Ommmmm . . .'

It was shortly after dawn when Hunt heard it in the early-morning quiet.

'Ommmmm . . . Bhur Bhava Sava . . . Ommmmm . . .'

Tim was performing some kind of ritualized chant out on his deck.

Hunt immediately went into the bathroom and threw some cold water on his face. He hadn't made it back to sleep after Herbie's goons returned him to the walled estate at four thirty a.m. No Neck had fetched a three-step aluminum ladder from the back of the Land Cruiser and set it up by the wall near the front gate. Then flipped open a laptop and punched in a set of codes.

'I've overridden their sensors, bro,' he told Hunt. 'When I hear you hit the ground I'll turn them back on. And next time I'll hit you first.'

After Hunt found his way back to the pool house he straightened up the furniture that got overturned in their scuffle, then sprawled out on the bed and wrote down everything he could remember about his conversation on the beach with the most powerful media baron in America. Herbie Landau had tried to buy his silence, then threatened his life. Hunt didn't want to forget one word. He no longer trusted that his own laptop was secure so he wrote it out longhand in a notepad, his body quivering with excitement. He'd wondered if Tim's shocking claims about Gary Dixon's sexual orientation and Kelly Graham's pregnancy were nothing more than a dying man's delusional ravings. Total bullshit. But if they were then why had Herbie just leaned on him so hard? Why had he tried to warn him off of a certain creaky old black and white movie that sure sounded a whole lot like *Monty and Me*?

Because it wasn't total bullshit, that's why.

When he was done scribbling Hunt phoned C.C. to tell her that she was being hacked. She had to know. He was dying to tell her the rest. That this was not just any story. That there was no turning back now even if he wanted to, which he didn't. But Herbie's minions might be listening in. So he kept quiet. It was for this same reason that he decided not to report back to Thayer yet.

It was good to hear C.C.'s voice – even if that voice was telling him he'd been the worst boyfriend in the world.

'Ommmmm . . . Bhargo Devasya Dimahi . . . Ommmmm . . .

He started up the stone steps toward Tim's glass house now, notepad in hand, his jaw working on a fresh piece of Bazooka.

He found the dying child star seated naked in the lotus position out on the deck that faced the rising sun, his shaved head bowed, eyes shut, hands pressed together at his heart center. Tim's neti pot sat before him on the deck, as did Rudy, who ran toward Hunt when he saw him, stubby tail wagging. A much warmer reception than yesterday. Hunt petted him, thinking Rudy pretty much sucked as a watchdog. All of those comings and goings in the night and not once had the famous Kerry Blue barked.

'What's that you were chanting, dude?'

'My Gyatri Mantra,' Tim answered softly. 'The words mean *Heaven. Earth. Space. I offer this prayer. That I may always remember. To turn to the light.*' Tim gazed up at Hunt with those ghastly yellow eyes of his. 'It's early, my friend. Duane's still asleep, and Lola doesn't get here until eight. Help yourself to anything you want in the kitchen.'

'I will, thanks. And then I'm anxious to see another DVD.'

'So you watched some last night?'

Hunt nodded. 'Volumes One and Two.'

'Is it . . .?' Tim cleared his throat uneasily. 'Did it hold your interest?'

The man had only weeks to live. A little thing called the White House was at stake. And yet here he was – still a needy, insecure actor. 'Dude, I'm hanging on your every word. Can't wait to see the rest of it. And when I have I'll be asking you a couple of hundred very specific questions. I've got to be satisfied that your charges are completely credible.'

Tim peered at him curiously. 'You think I'd make this stuff up? Why would I want to do that?'

'Easy: to destroy Dixon's candidacy. Look, I don't like the guy's politics. I don't like the kind of government he stands for. But I'm not going to help you Swift Boat him.'

'It's all true, Hunt. You can ask Duane. He was there.'

'Duane's word isn't good enough. He's your best bud. Speaking of which, are you sure you can trust him?'

'Of course I can. Why do you ask?'

'I have my reasons. Talk to me about this vintage porn film that you say the senator was featured in.'

'*Is* featured in.'

Hunt stood there, jaw working his gum. 'Are you telling me *Monty and Me* still exists?'

'It does,' Tim confirmed quietly.

'Can I see it?'

'I can get my hands on it if I need to.'

'You need to, dude. I have to watch it for myself, because there's one huge thing I don't understand.'

A faint smile creased Tim's face. 'Just one?'

'If Gary Dixon was such a gay player back in the old days then how come no one's ever outed him? He's been a Christian conservative standard bearer since forever. He's a shoo-in to be our next president. And yet there's never been a single whisper about him – or about Darren Beck's Trancas house parties. How is this possible?'

'It was almost fifty years ago, that's how. The Velvet Underground have all died of AIDS or old age. A few of them might still be hanging around in a nursing home somewhere, looking decrepit, but it's not as if they'd ever go public. They were pedophiles, remember? Besides, who in the world would believe them without proof?'

'Which you claim to have.'

'It's not a claim, Hunt. It's the truth.'

'You say you were Dixon's under-age squeeze for a while . . .'

'Correct.'

'Is there anyone – anyone at all – who can corroborate that?'

'Absolutely.' Tim gazed at him serenely. 'There's Gary himself.'

'And what about Kelly Graham? Every facet of her murder has been reported in painstaking detail. Yet not once has anyone ever alleged that she was seven weeks pregnant at the time of her death. How is that possible?'

'The results of her autopsy were sealed by the Santa Barbara County Coroner, that's how. It was part of the deal.'

'*What* deal?'

'The one that Herbie and Mort made with the Santa Barbara County District Attorney. He was a Republican hot shot who wanted a seat in Congress. They gave him one, too. Herbie and Mort *were* the California GOP, even back in seventy-two.'

'Is he still seated?'

Tim shook his head. 'Served his district without distinction for eight terms before he died back in the Nineties.'

Hunt jotted his name down anyway. Maybe there was something about this buried in the congressman's personal papers. Doubtless they'd been donated to some university library somewhere.

'By co-opting him,' Tim explained, 'they made sure that Kelly's pregnancy was kept from the public. Hell, they even got the bastard to agree to a joint criminal investigation with the LAPD – spearheaded by none other than Detective Lieutenant Duane Larue, who had big ambitions of his own in those days. Duane was on the team. We were all on the team.' He turned his face back to the sun that was rising over the parched, scrubby hills to the east. 'They thought *I* killed her.'

'Who did?'

'The jar-headed Sheriff's Deputies who showed up at the ranch. A real couple of porkers. They beat me up and threw me in a jail cell. Christ, I felt bad enough already – I'd lost both of my sisters in less than a week. And I was supposed to be watching out for Kelly. I failed her. I felt responsible. Always have,' he confessed. 'But they had zero proof I stabbed her, beyond the obvious fact that I was there when it happened. So when Herbie and Mort flew up that afternoon they started dealing.'

'Was Senator Dixon with them?'

'Hell, no. He had to protect himself.'

'Did that piss you off?'

'Not at all. I understood. You see, it was Herbie's world. In our own wildly different ways Gary and I were just trying to survive in it.' Tim paused, his sunken chest rising and falling. 'I had to submit to official questioning by Duane before I could leave. First thing he told me was that they'd reopened Tina's investigation.'

'Because of Kelly's murder?'

'Because of the results of Tina's autopsy. Her blood alcohol level was something like four times the legal limit. Which meant she must have been passed out drunk *before* she shot up that fatal overdose of smack. Tina couldn't have shot up herself. Somebody else did it to her. She was murdered, just like my K–Kelly . . .' Tim broke off, choking up. 'Duane . . . he told me that Parker Center was now lumping the two murders together as a single case. They were desperately afraid they hadn't gotten all of Charlie's followers. You know, that maybe some more Manson crazies were out there trying to wipe out the Bagley Bunch. It made sense. We were such beloved icons of white middle-class America. After that, the killings were front-page news across America. I was the "trouble-plagued former cast mate" who'd experienced "numerous brushes with law enforcement officials". I'd been at the ranch with Kelly. And my place in Laurel Canyon was the scene of Tina's death. I was all but guilty as far as the public was concerned. It was madness. Nothing but madness. The roller-coaster ride from hell . . .' He shuddered at the memory before he pulled himself back and said, 'You've only seen two volumes. There's much, much more to come.'

'About this fifth volume, the one that's not here. Is it in the same place as *Monty and Me*?'

'We'll talk about that when the time comes.'

'Let's talk about it now. Because I'm not into playing games.'

'This is no game,' Tim said crossly. 'If you think it is then we have a problem.'

Hunt heard footsteps behind him. Duane Larue came padding out on to the deck in gym shorts and a T-shirt, his face rumpled with sleep.

'You're up early,' Tim said, smiling at him.

'I heard your voices.' Duane ran a hand over his bristly gray crew cut, yawning. 'What's going on?'

'What's going on,' Hunt informed him, 'is your security around this place sucks. I got snatched out of bed in the night by two of Herbie's goons. They can override the system at will.'

Duane was wide awake now. And seemed very upset – unless he was fronting. 'I'll initiate an upgrade right away. That'll get us out ahead of them again for a few days.'

'Exactly what did Herbie want?' Tim asked with keen interest.

Hunt told them Herbie claimed he didn't want to see Tim get hurt. And had offered him $50,000 if Hunt would leave town immediately – or else.

Tim listened, his face impassive, before he said, 'I'm touched by his concern. It's total bullshit, but very moving. Are you planning to leave on the first stage out of Dodge City like Herbie said to?'

'Not a chance.'

'No one hands you your guns and tells you to leave town, do they? Looks like we have ourselves the right cowpoke, Duane. This is good. Very good. We've got Herbie exactly where we want him.' Tim gazed out at the rising sun, a look of supreme bliss on his face. 'He's scared shitless.'

TEN

After thirty-seven straight days and nights on the campaign trail Gary was enjoying that rarest of pleasures – a day off to do exactly what he wanted. Well, almost. The next president of the United States couldn't do *everything* he wanted. Not any more. But he was allowed to spend this bright, beautiful Pasadena afternoon all by himself in the darkened study of his mansion watching his favorite junk on television, sipping margaritas and smoking Marlboro Lights.

The voters didn't know that he smoked. It ranked as the least of the deceptions Gary was perpetrating on them.

On this day, he didn't have to speak to anyone about anything. He could just sit in blissful silence, the past weeks a dizzying blur of campaign speeches and handshakes punctuated by limo rides, plane rides and squirts of Purell antibacterial hand soap. On the TV before him was a DVD of Season Ten of *The Big Happy Family*, on which he'd played Walt Bagley, Jr.

Gary had grown thicker through the chest and shoulders since his youth. No longer had floppy blond hair. It was silver now, and elegantly coiffed. But to his public he still remained Walt Jr, the clean-cut boy next door who anyone would be happy to welcome into the family. The public images of Gary and Walt Jr were one and the same. Earnest. A good Christian. A good neighbor. *Good.*

Back in the old days, a lot of people in Hollywood thought Gary could turn out to be the next Jimmy Stewart. But Herbie had much bigger things in mind for him. Gary was destined to become that holiest of holy Republican things: the next Ronald Reagan. A successful actor who, with the help of the very same backers, would rise through California's GOP ranks to serve two terms as its governor and three more as a US senator. And now he was poised to take the White House on November seventh. The voters truly believed that he was going to lead America back to greatness.

Imagine how far we've fallen, he reflected, *if a fraud like me is America's Great White Hope. Was Ike a fraud, too? Was Reagan? Are all of us frauds?*

This was the unfortunate downside of a peaceful day off. Left alone for any length of time, drink in hand, Gary would begin to brood. Not that he was ever truly alone any more. The grounds of the mansion were crowded with Secret Service agents. Several were inside the house. There was even one right outside his study door.

The eight-bedroom mansion on Hillcrest Avenue in Pasadena's Oak Knoll section was a gabled 1907 Greene and Greene showplace with twelve acres of gardens, a swimming pool and tennis court. It was a home befitting America's next president. Gary's oak-paneled study was a hushed, cool chamber where serious men made serious decisions that affected the lives of millions. Displayed on the wall behind his massive walnut desk were photos of Veronica and himself with the Nixons and Fords, with President and Mrs Reagan, with both of the Bushes and their wives. Also a copy of the Ten Commandments that had been carved out of stone. Over by the leather sofa were vintage cast photos of *The Big Happy Family*. Most of that family gone now – all except for Tim, Gary and Veronica, who joined the cast in 1963 and was now perhaps the most admired woman in America.

His banjo was on display, locked away in a glass case like a fire extinguisher. And photos of Gary, Denny and Tom on stage at Ledbetter's in their matching cardigans back when Gary headlined his own folk trio. They'd had a couple of hits. Even played the Sullivan show. Tom was long dead. Denny he hadn't seen in twenty years until his advance team had arranged a campaign hootenanny in Greensboro, North Carolina last week. It was great to sing harmony with Denny again. Actually, no, it wasn't. Hearing his old band mate's pure, heartfelt voice just made Gary realize what a total whore he'd become.

He got up out of his leather chair and topped off his margarita from the chilled pitcher, peeking out through the shutters at the tennis court where his lovely bride was holding her own against the captain of the USC tennis team. Veronica looked amazingly trim and youthful in her tennis whites, shiny blonde hair pulled back in a ponytail. She could easily pass for a woman in her forties. Truly, the woman was a miracle of nature and cosmetic surgery. And a huge star with her own daytime TV chat show, her own magazine, a pair of bestselling books on marriage and motherhood, a line of clothing, beauty products. The woman was an industry unto herself.

Peering out at Veronica, Gary remembered the day Herbie suggested he marry her. 'She'll be a real asset to your political career, kid. And she ain't bad looking either.' Indeed, Gary had found Veronica quite desirable for a time. They'd had the two kids, Gary Jr and Brittany, who between them had produced five grandkids. But those nights of feverish desire were incredibly long ago. They hadn't slept together for at least thirty years. And when Gary looked out at Veronica now he felt only . . . fright. But Herbie had been right. She was a huge asset on the stump. Certainly more of one than Tucker Mayne, the drab Indiana governor who Herbie had chosen to be his running mate. The voters adored Veronica. Hell, *she* ought to be the one who was running for president.

Run, Veronica, run. Please run.

Gary sat back down with his fresh drink, feeling that same ache inside. The one that never went away. He reached for the remote, searching for solace in Season Ten. Came upon the episode when he'd approached Walt Sr in the garage for fatherly advice, his boyish, doltish face all scrunched with worry.

'Pop, I love Sandy so much that I can't even think straight.'

'You're going to be the man of the house, son. You have to think straight. A girl expects that. Let me ask you the very question Grandpa Bagley asked me about your mom way back when I was in your shoes: Is Sandy your best friend?'

'Why, yes. Yes, she is.'

'Then you already have your answer.'

Gary flicked it off in disgust. It was no help to be reminded that his entire career was built on infantile crap. He reached for the phone and summoned Jeremiah, hearing the reverend's footsteps out in the hallway as he approached. On Gary's nod, the Secret Service agent outside the door admitted him.

'Would you like to pray, my friend?' Jeremiah asked solicitously as soon as they were alone, his kindly blue eyes searching Gary's face.

'Not right now,' Gary replied glumly.

The Reverend Jeremiah Staunton stood there, bible in hand, and waited patiently for Gary to tell him what he did want. Jeremiah was nearly seventy but still as strapping and charismatic as ever. His short-sleeved white smock revealed the forearms and wrists of a man who'd done hard labor until he discovered Christ and started his Second Chance Ministry, which had grown from a Downey storefront into the magnificent Second Chance Cathedral and adjacent 3,700-acre religious theme park. Jeremiah had his own Second Chance cable network and his own Staunton University, a fully accredited institution of higher learning dedicated to the faith-based study of science, history, public policy and the law. He enjoyed more access to power than Falwell and Robertson had ever dreamt of. He was not merely the next president's spiritual guide. He was his closest friend.

Gary flicked the TV on again. Now he was at the malt shop blowing his proposal to Sandy. Kept babbling on and on about them being best friends. Sandy became so convinced he was breaking up with her that she ran out the door in tears. Gary hit the pause button and said, 'They called you my Billy Graham on CNN last night. How does that feel?'

Jeremiah smiled. 'There are worse things to be called by CNN.'

'They also called you "dangerous". The liberal media never called Graham that. You don't suppose they know something, do you?'

'Not a chance. I'm simply an outsider. Not of an established orthodox faith. Therefore, I threaten the ruling order. It's not personal. It's not *real*. Now, why don't you get out into the sunshine and have a nice, long swim? You ought to indulge yourself a little. Do something that makes you feel good.'

Gary raised an eyebrow at him. 'I was just thinking the very same thing.'

'Not a chance. Herbie's orders. You know that.'

'I *know* what I want, Jeremiah. Put out an SOS to Francesco. We could be on the beach in Cabo by sundown.'

'No,' Jeremiah said, shaking his head.

'Pick up the phone and do it, Jeremiah. Right now.'

'Look at me, Gary. Listen to me. You *know* it's not possible. Your Secret Service detail is with you around the clock.'

'They're paid to keep their mouths shut.'

'Publicly, sure. But they share everything with their superiors. The director of the FBI will know. And so will the good Lord.'

'I'm having a hard time, Jeremiah.'

'And He knows that. He's testing you.'

'Is this a pass-fail exam or can I squeak by with a gentleman's C?'

Jeremiah threw back his head and laughed. 'I'm stealing that for this week's sermon.'

'It's yours.'

'I wish we *could* hop on that plane and go. I'd love nothing better. He's testing both of us. We mustn't let him down.' He glanced at Gary uncertainly. 'Shall I get you one of your pills from the medicine chest?'

'I'm not supposed to take them with alcohol.'

'So you'll sleep for a few hours. You need the rest.'

Gary heard footsteps out in the hallway, approaching fast, and in barged Herbie. With him was his bloodless fixer, Mort Weingarten.

'Beat it, Reverend,' Herbie growled.

Jeremiah was no stranger to Herbie's gruffness. He retreated graciously, shutting the door softly behind him.

'We've got us some Timmy trouble, Senator,' Herbie announced, standing there in one of his loud Hawaiian shirts, hands stuffed in the pockets of his rumpled slacks. 'He's reached out to a reporter. A solid gold prick, I might add. The prick's being dealt with. Machinery's in motion as we speak.'

Gary could feel his stomach tighten. 'And what about Timmy?'

Herbie and Mort exchanged a look. Neither of them responded.

'You can't!' Gary insisted. 'Absolutely not. I won't allow it.'

'Believe me, I'm not happy about this either. But I warned you a long, long time ago that this day might come. We can't let him go public. He'll tilt the whole election to Oakley.'

'Nonsense. I'm leading by double digits.'

'Something like this can erase those double digits overnight. I don't have to tell you that, do I?'

No, he did not. Gary lit a cigarette, dragging on it deeply. 'How will you handle it?'

'It's better if you're out of the loop,' Mort spoke up.

'We never had this conversation,' Herbie agreed. 'In fact,

we were never even here.' He reached for the DVD remote and hit the play button. 'Oh, hey, good episode. That scene in the malt shop? You were brilliant.'

He and Mort left, closing the door behind them.

America's next president drank down the last of his margarita and gazed at those photos of himself and Timmy on the wall. Then he fell to his knees with a gut-wrenching sob and he wept, tears streaming down his cheeks as he knelt there on the carpet, hands clasped before him in fervent prayer.

Dear Lord, if only I could be honest just once in my miserable life. But the voters won't love me if they know who I really am. So they can't know. Mustn't know. Forgive me, Timmy. Please forgive me. Please, oh, please . . .

ELEVEN

should be the one who is running.

When her cell phone rang America's next First Lady was in the process of getting her sweet ass kicked by the lean blond captain of the USC tennis team, Ted, a good young Republican who'd been hand-picked by her campaign staff. Veronica's press secretary had escorted the camera people in for a photo op of them lobbing shots over the net to each other. Then escorted them out so that the two of them could play in earnest. Or at least Veronica could. Ted didn't so much as break a sweat as he sent her sprinting back and forth across the court. And the smug twerp was holding back, she felt certain, boiling inside.

Not so many years ago, sonny boy, you would have given your right arm for a taste of me. I was Miss Fucking America.

But that was once upon a time. Now she was a grandmother of five. And wife of the next President of the United States.

Gary was hiding in his study watching reruns of their moldy old show, which Veronica despised and never, ever watched. But he couldn't let go of it. And he needed his time alone to drink tequila and sneak cigarettes. The poor man was worn down by the campaign trail. As she chased down a cross-court volley and smacked it back across the net, Veronica found herself thinking it yet again: *I should be the one who is running.*

She thrived on the attention. Gary didn't. She was a role model, an *inspiration*, for millions of women. A poised and radiant campaigner. She looked great, felt great. Furthermore, she'd make a better president than Gary. She was smarter and tougher than he was. Never given to weakness or self-doubt.

Herbie had known what Veronica was made of way back when he'd cast her as Sandy in *The Big Happy Family*. Her reign had just come to an end that day she flew out to LA to read for the role. She was weighing a number of other career opportunities. Acting, she realized, was a long shot.

She landed the part, of course. And became one of Herbie's

girls, just like Tina Shea and countless others over the years. She still was one of his girls, even though the old goat was just talk now. Which was fine. Talk was cheap. And, Lord knows, Herbie had more than held up his end. He'd recruited a top production team to help her develop her talk show, and promoted the hell out of it. She was on hiatus for the duration of the campaign. Could return to it if they lost – not that they were going to.

I should be the one who is running.

Hell, she'd been training for the White House ever since her mother, the former Winnie Mae Dupree, started dragging her to rinky-dink beauty pageants back when Veronica was nine years old. Winnie Mae was a recovering hillbilly. Veronica's daddy, Billy, a self-made lumber tycoon, was a high school drop out. Yet Veronica took to being Miss America like she was seventh-generation royalty. Same as she did her role as the gracious, lovely wife of California Governor Dixon and then US Senator Dixon. As First Lady, she would be an advocate for the environment. Lady Bird had *Keep America Beautiful*. Veronica would have *Keep Us Green*. She would be looked up to. She would be loved. She would be what she'd always been – living proof that fairy tales do come true.

All except for her weak-kneed stand-in for a Prince Charming. She'd been propping up Gary Dixon for more than forty years now. Always standing there by his side. Always smiling. Never outshining him. Ambition wasn't ladylike.

'Nice try, ma'am!' young Ted called out when her weak backhand failed to clear the net. Now the twerp was taking outright pity on her.

Her phone rang as she awaited his next serve. She pulled it from the pocket of her shorts and glanced at the incoming number. It was Herbie, who'd just been to see Gary with Mort. The old bastard had seemed preoccupied when he left. Hadn't so much as waved goodbye to her.

She took his call, mopping her brow with a towel. 'Forget something?'

'I couldn't talk when I was there. Too many people around. You alone?'

The college boy was out of earshot, as was her Secret Service detail.

'I can talk.'

'I don't need you to talk. I need you to listen. Timmy's conscience has gotten to him.'

'We shouldn't be surprised, should we? The nearness of death often brings about a deep yearning to settle old scores.'

'Save the psychobabble for your viewers, will ya? Things may get a little rough for a couple of days. I want you to keep the senator focused and upbeat. Next week he'll be high-lighting his comprehensive immigration reform package. Why don't you go over his position papers with him?'

'That should consume a solid fourteen minutes. Any other suggestions?'

'Just keep him occupied, got it?'

'Yes, Herbie.'

'Why don't you invite some friends over?'

'We have no friends.'

'What are you talking about? Everybody has friends.'

'We don't.'

'Well, how about the grandkids? Can't they come for a visit?'

'They're in school, Herbie.' And scattered thousands of miles away. Gary Jr, Tippy and their three had settled in Hobe Sound, Florida. Brittany, Sean and the twins were in Harborside, Maine.

'Hey, I know, talk to Flynn Leverett. Maybe you can adopt a Casey. It'd make a great photo-op.'

'I don't want a damned dog, Herbie.'

'Well, what *do* you want?'

I should be the one who is running.

'Nothing. I'm . . . just tired of being Gary's keeper.'

'I know you are. It's been a long, hard slog. But we're almost there. Just stay strong for a couple more weeks. Can you do that for me?'

'Of course.'

'Atta girl. Tell me . . .' Lowering his voice now. 'What are you wearing?'

'My tennis whites. I was having a game.'

On the other side of the court, young Ted was downing a Gatorade while he waited for her.

'Have you got anything on underneath?'

'Why, aren't you just the sweetest thing? You do know I'm eligible for Social Security, don't you?'

'Are you touching yourself?'

'Now I am,' she whispered, her breath catching slightly.

'Are you wet?'

'Sopping. And I'm taking off my sneakers and little white socks now. My toes are pink and bare.'

'God, you're killing me . . .'

'From your lips to God's ear.'

Cackling, he hung up.

TWELVE

Mrs Pryor always contacted Wally on the cell phone she'd given him. No one else had the number, and Wally never used it to make personal calls. He kept the phone charged and near at hand at all times. Whenever she called he was ready. That's what he was getting paid for. And Mrs Pryor paid Wally Cooper very, very well.

Not that Pryor was her real name. Wally didn't know her real name. But the $10,000 that The Outfit direct-deposited to his Bank of America account every month was real. The top-flight health care at Cedar's Sinai for Mabel was real. The sunny penthouse apartment on Ocean Avenue in Santa Monica was real. And so was Rose, Mabel's live-in nurse. Wally never saw a bill for Rose's services. All he saw was the glow that had returned to Mabel's cheeks when they moved here from their dark little apartment in McLean, Virginia.

He and Mabel were sitting out on the balcony watching the sunset when the call came.

'You will fly to New York City this evening as John W. Norbis,' Mrs Pryor told him. She gave Wally the name of the airline, his flight and ticket confirmation numbers, all of which he committed to memory instantly. 'You will be given the details when you get there.'

'I'll get right on it, ma'am,' he replied in his soft, polite voice. 'Thank you for thinking of me.'

Then the line went dead.

'Mother, I have to go away for a couple of days to look into a claim.'

'Of course you do, munchkin,' said Mabel, who was of the belief that Wally earned his living as an insurance investigator.

He went into his room and shut the door. Unlocked his footlocker and sorted through the half-dozen wallets that were in there, pocketing the one that contained the California driver's license, credit cards and health insurance ID card for John W. Norbis, age forty-two, of Redondo Beach. All six of Wally's identities listed his actual age, though not his correct date of birth. He secured the footlocker and shoved it back under the bed. Got his carry-on bag out of the closet and packed the clothing he might need, including a warm V-neck sweater and his galoshes. No telling what sort of weather he'd run into. He dressed in a herringbone tweed jacket, blue button-down shirt, striped tie, gray flannel slacks and polished black wing tip shoes. Attired this way, Wally passed for a high school science teacher. Maybe an accountant. He was neither of these things.

Wally Cooper was paid to erase people.

He didn't look like a professional killer – or at least what people thought a killer would look like. Absolutely no one got nervous when they saw him coming. Wally was an owlish, meek little man with thick round eyeglasses, a weak chin and shoulders that were like two scoops of vanilla ice cream. He tried, but failed, to disguise his thinning mouse-colored hair with a comb over. He tried, but failed, to look fit. With his wide butt and short legs Wally never looked anything but pear shaped – even though he could still run three miles in under eighteen minutes, swim 500 meters and jump out of a plane into total darkness.

He carried his suitcase and belted trench coat to the front hall, then went out on to the balcony and told Mabel to be a good girl.

'Of course you do, munchkin,' she promised, which was how she replied to pretty much everything Wally said. The dementia was a part of her disease.

He stopped in the kitchen to say goodbye to Rose. Wally and Rose had an understanding – when Mabel was gone they would be together. They'd grown close ever since Rose arrived to take care of her. Wally, a lifelong bachelor, had always desired women, worshiped women. But the few romances he'd had were brief and unsuccessful. Naked, Wally felt jiggly, hairless and exposed – a turtle out of his shell. But with Rose he was himself. OK, she was a teensy bit older than he was. Sixteen years, to be exact. But tidy and energetic with milky white skin and vivid red hair. A devout Irish Catholic who believed him to be a good and religious man.

Rose didn't know what he did for a living and never would.

He paused in the kitchen doorway, watching her make dinner before he said, 'Mother's getting worse, isn't she?'

It wasn't only the dementia. Mabel had also lost control over her bowels. Difficulty swallowing would come next, then breathing. Then it would be over.

'Mabel's doing real well,' Rose promised him. 'She's not going anywhere. Don't you worry.'

'I never worry. Not with you here, Rose.'

She took his hand and held it to her smooth cheek. 'Well, I'm here. Now go do your work. And don't you think about anything else.'

Wally rode the elevator down to the parking garage with a lump in his throat, not knowing how he'd make it without Mabel, his big-boned gal who loved her Tammy Wynette records and those old Shirley Temple movies that she sobbed over no matter how times she'd seen them. It had been just the two of them ever since he was a boy growing up in Inwood, a little town in West Virginia situated halfway between nowhere and nowhere else. His dad, a long-haul trucker, overturned his eighteen-wheeler on I-81 near Allentown when Wally was nine. After that Mabel had to move them into a mobile home and work long hours waiting tables and slinging drinks. When Wally got out of high school she wanted him to go to college. Wally didn't see the point.

In truth, he hadn't cared what he did, Wally remembered as the elevator doors opened. He started toward his car, his eyes scanning the parking garage for anything out of the ordinary. An unfamiliar vehicle idling in wait. A person hanging around in the shadows. There was nothing. He unlocked his tan-colored Nissan Maxima and headed out.

Mabel had insisted he make a life for himself. Wally joined the Marine Corps to make her happy. He certainly didn't make himself happy at Camp Lejeune. The guys in his barracks ignored him no matter if they were white, black or brown. He didn't play poker. Didn't drink or go whoring. He kept his nose buried in paperback romance novels by Barbara Taylor Bradford and wrote long letters home to Mabel. Every Sunday, he attended church. Mostly, Wally's life in the Marines was about trying to get by.

Until that first day they were assigned to the shooting range with their M16s. To everyone's surprise – especially his own – Wally Cooper was a superfreak of a marksman. He graded out as the top shooter in the entire camp. His only equal was one of the instructors. Wally had no idea where this hidden talent came from. He'd never gone hunting in his life. Never even been around guns. It was simply a gift. They transferred him and his gift to a training unit for Scout Snipers. He excelled there with both the M40 sniper rifle and the older, specially fitted M14 Designated Marksman, which was still prized for its accuracy. They sent him to the Philippines, then Kuwait. Then came Desert Shit Storm, when the first fool of a Bush left Saddam in power even though they had him. After that Wally ended up in Somalia. He was right there in Mogadishu when the Black Hawks got shot down. After the first fool of a Clinton pulled the forces out Wally decided he was no longer proud to be a US Marine.

He took them up on all of that college aid money they'd been promising. Enrolled in the University of West Virginia in Morgantown, graduated in three years with a degree in criminology and got recruited by the CIA. They thought he had the makings of a top-flight covert operative. Not only due to his sharpshooting prowess but because he was a lone wolf who didn't drink, gamble or chase women. They even liked his unassuming physical appearance.

They sent him to The Farm outside of Williamsburg, Virginia, officially known as Camp Peary. When his training was completed he was designated as a non-official cover operative, or NOC, which meant if he got captured outside of the United States the US government would deny he worked for them. It also meant being overseas for long periods of times. But he was his own man, no one breathing down his neck, and Wally liked that. He liked living by his wits. Over the next three years he worked quietly and meticulously in Iran, Iraq, Yemen, Colombia and Nicaragua. Took out rebel leaders, tribal leaders, corrupt government officials, drug lords – twelve assassinations in all. He never failed to complete an assignment. Never got captured or detained.

Wally never asked whether his targets deserved to die. He did his job. It was very simple. Life can be if you keep it that way.

Until Mabel got the hand tremors. Then her speech became slurred. It turned out to be Parkinson's. She was fifty-eight years old. He asked to be transferred home so he could care for her. Langley put him to work as a desk jockey in the belly

of the compound. He happened to be working up an assess-
ment of Iraqi military capabilities when 9/11 hit. The finger
pointing from the politicians started even before the second
tower came down. Savvy agency infighters knew how to shield
themselves. Wally, a field man, was in the wrong place at the
wrong time. And so he was out.

He did spend a year trying to make it as an insurance
investigator, but he had zero knack for it. And Mabel's costly,
lousy health plan barely covered a fraction of her medical
care. On that cold, rainy March day when they reached out
to him The Outfit knew this. The Outfit knew everything.

They met out in plain sight at a Denny's coffee shop in
Falls Church. One of the men had been Wally's operations
officer before taking early retirement in 1999. The way the
other two kept squirming around in their business suits shouted
retired brass. The work they offered would call for Wally to
undertake the sort of clandestine assignments that he'd been
trained for. Sometimes he'd be undertaking these assignments
with the unofficial blessings of his own government.
Sometimes not. His sole contact would be a Mrs Pryor. He
was never to reach out to anyone else. All of which was fine
by Wally as long as they made good on the package of financial and medical benefits they were offering.

And they had. Wally savored every precious minute of life
with Mabel in the Santa Monica sunshine. He joined a nice
church a few blocks from the apartment. Became a literacy
volunteer through the public library. He and Mabel watched
Passions and *General Hospital* together every day. He bought
her a DVD player so she could enjoy her digitally remastered
Shirley Temple oldies.

And when Mrs Pryor called upon him The Outfit got its
money's worth. When it came to the fine art of covering his
tracks there was no one more cunning than Wally Cooper. It
was Wally who'd invented *46/33/21*, the shadowy domestic
eco-terrorist group that took its name from the chemical
composition of napalm – 46 per cent polystyrene, 33 per cent
gasoline, 21 per cent benzene – and claimed responsibility
for the Palm Beach firebombing death of the president of a
big three US automotive giant. It was Wally who'd taken out
that crusading New Hampshire attorney general, a rising young
star who'd been a sure bet to win a US Senate seat until his

unfortunate death in a skiing accident in the White Mountains. Apparently, the coroner found a great deal of cocaine in his system. Wally had erased the pampered mistress of the chief shareholder in a Dubai-based oil exploration company, an eminent psychiatrist in Singapore, a transvestite crack-whore in Omaha, a homicide investigator for the Baltimore Police Department and a Chicago-based producer of documentary films for PBS.

He never knew why any of these people had to die. It wasn't his job to know why. Simply to be careful and thorough and to leave no questions behind.

Tonight, Wally left the Maxima in long-term parking and made his way to the airline terminal, where he obtained his boarding pass from the automated check-in machine. Unfortunately, they'd assigned him an aisle seat for the overnight flight – and the machine kept bouncing him back to the main menu when he tried to change to a window. He could never sleep on the aisle. Those slender, pretty stewardesses always awakened him when they sidled past, their silky panty hose swishing seductively.

There was almost no wait at the security checkpoint. Wally took off his trench coat, tweed jacket and shoes. Deposited his suitcase on the conveyor belt, emptied his pockets into the plastic bin and padded on through in his black Gold Toe socks. He set off no alarms. The moving walkway took him most of the way to his departure gate, where the ground crew was all set up for business.

The young woman who changed his seat for him was crisp and efficient. Also really pretty. 'It's a good thing you wore your topcoat, Mr Norbis. The weather has turned cold back east. Have a nice trip, sir. Business or pleasure?'

Wally smiled at her bashfully and replied, 'Hopefully, a little bit of both.'

THIRTEEN

Tyrone made it to the Jack right after work just like Mr Gillis told him to. The man had left a voice mail on his cell phone specifying that he wanted Tyrone to meet him there *before* he picked up Lola. That meant he'd be a few minutes late getting her, and Lola hated to be kept waiting, but Tyrone didn't dare say no to the man.

Mr Gillis was seated in a candlelit booth near the back, looking huge in a sleeveless black muscle shirt. With him sat a broad-shouldered young fellow with long, scraggly red hair and a scowl on his face.

'How's it going, Tyrone?' Mr Gillis's nose was stuffed up. Also swollen and red. 'Say hello to my friend Steven.'

'Glad to know you, Mr Steven.'

'It's *Steven*,' he snarled. 'The name's Steven, not Mr Steven. Got it, bro?'

'Yes, sir,' Tyrone answered carefully as he sat down.

'Get you anything, Tyrone?' Mr Gillis and Steven were drinking beer.

'No, thank you. Got to fetch Lola in a minute.'

'Before you do I have a little business proposition for you.'

'Business proposition?' Tyrone repeated, glancing over at Steven.

'What are you staring at *me* for, numb nuts?'

'No reason, sir.' Quickly, Tyrone turned his gaze back to Mr Gillis.

'You're in a position to do us a major solid, Tyrone – in exchange for which I'm prepared to make your personal debt go away. The whole forty thou. *And* you'll come out sixty thou on the plus side.' Mr Gillis plopped a fat Manila envelope down the table. 'Take a look, my man.'

Tyrone opened the envelope. There appeared to be six tightly bound stacks of hundred dollar bills inside. He set it slowly back down on the table, his mind racing. Here it was, his shot at a week in Maui with Saundra. He'd tell Lola that he and his Nam buddies were having a reunion, no wives. A whole

week to lie on the beach together and rub oil on Saundra's
satiny skin. A whole week of Saundra's soft lips, the breeze
smelling of hibiscus. 'Mr Gillis, what could I do for you that's
worth that much money?'

'We'd like you to give us a ride to the house on Saddle
Peak Road,' he replied easily. 'Inside the trunk of your car.'

'Inside my trunk?' Tyrone shook his head at them. 'Is this
a joke?'

'Does it *sound* like a joke?' Steven demanded. 'Do we *look*
like a couple of fucking comedians to you?'

'No, sir. Absolutely not. But why do you want this ride?'

'What the fuck do you care?'

'Chill out, dog,' Mr Gillis told his hot-headed friend. 'My
man's a serious individual. He needs to evaluate the situation.' To Tyrone he said, 'If I tell you then you'll be in on it.
Is that what you want?'

'What I don't want is any trouble.'

'There's nothing to worry about, word of honor. All we
want you to do is let us out after you've passed through the
gate. There's a stand of sycamores at the first bend in the
driveway. You'll pause there, we'll hop out, then you and Lola
can go on your merry way while we do our thing. You're
wondering what our thing is. OK, that's a fair question. They
upgraded their security system this morning. We need to install
some sensory overrides. It's strictly about information gather-
ing, Tyrone. Same as my relationship with you has been.'

'You mean you're bugging Mr Tim's house?'

'That's it,' Mr Gillis said, nodding. 'That's exactly it.'

Tyrone swallowed. 'Exactly when would you be wanting
me to do this?'

'Tonight.'

'What, you mean right now?'

'Right now.' Mr Gillis studied him patiently. 'Are you in
or out?'

'I do this and the debt's gone?'

'All gone. I'm doing you a real solid here, Tyrone.'

'And I appreciate it,' he said slowly. 'I just . . . suppose I
say no?'

The big man heaved a sigh of disappointment. 'Then we're
back to figuring out how you're going to pay off that forty large.'

'Except you'll be dealing with *me* from now on,' Steven

said with a wolfish grin. 'I get all of you bad boys. And I ain't nearly as touchy-feely as my friend here.'

'What's it going to be, Tyrone?' Mr Gillis asked.

Out in the parking lot Tyrone popped open up the trunk of his green Buick Le Sabre. Mr Gillis grabbed a nylon gym bag from his black Toyota Land Cruiser and took out a power head screwdriver and a spring-loaded gadget of some kind. Steven went right to work taking apart the trunk's lock. He had the quick, expert hands of a master mechanic.

'What's that he's doing, Mr Gillis?'

'Fixing it so we can open the trunk from the inside. That way you won't have to let us out. Just toss the device when you get home.'

When Steven was done he jumped inside. Mr Gillis slammed the trunk shut on him. Tyrone heard a click – and the trunk popped open like a charm. Steven climbed out. Mr Gillis tossed the nylon gym bag into the trunk and closed it. Then the three of them got in the Buick and took off with Tyrone behind the wheel, Mr Gillis riding shotgun.

'This is a real grandad mobile, bro,' Steven observed, sprawled out in the back seat. 'You need to get yourself something hot.'

'I wouldn't say no to one of those PT Cruisers,' Tyrone allowed.

'*That's* what I'm talking about.'

Tyrone observed all speed limits as he made his way to the Ventura Freeway, feeling apprehensive yet hopeful. He was getting even. And when Christmas vacation rolled around there'd be Maui. Saundra stretched out beside him in a string bikini, her smooth flesh gleaming.

According to his dashboard clock Tyrone was running forty minutes late. Lola was no doubt leaving him angry messages on his cell phone, which was why he'd turned it off. He'd blame it on the traffic. It happened.

He got off the freeway at Topanga Canyon Boulevard and made the climb into the hills. There was a state park up where the mountains crested. Mr Gillis told him to pull over on to a deserted fire road near there. Tyrone eased the Buick on to the shoulder and they got out. Steven climbed in the trunk first, wriggling into a fetal position with his knees up near his chin.

Mr Gillis showed Tyrone that envelope with the $60,000 in it. 'I'll leave this in the trunk for you, Tyrone.' Then he stuck out his hand. 'It's been a pleasure doing business with you. I think you're a stand-up guy.'

Tyrone shook it. 'Same here, Mr Gillis.'

The big man climbed in with his friend. A tight fit, but they didn't have far to go. Tyrone closed the trunk, swung the Buick around and got back on to Topanga Canyon, feeling the weight of the two men in the car's rear end as he cruised around a bend and made his way toward Mr Tim's house.

FOURTEEN

'Dude, you have to tell me how it all ends!'
'You sound a bit anxious.' Duane was relaxing in a lounge chair on the deck with a long-necked bottle of Corona, Rudy flopped down next to him.

'Well, yeah . . .' Hunt had just watched Volumes Three and Four twice through. His fists were clenched, pulse racing.

Duane reached for a bowl of macadamia nuts and calmly tossed a handful into his mouth. 'Every single word is true. I was there. I lived through it.'

'Do you still blame yourself for the Kip McManus killing?'

He studied Hunt with his wide-set blue eyes before he grimaced and said, 'Kip was under the protection of the LAPD when he died. We should have had two men watching his house in Venice, front *and* back, instead of just the one parked out front. I begged them for two but I was told that the department lacked the manpower. There was an alley in back. Kip had old-fashioned sliding garage doors that opened right out into it. They weren't even locked. It was a snap to access the property from the rear, then climb through a back window and wait for him to come home. Kip's young Filipino girl-friend, Choochie Ochoa, was the one who found him.' Duane shook his head in disgust. 'We screwed up. *I* screwed up. The years don't change that.'

'Duane, what really happened that night on Stage Four at Panorama Studios?'

'I'm not going to get into that, Hunt. It's not how Tim wants to do things. I have to respect his wishes. Otherwise I have no honor, understand?'

'OK, but I've got to see that fifth volume. And *Monty and Me.*'

'Of course. We'll talk about it when Tim wakes up. He hasn't had a good day. He tries to exude yogic calm but he's truly terrified of death.'

'Can you at least tell me where the stuff's stashed? Is it at your Yslas Security offices? Because I'd like to see it tonight.'

'It's not at the office.'

'In a safety deposit box somewhere?' Hunt glanced at his watch. It was nearly six. 'Shit, the banks are closed until tomorrow.'

'Tim will answer all of your questions,' Duane reiterated patiently. 'But before you give yourself an aneurysm I can tell you this much – it's not anywhere nearby. He has his reasons. Volume Five is something of a parting gift. Tim wants to set things right before he moves on. For him, this is about much more than just Gary. You can appreciate that, can't you?'

'What I can appreciate is that we're talking about who does or doesn't become the next president of the United States. Herbie knows I'm here. If we don't move this story fast his Major Slime Squad will beat us to the punch. Get the mainstream media so tangled up in bogus, irrelevant accusations that they'll pay zero attention to the substance of what Tim is saying. That's Campaign Strategy One-oh-One. And these guys are real, real good at it.'

Duane took a long drink of his beer. 'Why don't you unclench your fists and grab a cold beer? Lola's still around here somewhere if you're hungry. I haven't heard Tyrone's car yet.'

'I need to blow off some steam first.'

'Suit yourself. Just make sure that you don't—'

'I know, I know. I won't leave the property.'

Hunt headed down the stone steps to the pool house, Rudy tailing him yet again. He began to wonder if the Kerry Blue's breeder was secretly in Herbie's employ. Maybe the dog had a miniature surveillance camera implanted under his bushy eyebrows. *Or maybe I'm just getting a little punchy.* Hard not to, given the outright weirdness of this situation. Trying to make responsible journalistic sense of Tim's shocking allegations. Getting leaned on by Herbie, whose geeks were hacking into the lives of everyone he knew and loved. Hunt hadn't slept a wink since he'd landed out here. His head was yo-yoing back and forth between the unfolding horrors of the summer of seventy-two and the major league deadline pressure of right now. He felt caged here inside of Tim's walled estate. Needed to run. A good, solid hour of road work to blow the tension from his system and clear his head. Hmm . . . Lola's husband, Tyrone, would be showing up any minute now to pick her up. What was to stop him from waiting down by the gate for the guy? When Tyrone passed on through he'd slip out before the gate closed. Run these canyons until he dropped, then ring the buzzer when he got back. So what if they got pissed? What could they do? Send him to bed without his supper?

Quickly, Hunt changed into his gym shorts and running shoes. Clipped his phone to his waistband, pocketed his wallet, then jogged down to the trees at the foot of the drive and stretched out his hammies, jaw working on a fresh piece of Bazooka. Within a few minutes he heard a car steaming up Saddle Peak. Tyrone had his own remote-control opener. Hunt heard a click and, slowly, the gate swung open. In rolled the green Buick Le Sabre, Tyrone looking very serious. He didn't notice Hunt waiting there in the trees. Just drove on in. As the gate swung shut Hunt darted out and took off down Saddle Peak.

The sun was sinking into the Pacific, infusing the blue water with an orange glow streaked with red and purple. As Hunt felt that first rush of fresh oxygen in his lungs, he knew he'd made the right call. Being around Tim had given him a powerful need to reaffirm he was healthy and alive. And he was. And it felt so damned good that he'd gone a couple of hundred yards before he realized he could hear another set of lungs gasping for air behind him – Rudy was still on his tail.

'Pick it up, little dude!' he called out to him, back-pedalling. 'Slackers never make it out of Round One!'

The dog happily sped up and joined him. Together, they ran the steep, twisting canyon roads surrounding Tim's estate, climbing their way past the trophy mansions that clung here and there to the hillsides. The air was clear and dry, and it was remarkably quiet. When the occasional car went by, Rudy would move over toward the curb to let it pass. He was plenty smart – for a dog.

Hunt ran, still trying to wrap his mind around what Tim had said about the murders, and so much else, in Volumes Three and Four . . .

After he got back to LA from Santa Barbara, Tim tried Kip's place in Venice and any number of Kip's favorite hang outs. But his missing co-star was nowhere to be found. Tim did hook up by phone with Gary Dixon, who was home in Pasadena – and, in Tim's words, devastated by Kelly's death.

'*Timmy, I am so sorry I got you into this. And I know what you must be thinking right now . . .*'

'*Never try to read my mind, Gary. It's much too scary a place for you.*'

'*But I didn't kill Kelly, I swear. I was here all night. Ask Veronica. Kelly should never have gone to that awful ranch. I've just phoned Jeremiah and told him everything about Kelly and me. He was incredibly understanding. He said that she was the best thing that's ever happened to him, and he'll always love her, no matter what.*' Gary let out an anguished sob. '*I'm getting out of politics, I swear. It's not a decent, moral career, Timmy. Just look at what it does to people.*'

Back home in Sepulveda Tim discovered he now had a policeman posted out front. He also had Kip McManus hiding in his trailer out in the driveway, freaked out but OK. Kip told Tim he'd dropped two hits of mescaline after they left him at the motel and totally flipped out. Hitched a ride north with some surfers and spent the night tripping on the beach at Gaviota State Park. In the morning, when Kip heard the news about Kelly at the Gaviota Truck Stop, he thumbed his way back to LA – but was afraid to go home. He'd been hiding in Tim's trailer all day.

'*Are you figuring Kelly's lunatic boyfriend killed her?*' he asked me. '*Because I sure am.*'

'*You think Jeremiah's a lunatic?*'

'*Well, yeah. He's into God, isn't he?*'

'*That doesn't make him crazy. Kelly wasn't crazy.*'

'*Kelly wasn't "Kelly". She was just another dirty girl trying to pass herself off as clean. Strictly about image, man. Same with Gary. Jeez, you're smarter than I am. Don't you see that?*'

The only flaw in Kip's theory was that the Reverend Jeremiah had spent the entire night in Buena Vista at the bedside of a dying congregant. Her family could vouch for the fact that he'd never left.

Darren Beck, the sexual predator who'd played Tim's on-camera father, reached out to him with yet another theory. On location in Pacoima, where he was filming an episode of his hugely successful private eye series, *Brock*, a frazzled Darren informed Tim that Herbie was now holding *Monty and Me* over *him* as well. The reason? Darren had filed a $20 million lawsuit against Panorama for defrauding him out of his share of the net proceeds of *Brock*.

'*I've got a top-ten hit here, kiddo*,' he complained, *seated there in his luxury trailer with his latest boy toy, a muscular blond would-be actor named Colin Gault. 'I'm shooting my fifth season, and I have yet to see one penny. Herbie employs full-time thieves on the Panorama payroll. He calls them accountants. But I'll be totally ruined if the public ever finds out I'm an ageing turd burglar. So I'm dropping my suit. Only I'm concerned that you may goad Herbie into leaking it. Can you tell me what you're thinking?'*

'*Absolutely. I'm thinking that I've just lost two people who I loved. I'm thinking that some lunatic's killing us one by one.'*

'*I know what you mean*,' *Darren said to me. 'I'm deathly afraid this psycho will come after me next. I've crossed paths with some pretty warped individuals over the years. Maybe one of them is trying to get even. Although an even more obvious candidate comes to mind.'*

'*Who, Darren?'*

'*Think about it. These deaths have focused so much attention on our old show that Panorama's syndication unit has gone through the roof. Panorama stock opened* five *points higher this morning – the goddamned corporation is worth seventeen per cent more today than it was yesterday. Herbie is making out like a bandit. We're talking tens of millions of dollars.'*

'*Do you honestly believe he'd kill Tina and Kelly over money?'*

'*Do you honestly believe he wouldn't?'*

Tim didn't know. He did know that he no longer wished to own his Laurel Canyon hideaway where Tina had died. His on-camera mom, Glory Wills, who had plundered him a decade earlier, met him there to talk over his options. Glory had become a top showbiz realtor after the acting gigs dried up. She urged Tim to keep the house as an investment.

'*Rent it out, dear. I know a party who'd be interested. And willing to go as high as a thousand a month.'*

'*Places rent for half of that on this street. What's the catch?'*

'*No catch. Nothing illegal. They're just anxious to rent an out-of-the-way place. Privacy is critical.' She arched an eyebrow at me. 'Get it?'*

I got it. Somebody she knew was looking for a hide out for trysts. Somebody who had deep pockets and a high profile.

I wondered if Darren was two-timing his boy toy, Colin.

Tim was at his house with Glory when the plainclothesman who was guarding him pounded on the door to tell him that they'd just found Kip dead on the bathroom floor of his house in Venice. Someone had split Kip's head open with a hatchet. Now three of the Bagley Bunch were dead.

Unlike Tina and Kelly, Kip had been murdered while under police protection. Unlike Tina and Kelly, Kip's murder had been accompanied by a chilling message that would be analyzed and debated for years to come:

THIS IS <u>NOT</u> THE END.

Those were the words Kip's killer had scrawled in foot-high letters on his living room wall with Kip's blood. It was generally accepted that the bloody warning was a reference to a Doors song called 'The End'. It was also accepted that the killer, or killers, had torn a page right out of the Manson family album. Absolutely no one had forgotten *Death to Pigs* and *Helter Skelter* and all of the other Beatles-based lunacy that the Mansons had left scrawled behind in blood. The handwriting on the wall made it clear to everyone that America's favorite TV sitcom family was being systematically obliterated by a person, or persons, on a deranged killing spree.

After that, the surviving Bagleys each had two members of the LAPD posted on their homes at all times as well as two officers with them wherever they went. All mail was intercepted and opened. All phone calls tapped and traced.

The morning after Kip died Tim received a call from Veronica Dixon, who invited him to lunch at the Oak Knoll mansion. Gary was putting in time at his district office that day. It was just Tim and Veronica, who quickly made it clear that she was a lot more clued-in than Tim had realized.

'I want you to tell me what Kelly was doing up at that ranch, Tim.'

'Taking a well-deserved rest. She needed to unwind.'

'Cut the crapola. Do you see any crow's feet under these eyes? No, you do not. I've been there myself. And I know that Kelly was there because my dear, sweet husband knocked her up. He's admitted everything to me.'

'So why are you messing with my head?'

Veronica cleared her throat uncomfortably. 'Because Gary wasn't home in bed with me that night. He was out. Didn't get home until dawn.'

'He told me you'd vouch for him.'

'And I will,' she vowed. 'Provided that I'm convinced he didn't drive up to Santa Ynez and hack Kelly to death. Mind you, he swore to me that he didn't.'

'You don't believe him, is that it?'

'Why should I? He's been screwing another woman for months and lying to me about it. I barely know him any more. I certainly don't know where he was that night.'

Me, I wondered if she knew that Gary was a switch hitter. Was she aware he'd had male lovers? That she was, in fact, sitting right across the table from one of them?

'I tried asking him where he was,' she went on. 'He told me it was personal.'

'You don't really believe Gary killed Kelly, do you? If he killed her that means he killed Tina and Kip, too.' Although how Gary could have gotten at Kip while being under police protection himself I couldn't imagine. 'You're accusing him of being a psycho killer.'

'I'm not accusing. I'm asking. I have a right to.'

Tim quickly realized that if Veronica couldn't vouch for Gary being home in bed when Kelly died then she had no one to vouch for her either. And if she'd been a patient at the ranch then she knew how to find her way around the place in the dark of night.

At his district office Gary didn't dispute her claim that he hadn't been home in bed that night.

'It's true, I wasn't,' he admitted freely, seated there at his desk.

'You told me that you were, Gary.'

'And I feel terrible about it. No excuse, I panicked. The truth is I was at Kelly's house until midnight in case she wanted to phone me from the ranch. It was her idea.'

'Did she call you?'

'She didn't, no.'

'Where'd you go after midnight? Veronica told me you've been staying out late a lot. Is there someone else, Gary? A boyfriend?'

'That's strictly off limits now, I told you.' Gary reddened sheepishly. 'Look, this is really personal, OK? I go to a funky

*old coffee house way out in Topanga Canyon called Spanky's.
They have a small stage with a stool and a mike. A lot of really
amazing people stop by late at night to try out new material.
Kristofferson's in there all of the time, Joni Mitchell . . .'*

'And you?'

*'I've never stopped writing new songs. I'm working on one
right now for Kelly.' He nudged at a lined pad on his desk,
his eyes moistening. 'The music's how I keep it together. Some
nights I just sit in on banjo. They close at two but we bolt the
door and cook until dawn. That's where I was the night Kelly
died. That's where I am every night. Ask Big Bear, the
bartender. He'll tell you.'*

'Gary, why won't you tell Veronica?'

*'Because it's mine. A man has to hold on to something
that's his.'*

'Even if it ruins your marriage?'

*'My marriage is already ruined. And I'd be thrilled beyond
belief if my political career ended tomorrow. I don't want to
live in a big mansion in Sacramento. Or anywhere else. I just
want to be me.'*

'Does Herbie know how you feel?'

'Kelly knew,' Gary replied forlornly.

Tim headed straight for Topanga with his police tail and
asked Big Bear, the burly bartender, if Gary had been in
Spanky's the night that Kelly died. And he hadn't. In fact,
Big Bear told him Gary hadn't been in for over a week. Gary
had lied to Tim yet again – even though he'd practically dared
him to check it out.

There was something else Tim needed to check out. He'd
raced over to Kip's place in Venice when he heard about his
murder. Saw that bloody handwriting on the wall for himself.
He'd also slipped into the backyard and checked out the old
incinerator where Kip hid his stash.

*Call it a hunch. Call it whatever you want. But Kip's stash
was gone. Whoever killed him had made off with five kilos of
prime weed, a dozen blocks of hash and a couple of hundreds
hits of purple mescaline.*

Choochie Ochoa, Kip's sexy, spacey, eighteen-year-old
Filipino girlfriend, had found Kip's body. Choochie worked
on the Santa Monica Mall at a T-shirt stall in a bookshop
called The Book Nook.

'It wasn't me,' she insisted, tossing her long straight black hair. 'I didn't rip off Kippy's stash.'

'Did you ever tell anyone where it was?'

'No way! I'd never fuck Kippy over like that. He was my sweetie. And now he's dead and the fucking cops are hassling me for my papers. Which I don't got, so now they'll send me back home. I ain't talking to them.'

'I'm a friend, Choochie. Not a cop.'

'And I'm freaking out, you showing up like this. What if somebody else comes looking for me?'

'Somebody like . . .?'

Choochie glanced at me uncertainly. 'Look, this dude started hanging around here a couple of weeks back, OK? Talking at me on my break. Do I got a big sign on me that says "Will Ball Anybody"? Hell no. Anyways, he asks do I know where he can score some mara-hoochie. I tell him, excuse me, but I don't even know you. Then last week I bumped into him again – coming down the street from Kippy's place. He says howdy. I say howdy back. Small world and all, right? But now I'm thinking did he, like, follow me to Kippy's? Like, if he knew Kippy dealt maybe he tried to score off him. Only, good luck, right? Kippy never sold to nobody he didn't know.'

Then again, maybe Kip already knew him. But if he did then why had this guy come at him by way of Choochie?

'What did he look like?'

'Anglo. Kippy's age. Maybe a little older, like thirty.'

'Tall?'

'Taller than me.'

'Did he have long hair?'

'Not really.'

'What color was it?'

'I wasn't into thinking about him that way, OK? I was with Kippy.'

'Well, would you recognize him if you saw him again?'

She gulped, her eyes widening. 'You think he killed Kippy, don't you?'

'What time do you get off work, Choochie?'

'I'm open until ten, why?'

Tim phoned Steve Yslas to tell him that Choochie had very likely seen the Bagley Bunch killer but was afraid of the police because she was an illegal. Steve told him he'd see the girl home, keep her safe for the night and try to coax her into sitting down with a police sketch artist in the morning.

'You done good, Timbo. Got dinner plans? Elvia and me would love to have you. Wait, what am I saying? Of course you've got dinner plans.'

Tim had the kids' table at Du-Pars all to himself that Friday night. But he didn't dine alone. The first visitor who sat down with him was Errol Landau, Herbie's slimmer, vastly better looking spin-off.

'Tim, did Glory get a chance to talk to you about me renting your house?'

'You *want to rent it?'*

'I do. My place on Crescent Heights has turned into the counter culture Friar's Club. Every writer and comic I know comes by to shpritz. Sometimes, I need a little privacy. See, I'm involved with somebody and our thing's not quite out in the open yet so we're . . .' He flushed bright red. The guy was madly in love. *'I totally understand if you'd rather not rent it for that.'*

'Really not a problem, Errol. I'm always happy to help out family.'

He looked at me in surprise. *'Is that what I am, Tim?'*

I slid the door key across to the table to him. *'Knock yourself out.'*

Moments after Errol raced out of there a grief-stricken Jeremiah Staunton joined Tim. The reverend's electric-blue eyes were pained, his shoulders slumped.

'Tim, I'm at your service day or night. We can pray together. Or just talk about Kelly.'

'You mean like you and Gary do?'

'We both loved Kelly. We both miss her. My ministry is holding a special Kelly Graham Group Healing at the Anaheim Convention Center tomorrow at noon. It will be telecast live by more than one hundred and fifty television stations across America, courtesy of Panorama Syndication. Karen Carpenter has offered to sing "Amazing Grace". And the Dixons have agreed to say a few words. Veronica couldn't have been more enthusiastic on the phone. Gary seems less so, but Herbie assures me the senator will pitch in. Tim, I'd like you to deliver her eulogy. This is your chance to tell the world about the real Kelly.'

*'Not interested. Lending my face to your televised freak
show is not me.'*

*He bristled, a malevolent black karma radiating off him. I
was reminded that he was a convicted felon whose combustible
old self still roiled away under that born-again surface. 'We're
all human, my friend. Kelly most certainly was. Gary told
me she was carrying his child. He's confessed everything.
I'd like to cut off the bastard's balls and stuff them down his
throat. I'd like to burn that so-called ranch to the ground.
But am I acting upon my very human impulses? No, I am
not. Would you like to know why?'*

*'Offhand, I'd say because Herbie warned you that if you
didn't play ball you could kiss your new relationship with
Panorama Syndication goodbye.'*

*Jeremiah's eyes flickered at me. Apparently, I wasn't too
far off the mark. Then he stormed out.*

When Tim left Du-Pars he ditched his police detail in a
maze of back roads off Benedict Canyon and headed for Laurel
Canyon. His bungalow was in darkness. He left his car a block
away, hid behind an overgrown oleander in his front yard and
waited. A half-hour later Errol pulled in and parked. Unlocked
the front door, went inside and flicked on the lights. Errol's
lover arrived ten minutes after he did, parked out on the street
and rushed inside. They were accustomed to grabbing their
love on the run. Were in there for less than forty-five minutes.
Errol took off first. Then his lover locked up and returned to
the white Jaguar XKE that was parked at the curb, top down.

*As the engine kicked over with a roar I jumped into the
passenger seat and said, 'Evening, Veronica.'*

She let out a startled cry. 'God, Tim . . .!'

'Did you have any trouble ditching your police protection?'

*'No trouble at all.' Veronica's poise clicked back into place
as she sat there, manicured fingers resting on the wheel. 'I
hope you ditched yours.'*

'Not to worry. No one knows you're here.'

*'You know. Why are you . . .? Oh, Lord, you're not going
to slit my throat, are you?'*

'Now you think I'm the killer?'

'What I think is that I'd like to go home.'

*'Sure, after you tell me something. You said you'd been to
that ranch . . .'*

'*So?*'

'*So how did you get there?*'

'*Gary drove me. Anything else?*'

'*Yeah. How long have you and Errol been getting it on?*'

'*Ever since I figured out that Gary's fling with Kelly was more than a fling. We've had to be so careful, Tim. People expect certain things of Miss America. And they just love to crap on her.*'

'*Veronica, Errol's a pot-smoking, anti-war gonzo satirist who hates everything you stand for. Is this you getting even or what?*'

'*I see a very different Errol. I see someone who is exceptionally gifted and ambitious. You would not believe how grateful he is to have me. How eager. I need that. I need Errol. True, he and Herbie can't stand each other. But that's just a phase fathers and sons go through. Errol will mature. Herbie will mellow, and before long he'll open every door he can. Errol Landau will be a major creative force in Hollywood. Together, we'll make a formidable team.*'

'*Get real. Herbie has huge plans for Gary, and those plans include you.*'

'*Gary has lost his way,*' she said sadly. '*He's about to take a huge fall. Herbie will have to find himself another boy. For all I know, he already has.*'

Tim said goodnight to Veronica, hiked back to his car and headed home for Sepulveda with the latest news on the radio for company. There was a breaking local story: at approximately ten p.m. Santa Monica police had rushed to the Third Street mall in response to a report of gunshots being fired. An unidentified young woman was critically wounded in the alley behind The Book Nook. A retired Los Angeles police detective named Steven Yslas, age fifty-four, was also hit. Both victims were pronounced dead on the scene.

So ended Volume Four of Tim's video memoir.

And now Hunt ran, sorting through the job ahead. His top priority, once he'd seen Volume Five, was to nail down Tim's story. Not just lay eyes on *Monty and Me* for himself. Something more, like a copy of that sealed Santa Barbara County Coroner's autopsy report – concrete proof that Kelly Graham had been pregnant at the time of her death. He could probably get it under the Freedom of Information Act. But that would take time. Unfortunately, he didn't have time.

Hunt ran, the dusk beginning to envelope him. Lights were twinkling down below now in Malibu. He'd just started wending his way back toward Saddle Peak Road when he heard the rapid *pop-pop-pop* of a semi-automatic handgun off in the distance. He knew the sound all too well from the streets of beautiful downtown Baghdad. Now he heard several more . . . *Pop-pop-pop* . . . *Pop-pop-pop-pop* . . . Admittedly,   the canyon echoes could have been playing tricks on his ears. But the shots sounded as if they were coming from the direction of Tim's place.

Next to him, Rudy let out a mournful howl. Absolutely no way that could be taken as a good sign.

Hunt sprinted his way back, Rudy racing right along next to him. As Hunt drew closer to Saddle Peak, his chest heaving, he heard a vehicle go rocketing down the hill. But he couldn't be sure where it had come from.

Tim's front gate was wide open.

He ran up the drive to the house and found Tyrone's Buick parked in the floodlit driveway near the front porch, the driver's door wide open. Tyrone Gilliam lay face down next to the car with the back of his head blown off.

Silence. Hunt could not hear a sound – other than his own heart thudding in his chest. Slowly, he made his way around to the other side of the car. He saw the blood trail streaming down the driveway before he saw her. Lola there on the pavement with her unseeing eyes wide open. She'd taken one in the cheek, another in her neck.

Rudy let out another howl – this time from inside of the glass house.

He dashed inside. Duane Larue was still out on the deck where Hunt had left him. The ex-cop had gotten up out of his lounge chair, maybe in response to those shots in the driveway. He'd taken three to the chest before he hit the deck, a look of utter surprise frozen on his dead face.

Rudy was in the master bedroom crouched low beside Tim's bed, whimpering. Tim Ferris lay under the covers with his hands folded across his chest. Aside from the bullet hole in his forehead he appeared to be resting comfortably. He didn't look surprised the way Duane did. He looked peaceful.

A Glock semi-automatic lay on the floor next to the bed. The killer, or killers, had left it behind.

The wall safe in Tim's study was open. It had not been blown – they knew the combination, apparently. The first four volumes of Tim's memoir were gone. There was nothing at all in the safe.

And no one left alive.

The mournful dog came over to Hunt and rubbed up against his leg. As Hunt reached down to pet him, it dawned on him that if he hadn't snuck out for that run he'd be dead right now, too. Of course he would. They'd killed Tim and Duane, Lola and Tyrone. They would have killed him, too. They wanted him dead. He was supposed to be dead.

He *was* dead.

Now he heard sirens in the distance. Someone had called the police. He had a few minutes. Not many. They were coming. Hunt stood frozen there for a moment. Couldn't move. Then he shook himself and dashed for the pool house.

His laptop was gone. His notepads were gone. His knapsack, too. The dresser drawers had been yanked open, his clothes removed. Everything was gone. They took it all. Wait, no, they hadn't. His leather jacket was still hanging in the closet. Strange. He put it on, hands searching through the pockets. Tucked inside of the breast pocket he found the computer print out with his flight information. His name, ticket confirmation number. Of course, they *wanted* the police to know he'd been here. Hadn't been able to kill him so they'd done the next best thing – made it look as if *he* killed these people and then cleared out fast. Which left Hunt wondering, as the sirens grew louder, if that in fact ought to be his very next move.

Stay or go?

His fingerprints were all over the pool house and main house. He'd been busted once in New York. His prints would be in the FBI data bank, so there was absolutely no way he could claim he hadn't been here. He ought to wait for the police and explain. Or try to, knowing full well they'd make him their prime suspect. They couldn't prove he'd massacred these people. But they could certainly hold him as a suspect and/or material witness. Tangle him up in this mess for God knows how long. Meanwhile, Tim's explosive tale would die with him and Gary Dixon would march to triumph on Election Day. That had to be what this was all about – the story Tim had been desperate to tell and now couldn't. Tim's version of history would never see the light of day. Herbie and his minions had just made sure of it. They'd eliminated Tim and Duane and taken possession of the DVDs. As for Hunt, well, he had a whole lot of explaining to do. But first he had to make the biggest decision of his life.

Stay or go?

True, they'd seized those DVDs from Tim's safe. But they didn't have Volume Five. And they didn't necessarily know that there was a second set of DVDs somewhere – complete with that missing fifth volume. Hunt couldn't imagine *where* but he had to find it and get it out there to the voters. Because Tim's story was all true. Had to be true. Otherwise Tim and the others wouldn't be dead now, would they? He owed it to Tim to keep on going. Owed it to the voters – not to get too melodramatic. But, hey, four people had just died here.

Stay or go?

Hunt stood there with his heart pounding, mouth dry. Those sirens growing louder. This wasn't about *him*. This was about Tim's story. The story meant everything. That meant getting the hell out of here and finishing the job, didn't it?

He ran back up toward the house. The keys to Tyrone's Buick lay on the pavement next to Tyrone's lifeless hand. Hunt grabbed them, jumped in and started up the car. Backed it up and turned around with a screech. He was just about to floor it when he heard Rudy let out a yowl. The dog came sprinting out of the house and leapt through the open window into the front seat with him.

He did not, apparently, wish to be left behind.

'Suit yourself, little dude,' Hunt told him as they went barreling out the open gate. 'But this makes us running buddies for real now.'

The old-school Buick was big and squishy with tons of play in its steering wheel. He lead-footed it down the canyon with the dog seated there next to him. Found his way to Topanga and took that to Pacific Coast Highway. He made a right at the stop light there just as a pair of LA County Sheriff's cruisers came screeching around the corner, sirens blaring, and headed up Topanga. He watched them in his rear-view mirror, exhaling with relief, then started north on PCH in the direction of Malibu.

He'd gotten out of tough jams before. He'd get out of this one. They wouldn't start looking for Tyrone's car until they'd pieced together the scenario and worked their way through each victim's driver's license and vehicle registrations. No one, as far as he knew, had seen him drive away. So the car ought to be OK for an hour or two. It had a full tank of gas. And no GPS navigation system on board – which was good because they could use the satellite to locate him. Hunt flipped open the glove compartment. Found a ton of road maps for LA County, Orange County, Ventura and Santa Barbara, a road atlas of all fifty states. In the ashtray he found a handful of loose change. He had his wallet on him with about $450 in cash. His credit cards, which he couldn't use if he wanted to stay on the loose. And his new smart phone. He was just about to speed dial C.C. with an SOS when he stopped himself. Herbie's geeks were very likely tapping her phone. Hers, Thayer's, Brink's, everyone he knew. If he placed a call to anyone they could zero-in on him. Hold on, this damned thing was equipped with GPS. They could do that even if he *wasn't* using it.

Hunt hurled the phone out his window into the middle of the highway and drove on.

Rudy was dozing with admirable calm by the time he reached Malibu, the luxurious playground of Hollywood's privileged few. Who wouldn't want to be in beautiful, care-free Malibu on a balmy October evening such as this one? Truly, it was everyone's dream destination.

Everyone who wasn't running for his life.

Hunt had somewhere else to be: wherever it was that Tim had stashed that second set of DVDs for safe keeping. *Not anywhere nearby*, Duane had told him. *A parting gift*, he'd called it. As if this were a big fucking game show. Hunt wondered who Tim might have sent the DVDs to. His cast mates were all dead, with the notable exception of Gary and Veronica. His best friend, Duane, was dead. Who did that leave? Who else had Tim mentioned?

The breeder. What was the guy's name again? Everett? No, Leverett. Flynn Leverett, son of Perc. Tim had called him a kindred soul. Said he lived in Santa Barbara, which was two hours north of Los Angeles. *Not anywhere nearby*. So be it. He'd head there and find Leverett. If he didn't have the DVDs maybe he'd know who else Tim might have sent them to. At the very least, Hunt could deposit Rudy with him. Because the last thing he needed right now was a famous dog for a traveling companion.

Hunt stayed on Pacific Coast Highway all of the way to Oxnard, where he picked up 101. He found an all-news station on the radio. They had a police report of a possible shooting at the Topanga Canyon estate of former child star Tim Ferris. Reporters were en route to the scene.

Santa Barbara scored higher on the quaintness scale than Malibu, but it was still plenty upscale and chic. He stopped at the first gas station he could find that had a pay phone. It was outdoors, just like everything else in Southern California. Which was a good thing. Inside, their surveillance cameras would get a much better look at him. He grabbed some of Tyrone's change from the ashtray and called 411. They had a listing in Goleta for an F. Leverett. Hunt got the address, too.

The breeder lived on a canyon road ten miles north of town off San Marcos Pass. Hunt drove past some new housing tracts into the foothills, where the road snaked its way through fragrant lemon and orange groves. The house lights grew farther apart. He eased his way along, keeping an eye out for the numbers, until he finally arrived at a wooden gate that featured the silhouette cut-out of a Kerry Blue Terrier.

Rudy started to whine excitedly. He was home.

Hunt lowered the window and buzzed the intercom. When he heard a crackly voice at the other end he said, 'I'm sorry to bother you, Mr Leverett, but Tim Ferris sent me. I'm a friend of his. It's real important that I see you.'

The gate swung open to let him in. A winding gravel drive took him through avocado groves before it arrived at a low-slung ranch house. The kennels were on the other side of the house. Hunt made out fenced enclosures and dog runs in the floodlights. And heard a whole lot of barking.

A tall, silver-haired woman waited for him out on the front porch, a pair of Kerry Blue puppies bumbling and stumbling around at her feet. Rudy whooped and pawed frantically at the car door. Hunt let him out and Rudy sprinted toward her. The woman bent down and made a huge fuss over him. She was a tanned, outdoorsy looking woman in her sixties with strong, handsome features. She wore a denim shirt, khaki slacks and work boots.

As Hunt approached her she ordered Rudy to *sit* in a booming, authoritative voice. Rudy obeyed, though he could barely contain his excitement.

'My name's Hunt Liebling. I'm here to see your husband, I guess.'

'That lame brain cleared out fourteen years ago with a blonde piece of fluff named Taffy,' she informed him dryly. 'Last I heard they were running a dude ranch near Durango. I'm Flynn. How can I help you?'

'Perc Leverett was your father?'

'He was. You say you're a friend of Timmy's?'

'Actually, it's a bit more complicated than that.'

'I should think so, Mr Liebling. Timmy's been murdered. He, Duane and the Gilliams. I just saw it on the news. They're hunting for the killer. And suddenly *you* show up.' Flynn reached inside the door for a shotgun she'd propped up against the wall. She raised it at Hunt. Held it comfortably. Knew how to use it. 'Tell me why I shouldn't call the County Sheriffs.'

Hunt swallowed, his eyes on the gun. 'If I hadn't gone out for a run I'd be dead, too. Rudy was with me. When we got back they were all dead. I'm no killer, ma'am. I'm a journalist. Tim had a story he wanted to tell.'

'What kind of a story?'

'About what really happened in the summer of seventy-two.'

'And why have you shown up here?'

'Because Tim said you two were close.'

'I see . . . And whose car is that?'

'Tyrone's. He wasn't using it any more.'

Flynn thought the matter over long and hard before she lowered the gun and said, 'Herbie and his thugs are behind this, aren't they? You'd better come inside. We'll do something about Tyrone's car later.'

Hunt didn't budge. For all he knew she'd already called the Sheriffs and was just stalling for time. 'Why do you believe me? You don't even know me.'

'I know Rudy. I raised him. If you'd killed Tim there's no way he would have gotten in that car with you. I'm trusting you because *he* does. So come on in. We're alone. My son has his own place in town.'

She returned the shotgun to a gun rack in the entry hall and led him down a long, tile-floored hallway. The living room was practically an art gallery of Casey paintings and sculptures. The kitchen was just a kitchen. Rudy headed right for the kibble and water bowls, the puppies circling him excitedly.

'I despise Herbie Landau,' Flynn informed him. 'That awful man gave my dad shingles, ulcers, high blood pressure and then a massive coronary. Dad was a man of great prestige in his field. Herbie treated him like crap, cheated him out of money and, Lord, how he used to *scream* at the poor dogs. Old Rex would get so scared he'd pee on the furniture. They must have gone through eight living-room sofas that first season.' She looked Hunt over, her tanned face creasing with concern. 'Have you eaten?'

'Not really,' he replied, his stomach rumbling.

She opened two bottles of Coors from the refrigerator and handed him one. 'There's leftover meat loaf from dinner. How does a sandwich sound?'

'It sounds great,' he replied, sitting down at the table with his beer.

Flynn slit open an onion roll and slathered it with mustard and ketchup. Cut off some slabs of meat loaf, built a sandwich and passed it to him on a plate. Found a Tupperware container of coleslaw and passed that to him, too.

'You're the Hunt Liebling who wrote those wonderful articles about the slaughterhouse industry, aren't you? I've only bought organic meat since I read them. That's free-range bison you're eating.' She sat across from him and sipped her beer, swiping at her mouth with the back of a work-roughened hand. 'I gave Rudy to Timmy because I felt sorry for the guy. I've felt sorry for him since we were both kids.'

'Why is that?' asked Hunt, wolfing down his sandwich.

Flynn's pale blue eyes studied him curiously. 'You don't know?'

'I know that his mother beat him. I know that his on-screen father, Darren Beck, sexually abused him. And that his real father . . .'

'What about his real father?'

'Tim never knew him, except as a man holding a cigarette lighter with a pin-up girl painted on it.'

'I've been crazy in love with Timmy Ferris since I was twelve years old,' she confessed, tears spilling out of her eyes. No sobs. No sniffles. They just started flowing. 'I can't believe he's gone. I was expecting it, naturally. But not this way. Did you . . . you saw him?'

'He had a smile on his face. He looked at peace.'

'I knew him practically my whole life. All of those kids. I grew up on the set just like they did. Well, not *just* like they did, but I helped dad with the Caseys,' she explained as Rudy and the puppies wrestled around under the table at her feet, growling and yapping. 'Gary hasn't changed one bit. He's still the same sanctimonious phoney. Kip was just plain squirrelly – always trying to get the dogs stoned. Tina was a wild child. Kelly a tormented little anorexic. And Timmy . . . Timmy I just wanted to hug. But Elvia was the one and only love of his life. After she passed I thought maybe he and I might have a second chance. I was alone by then, too. But he wasn't interested in starting over.' She swiped at her eyes, swallowing.

'You were writing a story about him?'

'Not exactly. He filmed a video tell-all memoir with Duane's help. Five volumes of DVDs that he wanted the public to see before the election. He wanted people to know what really happened that week. Do *you* know what really happened?'

'No, Tim always kept very quiet about that subject. He became quite the prosperous businessman for his silence, too. Turned Steve's little bodyguard service into a major operation. You don't do that without serious capitalization.'

'You're talking about Herbie, I assume.'

'You assume right.'

'I saw the first four DVDs. I didn't get a chance to see the fifth. And I really, really have to. He told me that a duplicate set was stashed somewhere else for safe keeping. Do you have it?'

'No,' Flynn said flatly. 'No, I don't.'

'Did Tim ask you to hold on to anything for him?'

'Such as . . .?'

'A safety deposit box key maybe.'

'I'm afraid not. Sorry.'

'Well, can you think of anyone else who he might have sent it to? Someone he trusted?'

'He trusted Duane, no one else. Except for Alicia, of course.'

Hunt raised his eyebrows. 'His daughter, right . . .'

'But she's dropped off the face of the earth. No one knows where Alicia is. She could be in Timbuktu.'

That's when Hunt remembered the letter Tim had sent Thayer, the one that was postmarked Balltown, Iowa. 'No,' he said quietly. 'No, she's not.'

FIFTEEN

The flight to New York touched down at JFK right on time. It was a few minutes past eight a.m. when Wally ventured outside to the passenger loading zone, his eyes flicking around until he caught sight of the black man in the Cablevision bucket truck that was idling out beyond the taxi stand.

Cloverdale Millington was employed by The Outfit. Often, they were teamed together on major operations. Clover was the best scrounger and wheelman Wally had ever come across. He was also a functioning psychotic.

Wally shoved his thick, round glasses up his nose and headed toward the truck, glad for his trench coat. It was quite blustery out. He opened the passenger door and got in next to Clover, a tall, erudite man in his late forties whose neatly trimmed goatee was flecked with silver. Clover was a man of highly sophisticated tastes and, ordinarily, an elegant dresser. Right now, he had on blue coveralls and a pair of buckskin work gloves.

'Welcome to the Big Apple, Coop,' he exclaimed with a warm smile.

'A pleasure to see you, my friend,' Wally responded, parking his overnight bag at his feet.

Clover opened the fragrant take-out bag that was on the seat between them. 'Got you a genuine New York bagel. You want onion or sesame? I'll take the other one.'

'Sesame, please.'

'You got it, Coop.' Clover passed it to him. 'Here's your coffee – black, two sugars, just the way you like it. And our file.' The Manila folder contained all of the character particulars and photos Wally would need. It was unusually thick, meaning more than one target. 'Oh, and I got you this,' Clover added, handing Wally a small, gift-wrapped box. 'Your birthday's next week, right?'

'Why, yes.' Actually, Wally's birthday was in March, but he saw no point in being impolite. He tore open the wrapping paper to find a boxed DVD collection of the films of director Douglas Sirk.

'I know how much you and Mabel enjoy your romances,' Clover said, pulling out into the airport traffic. 'These here are considered the apotheosis of Fifties romantic melodrama. You've got your *Magnificent Obsession* with Mr Rock Hudson. Your *All That Heaven Allows* with Mr Rock Hudson. *Written On The Wind*, also with Mr Rock Hudson. I sure do hope Mabel likes him.'

'Loves him. This is so thoughtful of you, Clover. I'm touched.'

'How is Mabel feeling?'

'She's fine. Thank you for asking.'

'I've missed you, little man. What's it been – eight months, ten?'

'More like four. The job in Aspen, remember?'

Clover shook his head. 'No, no. I've never been to Aspen.'

'Clover, I don't mean to be rudely contradictory but you were there with me in June.' Wally bit into his bagel, nodding to himself. 'You were off of your meds, weren't you? I had a feeling.'

Clover was bipolar. As long as he stuck to his hefty daily regimen of meds he did just fine. But if he got feisty and stopped taking his pills then all bets were off. On more than one occasion he'd undergone electroconvulsive therapy.

'How did you know, Coop?'

'Because you introduced yourself to me as if we'd never met before.' Temporary memory loss was a side effect of the ECT. 'And when we disagreed over strategy you bit me.' Wally held up his freshly scarred pinky finger. 'I had to get eight stitches and a tetanus shot.'

'Jeez, I'm sorry, man. But those damned drugs can make me feel like I'm sleepwalking. Not to mention limp between the legs. I am talking *severe* man trouble. Sometimes I just can't go on living like that, know what I'm saying?'

'Perfectly. But are you taking them now?'

'Without fail. And there's no need for you to worry about my rage response. I'm all done with that kind of behavior.'

Wally studied him closely. 'Forgive me for asking, but is there a new kind I should know about?'

'Coop, it's under control. No point in us even talking about it. But all we've got out here is each other, so if anything *does* happen – not that it will – it's all in here.' He handed Wally a sealed letter-sized envelope. 'The correct dosage to give me and so forth. I'd appreciate it if you wouldn't open that until the time comes. Which it won't.'

'As you wish.' Wally stuffed it, unopened, into the breast pocket of his tweed jacket, then opened the Manila folder in his lap. 'Who's up first?'

'Lady in Mineola. I figured we'd save time by doing her before we head into the city. We have a pretty full day.'

Wally read the Mineola assignment over while Clover worked them out of the airport and on to the Southern Parkway.

'I disconnected her cable last night,' he explained when Wally was finished. 'Phoned her at seven this morning to tell her we had an automated alert that it was out, which she confirmed. She's expecting us there by nine. Your coveralls and tool belt are behind the seat. Got you a fine claw hammer.'

'Clover, my friend, you think of everything.'

Clover took the Southern Parkway to the Cross Island in the direction of Floral Park, where he picked up the Jericho Turnpike. He did not need to consult the enclosed Long Island road map or any sort of GPS device. When it came to directions he had a photographic memory. Wally changed from his businessman's attire into the coveralls and work boots while they drove.

Their destination was a quiet, well-maintained street of raised ranches. Marie Farlese, age fifty-four, lived in the third house from the corner on the right. Her Honda Accord was parked in the driveway.

Clover pulled up at the curb and got out, wrapping his own tool belt around his slim hips. 'It'll just take me a sec to hook her back up, OK?' He was unfailingly diligent. Put down orange safety cones around the truck because that's what an actual cable guy would do. Then he stepped into the bucket and powered his way up, up to the utility lines with so much practiced ease you'd swear he'd been doing it for years.

Wally headed up the walk to the front door and rang the bell.

The woman who answered was trying a bit too hard to look younger than fifty-four. Her business suit was on the flashy side. Her hair an unlikely shade of blonde. And she wore way too much make-up for Wally's taste. A widow, according to her file. One daughter living in Tucson, a son deceased.

'Good morning, are you Mrs Farlese?' he asked politely.

'Can we make this fast, kiddo? I have a million appointments today.'

'We'll have you out of here in a jiffy, ma'am. Would you check to see if your cable's back on now?'

'No problem. Do you need to come inside?'

'I'm afraid so – just to make sure there hasn't been a surge.'

Wally followed her in, nudging the door shut with his elbow. The living room had the spotless, showroom look of a room that no one ever used. One entire wall was lined with photos of her late husband and son.

She flicked on her flat-screen TV with its remote. 'Seems fine,' she said when it came on.

'Are there any other TVs in the house?' He needed to make sure there was no else around. There could be a boyfriend staying over or a neighbor coffee-klatching. There could be a dog, though he'd heard none barking.

The little television in the kitchen came on loud and clear.

'Good, good,' he said, glancing about. One juice glass and one coffee cup in the dish drainer. No pet dishes in sight. Good, good indeed.

'There's also a TV in the master bedroom,' she said, hurrying down the long hallway off the living room.

He followed her, peering into empty bedrooms as he made his way along. By the time he'd joined her in the master bedroom she'd already flicked on the set at the foot of her bed.

'Fantastic,' he exclaimed. 'You're good to go, Mrs Farlese.'

Marie Farlese turned off the TV and started out of the bedroom. She didn't make it. Wally hit her over the back of the head with the claw hammer and shattered her skull. The lady went down and stayed down. Wally pounded her two more times just to make sure, calmly wiping her blood and brain matter on to the rug before he returned the hammer to his tool belt.

Clover had stuffed a pair of latex gloves into the pocket of the coveralls. Wally put them on and ransacked her dresser and nightstand drawers, yanking them open wide. There were four king-sized pillows on the bed. He removed the pillowcases and emptied the contents of her jewelry box into one of them. Then he returned to the body and removed Marie Farlese's gold wristwatch, gold rings and pearl necklace. These items went in the pillowcase, too.

Her laptop computer was on the desk in one of the spare bedrooms. Wally stuffed it into a second pillowcase. Her computer files were backed up on CDs that were stored alphabetically in a rack. He found the CD labeled *secondchances.com* and tossed it into the pillowcase with her computer. Slid open the drawers of her filing cabinet and discovered personalized file folders that contained printouts of the emails she'd received from men she'd met online. Wally bagged all of them before he went in the dining room and emptied Marie Farlese's good silver into another pillowcase. Her purse and car keys were on a table in the entry hall. Wally dumped the purse's contents out on to the floor. Took her wallet, left the rest.

Clover had pulled the truck into her driveway. Wally jumped in and Clover drove them past several shopping centers before heading out in the direction of an industrial park. They went by a plastics factory and a printing plant, then the road dead-ended at a cluster of vacant warehouses. The *For Lease* sign out front was spray painted over with graffiti, and weeds grew in the parking lot. Clover eased the truck around back to a loading zone. A late-model dark blue Volvo 850 sedan was parked there.

They got out of the truck with the pillowcases and got busy. Clover flipped the laptop open on to the pavement and smashed it to pieces with his claw hammer. Likewise the CD that Wally had lifted. Wally poured lighter fluid on to the email print-outs and set them ablaze with a disposable cigarette lighter.

Clover had purchased a box of heavy-duty black plastic trash bags with drawstrings. He stuffed the broken bits of the laptop and CD into one of these, then shoved the pillowcases full of jewelry and silver into another. Wally trash-bagged his tool belt, overalls and boots. Changed back into his tweed jacket and wingtips, knotting his necktie in the truck's side-view mirror. He tossed his suitcase into the back seat of the Volvo next to Clover's Il Bisonte bag and a Samsonite briefcase.

Clover changed into a dark blue uniform that had the word *Maintenance* stitched over the right breast pocket and *Rico* stitched over the left. He'd stashed a duffel bag behind the seat of the truck. In it was Wally's standing order for weaponry: a pair of SIG-Sauers, a Tec-9 and an Italian-made Beretta AR-70 semi-automatic rifle with a thirty-round magazine and a pistol grip. This went into the Volvo's trunk, as did all of the trash bags. Those would be tossed into a dumpster somewhere on the way into New York City. Clover would have worked out where already.

They wiped down the cab and door handles of the truck for prints. Then got into the Volvo, which had heated front seats, and drove back the way they'd come.

'Is this car OK with you, Coop? Because if you don't like it I can steal us another one.'

'No, no, it has a very nice ride,' Wally said, shifting his wide, spongy bottom comfortably. 'And I'm crazy about these heated seats.'

SIXTEEN

The cheery uniformed doorman, whose name was either Ken or Len, held the apartment building's front door open wide for Thayer when the world's oldest living Pulitzer Prize winner emerged from the elevator.

'Lovely day, Mr Thayer,' Ken or Len exclaimed with a broad grin.

'Easy for you to say,' Ernest Ludington Thayer snapped, smelling the man's Aqua Velva as he tottered across the marble-floored lobby toward him. 'You're not the one who's circling the drain.'

'Yessir,' Ken or Len chuckled. 'Always ready with a quip you are.'

'Young man, I'm talking verifiable hard news,' grumbled Thayer, who was in no mood for chirpy banter today.

That morning's news had been saturated with coverage of what they were calling the Saddle Peak Massacre, with details of all four gruesome deaths. The murder weapon, a Glock semi-automatic handgun, had been left behind at the scene. The LA County Sheriffs were attempting to trace its owner. Hunt Liebling's airline boarding pass had been found in a bathroom wastebasket in the estate's pool house. And Hunt's fingerprints were, reportedly, all over the damned place. Yet Thayer's gifted young protégé was nowhere to be found. Thayer hadn't heard from him. Didn't know if he was on the run or dead or what. All he knew was that the finger of blame was being pointed right at Hunt. And that this was *his* damned fault. He'd gotten the kid into it.

Little Mike idled out front at the curb in the Rolls as Thayer made his way out into the chilly October morning. A gusty wind blew off the Hudson. Thayer was glad he'd chosen the tan duffel coat that he'd bought in London when he was bureau chief there in the late Fifties. Around his throat was the red scarf Elly had knitted for him. On his head was his favorite blue beret.

The Rolls was a 1957 Silver Wraith touring limousine, black with tan leather upholstery. Belonged to Elly's father. Thayer had kept it out of sentiment. Little Mike loved the damned car. Donned his old black livery driver's suit whenever he was behind the wheel, and refused to let Thayer ride up front next to him. The old fighter insisted upon chauffeuring him around like a grand pooh-bah.

'You OK back there, Ernie?'

'Fine,' Thayer answered heavily.

'You're worried about young Liebling, aren't you?'

Hunt hadn't killed anyone, Thayer felt certain. Someone had murdered Tim Ferris to keep him from telling Hunt what he knew. Thayer also felt certain that this someone was connected up with Herbie Landau, who'd revealed at a raucous morning press conference that he'd personally confronted Hunt the night before the murders. 'I begged him to leave Tim alone,' Herbie claimed, his crocodile tears flowing. 'This poor guy had terminal cancer. The last thing in the world he needed was to be harassed by some left-wing extremist. But Liebling wouldn't listen to me. He seemed incredibly agitated. Frankly, I was concerned about his mental stability.' Senator Dixon had cancelled all campaign activities and gone into seclusion until further notice.

The LAPD, meanwhile, was flying flags at half-mast in honor of Duane Larue, the highly decorated retired homicide detective who broke the Tate La Bianco case and was credited with bringing an end to the Bagley Bunch killing spree.

'The kid will be OK, Ernie,' Little Mike promised. 'They stuck him with a knife in the South Bronx and he lived to tell about it, remember?'

'I don't like it,' Thayer said, peering bleakly out of his window as they cruised downtown on Broadway. He barely recognized his neighborhood any more. The shoe repair stand was gone, the Jewish bakery, the butcher, the fishmonger. Replaced by desperately chic restaurants with catchy names like Zoot. Broadway wasn't *Broadway* any more. Then again, if all you can see is the world as it used to be then maybe it's time to move on. *Soon, Elly. Soon, my love . . .*

His dentist, young Dr Siegel, practiced out of a pocket-sized office in a narrow building on the corner of Madison and East 49th Street.

Little Mike pulled up out front and said, 'I'll wait for you right here, Ernie. Dr Siegel's office is on the third floor, remember?'

'I haven't forgotten. And I regard this appointment as the epitome of wasteful spending. Who needs a "permanent" crown at my age? A temporary one is plenty adequate. Hell, a well-targeted wad of saltwater taffy will do.'

Little Mike opened Thayer's door and helped him out. 'Just be a good boy, will you? Maybe the dentist will give you a lollipop.'

'If he does then I have a damned good idea where I'd like to stick it.'

It was a dingy old building with not much of a lobby. Just a front desk where a security guard sat dozing over a sports magazine. Since visitors were not required to sign in or phone upstairs for admittance Thayer had never fathomed what the guard was there to do – aside from use up oxygen. One of the two elevators was out of order. When the elevator finally arrived he took it up to the third floor. The elevator door opened on a meek little man in a trench coat who stood waiting there with a hopeful expression on his face. When the little man saw that the elevator was heading up, not down, he let out a crestfallen sigh.

There were two other office suites on the floor besides Dr Siegel's. One belonged to a dermatologist, the other to an accounting firm.

Thayer pressed the buzzer and was admitted to young Dr Siegel's waiting room, which was barely large enough to seat four patients. None were seated there right now. A flat screen, wall-mounted television played a video of brightly colored fish swimming about in a coral reef. It was, Thayer observed, painfully illustrative of this new American age. Why bother with a real fish tank when you can have a trouble-free two-dimensional image instead?

Linda at the reception desk showed him her gleaming white smile. 'You can go right in, Mr Thayer! Doctor Bob is ready!'

Thayer abhorred the way young Siegel called himself Doctor Bob. Felt it unseemly to be on a first-name basis with anyone who'd had his hands in either his mouth or his rectum.

'I just need a moment,' he said, feeling the urgent need to pee that struck him virtually every half hour. 'May I please borrow your lavatory key?'

'Absolutely, sir!' She handed him the key, which was attached to a clumsy block of wood so that no one would mistakenly pocket it. 'Do you remember where the men's room is?'

It was in the service stairwell. When Thayer went back out into the hallway that same little man was still waiting for the elevator, one hand clutching a Samsonite briefcase. He was in his forties with thick round glasses, thinning hair and the slump shouldered air of a man who often got yelled at. Thayer pegged him as an office drone at the accounting firm, though his trench coat was a top of the line Burberry and his gloves good kid leather.

'Sometimes the old-fashioned way is the best way,' Thayer advised him, pushing open the door to the stairs.

'I guess this is one of those times,' the little man acknowledged, his shoes squeaking as he started toward Thayer. He had on galoshes, which one didn't see very often any more. Apparently, there was rain in the forecast. 'After all, it's only three floors down.'

'And this way you can be sure you'll arrive in one piece.'

'You make a good point, sir.'

'Of course I do,' Thayer said loftily.

The cement stairwell was chilly and somewhat sooty. The men's room was right there on the third-floor landing.

'Say, there's another good idea,' the little man said as Thayer unlocked the door. 'I'm afraid I can't hold it like I used to.'

'Wait until you're my age. Better yet, hope that you never are.'

The men's room had a sink, a toilet stall and a urinal – all in need of a good scrubbing. The smell in there was quite revolting.

'Take your pick, sir,' the meek little man offered, crinkling his nose.

'I shall use the urinal if you don't mind. If I sit down it can take a crane and a husky work crew to get me back up.'

Thayer leaned a shoulder against the tile wall above the urinal to steady himself, unzipped his pants and felt around in his boxer shorts for his shriveled self. Then he stood there and waited for the stream to come. And waited, glancing idly at his companion in the mirrored wall above the sink.

The little man parked his briefcase by the stall door and pocketed his kid leather gloves. He wore a pair of white latex gloves underneath them. Suffered from a skin disorder, evidently, which suggested that he wasn't an accountant after all. He was a patient of the dermatologist.

One other thing Thayer observed: in the palm of his white-gloved right hand the little man was clutching a narrow wood chisel.

It was the last thing that Ernest Ludington Thayer ever saw.

With swift, sudden ferocity the man with the thick round glasses rushed at him and drove that chisel once, twice, three times deep into the base of his skull.

Thayer felt the intensely sharp pain of the first stab. After that he experienced . . . nothing at all. No pain. No awareness that something terrible and final was happening to him. No glimpses of his long, distinguished life passed before his eyes. Elly did not beckon to him, smiling sweetly. Thayer's brain had already ceased to function as his ancient body slid slowly down the wall. By the time he'd crumpled to the filthy, urine-soaked men's room floor the world's oldest living Pulitzer Prize winner no longer qualified for that title.

Downstairs at the curb, Little Mike sat behind the wheel of the Rolls fretting like crazy over Hunt Liebling. He wasn't nearly so confident about the kid's chances as he'd let on to Ernie. True, Hunt knew how to get out of a scrape. And maybe, just maybe, the kid had vanished into thin air because he was working the story in his own way. Preparing one wowser of a knock-out punch. But Little Mike's mind kept playing the flip side: what if Hunt had been shot dead along with the others? What if the police couldn't find his body because whoever killed him was purposely trying to make him look like the culprit? God, he sure hoped the kid was alright. Because if anything bad had happened to Hunt then Ernie would never forgive himself.

With a heavy sigh Little Mike flipped open his laptop computer. He carried it whenever he chauffeured Ernie around. The sports section of the *New York Daily News* barely even mentioned boxing any more. If you wanted to keep up with the sweet science you had to go online. But first he checked his email.

Still nothing from Marie. He hadn't heard back from her in a couple of days, and couldn't understand why. He really wanted to see her again. Maybe take her to the Poconos for a weekend. And maybe, if she was ready, take their relationship to the next level. She was such a nice, classy lady. Stacked, too. And he'd thought the two of them had really hit it off.

Little Mike was thinking maybe he should just pick up the phone and call her when a guy in a maintenance uniform came rushing out of Dr Siegel's building and tapped on his window.

Little Mike lowered it and said, 'Help you, pal?'

'The dentist's office just called down,' he said, a black guy with the name *Rico* stitched on his chest. 'Mr Thayer is having a little problem in the third-floor men's room. They wondered if you could give him a hand.'

'Is he OK? Did they call an ambulance?'

'I don't know, man. They just said he needed you.'

Little Mike locked up the Rolls and hurried toward the front door of the building.

'One of the elevators is out of order,' Rico called after him. 'If you take the stairs you'll get there faster.'

The sleepy security guard at the front desk barely looked up when Little Mike lumbered by him to the stairs and started climbing, snuffling for breath through his broken nose. He was halfway up the second flight of steps when he encountered a businessman with thick, round eyeglasses who was on his way down, Samsonite briefcase in hand. Little Mike was too worried about Ernie to pay him much mind.

Not until the businessman stuck out his leg and tripped him.

Little Mike went down hard. 'Hey, what the hell?' he protested, raising his head just in time to see the wood chisel coming down at him fast.

He raised his left hand to block it – and felt an unbelievable stab of pain as the guy drove the chisel into his palm, shattering several small bones. Staggered, Little Mike was defenseless against the savage thrusts that pierced deep into the base of his skull. With a groan he pitched over on to his back, arms and legs twitching, and gazed up at those familiar bright lights that were floating up there high above the canvas. In the last precious few seconds of his life Irish Mike O'Brien, pride of Far Rockaway, Queens, vowed to get back up on his feet one more time and do his mom and his pop proud. He was fighting for them. Hell, he was fighting for the whole damned neighborhood. They were all there to cheer him on. Irish Mike could hear their mighty roar.

But he couldn't get back up. Irish Mike O'Brien twitched once more and stayed down for good.

SEVENTEEN

This is the greatest day of my life, Brink realized as he ran his team of Park Avenue dogs through the Central Park Ramble. *And by a strange twist of fate it's also the worst.*

Never before had he experienced so much elation and sheer anguish at the same time. His heart was racing much, much faster than usual. His innards were roiling. His whole being was in turmoil.

As of today Brink Liebling was now an official cast member of *By Any Means Necessary*. No more flea killer commercials. He'd finally arrived. A certified prime-time television star.

He'd jumped on his Indian Chief that morning and zipped on out to Silvercup Studios in Long Island City to read for the show runners of *BAMN*. Brink knew them already. He'd auditioned for a role in the gritty cop drama back when they were initially casting. Nailed it, too. But the network wanted a proven West Coast leading man, which was painfully typical when the networks were casting New York shows. They wanted edgy authenticity. Just not too much.

Today, the show runners didn't want him to read. They just wanted him to say yes. Apparently, their proven West Coast leading man had suddenly dropped out. Or been fired. It wasn't exactly clear to Brink. And totally didn't matter. What mattered was they wanted *him* to play the newly created Joey Murtaugh, a detective with a drinking problem and a junkie for a wife. The part was his. He even had network approval. He couldn't imagine how. Or believe his luck.

One of the producers noticed the shock on his face and said, 'You were always our first choice. We just had to wait for the network to come around.'

His agent would be hearing from their money person very soon, they assured him. Which Brink sincerely doubted because, let's face it, *none of this is really happening*. But his agent had already texted him the details of their generous offer by the time he'd made it back across the Queensborough

Bridge. It was real, alright. He started shooting on Monday. Had a wardrobe fitting tomorrow at ten a.m. followed by a publicity photo shoot. He still hadn't broken the news to Luze. Couldn't wait to.

This was the good part of his day. But there was a really, really bad part.

Remember the Alamo.

Hunt was in deep shit. It was all over the morning news that Tim Ferris of *The Big Happy Family* had been murdered in Topanga Canyon along with three others. According to Herbie Landau, the Panorama Communications tycoon – and Brink's new uber-boss – Hunt had been out there trying to get some dirt on Senator Gary Dixon from Ferris. Hunt had even been staying at the very house where the murders took place. Now he was missing and the police were looking for him. And Brink had yet to hear a single word from him. No phone call or text message. No email. Nothing. He'd tried calling his brother's cell a zillion times but the phone just rang and rang – didn't even go to voice mail. Every moment that Brink was in with those *BAMN* producers he'd been consumed by worry. *Where's Hunt? Why hasn't he reached out to me?*

When Brink arrived on Park Avenue to run his dogs one last time he got some answers from Pat the doorman, who'd been sneaking looks at Panorama News Channel.

The murder weapon had belonged to Hunt.

According to the LA County Sheriff's Department, the Glock semi-automatic handgun used in the massacre had been registered to Hunt by the state of California. Which Brink refused to believe. Hunt had never owned a gun in his life. But as far as the authorities were concerned, Hunt had murdered four people, was a dangerous fugitive, and that wasn't all.

Hunt was now in New York.

A computer search of the airline passenger manifests had turned up his name on a red-eye flight out of LA late last night that landed at JFK at eight a.m. Officials were scouring the security camera feeds at both airports for a glimpse of him. And a massive FBI-NYPD manhunt was under way throughout the city.

'You haven't heard from him?' Pat asked Brink.

'Nope. I've checked my phone eight times.'

'Well, you'll be hearing from the law. Count on it.'

'They've got it all wrong, Pat. Hunt wouldn't kill anyone.'

'Of course he wouldn't,' Pat said reassuringly. 'I wouldn't worry.'

But Brink did worry. He was so worried that he almost didn't notice the new pair of benchwarmers who were hanging out in the Ramble today. Brink saw a lot of the same faces there when he ran. Park Avenue nannies who congregated on the same benches every day with their little charges. Elderly people catching a few rays, often accompanied by a nurse or paid companion. But he'd never seen a pair quite like the New Odd Couple.

One was a soft-looking middle-aged businessman whose thick round eyeglasses made him look like an owl. The other was a dapper, goateed black man wearing a belted suede jacket, yellow turtleneck and tan slacks. The two men were chatting. Seemed to be together. But why would a white bureaucrat and a sharp black guy be sitting on a bench together in the middle of Central Park? Were they out-of-town convention-eers? Secret gay lovers?

None of the above. Their eyes gave them away.

When Brink ran the dogs everyone in the park looked *at the dogs*. Hardly noticed Brink at all. Yet the New Odd Couple never so much as glanced at his half-dozen charges. Just stared right at Brink as he ran by them. *Because they were cops.* Of course, they were hoping he'd lead them to Hunt.

Remember the Alamo.

Brink checked his phone again. Still nothing from Hunt. Luze would be home from school soon. Brink texted her to let her know he was on his way. God, he had so much to tell her. He cut his run short, returned the dogs to their apartments and settled up with Pat. Then Brink climbed on to his Indian Chief and kick-started it, his eyes searching up and down Park Avenue. He didn't spot the New Odd Couple anywhere. Good. He started his way home to Harlem.

Brink was cruising up Madison near E. 87th Street when he felt his phone vibrate in his chest pocket. He pulled over right away and flicked on his Bluetooth, hoping it was Hunt.

It was one of the executive producers of *BAMN*, sounding a whole lot chillier than she had this morning. 'Listen . . . are you related to Hunt Liebling?'

'He's my brother, why?'

Silence. Really long silence. 'We need to supply you with a response . . .'

'To what? My brother's no criminal. He's a really distinguished journalist. This mess will be cleared up by the end of the day, I guarantee it.'

'I'm sure you're right, Brink, but the network doesn't like to cast anyone who has personal problems.'

'I don't have personal problems.'

'Brink, I'll have to get back to you, OK?'

'Wait, are you saying I don't have the part now?'

'I'm saying I'll get back to you.'

The line went dead. Brink felt as if he'd just been punched in the gut.

It was getting to be rush hour. The one-way uptown traffic on Madison inched slowly along. Brink made decent time by weaving his bike in between the taxis and commuter busses. But as he got close to home the traffic became completely snarled. His block of Madison between 122nd and 123rd was closed off with police barricades. A half-dozen blue and whites were parked in front of his building, along with an EMT van and a couple of unmarked sedans. Something had gone down – not an unusual state of affairs if you lived in Harlem.

'What's happening?' he asked the beefy uniformed cop on the barricade.

'They don't tell me a thing. I'm just supposed to secure the block.' The cop checked out Brink's Indian Chief with keen interest. 'That an old Harley?'

'I live on this street, man. I have to get home.'

He pulled the barricade aside so Brink could get through. 'Just try to stay out of the way, OK?'

Brink eased the bike toward his building, engine burbling. His neighbors were standing out on the sidewalk gawking at the policemen who were going in and out. He spotted Mrs Washington from across the hall, who didn't like him. And sweet Charmaine from next door, who danced with Alvin Ailey. Both women looked wide-eyed with fear.

'Yo, Flea!' Kareem, the super's son, came darting out of the service gate toward him. 'You got to book *now*, man. They looking for you.'

'Who's looking for me?'

'The police. They think you stuck her.'

'Stuck who, Kareem?'

'Your old lady. She *dead*.'

All of the oxygen rushed out of Brink's body. '*What . . .?*'

'Somebody killed her, Flea, like a half-hour ago. I heard 'em say they was looking for you. That nasty old Mrs Washington? She told 'em you was a no-good unemployed actor. And I'm like, yo, what's up with that? I *seen* you on the TV like *all* the time and . . .'

Brink no longer heard a word the kid was saying. There was such a loud roar between his ears that he thought his whole head would explode. *Luze is dead.* His love *gone*. His life *gone*. How could this have happened? Who would hurt Luze?

Now Mrs Washington spotted him there on his Indian Chief. She told a policeman at the front door, who turned and looked at Brink.

Someone else was looking at Brink, too. That same middle-aged plainclothesman with thick round glasses who'd been sitting in Central Park with his black partner. The little owl stood right there next to Mrs Washington staring at him, a look of cool detachment on his face.

Two cops in uniform started their way toward Brink, hands on their holsters. Brink watched them, then glanced back at the little owl – except now the guy was gone. Vanished into thin air.

'Sir, please shut off your engine and dismount,' one of the cops barked.

He didn't dismount. He tore out of there with a roar – jumped the sidewalk, veered around the barricade and sped his way down Madison *against* the one-way uptown traffic. Steering in and around the honking cars and buses. Sending alarmed pedestrians diving out of his way, hollering, until he'd managed to make it below Marcus Garvey Park and on to E. 119th at North General Hospital. He took that over to Fifth Avenue, where he made a screeching left so low that he nearly scraped pavement, then rocketed his way downtown through the projects.

Brink fled, his eyes stinging with tears. He had no idea where he was going. Just away.

But they weren't going to let him go, he realized, noticing

the dark blue Volvo in his rear-view mirror. It was staying right with him, running every light he ran, bearing down on him hard as he raced his way in and out of the downtown traffic. Brink could make out a black man behind the wheel, and a white man with round eyeglasses riding shotgun. *Them.* Except they weren't acting like any kind of law enforcers. No flashing lights, no siren. Which could mean only one thing. *They are Luze's killers. And now they are after me, too.* But why? Why had these two complete strangers killed the woman he loved? Who they fuck were they?

No time to find out now. Had to get away. His agent was a lawyer. Her office was on W. 57th Street. He'd go there and talk over this madness with her before he turned himself in. He was an innocent man, after all. But first he had to lose these maniacs. He liked his chances. He had the Indian Chief. They didn't. And he knew every single path in Central Park. They couldn't. Not like he did.

The Malcolm X Boulevard entrance was open to vehicular traffic after three. Brink plunged into the park there, went around the first bend then jumped the curb and zoomed his way across open ground toward the Harlem Meer, which was what they called the lake up in Central Park's northeast corner.

In his rear-view mirror, the Volvo peeled off and came right after him.

There were footpaths below the Meer that led toward the Conservatory Garden. He hurtled his way down one of them, pedestrians screaming at him in angry protest. Until they caught sight of that blue Volvo squeezing its way down the narrow footpath after him and had to dive out of its way or get run over.

Luze is dead.

Brink tumbled on to East Drive and joined the car traffic winding its way toward Lasker Pool before he jumped the curb once again – the blue Volvo hot on his tail – and found the unpaved swathe of the park's Bridle Path, the bike's wheels spinning in the loose cinders before they caught hold. He tore his way downtown on the Bridle Path, the Volvo staying right with him as he veered around startled dog walkers and joggers. And now he was overtaking a guided equestrian tour. The roar of the Indian Chief scaring hell out of a half-dozen horses. And really scaring their riders. Somehow, the Volvo was

gaining on him. Glancing in his rear-view mirror, Brink saw
the little owl leaning out his window with a weapon that he
held like a pistol except it looked like a rifle. It *was* a rifle.
A shot slammed into one of Brink's leather saddle bags, the
impact almost knocking him over. But Brink kept the Indian
Chief righted, kept on going, faster and faster, letting the
Indian Chief run full bore.

Snapshots . . . It was all happening so fast he could take in
only snatches . . . Streaking around the Central Park Reservoir
. . . Across the Great Lawn . . . Guys throwing Frisbees, lovers
walking hand in . . . Plowing right through a touch football
game . . . The Volvo still gaining on him . . . Jumping on to
the 79th Street Transverse, shooting in between two onrushing
taxis, their brakes screeching . . . The Volvo smashing into
somebody back there and spinning out. Yet still coming
after him, dented, one headlight broken, not slowing, never
slowing . . .

Until Brink disappeared back into the maze-like confines
of the Ramble for the second time that day. Roaring his way
through the people. Hearing more yells of protest. Not caring.
He was safe now. No way a car could make it through the
Ramble. Too narrow. He'd finally shaken them. Just had to
make it over the Rowboat Lake on the Bank Rock footbridge
– setting for a million on-screen romantic clinches – and he'd
be out of the park free and clear.

It was quiet there at the scenic little humpbacked bridge.
No people. As Brink sped his way across it, the luxury apartment towers of Central Park West looming before him in the
sunset, he allowed himself a small sigh of relief. Yes, his entire
life had been destroyed. Luze was dead. Hunt was God knows
where. Nothing, but nothing made sense. But at least he'd
beaten back these bastards and lived to tell about it.

'Remember the Alamo!' he cried out exultantly.

He didn't see the barricade at the other end of the bridge
until it was too late.

It was a heavy wooden Parks Department barricade and
the bike crunched right into it at full speed. Brink kept on
going. Flew some thirty feet through the air before he
slammed face-first into a tree and fell, broken, to the ground.
Brink lay there, barely conscious, not wholly aware of how
much pain he was in. He did know that it was incredibly

hard to breathe. He had to gasp for air, hearing the bike's engine burbling somewhere nearby.

And footsteps. Someone was coming. Brink could make out a pair of highly polished black wingtip shoes. The owner of the wingtips was turning him over on to his back. Brink squinted up at him. It was the little owl. He and his partner must have separated back when Brink lost them in the Ramble. Except he hadn't lost them. The owl had simply gone up ahead on foot to set up the barricade. They'd been up inside his head the whole way. How?

Brink tried to ask him, but all he could manage was a half-choked gurgle.

The little owl had a chilly, professional look on his face as he snatched Brink's phone from him and pocketed it. Now he was clutching something heavy in his gloved hands – a large, flat granite fieldstone, the kind that the old Vermont farmers used to make stone walls. And he was raising that heavy stone high over his head, pausing to gather his strength before he brought it rushing downward toward Brink's face.

Brink didn't see anything after that. Didn't see the little owl fling the bloodied fieldstone into the lake where it landed with a plop and sank to the bottom, sending ripples across the still water. Didn't see him stride calmly out of the park, Samsonite briefcase in hand, and on to Central Park West, where he joined the flow of people walking home from work. He was unaware of these things because Brink Liebling, distinguished graduate of the Yale School of Drama and – for a very few brief hours – a star of the acclaimed police drama *BAMN* had already been cancelled.

EIGHTEEN

Clover parked the Volvo on West 83rd Street near Amsterdam, his nerves still jingle-jangling from that high-speed chase through Central Park. Not to mention slamming into that damned taxi. He wiped the Volvo clean of prints before he removed their overnight bags, slinging the canvas duffel of weapons over his shoulder, and hoofed it toward Broadway. Coop had their assignment folder in his Samsonite briefcase, along with the old prize fighter's laptop and the computer hard drive he'd boosted from Brink Liebling's apartment. When Clover got to Broadway he caught a cab downtown, instructing the turbaned driver to pull over at the corner of West 77th to pick up that little fellow who was waiting patiently there, the one with the round glasses.

They rode downtown together in silence. Coop had been quiet ever since Clover picked him up around the corner from the Harlem apartment building. Not because he was upset about taking a kitchen knife to the man's beautiful dark-skinned wife. Coop was simply a quiet little dude as a general rule. Which suited Cloverdale Millington just fine.

Clover couldn't abide nervous chatterers. Especially when you were up against a busted play. Absolutely nothing had gone according to script when it came to the disposition of Mr and Mrs Brinkley Liebling. They'd planned to do the man first while he was dog running in Central Park, then deal with the wife and the hard drive. But there'd been too damned many nannies there in the park. So instead they did the wife first. Easy pickings for Coop, who knocked right on her apartment door saying he was an insurance adjuster checking out a neighbor's break-in claim. The wife let him in. That was the beauty of Coop. He looked like a harmless mama's boy. But he was the coldest killer Clover had ever met.

The wife did some screaming and a neighbor called the cops. Not a big deal. They just waited downstairs for her husband to come home – except he went cowboy and took off on his motorcycle. They had to chase the bastard over hill and dale. Still, it all worked out OK because Clove was thorough and prepared. He'd memorized those pathways through Central Park while he was waiting for Coop's flight to land. That was how he'd anticipated the man's escape route and arranged for Coop to barricade the footbridge. Mission accomplished.

As they rode downtown in the cab Clover noticed how his knees kept jiggling. His good, pure adrenaline was flowing, which was a mighty positive sign. Meant that he had his edge back. He needed his edge if he was going to make it through this assignment to the end. Still had a long drive ahead of him tonight. Needed to be alert and up. *Himself*. That's why he stopped taking his meds last night. No more damned meds until the job was done. Being straight felt good for a change. He was staying in the moment. Keeping it real. No worries. Hell, he was fine without those meds. Just needed to stay awake, that's all. As long as he stayed straight and awake he'd be fine.

The cab dropped them at a garage on Eleventh Avenue near the Javits Center. Clover had stashed a fresh 2004 Mercedes Benz S430 there last night.

Mrs Pryor had summoned him to New York City from Boca one full day ahead of Coop. The Fed Ex package was already waiting for him downstairs at his front desk. Clover had packed a bag for fall weather. Kissed his third wife, Anita, and left their twelfth-floor ocean-front condo, complete with twenty-four-hour security, heated pool and Isis, his bug-cute sixteen-year-old Cuban girlfriend, who lived three floors below in another unit that he owned.

It was a sweet arrangement. Anita didn't know about Isis. Didn't know exactly what Clover did for work any more, either. She still thought he was with Army Intelligence, which had drop-kicked him four years back because of his various and sundry psychological challenges. Happily, The Outfit didn't care so long as he got the job done. Isis? That girl was strictly interested in nice clothes and a steady flow of Colombian marching powder. And damn could she make love. Which was another reason why he was laying off those fool meds. When he got home tomorrow he wanted his cobra to be rising.

He'd caught the eleven forty-five a.m. flight out of West Palm.

After he landed at La Guardia he jacked the Mercedes from long-term parking, switched its plates with somebody's Mazda and drove it into Manhattan, where he parked it in that garage by the Javits Center. The Fed Ex package had contained the key to a locker in the Port Authority Bus Terminal, inside which he'd found their assignment folder and $50,000 in cash for expenses.

While he was in midtown he did his recon on the dentist's building on Madison. He knew the time and place of the old man's appointment thanks to The Outfit's phone taps. The plan he devised required a maintenance man's outfit. He scored that from a uniform store on Sixth Avenue along with two pairs of coveralls for the Mineola job. Bought Coop's Samsonite briefcase at a luggage shop nearby. Then boosted a Nissan Altima and drove it over to Newark to score their firepower from a gun seller he knew who fronted as a second-hand kitchen appliance dealer. He drove the Nissan back to a parking garage near the bustling Times Square theater district, where he swapped it for the blue Volvo sedan.

Clover always chose a sedan when he was on assignment. You just never knew when you might need to cram a big something, or someone, into the trunk.

He drove the Volvo out to Mineola and parked it behind some abandoned warehouses. Walked two miles to the nearest shopping mall, boosted a Subaru Outback and took that to the Cablevision Service Center's parking lot, where he borrowed one of their bucket trucks. Then he drove the truck to JFK to meet Coop's flight.

The fresh Benz was right where he'd left it. It was gunmetal gray, with black leather. A good highway car. They got in. He steered them out of the city through the Lincoln Tunnel and on to the New Jersey Turnpike, heading south for Washington, DC. It was not quite six p.m. They had a four- to five-hour drive depending on the traffic, which was never light on the Jersey Turnpike. Same as there was never a single square foot of anything nice to look at. But Clover wasn't getting paid ten grand a month to gaze at the scenery.

'You doing OK over there, Coop?' he asked him after a solid hour of silence. The little dude was so quiet it was easy to forget he was sitting there.

'Fine and dandy, my friend.'

'Feel like stopping for dinner soon?'

'If you'd like to. Whenever you're hungry.'

Both of them detested the greasy fast food that was indigenous to interstate rest stops. 'If you can hold out a while there's a nice little Italian place outside of Cherry Hill that serves killer veal piccata.'

'Sounds wonderful. Do we have the time?'

'Plenty of time. We'll have ourselves a nice meal, wash it down with a bottle of Chianti Classico. I'll even spring for a ninety-eight if they've got one. That was the best vintage for Chiantis in I don't know how long.'

Coop was staring at him from behind those thick, round glasses of his. 'Clover, I don't mean to be rude but are you sure it's OK for you to drink alcohol on that medication you're taking?'

Clover smiled at him. A secret smile. 'Oh, a glass or two won't hurt. In fact, scientists say it's the ticket to a long and healthy life.'

NINETEEN

C.C. heard the lock turn in Hunt's front door just after one a.m. She'd been at work when the shit hit the fan and never left. Just stayed there surfing frantically for every morsel of late breaking news – and taking a nail file to her fingernails, which she'd started to chew on for the first time since she was a high school geekette. C.C. was so upset she could barely focus. Didn't know what to believe. But she did know this: Hunt wasn't merely being blamed for the Saddle Peak massacre now. It was so much worse than that. According to the FBI, he'd fled LA for New York and slaughtered everyone there who was near and dear to him. Thayer and Little Mike. Hunt's sister-in-law, Luze. Supposedly, his brother Brink was a victim of Hunt's rampage, too. According to the news reports, the poor man had gone mad when he found out about Luze and had crashed his motorcycle into a barricade in Central Park.

This made a total of eight people who were gone.

And now Hunt was a wanted man, his picture all over the TV and the Internet. C.C. had been fielding emails and phone calls all day from his worried online friends. Also from opportunistic reporters who were jonesing for a career-making scoop. She fended off friend and foe alike, pleading ignorance. Which was no stretch of the truth: C.C. had no idea what the hell was really going on. All she knew was that the man she loved was not a crazed killer. Hunt had brains. Hunt had integrity. She believed in him. So here's what she kept thinking:

He'd gotten some major dirt from Tim Ferris on Gary Dixon. Dirt that could topple Dixon's bid for the presidency. '*I'm up against something really huge*,' he'd said to her on the phone. He'd sounded worried, and with good cause – people with some serious chops had been hacking into her personal financial accounts. And now those same people were framing Hunt for these murders. It wasn't that much of a stretch. They'd have no problem planting the serial number of a Glock registered to Hunt in a State of California database. Or inserting his name on the passenger manifest of a red-eye flight from LAX to JFK so as to place him in New York. Chances were he'd never even left LA. Hell, for all she knew Hunt had died right along with the others on Saddle Peak. But *why*? What on earth did Tim Ferris have on Dixon that was *so* damaging that Ferris and his Saddle Peak household had to be wiped out – along with virtually everyone who Hunt might have reached out to in New York?

This is what C.C. was wondering when she heard the front door open.

'Hunt, is that you?' She dashed from the dining room, nail file in hand. 'I've been calling you and calling you. Where've you been? Hunt . . .?'

But it wasn't Hunt.

Two men stood there in his entry hall. One looked just like Mr Klein, her high school geometry teacher. The other was a tall, nicely dressed black man. Both men wore latex gloves. The one who looked like Mr Klein had galoshes on over his shoes.

With a sudden chill of certainty C.C. realized what should have occurred to her much earlier: *I am one of the people who Hunt contacted.*

The black man said, 'We tried you at your apartment, sugar lips, but we should have figured from the very get-go that you'd be here, seeing as how you loved this particular guy and all that.' He talked very fast. Seemed high on something. His eyes had a glint to them. 'You're hanging close in case he checks in. That's awful sweet. Isn't that sweet, Coop?'

Coop shot a surprised look at him before he murmured, 'Very sweet.'

'How did you get in?' C.C. demanded, keeping her voice steady.

'Sugar lips, there isn't a lock on this planet I can't open in less than ten seconds.' The black man was clutching a plastic jug of barbecue starter fluid, she now noticed. He unscrewed the cap and began squirting its contents around the dining room, soaking the computers, the network of towers, printers and server hook ups, the rug under the desks, the heavy drapes over the windows. Within seconds the whole room stank. 'By the way, do you folks generally back up your emails on CDs?'

'You won't get away with this,' she told him.

'Yes, we will. Bad shit happens. Sorry to be the one to tell you.'

She made a run for the front door but the other man, Coop, was no geometry teacher. He kicked C.C.'s legs out from under her with so much force that she flew up into the air before crashing hard to the floor. Coop reached down and tried to grab her. She stabbed him in the back of his hand with her nail file, drawing blood.

He stared at her with no expression on his face. Didn't register any pain.

'That wasn't nice, sugar lips,' the black man clucked disapprovingly. 'But you have to admire the spunk, don't you, Coop?'

Coop said nothing. Just bent her hand back so that she would let go of the file – bent it back so far that C.C. could feel her wrist about ready to snap. Groaning, she gave it up. He pocketed it, then kicked her in the ear so hard that she practically passed out. Then he stuffed a rag in her mouth and bound her wrists and ankles with rope.

The black man fetched Hunt's mildewy shower curtain from the bathroom. He bent down and laid it over C.C. gently, almost tenderly, like when her father used to tuck her into bed at night. 'This is to protect my man Coop's clothing,' he explained. 'He's always real careful about keeping his person tidy. Did the same thing when he stuck that pretty wife up in Harlem. Not one spot of blood on him. Am I right or am I right, Coop?'

Coop shot an annoyed look at his partner. Then he went into the kitchen. C.C. could hear him rummaging around in the drawers in there.

He returned with a steak knife.

C.C. screamed and screamed into that rag in her mouth as he kept stabbing her in the neck – until finally he severed her carotid artery and her blood, her *being*, came gushing out on to the musty carpet. The two men backed slowly out, the black man pausing in the doorway to set fire to a rag and toss it under Hunt's desk. Then he closed the door behind him and, with a *whoosh*, C.C. Reiter's brilliant and beautiful young life went up in flames.

TWENTY

'What a load of crap!' Herbie hollered at the television set, flinging his uneaten hot fudge sundae across the elegant master suite of the Ronald Coleman house. It landed near the foot of his bed, fudge sauce exploding all over his spotless white carpet. As if he cared. He was too upset to care.

Somehow, Liebling had gotten away. And so had Volume Five of Tim's memoir. There were only four DVDs in the damned box. The crucial fifth volume was missing. The one that would put the White House out of reach forever. And now he had a total fucking mess on his hands.

He'd forced himself to sit through the first four volumes of Timmy's poisonous video diatribe. Most of that poison was directed at him personally. Herbie couldn't believe how bitter and hateful the cancer-stricken brat remained after all of these years. Not once did Timmy mention all of the positive things he'd done. The sheer joy that his beloved creation, *The Big Happy Family*, had given to countless millions around the world. The children's hospital wing he'd bankrolled at Cedars-Sinai. The tens of thousands of computers he'd donated to the LA public schools. The Herbert Landau scholarship fund he'd endowed at USC.

Herbie slumped back in his black leather recliner with a weary groan. It was three a.m. but there was no time to sleep. He was the public face of this disaster. Making one grim-faced appearance after another for the media horde. Going on-air live with Matt Lauer, with Larry King. Meanwhile working, working, the phone. Shpritzing a story line out of thin air to account for the Liebling fuck-up, then retrofitting the evidence so that it would stand on its feet. The geeks in La Mirada made it happen. Everywhere Hunt Liebling had gone he'd left dead bodies behind – or so it appeared. And with Herbie's own Panorama News Channel out in front, pushing the hell out of it, the story had taken hold.

The unvarnished truth, sad to say, was a whole other plot:

Hunt Liebling had disappeared off of the face of the earth. Hadn't tried to email anyone. Hadn't used his cell phone or touched his credit cards. He'd simply vanished. So had Tyrone Gilliam's Buick Le Sabre.

Liebling's laptop computer had been on the bench at the lab in La Mirada all day and night, the kids poring through his emails and address book for possible leads. Herbie had ordered Mort to bring him the rest of his possessions so he could have a look at them for himself.

'Mr Weingarten, sir,' Milton the butler announced dryly.

Mort came into the master suite toting Hunt Liebling's rumpled knapsack and overnight bag. Despite the late hour the attorney looked as alert and unflappable as ever. Herbie swore he had formaldehyde in his veins. Mort deposited Liebling's bags on the coffee table and reported, 'The kids have located three journalists in the LA area with whom Liebling has been in regular contact over the past several months. Two work at the *Times*, one is a freelancer. They're monitoring the computers and cell phones of all three, and Baer has men watching their houses. But Liebling hasn't reached out to any of them yet. He's also very tight with a left-wing blogger up in the Bay Area. A self-styled muckraker like himself. The kids are monitoring her, too. And Baer has her under surveillance.'

'What else?' Herbie demanded testily.

'They've gone through Liebling's notepads.'

'And what have they found?'

'Nothing that we'd want made public. A blow-by-blow account of his conversation with you at the beach, right down to the Gulden's mustard you like. Detailed descriptions of Volumes One through Four . . .'

'What about Volume Five?'

'Nothing. Not a word.'

'Damn . . .' Herbie ran a hand over his jowly face. 'Let me see that knapsack.'

'It's empty, Herbie. I don't see why you—'

'That's why you're you and I'm me. I want to get inside his head, OK?' He tore open Liebling's black nylon knapsack and peered inside. Like Mort said, there was nothing in there – beyond a gooey sludge at the bottom of its main zippered compartment. Herbie felt around down there and came up with several wads of chewed bubble gum, a half-eaten Snickers bar and an aged throat lozenge that had fused to its wrapper. 'Jesus, this guy's a human cockroach.' Disgusted, Herbie tossed the knapsack aside and opened Liebling's overnight bag. Inside were a few T-shirts, a pair of jeans, a ragged old sweater. 'And he lives like a fucking teenager. No wonder I couldn't do business with him. Where are all of the grown-ups, Mort? Are we the only ones left?'

Mort didn't answer. Just lurked there in his black suit.

'Siddown, will you? You're giving me the willies.'

Mort perched on the loveseat awaiting Herbie's orders.

'OK, we know Liebling doesn't have Volumes One through Four,' Herbie asserted, stabbing the coffee table with a blunt index finger. 'Because *we* have them. But where the fuck is Volume Five?'

'We must assume Liebling has it,' Mort replied, grayish tongue moistening his thin, dry lips. 'It's his best leverage, after all. And here's one more troubling thought: We may not be in sole possession of these first four DVDs.'

'What's that supposed to mean?'

'It means we can't be certain that there's only one set of them in existence. We won't know that until we locate Liebling – assuming he'll tell us.'

'Oh, he'll tell us,' Herbie said darkly. 'What I'd like to know is how the fuck he got away. Where was he when the hit went down?'

'Hiding somewhere on the estate, presumably.'

'Did Rudy turn up yet?'

'The front gate was left open for quite a while. Odds are the dog got frightened and ran for the hills. Coyotes will probably get him.'

'Christ . . .' Herbie still couldn't get used to the idea that wild animals lived all over Southern California. 'Flynn Leverett's been questioned, right?'

'By a Santa Barbara County Sheriff's investigator. Apparently, she was quite upset about Timmy.'

'Yeah, she always had a thing for him. I tried to shtup her back when she was seventeen, eighteen. Real cute kid, even if she did have a pair of hands on her like Burt Lancaster. I took her to dinner at Scandia, but she gave me such a fish eye I figured her for a dyke.' Herbie's googly eyes narrowed. 'Can we trust her?'

'Flynn falls under the category of "trust but verify". Baer is keeping a tap on her phone and a man on her place.'

'A neat, surgical operation,' Herbie grumbled. 'That's what Baer promised us. Now look what we've got.'

'Herbie, I know the situation appears perilous but bear this in mind: wherever he is, Hunt Liebling is a marked man. No one will believe a single word he has to say.'

'They'll believe him if he has that fifth DVD on him. If that thing gets out the Dixon campaign is toast.'

Mort considered this for a moment. 'He hasn't tried to put it out on the Internet yet. Puzzling, don't you think?'

'What are you getting at?'

'What if he *doesn't* have it?'

Herbie sat up in his chair. 'Doesn't have the DVD?'

'That's what I'm saying.'

'If we don't have it and Liebling doesn't have it then where is it?'

'I haven't the slightest idea.'

'Hold on, maybe I do . . .' Herbie said slowly. 'Knowing Timmy, there *is* another possibility. What if it wasn't in his safe with the other DVDs because he sent it to somebody? What if he wanted this somebody to watch it before he died and maybe, just maybe, forgive him a little bit?'

'Are we talking about who I think we're talking about?'

Herbie stared at him in reply.

'Alicia has jumped the grid, Herbie. We can't find her. We've tried.'

'Try harder,' Herbie ordered him. 'Find Alicia Ferris. And find that bastard Liebling, will you? Christ, where in the hell is he?'

TWENTY-ONE

T he slam of a car door in the next parking space woke
him with a start. Briefly, Hunt was confused as to why
he was lying wrapped up in a blanket in the back of
someone's freezing cold van. It took him a moment to
remember that he was a wanted man who had driven this van
all night. That right now he was in the middle of a Wal-Mart
parking lot in the suburbs of Reno, Nevada. And that the hot,
sour breath approximately three inches from his face belonged
to Rudy, who was wide awake and anxious to be let out.

'Yeah, I'll get right on that, little dude,' Hunt groaned.

He was on the run. His destination a tiny dot on the map
2,000 miles away called Balltown, Iowa. Hunt's hope – his
prayer – was that he'd find Alicia Ferris there. That it was
Alicia who had forwarded Tim's letter to Thayer. And that
when he found Tim's estranged daughter he'd also find the
duplicate set of Tim's memoir, including the missing Volume
Five and maybe even *Monty and Me*.

Alicia had it. Alicia *had* to have it.

Hunt knuckled his bleary eyes, yawning, and glanced at his
watch. It was eleven thirty a.m. He'd grabbed two whole hours
of sleep. Rudy pawed at the van's sliding side door again,
whimpering.

'I heard you the first time, little dude.'

He poured himself some strong black coffee from the
Thermos and climbed back behind the wheel of the van,
blinking in the bright morning sunlight. Then he started it up
and pulled out of the parking lot, his memory of the last twelve
hours a chaotic freakfest.

First, Flynn had helped him dispose of Tyrone's Le Sabre.
Climbed in her Jeep and led Hunt up San Marcos Pass to a
dirt road that twisted its way deep into wild, rocky country.
Hunt drove the Buick down into a ravine there. No one would
spot it for days, she assured him.

They worked fast after that, fearing the law would come
knocking on her door any minute. She took a pair of dog

grooming shears to Hunt's head of unruly black curls and fashioned him a crude, hasty crew cut. He shaved off his two-day growth of beard, leaving himself with the beginnings of the goatee he'd worn when he went underground as a Latino migrant worker.

There was no way he could fly to Iowa. Not without showing his driver's license to airport security. So Flynn gave him the keys to the fourteen-year-old white Ford Econoline van she used for hauling kennel cages. She gave him a couple of wool Navy surplus blankets to curl up in. The big Thermos of coffee, gallon jugs of water. A Coleman cooler that was stuffed with bison loaf sandwiches, a wedge of Cheddar cheese, a jar of peanut butter, a loaf of wholewheat bread, apples and bananas.

It was cold where Hunt was heading and he was still wearing his running shorts. Flynn found him some baggy jeans of her son's, a plaid flannel shirt, a bandanna kerchief. Also an old dark blue turtleneck sweater of hers that fit Hunt under his leather jacket.

Lastly, she produced two plastic bowls, a bag of Casey's Own dog chow and a leash. 'He doesn't really need the leash,' she explained. 'But they require them at those roadside rest stops, and the last thing you need is someone—'

'Wait, wait. What's up with all of this dog stuff?'

'Rudy's going with you.'

'No way. Uh-unh.'

'You have to take him, Hunt. Otherwise, you won't get within a hundred feet of Alicia. And he *can't* stay with me. Trust me, if Rudy's here when the Sheriff's deputies show up I'll get all flustered and blow it. I'm the world's worst liar.' Flynn opened the van's door. Rudy promptly jumped up on to the passenger seat, stubby tail thumping. 'Besides, he wants to be with you, see? So don't fight it. The matter is settled. Do you need money?'

'I'm good.'

She handed him a half-dozen folded twenties anyway. 'The mileage on this old bucket stinks. And the steering wheel shakes like hell if you push her over seventy, so don't. But she'll get you there.'

He got in and started it up. It rumbled and rattled but it ran.

Flynn patted Rudy goodbye through the open window. 'Take good care of this man, old thing.'

'Flynn, I don't know how to thank you for all of this.'

'I do,' she responded. 'You can crush Herbie into primordial ooze.'

'Count on it.'

It was past midnight by the time Hunt headed north on 101 with a half-tank of gas and Rudy curled up contentedly there in his own seat. Just outside of San Luis Obispo he turned inland on a two-lane road that hooked up with Interstate 5 after a couple of hours at Kettleman City. By now a radio station out of Bakersfield was saying that the LA County Sheriffs were interested in the whereabouts of an online journalist named Hunt Liebling who, it was believed, had been staying at the Saddle Peak estate at the time of the murders.

The van was running on empty as he closed in on Stockton. Time to stop at one of those brightly lit twenty-four-hour gas station/mini-marts. He'd be paying cash, which meant he'd have to go inside. And that meant smiling for the security cameras. So before Hunt stopped he yanked the bandanna out of his pocket and tore off two strips. Wadded them up and stuffed one in each cheek so as to subtly alter the shape of his face, recalling the kernel of acting advice Brink had shared with him. *The most important change in your appearance comes from inside.*

The station he chose was deserted at three in the morning. From the moment he climbed out of the van Hunt was in character. His walk was a rolling, hipshot barrio strut, his baggy jeans rode low, chin high as he stood there at the gas pump filling his tank.

The pimply kid behind the counter eyed him warily when he came in.

As Hunt paid him he spoke to the kid in a rough, raspy voice. '*Por favor, amigo. Que hora es?*'

'Don't speak no Spanish here,' the kid muttered in response.

Hunt tapped at his wrist quizzically. The kid pointed to the clock over the door.

'*Gracias, amigo,*' Hunt said as he swaggered back out.

It took him another hour to get to Sacramento, where he picked up Interstate 80. Now all he had to do was ride I-80 due east for two or three days and he'd be in the land where the tall corn grows. Outside of Sacramento he started climbing into the Sierra Nevada. At the Donner Summit, elevation 7,239 feet, the van ran hot as it chugged its way up the steep grade, just him and the big rigs making the climb in the middle of the night. North of Lake Tahoe he pulled off at a rest stop to cool the engine and walk Rudy around on his leash. It was the morning rush hour by the time he crossed over into Nevada. A Panorama Radio Network all-news station out of Reno was reporting that the Sheriff's Department believed Hunt Liebling had fled the murder scene in a green 2005 Buick Le Sabre belonging to one of the victims. Liebling was now wanted for questioning in connection with the four deaths.

He'd just about cleared Reno when he realized he could no longer keep his eyes open. He'd logged eight straight hours on the highway since he left Flynn's. Gone two nights in a row without sleep. That was how he'd ended up in the Wal-Mart parking lot.

There was a weedy vacant lot next to the on-ramp to I-80. Hunt put Rudy on his leash and let him tromp around in the chilly morning air for a few minutes, snuffling, snorting and leaving deposits here, there, everywhere. He put down kibble and water for him in the back of the van. Made himself two peanut butter and banana sandwiches. Then got back on the highway, feeling strangely cut off from the world without his laptop and cell phone. He couldn't email or talk to anyone. Not if he wanted to stay a free man.

He felt crushingly alone.

He had maybe ten hours ahead of him before he hit Salt Lake City. After the tacky sprawl of Reno the natural beauty of the majestic snow-capped peaks outside of town was staggering. He chugged his way to Two Tips North Summit, elevation 7,090ft, before he found himself in the remote high desert near Pyramid Lake. As he passed through the lunar landscape of the Black Rock Desert, Hunt picked up the Panorama Radio Network's all-news station out of Salt Lake City. Panorama, he soon discovered, had cornered the news radio market across the West.

Absolutely none of the news was good for Hunt. Or real. They were now alleging that the murder weapon had been registered to *him* by the State of California. *And* an airline computer had him fleeing Los Angeles on a red eye flight to New York. The FBI was now calling him the prime suspect in the four killings. Also 'dangerous'.

Hunt couldn't believe how swiftly Herbie had concocted a fictional narrative and gotten it out there as the undisputed truth. The man's La Mirada geek squad had to be behind the trail of so-called evidence. But why had they put him on a plane to New York? Hunt didn't get that part.

Not until he heard the next update when he was outside of Elko. That's when Hunt found out how breathtakingly evil Herbie's intentions were. So evil Hunt couldn't believe what he was hearing. *Wouldn't* believe it.

Thayer and Little Mike had both been stabbed to death in a midtown office building.

It was Thayer who Tim Ferris had reached out to. And now the old man and Mikey were dead, just as Tim, Duane and the Gilliams were dead. That was why Herbie's geeks had planted him on the red-eye to New York. *To make it look as if I murdered them, too.* Truth had nothing to do with it, Hunt realized, consumed by fury and grief, his fists clenching, stomach in knots. The noose just kept tightening around his neck as Hunt inched his way across this vast, barren landscape – with no way to fight back and only the slimmest of hopes that somewhere out there he'd find a woman named Alicia who possessed the video evidence that would expose the truth and maybe clear him.

After he crossed into Utah Hunt found himself in the Great Salt Lake Desert. He'd thought Nevada was barren, but that was nothing compared to the Bonneville Salt Flats, the stark white wasteland that was home to the Bonneville Speedway and virtually no living life form. The late-day sun was sinking below the horizon in his rear-view mirror when a breaking news update on the radio made him realize that his nightmare had only just begun: Brink and Luze were now dead too.

Hunt pulled over into the breakdown lane, hit the brakes and totally lost it. Roaring with animal rage, he pounded the steering wheel and dashboard with both fists, punching wildly, blindly, tears streaming down his face. His brother Brink, his best friend in the whole world . . . *dead.* Brink's dear, beautiful wife, Luze . . . *dead.* Hunt couldn't deal with it. He was in such a frenzy that he nearly put his fist through the windshield. Rudy saved him. Climbed into his lap, whimpering, and started licking his face. Hunt hugged the dog to his chest and sobbed and sobbed, very glad indeed that he was along for the ride. Because if Rudy hadn't been there to comfort him at that moment Hunt felt certain he would have jumped out of the van and hurled himself in front of an onrushing car.

Instead, he resumed driving, blown away by Herbie's barbaric disregard for human life. The man was willing to kill *anyone* who got in the way of his quest for the White House. Brink and Little Mike had received emails from Hunt about his trip to LA. Therefore they had to be eliminated, as did Thayer, Luze and all traces of those emails. True, the big Internet Service Providers saved every single email. Millions and millions of them. But Panorama *owned* the two largest ISPs. Herbie's geek squad could expunge his emails, no problem. What they couldn't do was erase them from the hard drives of the computers themselves. The radio reports hadn't said so but Hunt was willing to bet that their computers had disappeared when they were killed.

The Unablogger.

That's what they were calling him on the radio now. They had nothing more than fabricated circumstantial evidence. No actual proof he'd murdered Tim, Duane and the Gilliams. No proof he'd flown to New York and slaughtered four more people who were close to him. But no proof was required. They had a story. And Herbie had Panorama's media might to light a fire under it. Virtually overnight, Hunt had been transformed from an independent-minded, Pulitzer Prize winning journalist into the blogosphere's own answer to Ted Kaczynski.

The Unablogger.

Naturally, sober law enforcement authorities were hastening to point out that Hunt could only be classified as a suspect at this point. Naturally, sober radio reporters kept shoehorning the word 'alleged' into every feverish sentence of their so-called news copy. But there could be no doubt that Hunt was a monster. All you had to do was connect the dots. Four dead in Topanga. Four more dead in New York City. Hell, it was obvious he was guilty. Otherwise the media wouldn't have given him such a fiendish nickname, would they?

As Hunt drove on and on through the Utah night, his head spinning, it suddenly smacked him in the face that there was still someone else out there. He had to call C.C. and warn her to get the hell out of Washington. Somewhere, anywhere far, far away. So what if Herbie's geeks traced his call to a roadside pay phone somewhere in Utah? He'd be long gone by the time the police descended on it. And they had no clue where he was heading.

By now he'd reached the Great Salt Lake's south shore. It was around midnight. It would be two a.m. in Washington. He pulled off at a gas station, charged inside and jammed a bunch of coins into the mini-mart's pay phone, ignoring the chilly looks of the clerk behind the counter. Being recognized was the least of his worries right now. Hell, the Unablogger was in New York City. Everyone knew that.

C.C.'s cell phone just rang and rang. No voice mail. He tried his office number. It rang once before there was a harsh beep, followed by a recorded announcement that the number was not in service at this time.

Hunt slammed down the phone and stormed back out to the van. He didn't like this. Not one bit.

He was making his way through Salt Lake City when he heard the news out of Washington about the Unablogger's ninth victim. Not that they were confirming C.C.'s identity yet. Merely reporting that Hunt's basement apartment in Georgetown had been firebombed. The whole building had gone up in flames. Hunt's landlord and his family had gotten out alive, but the body of a woman had been found in the charred wreckage. A forensic examination would have to be undertaken to determine the victim's identity.

Hunt needed no forensic science. He knew exactly who it was.

The FBI, meanwhile, was confirming that Hunt Liebling had been a ticketed passenger on the eight fifteen p.m. Amtrak Acela out of Penn Station. The train had arrived in DC at Union Station in plenty of time for him to get to Georgetown and destroy his home plus everything and everyone in it.

Hunt reached over and flicked off the radio, his hands wrapped tight around the wheel. Chugged his way out of Salt Lake City and started climbing into the Wasatch Range toward Wyoming. He'd put in over twelve hours behind that wheel since he'd left Reno but he wasn't tired. Or frightened. Or grief stricken. Not any more. He couldn't allow himself to be any of those things. Couldn't give in to such weakness.

He was back in the ring again, fighting for his life. And not for a single second could he let himself think that Herbie Landau would get the best of him. The moment you begin to doubt yourself is the moment when the fight is lost. And so Hunt Liebling, aka The Unablogger, drove on into the blackness of the night, his eyes burning with intensity as he recited a mantra of his own:

They can't stop me. I still don't know what they're hiding, but I'll find out. And when I do I'll destroy these people. They can't stop me. I still don't what they're hiding, but I'll find out. And when I do I'll destroy these people. They can't stop me . . .

TWENTY-TWO

After the doctor was gone Veronica phoned Herbie from Gary's bedroom for the umpteenth time. 'He refused to give him another injection,' she reported. 'He just wouldn't do it.'

'Why the hell not?' Herbie demanded, sounding just a tiny bit fed up. Veronica didn't blame him. It was four a.m. and they were now entering Hour Thirty-Six of the next President's emotional meltdown.

'Because it so happens that your candidate has already gone through a half-bottle of tequila and twenty milligrams of Valium.'

'Is the senator asleep, please God?'

'Not exactly.'

Gary lay propped against some pillows on the bed, his silver hair uncombed, a half-smoked cigarette burning down between his fingers as he gazed vacantly at another episode of their miserable old show – an early one when little Beanie tried to give Casey a bath by wrestling him into Mom's new Kenmore washer. Mercifully, Gary was quiet for the moment. More than quiet. He was in a stupor. Veronica took the cigarette from him and stubbed it out, thinking he really didn't look America's next President.

What he looked like was a great big wooden ventriloquist's dummy.

Gary's bedroom was upstairs in the south wing of the Oak Knoll estate. Several years earlier Veronica had converted the wing's four bedrooms into a master suite. She and Gary each had their own bedroom, bath and dressing room. The mansion had four more bedrooms in the north wing for guests, plus maids' quarters, the caretaker's cottage and chauffeur's apartment over the garage, which the Secret Service was using as its headquarters. Agents were detailed to the estate around the clock. Three were stationed inside of the house. When Gary retired to the master suite for the night, one of them sat on a chair in the hallway right outside of his bedroom.

'What the hell's keeping him awake?' Herbie wanted to know.

'What have we done to Timmy?' Gary cried out suddenly. 'Lord, what have we done?'

'Listen to me, princess. I've been directing this guy since puberty. When he gets upset you've just got to let him vent. He needs to think that his input matters. Never, ever forget that he began his career as an actor.'

'Believe me, I haven't,' she assured him, her temples throbbing.

'I want to f–feel!' And now Gary's tears started coming again. Huge, wrenching sobs. 'I want to feel like *me* again!'

'What'd he say?'

'That he wants to feel like "me" again.'

'What the fuck's that supposed to mean?'

'How should I know? I've only been married to him for four decades. I'm at my wit's end, Herbie.'

'What did the doctor tell you to do?'

'To comfort him. But he doesn't *want* to be comforted. Not by me anyhow . . .'

Herbie exhaled audibly. 'Don't go where you're going, OK? I've got enough on my mind.'

'Could you at least come over here and give me some back up?'

'I would if I could, but I honestly can't right now. This is a *very* serious situation. If things don't play out just right there won't be a November Seventh. Not for us.' Adding in a hushed voice, 'And something major just broke in the last few minutes.'

'Something major as in . . .?'

'It's better if you don't know the details.'

'Damn you, Herbie, it's my future, too. What's going on?'

'Alright, alright. But keep this to yourself, OK? Joe Baer's contact on the NYPD just came through. They found a letter from Timmy in Ernest Ludington Thayer's desk when they searched his apartment.'

'And what's so significant about that?'

'The postmark on the envelope it came in. We think we know where Liebling's heading. If we're right, the story ends there. And the campaign's back on track.'

'Why, that's wonderful news, Herbie! Will you please tell Gary?'

'Tell him what?'

'I'm putting you on speaker, Herbie.'

'No, no, don't you fucking put me on the—'

'Gary, darling, Herbie has some terrific news for you!'

'How are you, Senator?' Herbie's voice sounded calm and reassuring over the speaker phone. 'Senator, are you there?'

'Timmy's *gone*, Herbie,' Gary blubbered in response. 'He's *dead*.'

'And it's a horrible crime, Senator. But the lunatic who's responsible for it, this Hunt Liebling, we know where he's going now. He'll be behind bars – or dead – within the next twenty-four hours. Scout's honor.'

'Don't piss on my leg and tell me it's raining, Herbie.' Gary's eyes were no longer blank. They were icy blue pinpoints of rage. '*You* told me Timmy was planning to talk. *You* told me you'd take care of it. *Your* goons killed him. Don't bother to deny it, you miserable piece of human filth. You're a waste of skin, Herbie. And it's high time the whole world knows it. I'm telling them, hear me? I'm running outside right now and telling the whole damned press corps the truth . . .'

Gary wasn't kidding. He actually tried to get up off the bed. It took all of Veronica's strength to shove him back down. He stayed down, thank God, his chest heaving.

She flicked off the phone's speaker button and said, 'I give up, Herbie. I'm calling him.'

'Wait, wait, calling who?'

'You know who.'

'What are you, crazy?'

'Actually, I may be the only one among us who isn't.'

'Veronica, sweetie, your house is crawling with Secret Service agents.'

'None of whom will question a thing. It's entirely appropriate. And I think I can handle the one who's out in the hallway.'

'You *think* you can handle him?'

'I'm certain I can.'

'You'd better be,' he warned her.

'Herbie, have I ever let you down?'

He had to think about it for a moment. 'No, you haven't,' he finally acknowledged. 'Sometimes I wish *you* were the one who was running. God knows you've got the balls.'

'Are you just realizing that?' she demanded, hanging up on him.

The Reverend Jeremiah Staunton arrived in twenty minutes to provide Senator Dixon with the spiritual counsel that would, it was hoped, help him to process his grief. Jeremiah had to pass through an LAPD perimeter checkpoint outside of the estate. And then pause to speak briefly with the skeleton crew of media people who remained out there even in the dead of night, speaking of a waste of skin. On Veronica's say so, the Secret Service let him in the house. Agent Rosenthal, who was stationed outside of Gary's room, admitted him to the master suite.

Agent Rosenthal was one of the older ones. He was quiet and discreet. Also divorced and very lonely. On more than one occasion, Veronica had caught him gazing at her like a love-struck schoolboy.

Jeremiah greeted her in the hall outside of Gary's room with a pained, caring look on his face.

'This must be agonizing for you, my dear,' he intoned, taking her slim, manicured hands in his large, hairy ones. 'Being strong for the senator when there's no one for *you* to lean on.'

'I'm fine, Jeremiah,' she assured him, feeling Agent Rosenthal's worshipful eyes on her. 'But the senator can't sleep. Will you sit up and talk with him for a while?'

'Of course I will. I'll stay by his bedside all night if I have to.'

She led him into Gary's bedroom, closing the door behind them.

'Timmy's *gone*, Jerry!' Gary sobbed when he caught sight of him. 'They *killed* him!'

Jeremiah crossed the room to the bed and perched there next to him, gripping Gary by the shoulders. 'I'm so sorry, my friend.'

'Your *friend*? Is that all I am to you now?'

Jeremiah shot an inquiring glance over at Veronica. She gave him a quick nod, her nostrils flaring.

'No, of course not,' he replied, swallowing.

'Prove it,' Gary commanded him.

The two of them gazed deeply into each other's eyes for a long moment. And then, feverishly, they kissed.

Veronica looked away, shuddering with revulsion.

'Don't leave me tonight, Jerry,' Gary pleaded, clutching on to him. 'I won't make it without you. I'll die, I swear.'

'I'm not going anywhere, OK? I'm here now. Jerry's here.'

She left them alone in there, closing the door softly behind her. Agent Rosenthal gazed up at her from his chair in the hall, so eager to please. And so damned likely to overhear what those two were about to engage in on the other side of that door.

'I wouldn't be surprised if they talk straight on through the night,' she said, tilting her head at him fetchingly. 'It's Ron, isn't it?'

He reddened, poor bunny. 'Why, yes, Mrs Dixon.'

'You look as though you could use a bit of cheering up yourself, Ron. I guess we all could tonight. Tell me something,' she said, holding her hand out to him. 'How would you like to see Miss America in a tiara, a pair of high heels and absolutely nothing else?'

TWENTY-THREE

Annie was seated in the lotus position out on her enclosed front porch, her eyes closed, mind and body fully connected to her sunrise practice. Annie performed her morning practice in the nude, a truly liberating ritual that she'd picked up from her dad a long time ago. It was maybe the only positive thing he'd ever taught her.

Keeping her eyes shut, Annie used her third eye to observe the sun rising over the Mississippi before her, its light diffused by the wisps of low fog that lingered over the river. Her perch was high on the bluffs above the river on Balltown Road, the second highest spot in all of Iowa. She didn't know what the highest was. She only knew this hilltop with its panoramic view all of the way across the river to Illinois. She knew the rich, rolling hills of the dairy farms that tumbled down toward the river's banks. The deep green grass that glistened with dew. The bright, brilliant splashes of fall color on the trees. She knew the calm and the serenity. Knew this porch where she sat, sit-bones grounded to the earth. She knew this morning, its golden sunlight warming her bare shoulders and breasts.

Annie was full-breasted and curvy like her mom had been. She also had her mom's gleaming black hair and big, dark eyes, although on Annie it didn't necessarily cry out Chicana. Thanks to her dad's Anglo features and fair complexion Annie passed for Italian, Greek, Jewish, whatever. Right now she was Annie Ferrarro, a nice Italian girl from Brooklyn, New York. When she'd moved here six months ago she told the realtor that she'd visited Balltown as a child and had dreamt ever since about fixing up an old farmhouse here. She did not tell the realtor that her real name was Alicia Ferris. That she'd been living and working in Chicago for the past eleven years, and that she'd chosen Balltown because she felt certain it was a place no one would ever think to look for her.

Alicia Ferris was no more. A friend in the wireless under-world had disappeared her. Annie had a new social security number, driver's license, credit cards, credit history and bank accounts. Alicia's assets, which had been electronically laundered through three different offshore accounts, were now Annie's assets. Not a fortune, but enough to live on for ten years if she was careful.

Her dear little upended shoebox of a farmhouse had been built in 1921 on 7.3 acres of land. It had a small parlor with a pot-bellied stove. An eat-in kitchen. Two small bedrooms upstairs and a bath with an old claw-footed tub and a brand new Toto low-flow toilet. Annie had installed the Toto first thing. She had a hang-up about wasting water. She'd left her car, furniture and most of her clothes behind in Chicago. Bought a bed, dishes and a used Ford F-150 pickup when she got here. Found a battered kitchen table and chairs at a flea market, a chest of drawers, a couple of overstuffed chairs for the parlor. Didn't need much else. She had no visitors.

Annie had worked hard on the house all summer long. Enclosed its front porch so she could practice her sunrise yoga year-round. Pried off its ugly pea green asphalt shingles and hauled them off to the dump. She was still in the process of re-shingling it with beautiful red cedar. Doing all of the work herself. She had gotten to be quite handy with her table saw and nail gun, thank you. Actually, Annie enjoyed the long, hard hours of outdoor work. It was honest and satisfying. A far cry from the life she'd left behind when she said goodbye to her start-up company. Goodbye to the twenty-first century altogether. She didn't own a computer or cell phone. Didn't have a TV. Never listened to the news on the radio of her pickup. Never picked up a newspaper. She simply *was*.

It was incredibly liberating to no longer be Alicia Ferris. Finally, she was free of her morally bankrupt dad, a man so haunted by his past that he could suck her *prana* right out of her. Finally, she was free of his lord and master, Herbie Landau, the ruthless sleaze who'd been chasing after her ever since she'd grown breasts. That googly-eyed old creep just wouldn't leave her alone. And, God, did he make her skin crawl.

Now she was free of both of them, Annie reflected, gazing inwardly. Seeing those remarkable layers of peeling paint with her third eye, touching them. Annie was totally into the abandoned old farmhouses and barns she'd found sinking into the landscape in and around Balltown. One of the only things she'd carried with her was her camera gear. When she wasn't working on the house Annie was off in her truck with her camera in search of wooden remains. She rented darkroom time from a retired commercial photographer in Dubuque. Annie completed her meditation by focusing her intention on the day ahead. On the shingling she would do. On the new and beautiful textures she would find in the darkroom. She placed her hands before her heart center and said, '*Namaste.*' Then she opened her eyes to gaze out at the day and . . .

And some guy was standing right there outside of the porch staring at her naked self. A grungy, unshaven guy in a rumpled flannel shirt and baggy jeans. Very intense, with dark smoldering eyes that were . . . OK, *gorgeous*. He looked very angry. His fists were clenched. And he had to have the single worst haircut Annie had ever seen in her life. It looked as if someone had taken a power mower to his head. And that wasn't even the weirdest part about him.

The weirdest part was that standing next to him, stubby tail quivering, was Rudy.

TWENTY-FOUR

It was the middle of the night when Hunt made it to Balltown. Not that there appeared to be anything more to Balltown than a Roman Catholic church, a scattering of farmhouses and something called Breitbach's Family Restaurant, which served breakfast, lunch and dinner. None of them at four-thirty in the morning.

He had, according to his bleary-eyed reckoning, pulled out of Flynn Leverett's driveway something like fifty-four highly caffeinated hours ago, the final eighteen-hour stretch from Cheyenne an endless ribbon of highway, the landscape so vast and desolate that Hunt couldn't imagine how anyone had survived there before there were things like phones and cars and electricity. Winter's frozen isolation must have been overwhelming. Truly, Hunt had never felt so alone in his life as he did on that final six-hour leg from Omaha to Dubuque in the black of night, Rudy fast asleep next to him, legs twitching.

Hunt now sat atop the FBI's Ten Most Wanted List – right there with Osama Bin Laden. The FBI had posted a reward of up to $100,000 for information leading to the capture of Huntley Havlicek Liebling, aka The Unablogger, who was wanted in connection with nine murders. And was considered to be extremely dangerous.

It amazed Hunt just how neatly every facet of his life was dovetailing into the fictional Unablogger scenario that continued to dribble out over the Panorama Radio Network. From the smoldering remains of his Georgetown Federal row house, Hunt's shaken landlord described him as 'surly', 'confrontational' and 'chronically delinquent' on his rent. In Radnor, Pennsylvania, C.C.'s grief stricken parents revealed that she'd been planning to leave Hunt's employ – a clear indication that she thought he was becoming unstable. From Coral Gables, Florida, Hunt's old boxing coach at Columbia, now retired, recalled, 'Nobody wanted to fight that kid. Once he climbed into the ring, Hunt Liebling had something you can't teach. I call it the killer instinct.' Hunt's editor back when he'd written his Pulitzer-winning series on the meat packing industry called him, 'A guy who lives each story to the max, no matter where it takes him. And the ice can get pretty thin out there sometimes.'

The media had already descended on his hometown of Brattleboro where, according to one report, 'the suspect's parents died of apparent natural causes some years back.' As if to retroactively implicate him in their deaths. Mr McDowell, their next-door neighbor, grumbled that 'the Liebling brothers both had a mean streak,' having hated them ever since he found his fifteen-year-old daughter, Barbara, boinking Brink on the living-room sofa. Mrs McKenna, Hunt's high school journalism teacher, called him 'a fine young man of high integrity' and 'the best pupil I've ever had.'

She was the only person who stood up for him.

There was a fine, touching AP obituary of Thayer in the copy of *USA Today* that Hunt bought when he stopped for gas outside of Ogallala. No surprise there – the old man had filed it himself several years earlier. 'He did not wish to be remembered as a giant of American journalism,' Thayer's obit concluded. 'Simply as a reporter who tried to tell a story honestly and fairly.'

Hunt had no one now. No family. Not even an apartment to call home. Part of him, a really huge part, felt as if he'd gotten trapped inside Tim's nightmare from the summer of seventy-two – when it was Tim's own loved ones who'd been picked off one by one. In fact, the parallel spooked the hell out of Hunt. But he could not give in to his fear. He needed to find that second set of DVDs and get them out there to the American voters. Tim had tried to tell them about the real Gary Dixon. That's why he was dead. That's why they all were dead. It was up to him to finish what Tim had started.

Balltown was fifteen miles outside of Dubuque on the Great River Road. As Hunt steered his way there in the dark country night he wondered what Herbie was up to at this very moment. By now, the old bastard must have watched the DVDs they'd stolen from Tim's safe. Had to know he didn't have Volume Five. Would it occur to him that Alicia might have it? Did his assorted geeks and goons know where she was living? Would Flynn Leverett give her up? Had they already beaten him to her door?

No, they hadn't. There was only an old Ford pickup parked

in the driveway when he found her place. Alicia was sitting
right there on her glassed-in front porch soaking up the early-
morning sunlight. Hunt stood and looked at her, transfixed.
She was lovely to look at. She was . . . OK, *naked*. Unless he
was seeing things. Hey, after so many days and nights on the
road he couldn't be sure.

'You don't look like him at all, Alicia,' he said finally, his
voice sounding rusty and strained.

'My name is Annie,' she responded coldly. By now she'd
thrown on her robe and opened the porch door a crack. 'You
have me confused with someone else.'

'Sure, whatever,' Hunt said, knowing he didn't. Not the way
Rudy was jumping excitedly against the door and barking his
head off.

She pretended she didn't notice it. Her face gave away
nothing. It was a nice face, her huge dark eyes and full lips
framed by a wild mane of lustrous black hair. She was in her
thirties, almost but not quite plump. *Zoftig*. 'What do you want?'
she demanded, her eyes locking on to his. 'Who are you?'

'Hunt Liebling, who do you think?'

'You say that like I'm supposed to know you.'

'Are you trying to tell me you don't?' he shot back, his jaw
working a piece of Bazooka as she continued to stare at him.
'OK, then let's do it this way: you mailed a letter to Ernest
Ludington Thayer in New York City a few days ago, am I
right, Alicia?'

'My name's *Annie*, I just told you.'

'Fine, your name's Annie,' he sighed as the dog continued
to hurl his body against the glass door and yap. 'Chill out,
will you, Rudy? You're making a bad first impression.'

Annie softened, smiling at the dog. It was quite a smile.
Her whole face lit up from inside. 'I'd hardly call it a first
impression.' She opened the door wide and he charged her,
whooping with delight as she hugged him and cooed, 'He's
my Rooty-Tooty. Aren't you my Rooty-Tooty?' To Hunt she
said, 'We used to live together.'

'Flynn was right. She promised he'd get me inside.'

'You're not even close to inside.' Annie cocked her head at
him curiously. 'Did Flynn give you that haircut, too?'

'How did you know?'

'Because you look just like Rudy – minus the bangs.'

'It was Flynn who helped me get away.'

'From what?'

'You mean you don't know?'

'Don't know *what*? Who are you? What do you want?'

'Your father is dead.'

'Well, that was expected,' she said quietly. 'His cancer was spreading and the doctors figured he—'

'It wasn't the cancer, Annie. He was shot. So were Duane, Lola and Tyrone.'

She gulped, her eyes widening. 'My God, who would . . .?'

'The murder weapon was registered to me even though I've never owned a gun in my life. Supposedly, I also caught a flight to New York and murdered Ernest Ludington Thayer, his friend Mike and my sister-in-law, Luze. And my brother died in a motorcycle accident that you can bet was no accident. Supposedly, I then took a train to DC, murdered my intern and torched my apartment. They're calling me the Unablogger. That's because I'm a journalist. Or I used to be. Now I'm just the most wanted man in America. They think I've killed nine people.'

Annie looked at him, her eyes huge and probing. 'Did you?'

'Hell no. I'm being done in by Herbie, same as your dad was. Forgive me for asking, but how is it possible you don't know any of this?'

'I don't own a TV or a computer,' she answered, stroking Rudy. 'I don't talk to anyone either. I've kind of disappeared.'

'So have I, although it wasn't by choice. Did you read that letter you forwarded to Thayer?'

She shook her head. 'It arrived here in a Manila envelope all stamped and sealed. I just put it out for the postman. You found me because of the Balltown postmark, didn't you?'

'I hung out at Breitbach's until they opened and asked my nice breakfast waitress, Dot, if anyone new had moved to town lately. Two or three new families, she said. And Annie Ferraro at the top of the hill. Annie Ferrarro, Alicia Ferris – same initials. I left the van in their parking lot and walked here. Needed to stretch my legs. The countryside around here isn't at all like the rest of Iowa, is it? I've never seen flat like that – and I've spent time in Iraq. But this area around here, this really, really reminds me of Brattleboro. The hills and the way the leaves are turning and . . . hello, I'm jabbering, aren't I?'

'Kind of.'

'Sorry, I haven't talked to anyone in three days who doesn't have a wet nose and a tail.' His gaze fell on the shingles piled there on her lawn under a blue tarp. 'What time do your workmen get here?'

'There are no workmen. I'm doing it all myself.'

'Good,' he said. 'Your dad wrote to Thayer about the Bagley Bunch killings. He wanted to tell people the truth about what really happened in the summer of seventy-two. Wanted them to know the real Gary Dixon before they elect him president. But Lola told me Tim didn't know where you were. How did his letter get to you?'

'Duane knew. I thought someone ought to, just in case.'

'So you trusted Duane?'

'Totally. Why do you ask?'

'I'd been wondering if he was feeding Herbie information.'

'Not a chance.' Annie was emphatic. 'Herbie would know where I am. And he doesn't – or he'd have been all over me months ago.'

'Oh, yeah? Why's that?'

She considered her reply long and hard before saying, 'I was going to put water on for tea. Would you care for some?'

'Does that mean I'm inside?'

'You're inside.' She started in with Rudy on her heel.

The enclosed porch was crowded with power tools. A heavy-duty DeWALT table saw, a Paslode nail gun with a coiled fifty-foot hose that was hooked up to a Hitachi electric air compressor. Serious stuff. This Annie was no wuss, although she was kind of on the small side. No more than five-feet three as she stood there barefoot, wrinkling her nose at him.

'Yeah, sorry,' Hunt acknowledged. 'I don't have a change of clothes.'

'I could wash those for you if you'd like.'

'No time, but thanks.'

She put the kettle on in the kitchen, then went up the steep, narrow stairs to get dressed, Rudy in hot pursuit, while Hunt paced around her parlor, which had a couple of moth-eaten chairs for furniture. Dozens of eight-by-ten black and white photos were push-pinned to the parlor's walls. All of them were extreme close-ups of weathered barn siding, exceptionally grainy, textured and interesting.

Annie returned wearing a khaki work shirt, blue jeans and lace-up boots. She looked downright stocky in her work clothes. Hunt would never have guessed that her form was so ripe unless he'd seen it for himself.

'Way cool photos. What do you use?'

'An old Nikon twenty-twenty,' she answered, coloring slightly. 'With a fifty-five millimeter micro lens.'

'Tripod?'

'Have to. The shutter speed's way slow. So is the film.'

'What is it, ASA twenty-five?'

She nodded. 'You're into photography?'

'I was when I first got into reporting. But I drifted away from it when I started going underground. Once you point a camera at somebody it's kind of hard to blend in. Have you got your own darkroom?'

'Not yet. I'd like to install one down in the cellar. Just have to run water pipes down there for a sink.'

'That's something I can help you out with. There's nothing I can't do when it comes to plumbing. Which reminds me . . .'

'It's at the top of the stairs. You'll find towels in the cupboard.'

She had a nice old claw-footed tub and a truly exciting new low-flow Toto. As he washed up Hunt stared at his reflection in the mirror, barely recognizing himself. It wasn't just the doggie haircut and the scraggly goatee. It was the crazed look in his red-rimmed eyes.

Annie's sun-splashed kitchen hadn't been modernized since the Eisenhower era. His steaming mug of tea awaited him on the beat-up kitchen table. Annie sat there sipping hers, Rudy by her side.

'Awesome new Toto. That's their Drake model, am I right?'

She nodded her head. 'The place had an old American Standard that used up *six* gallons of water per flush. I pulled that sucker right out of there. I'm something of a whack job when it comes to wasting water. I just don't see how the planet will survive if we keep . . . Why are you looking at me that way?'

'No reason,' he said. 'That sink's not draining real well. I don't believe in chemical drain cleaners, but if you've got some wrenches I can open up that drain pipe for you and—'

'OK, but right now would you please sit down? You're making me nervous the way you keep prowling around.'

He flopped down in a chair while Annie sat there petting Rudy. Whenever she stopped the dog would poke her hand with his head.

'I guess I should be crying my eyes out right now,' she said slowly. 'But I'm actually relieved that my dad's gone. Do you think that's weird?'

'I'm the wrong person to ask. I left my emotional equilibrium somewhere back in Utah.' He tasted his tea, which was some kind of fruity herbal shit but not too bad. 'You and your dad weren't close, I gather.'

'You gather right.'

'Did he ever talk to you about the Bagley Bunch killings?'

'Not a word. Neither did my mom. It was a very, very sensitive subject with them. She lost her father that week, and he lost *everyone*. All they had left was each other. I guess that's how they ended up together.'

Yet another eerie parallel. Now it was he and Tim's daughter who'd been left alone with each other. As Annie gazed across the table at him, wide-eyed, Hunt wondered if she was thinking the very same thing. He doubted it. She'd just found out her father was dead. 'You said Herbie would be all over you. How come?'

'That old lech has been trying to get in my pants since I was thirteen,' she explained, her mouth tightening. 'I went away to college in Chicago partly to get away from him. Fat chance. He'd show up there at my dorm. Tell me he wanted to buy me things and take me to Europe. And he's never, ever given up. I used to move from one apartment to another, change my phone number . . . He'd always find me. And after I started my own business, forget it. No way I could hide from him. He's the one who gave me the news that my dad was sick. Flew to Chicago last year just to tell me that I should forgive him.'

'For what?'

'Selling his soul to the devil, same as Gary and Veronica did. Well, not Veronica. She never had a soul. Know what my mom told me when she left Dad? That he was dead inside, and had been for years. She moved back into her old house in Glendale. I stayed there with her after she had her heart attack. Flynn gave her Rudy to cheer her up. That's how come we're old friends.' Annie smiled down at the dog before she looked back up at Hunt and said, 'Dad's funeral will be a horrorpalooza. Herbie will be all weepy. Gary and Veronica will be grief-stricken for the cameras. And that pious douche bag Jeremiah Staunton will probably deliver the sermon. I'm not going. They can't make me go. And they can give all of his money to a homeless shelter as far as I'm concerned.' She ran her hands through her mane of hair, studying Hunt thoughtfully. 'You found me because of the Balltown postmark. Is there any chance someone else will, too?'

Hunt glanced out the kitchen window at the quiet country road out front. He hadn't forgotten that Thayer had stashed the envelope in his desk. Would the police search the old man's apartment and find it? No doubt. Would the FBI follow up on it? No doubt. How much time did he have before carloads of G-men descended on this tiny town in search of him? Enough time, he told himself. There had to be enough time.

'Will they?' she pressed him.

'I hope not,' he answered her finally.

'So do I, Hunt, because I like being Annie.'

'Listen, I need to know something . . .' Hunt's mouth was suddenly very dry. 'Did Duane send you anything else besides that letter?'

'Like what?'

'Your dad produced a video memoir about the Bagley Bunch slayings. It's explosive stuff, Annie. It'll destroy Dixon. There's a set of five DVDs, each about ninety minutes long. I've seen the first four. I didn't get to see the fifth. He told me there was a duplicate set somewhere. I've been figuring he sent it to you. He definitely wanted you to see it before he died. It was important to him.'

'It couldn't have been that important. Duane never wrote me about any DVDs.'

'He didn't?' Hunt felt himself sag inwardly, his hopes dashed. What would he do now? Where would he go?

'Although he did send me a huge carton of stuff last week,' she added.

He jumped to his feet, his heart pounding. 'Duane sent you a *carton*?'

'Yeah, some family keepsakes my dad wanted me to have. As if I'd ever be—'

'What kind of keepsakes, Annie?'

'My first impulse was to just toss it. But, who knows, maybe twenty years from now I'll get sentimental. Or my kids might want to check it out, if I ever have any. Not that I'm getting any younger. Or have a man in my life. But, hey, never say never, right?'

'What *kind* of keepsakes, Annie?' Hunt said, louder this time.

'No idea. I didn't open it. Just stuck it down in the cellar.' She peered at him curiously. 'You think those DVDs are in it, is that what you're saying?'

'Kind of. Could we please fast forward those twenty years and tear it open right this second?'

The cellar door was in the kitchen. It was a deep, dry cellar with fluorescent lighting overhead. Against one wall there was a huge workbench laden with hand tools. Above it were built-in shelves crammed with paint cans and solvents.

'Damn, you don't fool around, do you?'

'Most of this stuff was already here,' she said as Rudy made a full circuit of the basement, nose to the cement floor.

It was a big carton, at least thirty-inches square. Weighed at least twenty pounds, Hunt decided as he hoisted it up on to the workbench.

Annie wore a Leatherman all-purpose knife in a sheath on her belt. She used it to slash open the top of the carton. Hunt watched her, trying to remember if he'd ever known a woman who carried her own knife. The short answer was: *No way.*

Inside, they found a tightly packed layer of bubble wrap. A plain white envelope was taped to it with *Alicia* written across its face. She opened and unfolded a handwritten note.

Dear Alicia – Please hold on to this. If anything should happen, you may need it. All my love, Uncle Duane.

Hunt removed the layer of bubble wrap. Underneath it was a sealed clear-plastic storage bag. A yellow Post-it was stuck to the bag on which Duane had written: *Do not touch any of these contents. Leave them to the authorities.* Hunt held the bag up to the light. It contained dirty, bloodstained clothing and a hunting knife encrusted with dried blood. There was a tightly coiled rope in the bag, too.

'What do you make of this?' Annie was gazing down into the carton.

A five-by-seven-inch mailer pouch had been stuffed in there beneath the storage bag. Something small and cylindrical was wrapped inside. There was no *Do Not Touch* warning on it so Hunt tore the pouch open – and found an old cigarette lighter. An unusual one that was shaped long and narrow. Had a pin-up girl painted on it, one of her breasts exposed.

Hunt tried flicking it with his thumb. Didn't work. It was dry. He found a can of lighter fluid on a shelf over the workbench and filled the lighter's reservoir. Then flicked it three, four, five more times until he got a flame. He stared down into that flame for a long moment, his wheels spinning, before he snapped the lighter shut.

He dug deeper in the carton. There was another layer of bubble wrap. Beneath that he found the duplicate boxed set of five – *five* – DVDs with *Tim's Story* written on the side in marking pen. Breathless, Hunt yanked the fifth DVD from the box and clutched it in his hand. Here it was, the DVD he had traveled 2,000 miles to watch. The DVD that had cost nine people their lives.

'Annie, I've got to see this right away. And then we've got to get it out there to the public.'

'What's in *this* box?' she wondered, searching still deeper in the carton.

It was a tin strongbox. Hunt pulled it out by its handle, set it on the workbench and opened it. Inside was a boxed VHS tape on which were scrawled the words: *'Monty and Me'* – *transferred from 16mm to VHS 2-22-88*. There was also a round film canister in the strongbox. Hunt pried the canister open and found a brittle, ageing reel of 16mm film. The movie itself. The original of *Monty and Me*, which appeared to be in an advanced stage of decomposition. The videotape wasn't exactly in its first youth either, come to think of it.

'I hope this tape hasn't gone bad. They turn to shit after ten or fifteen years, don't they?'

'If it's been stored in that thing it's probably OK,' Annie said, squinting at it. 'What's *Monty and Me*?'

'Something pretty awful from out of your dad's past.' Hunt shoved it back into the strongbox, unwrapped a fresh piece of Bazooka and stuck it in his mouth, his jaw working on it. 'Annie, do you trust me?'

'I've known you for, what, twenty minutes? You say

everyone thinks you killed my dad. You say you're a wanted
serial killer . . .'

'Spree killer, technically.'

'You show up here out of nowhere looking like a wild man.
You smell really, really—'

'Been there, move on.'

'Why on earth should I?' she demanded, raising her chin
at him.

'No reason,' he conceded. 'Same as there's no reason why
you should care about any of this. You had major issues with
your dad. OK, I get that. But he really wanted you to watch
this final volume. He didn't even have a copy of it at his place.
This is the only one in existence. Want to know what I think?
I think Duane was hoping you'd fly out there with it so you
and your dad could watch it together. Tim wanted to set things
right, Annie. Foil Herbie's plans. Keep Dixon out of the White
House. He wanted the world to know the real truth, and it got
him killed. Now it's up to me to finish what he started. If I
don't then his death – all of these deaths – mean absolutely
nothing, understand?'

Annie studied the floor, scuffing at it with the toe of her
boot before she looked up at Hunt and said, 'What do you
need exactly?'

'A laptop, for starters. I can't use my credit cards. You could
buy us one in Dubuque. We could watch Volume Five together
and then send the whole package out to all of the major news
outlets *and* every single blogger who—'

'Whoa, cowboy, *how* are you planning to send it to them?'

'We can find a Wi-Fi signal somewhere in town, can't we?'

'What, you mean just war-drive around Dubuque until we
latch on to someone's signal?'

'Well, yeah. There must be like a library or a Starbucks we
can hit.'

'OK, you're not a techie, are you?'

'Not exactly. Why, are you?'

'I used to design and install computer systems for ad agen-
cies, law firms, all sorts of businesses. I had twenty kids
working for me.'

'Good, so tell me what my problem is. Won't they be able
to download it?'

'No, no, they'll be fine as long as they have a high-speed line.

They can stream it as it downloads. The problem is at our end, Hunt. You're talking about uploading hours and hours of *video*. Ninety minutes of camcorder video translates to four-point-seven gigabytes of data. Which is to say, um, thirty-seven-point-six million kilobits. The typical max upload limit for a high-speed home user is seven hundred and sixty-eight kilobits per second. Do the math. You're talking forty-nine thousand seconds per DVD. That's . . . eight hundred and fifteen minutes – roughly thirteen hours – for *each* DVD. A business office with a T-One line might be twice as fast, but you'd still need six hours and change to upload each DVD.'

'I don't have that kind of time, Annie. Isn't there anything faster out there?'

'Sure. A T-Three line has an upload speed of forty-four *thousand* kilobits per second. That's a fifteen-minute upload per DVD.'

'Now you're talking. That's what I need. How do I—?'

'You don't. You'll never get access to a T-Three line.'

'Why not? Who has them?'

'The big boys with server farms. People like, say, your federal government. And a handful of major, major university labs.'

He looked at her blankly. 'OK, server farms are . . .?'

'Clusters of grid slaves.'

'If you could please dumb that down just a teeny bit more . . .'

'We're talking about a supercomputer.'

'Gotcha, thanks.' Swiftly, Hunt repacked the carton and gathered it up in his arms. 'Here's the deal. I have to get this stuff out into cyberspace before I'm arrested and/or shot. Do you know *anyone* who has access to a supercomputer? Someone who you trust with your life? Well, not your life but mine.'

Annie hesitated. 'I do, as a matter of fact. And I want to help you, Hunt. Really, I do. But I gave my word that I'd never show up there again. I can't. I just can't. It would be . . . I mean, it's a huge breach of trust and I . . .' She trailed off, her chest rising and falling. 'Oh, hell, we can take my truck.'

TWENTY-FIVE

W ally and Clover were on Route 20, closing in on historic Galena, Illinois, home of America's eighteenth president, Ulysses S. Grant, when Wally's cell phone rang. It was just after eight a.m. They'd been on the road since they left their Courtyard by Marriott in a suburb of Chicago before dawn. Wally listened to what Mrs Pryor had to say, thanked her politely and hung up.

'I'm afraid they still can't find us accommodations for this evening,' he reported to Clover across the seat of their stolen silver-colored Ford Crown Victoria. 'It seems every single motel room within a radius of one hundred miles of Dubuque, Iowa, has been booked for months.'

Clover watched the road ahead, his eyes fixed in a thousand-yard stare. He didn't ask Wally why. Had hardly spoken to him at all since that hyper talking jag of his when they were torching the apartment in Georgetown. Nor had he slept. He was still wearing the same clothes, which reeked of lighter fluid.

'It's leaf-peeping season. People drive here from cornfields hundreds of miles away to take in the fall color in these hills near the Mississippi River.' Which were, Wally noted, quite lovely to behold. Mabel would adore them. 'There also happens to be a major car show tomorrow in Prairie du Chien.'

'That's in Wisconsin,' Clover said hoarsely.

Wally nodded. 'Across the river from Dubuque. It's a vintage Corvette show. The largest in the Midwest, apparently. Owners from as far away as St Louis and Cleveland drive their old Vettes there to show them off.'

'I'm tingling all over.'

'Exciting stuff indeed.'

'No, I'm tingling all over,' Clover said, big hands shaking on the wheel.

'Clover, have you gotten any sleep at all?'

'Awake and straight. It's all about the dreams, baby.'

'Certainly,' Wally sighed. 'Whatever you say.'

Things hadn't been going particularly smoothly since they'd left Washington. Make that *tried* to leave Washington. Per Mrs Pryor's last-minute instructions, they'd headed out to Reagan National Airport to catch a one fifty-five p.m. flight to Chicago – only to discover that the plane had been grounded back in Houston due to a thunderstorm. The next direct flight to Chicago wasn't for another two hours, and there were no seats available.

As Wally hashed over their limited options with a ground-crew person, Clover's breathing became increasingly rapid and uneven.

'Milwaukee,' he growled at Wally between gritted teeth.

An excellent suggestion, in fact. Milwaukee being a mere ninety minutes north of Chicago by car. And a direct flight to Milwaukee was leaving in less than one hour. Clover said nothing the whole way there. Just sat in his seat next to Wally, grinding his molars against each other.

In Milwaukee, Clover liberated an Audi Quattro from long-term parking and they headed south on Highway 94 to the upscale Chicago suburb of Winnetka. Clover's arms contact there fronted as the owner of an extreme sporting goods store. Mountain bikes, snowboards and such. The store stayed open evenings. It was boiling over with loud, pimply teenaged boys when Wally and Clover got there. They placed their order in the back room – the usual plus the Barrett .50-caliber long-range semi-automatic sniper rifle Wally had requested. It had been a priority to portray the New York and Washington assignments as the work of a deranged amateur. This was no longer an issue. And Wally was a huge fan of the Barrett. With one well-placed armor-piercing bullet it could turn a moving vehicle into a fireball from a half-mile away.

Clover's dealer needed a few hours. They ate porterhouses at a nearby steak house while they waited to take delivery. Traded the Audi for the Crown Vic. But it was past eleven p.m. by the time the dealer finally made good. Since there was no point in arriving in Balltown in the middle of the night they checked into a nearby Courtyard by Marriott and ordered an early wake-up call.

Clover had been silent from the moment they hit the road. And seemed to grow even more withdrawn the closer they got to Balltown. Wally wasn't sure which of his partner's

mood swings he found the most worrisome. Clover had truly
alarmed him the way he'd called him *Coop* out loud in front
of the Georgetown target. You never, ever used a colleague's
name. What if the target survived? What if a bystander
happened to be witnessing the entire operation? It was shock-
ingly unprofessional, and had definitely put Wally on high
alert. He hadn't forgotten the bite scar on his pinky finger.
Nor the envelope of medical information Clover had passed
him. Which, as promised, remained in his jacket pocket,
unopened. But as long as Clover did the job they were being
paid to do then Wally had no real grounds to complain. And
Clover's driving remained top drawer – even if his gaze was,
well, disturbingly blank.

'With any luck,' Wally told him as they neared Galena, 'we
won't even need to book accommodations. We'll find our
targets today, take them out and head for home. How does
that sound?'

No answer.

'I suggest we start out at the local town hall or whatever
they call it in these parts. Research any and all land transac-
tions over the past two years. There can't be very many in a
place the size of Balltown. Particularly to a single woman.'
Wally studied Clover carefully. 'Unless you have a better idea.'

Still no answer.

'Clover, do you have everything you need this morning?'

After a *long* silence: 'Like what, Coop?'

'Like water for your pills, for instance.'

Clover unlocked his gaze from the road, glaring across the
seat at Wally. 'Why are you asking me about my damned
pills?'

'I just want to make sure you're OK. You seem a bit down
today.'

'I'm tired.' His eyes returned to the road. 'Didn't sleep last
night.'

'Awake and straight, right?'

'Awake and straight. Can't let them mess with me. They
will if I let them.'

'Who will, Clover?'

Clover shook his head, as if to clear it. 'Excuse me for
asking, Coop, but did I just say that out loud?'

'You did, as a matter of fact.'

After that, Clover said nothing out loud to him. Not one word.

Shortly before nine a.m. they crossed the mighty Mississippi at Dubuque and took a winding road north to Balltown, which seemed to consist of a place called Breitbach's Family Restaurant and not much else. They hadn't eaten breakfast along the way. It made sense to stop now. As they pulled into the lot Wally noticed a white van with California plates parked there alongside of a tour bus. Wally, who didn't believe in elves or coincidences, called Mrs Pryor at once to have the plate run. The van belonged to a Flynn Leverett of Santa Barbara. According to Mrs Pryor, it was exceedingly likely that one of their two targets, Hunt Liebling, had made his cross-country escape in it.

And now Hunt was inside eating breakfast at this very moment. Good, good.

Wally glanced around the restaurant as he and Clover were being seated, his eyes taking in every customer. He didn't spot Liebling. Nor anyone who so much as matched the journalist's general description. After he'd placed his order Wally shoved his thick, round glasses up his nose and visited the men's room, patiently checking out the adjoining dining rooms. A tour group of chattering old ladies in festive pastel pant suits was gathered in one of them. No Liebling.

Their young waitress, Dot, brought Wally his oatmeal as he was sitting back down. The oatmeal was Rose's idea. Wally's cholesterol levels were trending a bit high, plus he suffered from frequent irregularity when he traveled. Clover had ordered only coffee. Which he wasn't drinking. Just staring at.

Wally smiled up at Dot and said, 'I see from the license plates out in the parking lot that you've got customers here all of the way from California.'

'That must be the real cute guy who was asking about Annie.' Dot had a pretty smile and a peaches and cream complexion. Body on her like a young heifer. 'He was waiting here for us when we opened up.'

'And Annie is . . .?'

'She bought the Blackwell place a few months back. It's up the road past St Francis of Assisi. It'll be real cute once she finishes re-shingling. Can I get you gentlemen anything else?'

Wally said, 'No, thank you,' and dutifully put away his oatmeal before he and Clover went back out into the crisp fall morning.

The duffel bag of weapons was in the trunk of the Crown Vic. It was exceptionally heavy because of the Barrett, which weighed thirty pounds on its own. Wally got in the back seat with the duffel and unzipped it. Clover took the wheel. Wally passed one of the two fully loaded Sig-Sauers over the seat to him. Then, as Clover pulled out of the parking lot, Wally loaded the Barrett with its ten-round magazine of .50-caliber armor-piercing cartridges.

There was a Catholic church just around the bend from Breitbach's. Then a few houses that were spaced pretty far apart. It was about a mile down the quiet country lane to the one that was half-shingled, a tiny place that sat up on a rise with a commanding view of the river. A green Ford-150 pickup was parked out front.

'Just keep right on going,' Wally told Clover as they drew nearer. 'We'll circle back and find a place to roost. That stand of oaks back near the Catholic church should make for an ideal . . .'

Before he could get another word out their targets came marching right out the front door, accompanied by a charcoal-colored terrier. Liebling was toting a large carton. The woman got in behind the wheel of the pick-up. The dog jumped in beside her, then Liebling got in.

'Positively our lucky day, my friend,' Wally exclaimed brightly. 'We'll be jetting home to our loved ones before lunchtime. How does that sound?'

Clover wouldn't say. He was really starting to piss Wally off.

She backed the pickup out of her driveway and took off in the direction of Breitbach's. Clover turned around and followed her north on Route 52 through lush dairy farmland in the direction of Guttenberg. It was a twisting two-lane road, a quiet road. Clover stayed a steady, cautious quarter-mile back. Wally laid the barrel of the Barrett over the front seat and peered through its optic sight, adjusting the focus, getting used to it, loving the potent feel of the weapon in his hands.

After a few miles she pulled over at a convenience store, got out and went inside. Clover eased over on to the shoulder

and idled there until she returned to the truck with a newspaper tucked under her arm. She and Liebling remained there
for several minutes before they finally continued on.

There were no other cars in sight.

Wally set the Barrett on the seat beside him and opened its
bipod. 'Let's get this done, Clover. Go ahead and cozy up to
them at the next stop sign that they come to. After we've
crossed the intersection I'll need you to make a hard left so
that my passenger-side window swings around and faces the
road. I'll put one right in her gas tank. Then we can skedaddle
back, torch the house and we're gone. Sound like a plan?'

Clover didn't answer him.

'Clover . . .?' Wally couldn't wait to be done with this
psychotic mute. Next assignment, he was saying something
to Mrs Pryor. Enough was enough. 'Clover, I need a direct
answer out of you right this second. Are you on board?'

Finally, Clover gave him a single nod of his head.

'Thank you,' Wally snapped.

Just outside of Monona they approached an intersection
with Route 18, which went eastward to Prairie du Chien,
according to the road sign. Route 18 had the right of way. Up
ahead of them, the Ford pickup slowed at the stop sign and
came to a halt. Clover eased right up on to its tail. Wally
rolled down his back window. Several cars were heading
toward Prairie du Chien on Route 18. The pickup had to wait
for them to pass before it could cross the intersection. After
it had, Clover inched forward and waited to cross, too. Except
more cars were coming now. A whole slew of them – all
headed for Prairie du Chien. Clover had to idle there and wait
for them to pass on by.

'Not a problem,' Wally assured him, gazing calmly out of
his window. 'We can catch up to them. The road looks nice
and clear up ahead. Easy pickings.' When the moment arrived
he would poke the barrel of the Barrett out the window, steady
the bipod on the arm rest and nuke that green Ford pickup into
oblivion. When the moment arrived. 'Nice and easy, Clover.
Just two more cars . . . One more . . . OK, here we go . . .'

TWENTY-SIX

'So where the hell are we going?' demanded Hunt who, it seemed, never got tired of chewing Bazooka bubble gum with his mouth open.

'A little farm town about an hour up river called Waukon.' Annie was still trying to wrap her mind around the harsh reality that her dad was dead. The surprising part was that she felt zero sense of loss. None. When her mom died she'd ached inside for months. She'd have to meditate on this later. And, for now, try not to judge herself too harshly. She already had enough to deal with.

Rudy lay curled up next to her as she drove. Hunt clutched that carton of her dad's stuff in his lap. Wouldn't let go of it.

'And what's in Waukon?' he asked, chewing, chewing. His right knee jiggling, jiggling. Hyper didn't begin to describe this man.

'It's more like a *who*,' responded Annie, who was even more surprised by her reaction to this fugitive who'd shown up at her door.

She wanted him. In fact, she felt such an intense physical desire for Hunt Liebling that she'd practically jumped him right there on her kitchen table. Which was *so* not like her. Annie was always very cautious when it came to men. In her own defense, she hadn't been with one in over ten months. And Hunt was undeniably sexy. And smart. And really, really hurting right now. Plus there was this weird symbiotic thing happening – the two of them ending up together after so much death just like her parents had. Annie wondered if that had occurred to him, too. Probably not, the poor guy was so shell-shocked. She wanted to hold him in her arms and comfort him.

And then make love to him non-stop for three solid days and nights.

But Annie *was* cautious. Downright suspicious even. What if this man who called himself Hunt Liebling was just another private detective hired by Herbie to reel her in? She doubted it.

He seemed genuine. And he did have Rudy. Nonetheless, she stopped at the first convenience store she came to and bought that morning's *Dubuque Telegraph-Herald*.

And it was plastered all over the front page just like he'd said. The Unablogger murder rampage. The nationwide manhunt. Hunt's photograph right there on page one. A two-year-old picture in which he had nicer, less terrier-style hair. One of the articles mentioned that Gary would be delivering the eulogy at her dad's funeral tomorrow at Forest Lawn. Herbie was quoted as saying he still hoped to locate her in time for her to attend. 'Tim had lost touch with Alicia. I'm praying she'll reach out to me. It won't seem right if Alicia's not here.'

'Do you believe me now?' Hunt asked her as he scanned the articles right along with her. Rudy lay beneath the open paper, poking at it playfully.

'What makes you think I didn't?'

'Because *I* wouldn't have. If you hadn't checked it out for yourself I'd have wondered if maybe you were going to sell me out.'

'Sell you out how?'

'By driving me straight to the nearest police station.' Hunt's soulful eyes locked on to hers. Annie felt herself shiver inside. 'You're not, are you?'

'No, I'm not.' She released the parking brake and got back on the road, heading north. 'But I am taking a huge chance. I promised I'd never, ever show my face in Waukon again.'

'And *who* is in Waukon?' he asked, studying the road behind them in the truck's side mirror. He was making sure that no one was tailing them.

No one was. There wasn't a soul in her rear-view mirror.

'Sharon Combs,' she said in an appropriately reverent voice. 'And Sharon does not like drop-ins. She's intensely paranoid. I'm talking way, way twitchy. Which is to be expected, I guess.'

'Why is that? Who is she?'

Annie glanced at him in surprise. 'You've never heard of Sharon Combs? God, Sharon is . . . I guess you'd call her an iconic figure in the geek universe. An off-the-charts genius. She got her PhD before her twentieth birthday. Was a fellow at the Computation Institute when I was an undergrad at the

University of Chicago. She taught some of my classes, and we became friends. Don't tell anyone this, but it's Sharon who disappeared me. And that's the least of what she can do. There's no one on the planet who knows as much as Sharon does about data mining. The National Science Foundation wanted her working for them full time. So did every multinational corporation you can think of. And she did design a supercomputer for one of the pharmaceutical giants a while back. I'm talking monster. That bad boy can practically sit up and say—'

'Again, if you could just dumb this down a bit. Data mining is . . .?'

'Oh, sorry. Pharmaceutical companies have very, very complex scientific research problems to solve, OK? Like human genome research where there's a *huge* number of changing variables and only a unique combination will solve it. Data mining, quite simply, is the application of brute force. Bunches and bunches of computers all linked together by a mondo bandwidth that are sharing and updating from a common data storage pool. We call that grid computing. Grid controllers distribute the data. Grid slaves do the processing. The slaves are stacked one atop the other, OK? And they're all clustered together in a room that's the size of a football field. We call that a server farm.'

'And that's what this Sharon Combs designs?'

'*Used* to design. Now she's strictly an insurgent who rages against the machine. The cool part is Sharon set it up so that some of those slaves in the big pharma supercomputer are actually running her outlaw site. How, you may be wondering.'

'And the answer is . . .?'

'That the grid network's so interconnected with so much bandwidth in use at once that no one notices if a couple of renegade slave servers are bogarting more than their fair share. She held on to her own passwords and access codes. And, somehow, established a remote connection to the network. She's hooked right into the grid from her set-up in Waukon. That's how she and Big Bob, her partner in crime, power their web site. Which, you'll be happy to know, specializes in streaming digital videos. You'll also be happy to know she hates Herbie, hates Gary Dixon, Jeremiah Staunton, the whole lot of them.'

'Sounds perfect, Annie,' Hunt said, studying the road sign up ahead as they neared an intersection with Route 18. 'Prairie du Chien,' he read aloud, his French pronunciation excellent. 'There's a town in Wisconsin called Prairie of the Dog?'

'There is. Except it's pronounced Prayer-du-sheen.'

'No, it's not.'

'I assure you it is. You're in the Midwest now.'

'What kind of a website does Sharon operate? Something to do with the computer underworld?'

'Not exactly.' Annie cleared her throat. 'In fact, you may find it a bit shocking.'

'Why, what could be so . . . *shit*!' His eyes were on his side-view mirror. 'No, no, don't turn around. And *don't* look at them in your rear-view mirror.'

'Don't look at who?' she asked, slowing to a stop at the intersection.

Hunt stared straight ahead, his fists clenching. 'The same silver Crown Vic's been dogging us for the last ten miles. It's just pulled up right behind us. There are two guys in it, one white, one black. They have G-men written all over them.'

'Maybe they're not following us,' she said, her heart racing as she idled there, waiting for the cross-traffic to pass. 'Maybe they're turning here for Prairie du Chien.'

'The dude doesn't have his turn signal on.'

'Hunt, what should I do?'

'Not a thing. You're not the one who's in trouble, I am. Just keep calm.'

'I *am* calm,' she assured him, even though she was clutching on to the steering wheel so tight her knuckles were white.

'I didn't say you weren't. You're an awesome wheelman, Annie. You're doing great. Sure could have used you when we were powering cross country, right, little dude?' Rudy nuzzled Hunt's hand with his nose in response. 'OK, here's the thing, here's the thing – just wait for these cars to go by and then keep right on going like everything's normal. Can you do that?'

'I can do it.' Annie waited as one, two, three cars passed by them en route to Prairie du Chien. But she couldn't go yet. There were still several more to come. As she waited she sneaked a peek in her rear-view mirror. The black man behind the wheel was staring straight ahead, his face a blank.

The white man, who wore round eyeglasses, was riding in the back seat for some reason. And appeared to be lowering his window.

Hunt watched the passing cars go by. 'Damn, there's sure a lot of traffic here. Considering that we're in the middle of Butthole, Nowhere. And, OK, is this getting weird or is it just me?'

Annie swallowed. 'What do you mean?'

'Every single one of these cars is a cherry Corvette Stingray from the Sixties. See? Here comes another one . . . And there's two more . . . What's up with all of these Vettes?'

'Maybe they're in a club together,' she said tensely.

Finally, the road cleared. Lower lip fastened firmly between her teeth, Annie crossed over Route 18 and continued on toward Waukon – just like everything was normal.

TWENTY-SEVEN

The single most important thing? He couldn't let them know just exactly where inside of his head he was hiding. As long as they couldn't find him in there he'd be OK. So Clover kept very quiet and very, very still. Had to. Because if he didn't then they would find him – and mess with him.

I'll be OK as long as they don't mess with me.

And, hey, so far so good. His driving was smooth and steady. Eyes forward, hands strong on the wheel as he stayed a careful distance behind that Ford pickup. Within the job. Invisible. And trusting no one.

Can't trust anyone. For damned sure not those doctors with their poison pills. If he took one it would kill him instantly. Clover knew this for a fact. So he stayed awake and straight. Getting his job done even though they were becoming stronger and bolder as he grew more tired. But he couldn't, mustn't sleep. The instant he fell asleep they'd find him. So he stayed awake. And quiet. And very, very still.

I'll be OK as long as they don't mess with me.

But, damn, they were right out in the open now. As he drove across Illinois on Route 20 in the misty light of dawn Clover could see them out of the corner of his eye – dashing right alongside the Crown Vic, saliva dripping from their sharp little teeth, yellow eyes gleaming with vicious delight. They were laughing at him. He could hear their laughter. Hear them murmuring to each other in hushed tones. And see their flickering shadows there – *right there* – behind the trees.

Coop was in direct contact with them again, he felt certain. Just like that time when they were in Aspen. Clover had sunk his teeth into the little guy just to let to let him know he was on to him. He couldn't trust Coop. Not then, not now. Can't trust him. Damn, what was he *doing* in the back seat? And wait, now he was *talking* at him again. Trying to break his vital concentration. Some shit about swinging around hard left after they crossed this intersection. Clover nodded his head so the little guy would shut the fuck up.

I'll be OK as long as they don't mess with me.

Up ahead, the pickup slowed at a country crossroads and came to a stop, waiting to cross. Clover snugged up behind it and waited there like Coop said to. A whole lot of traffic had to go by. Car after car after car. Clover sat quiet and still, eyes forward. Until, ever so slowly, it dawned upon him that something a whole lot wrong was going on . . .

It was those cars. The ones crossing in front of him. They were . . . They were *all the same.* One after another after another. All of them antique Vettes. All of them throaty and alive. Eight Vettes, ten Vettes, twelve . . . No end to them. They didn't stop. Just kept on coming and coming and . . .

They're messing with me. Lord, they are most certainly messing with me.

Laughter. He could hear their roars of laughter now. Because they'd been waiting here for him all along. They were on to him.

They've found me.

Too strong. Too damned strong for him. They'd won again. Gotten the better of him despite his best effort. And Clover knew what that meant. They were going to chew their way right into his brain now with their sharp little teeth – unless he shut himself down. Had to shut it down right this second or they'd eat his brains for breakfast on toast, smeared with farm-fresh butter and home-made apricot jam.

So I'll shut myself down. Not move one muscle. If I so much as twitch I will give myself away. But as long as I stay perfectly still they will not know I'm in here. I mustn't let them know. So I will not move one muscle or speak a single word or so much as blink, so help me God . . .

TWENTY-EIGHT

'Step on it, Clover.' Wally had the Barrett's bipod positioned on the armrest, its barrel sticking out of the open window. 'The coast is clear. I'm loaded and ready. Hit the gas.'

Clover didn't hit the gas. Didn't so much as respond at all.

'Darn it, Clover, they're getting away. *Go*, will you?'

Clover didn't go. Just stared straight ahead.

Wally shook him by the shoulder. 'Clover?'

Nothing. Absolutely no reaction. It was like talking to a statue.

Wally leaned over the seat and waved a hand in front of Clover's eyes. Clover didn't blink. He'd gone into some form of a catatonic trance, damn him.

Wally jumped out of the car, flung the driver's door open and pulled the parking brake. He shoved the seat back as far as it would go and climbed on to Clover's lap, feeling Clover's moist breath on the back of his neck. No other sign of life. Clover didn't move a muscle under him. Wally released the parking brake, kicked Clover's ankle boot from the brake pedal and hit the gas with his own foot, powering the Crown Vic across the intersection. He turned in at the first dirt farm road he came to, went in about a hundred yards, stopped and got out.

Clover continued to stare straight ahead, not blinking, not *there*.

The envelope. Clover had told him its contents would explain what Wally should give him should any problematic symptoms arise – *not that they would*. Wally sincerely hoped Clover had brought the proper medication with him. The man's overnight bag was stowed in the trunk. But first Wally snatched the envelope from the breast pocket of his tweed blazer and tore it open. Inside, he found a two-word handwritten note. The note read:

Shoot me.

He grabbed Clover under both arms, pulled him bodily from the car and dumped him on to the ground, face up. Clover stared directly at the sun, not so much as squinting. Wally riffled through his trouser pockets. Removed a wallet with a driver's license and credit cards that identified him as Calvin Lamar Samuels of West Palm Beach, Florida. Wally took his money and house keys, removed his Rolex and gold rings. Stuffed these items into the pockets of his tweed blazer for disposal. Then he fetched the Sig-Sauer from the front seat and shot Cloverdale Millington once in each unseeing eye.

Wally got back in the car immediately, backed up to the paved road and went tearing off after the targets, pedal to the metal. He drove the Crown Vic hard for several miles but couldn't catch up to them. And then, unhappily, he reached a fork in the road. Wally took the right fork and gave himself five miles. But he saw no sign of the green pick-up. They'd either taken the other fork or turned off somewhere else along the way. Didn't matter which. What mattered was that he'd lost them.

Not good.

He came to a stop on the deserted road and puffed out his cheeks, weighing his options. His best hope was that they would return to the house in Balltown. Didn't know that its location had been blown. Weren't fleeing. She was fixing up the place, after all. Putting down roots. She'd come back. *They'd* come back. Sure they would.

And when they did he'd be ready for them.

TWENTY-NINE

'Shit, did you just hear that?' Hunt cried out as Annie steered them north toward Waukon, Rudy dozing between them. 'Sounded like gunshots. Two of them.'

'Hunters,' she responded calmly. 'That's not so unusual around here.'

'That didn't sound like any shotgun to me. More like a handgun.'

'Also not so unusual. This is farm country, Hunt. If you have livestock then you have mice, and if you have mice you have snakes. Some are poisonous and have to be dealt with. Chill out. It's nothing to worry about.'

But Hunt did worry, his eyes remaining glued to the truck's side mirror. That silver Crown Vic no longer seemed to be on their tail, thank God. Maybe the G-men had been heading for Prairie du Chien after all. Not a big deal. Just as those shots were not a big deal. They were in farm country, like Annie said. Could be he was just spooked. Not that he didn't have good reason to be. He was the most wanted man in North America. Everyone he knew and loved was dead. The outcome of the presidential election was hanging in the balance.

Chilling out? Not really an option.

Outside of Waukon they encountered the usual collection of charm-free fast food franchises, motels and mini-marts. The old-timey center of Waukon was still thriving. Annie rolled straight on through town, which really didn't take long, then got on to Round Prairie Drive and kept on going until they reached a huge dairy farm. Just beyond it she turned in at a dirt driveway where a rather flat ranch-style home had been plunked down in the middle of a cleared five-acre plot of land. There was no garage. And no car sitting out front.

'It doesn't look like Sharon is home.'

'Sharon's always home,' Annie said apprehensively.

She parked in a muddy clearing next to the house. From there, Hunt spotted a mobile home around back that was joined to the main house by huge electrical cables. Annie got out and started for it. Hunt and Rudy followed her.

Annie tapped on the mobile home's door. No one answered. She tapped harder.

Finally the door was flung open by the palest, skinniest woman Hunt had ever seen in his life. Based on what Annie had told him, Sharon Combs, PhD, had to be in her thirties. But she could easily pass for under twenty-one. She was barely five feet tall and dressed like a pint-sized Goth outlaw in a sleeveless black T-shirt and tight black jeans. Several clunky bracelets jangled around her puny wrists. Sharon's face was narrow, nose long, her black hair spiky and tinged with purple.

She peered out at them with pale blue eyes that were piercing and intensely hostile. Her gaze took in Hunt standing there with the big carton in his arms. Then Rudy, who was sniffing around the trailer, nose to the ground. Lastly, it settled on Annie.

'You promised you'd *never* come back here. You gave me your word.'

'I know I did, I know,' Annie blurted out. 'And I'm incredibly sorry. But something major has come up.'

'Not interested,' Sharon snapped at her. 'Go away – and take your boy toy with you.'

'Her boy toy's name is Hunt Liebling,' he said just as the great Sharon Combs was about to slam the door in their faces. 'That particular kernel of information is worth a hundred thou cash money. You can pick up the phone right now and collect your reward. Or you can listen to what I have to say. The choice is yours. But make up your mind fast because I don't have a lot of time.'

Sharon's eyes narrowed at him. 'Holy shit . . . it *is* you. I must read your gnarly rants two, three times a day. Or I did until you stopped posting and became public enemy *numero uno*.' She hesitated now, her mouth drawn tight. 'OK, get your asses in here. In, in. Your dog, too. Everybody in.'

Hunt hurried through the narrow doorway after Annie and Rudy. Sharon closed the door behind them, then whirled and clamped something hard and flat against Hunt's right bicep with the palm of her hand. Something that resembled a black plastic cell phone.

Except it was no cell phone. It was a Stun Master Hot Shot.

Annie said, 'Sharon, what the hell are you—?'

'Shut up! Move one single muscle, Mr Unablogger, and I will zap you like you've never been zapped before. Do you believe me? Say you believe me.'

'I believe you.' Hunt made no move to knock the palm-sized stun gun out of Sharon's hand. Just stood there very still. He wanted this woman on his side. And he didn't want a 975,000-volt charge coursing through his body.

'Now tell me what you're doing here,' Sharon commanded him.

'I'm in trouble.'

'Duh, I *know* that.' Sharon's pale eyes probed his. 'Why should I care? Why should I trust you?'

'*I* trust him,' Annie offered.

'Which means shit. You already broke your word to me.' To Hunt she said, 'Did you kill all of those people? Tell me right now. And *don't* lie or I'll really, really hurt you.'

'I haven't killed anyone. Tim Ferris reached out a few days ago with a story. That story would have ruined Herbie Landau's best-laid plans for Senator Gary Dixon. I'm talking total polit-ical annihilation. So Herbie destroyed Tim and now he's trying to destroy me – unless I get him first.'

Sharon nodded her spiky head slowly. 'I'm hearing you so far . . . But if you're waging a one-man jihad against Herbie Landau then what are you doing in Waukon, fucking Iowa? Nobody comes here.'

'I had to find Annie.'

Sharon glanced over at her. 'You mean Alicia Ferris.'

'I mean I'm trying to bring down the curtain on Gary Dixon's bid for the White House. And I desperately need your help.'

'Why, what can *I* do?'

'Lighten up on the stun gun and I'll tell you,' Hunt said. 'Deal?'

She stared deep into his eyes for a long moment before she released the Hot Shot from his arm, her chin raised at him challengingly. 'Come on in. We'll talk. But I'm making you no promises, understood?'

'Fine,' he said, breathing a whole lot easier. 'Whatever you say.'

The mobile home's room dividers had been pulled out. What remained was one long, narrow space that was lined from floor to ceiling with computer monitors. There had to be a hundred of them – all of them actively displaying streaming videos. *Porn* videos. Porn, porn and more porn. Slick, professional porn. Wobbly, home-made porn. Straight porn. Gay porn. Black, brown and Asian porn. There were threesomes. There were web cam feeds of solitary naked hotties diddling themselves. It was such a dizzying smorgasbord of virtual sex that Hunt couldn't even take it all in. But one thing he did notice was that each and every monitor featured the logo of a hairy, drooling ape in the lower right corner of its screen.

'No way . . .' he gasped. 'You're *gorillaboink.com*.'

Everyone in the online universe knew *gorillaboink.com*. It was the world's largest and most audacious free porn Internet site. The Feds had been trying, and failing, to shut it down for years. The site's snarky invincibility made it the stuff of Internet legend, not to mention the scourge of the Christian right.

'I always figured it came out of Singapore or maybe Russia.' Hunt shook his head in awed disbelief. 'I had no idea you were right here in America's heartland.'

'Only a very, very small circle of people know,' Sharon told him in a low, threatening voice. 'I'm letting you into that circle. I respect you. I respect the work that you do. But if you break the circle I swear I'll track you down and punish you.'

'I won't break it. You have my word.' Up on one of the monitors a naked foursome of what appeared to be Chinese gymnasts were in the process of joining together in a way that Hunt had previously believed to be anatomically impossible. 'And all of this is powered by a big pharma supercomputer?'

Sharon glowered at Annie. 'Is there anything you *didn't* tell him?'

'He's on the run. I had to convince him that you were cool.'

'True that,' she admitted to Hunt grudgingly. 'They're busy doing research on a new erectile dysfunction drug. Spending trillions trying to figure out how to get a guy's dong hard while I'm pirating their system to put videos out there that do it for free. It's all free. I haven't paid an electric bill in three years. But enough about me – does the law have *any* idea where you are right now?'

'You tell me. I'm not hooked up.'

Sharon sat down at a computer, lit a Marlboro and went to work, her fingers flying over the keyboard as she searched the twenty-four-hour news sites. 'They think you're hiding in Washington,' she reported, cigarette smoke curling from her lip. 'Your friends and associates are being urged to contact the FBI if you reach out because you are one bad mother-fucker.'

Rudy started barking excitedly now – a car was coming up the driveway. Hunt went to the window, tensing. Sharon right there alongside of him. A dark blue Toyota Corolla was pulling up alongside of Annie's pickup.

'It's just Big Bob. We're good.'

Although Big Bob didn't exactly think so. Sharon's partner in crime came charging through the door on high alert. 'Babe, there's somebody's green pick-up parked out front!'

'It's OK, it's OK!' Sharon called back. 'We have guests.'

Big Bob stood there holding a large, fragrant pizza box and a six-pack of Old Milwaukee. She was a hulking blonde six-footer in her mid-twenties dressed in a flannel shirt, corduroy jeans and work boots. 'Alicia? What are *you* doing back here?' she demanded suspiciously.

'Believe me, it wasn't my idea. And it's Annie now, remember?'

'Shit, I always forget that stuff. I'd make the world's worst spy. Hey, you brought a Casey dog.'

'Actually, he's not *a* Casey,' Hunt said. 'He's *the* Casey – although he goes by Rudy.'

'OK, I'm nodding my big fat head even though I didn't understand one word of that,' Big Bob said, looking Hunt over from head to toe.

'It's a Hunt Liebling,' Sharon informed her.

Big Bob's eyes widened. 'The Unablogger?'

'He's wanted by the FBI in all fifty states and, fuck me, I'm actually thinking about aiding and abetting.'

'Slow this way, way down,' Big Bob cautioned her. 'I'm not on board yet.'

'You will be.'

'Babe, we're talking about some serious shit here.'

'I know this.'

'Well, did you check him out?'

'Totally. I gave him the Stun Master test. He passed it.'

Big Bob considered this, shoving her lower lip in and out

thoughtfully. 'Then in that case, let's eat.'

She opened the pizza box on a cluttered desk and all four of them dove in. The pizza was plenty good, although unlike any Hunt had eaten before. Topped with smoked sausage along with something else that tasted vinegary and kind of familiar although he absolutely couldn't place it.

'What's on this pie?' he asked, munching.

'Bratwurst and sauerkraut,' Big Bob answered around a full mouthful.

'That's funny, I could swear you just said *sauerkraut*.'

'Get used to it. You're in the—'

'I know, I know. I'm in the Midwest now.'

'Hunt, it pains me to admit this,' Sharon said, taking tiny rodent nibbles out of her slice, 'but you're exposing my soft white underbelly. Any opportunity to man up against a totalitarian shithead like Herbie Landau is my idea of a party. So break it down for us – what kind of help are you looking for?'

Hunt wiped his fingers on a paper napkin and removed the boxed set of DVDs from the carton. 'Tim Ferris wanted to tell the world a story. That story's right here in a five-volume video memoir. There's maybe seven hours of material altogether. I've seen the first four volumes. I haven't seen Volume Five yet. For starters, I need to sit down and watch it.'

'And then . . .?'

'I need you to upload them *fast*.'

'With email links to all of the major news outlets,' Annie added. 'Plus every blogger he knows.'

Sharon said, 'Not a problem. We could do that for you. What else?'

Hunt dug deeper into the carton for the strongbox that contained the videotape of *Monty and Me*. 'I need to transfer this on to a DVD and put it out there, too.'

'I'll run it through my digitizer while you're watching Volume Five. What is it?'

'Something right up your alley, according to Tim – an authentic underground porn classic. Gay Hollywood legends engaging in X-rated fun at Darren Beck's Trancas beach house, circa-1960. The young Gary Dixon is on it, as is Tim himself . . .' Hunt glanced uneasily over at Annie. 'I'm sorry. I didn't mean to break it to you this way.'

'It's OK,' Annie said quietly. 'My dad was into pretty much

everything at one time or another.'

Big Bob frowned at him. 'Hang on a sec . . . exactly how old were they when this was made?'

'Gary was in college. And Tim said he was thirteen.'

'We can't help you,' Sharon said abruptly.

Hunt frowned at her. 'You can't? Why not?'

'You're talking about kiddie porn, that's why not. We don't do that. Kiddo porn is a sickness. It's evil, mean and nasty.'

'Also way felonious,' Big Bob added. 'If we so much as dip one toe in it we'll be giving the Feds an excuse to throw our asses in jail for all eternity.'

Hunt had been so wrapped up in the madness of it all that this rather obvious stumbling block hadn't occurred to him. 'But it's *news*.'

'Doesn't matter,' Sharon said. 'We won't do it. You'll have to handle it some other way.'

Silence fell in the trailer, which throbbed with so much electrical current it practically hummed.

Hunt unwrapped a fresh piece of Bazooka and popped it into his mouth, his wheels spinning. 'OK, we'll come back to that. Right now, Annie and I are going to watch Volume Five.'

'Know what? I really don't need to see it,' Annie said hurriedly. 'It's such a pretty day out. I think I'll take Rudy out for a nice long walk instead.'

'No, you won't,' Hunt said. 'Your dad wanted you to watch this. That's why he sent you the only copy in the whole world. The man was holding his hand out to you one last time. You've got to take it.'

'I don't believe what I'm hearing,' Big Bob grumbled. 'He's an outlaw, he's gorgeous *and* he's sensitive?'

Sharon nodded. 'I'd do him myself if I was still into meat.'

'Sit and watch this with me, Annie,' Hunt implored her. 'Please.'

Annie looked at him long and hard with those huge dark eyes of hers. 'OK, Hunt, we'll watch it together. But only under one condition . . .'

'Name it.'

'Would you please get rid of that fucking gum?'

VOLUME FIVE

(Tim is seated in his den wearing a tie-dyed Grateful Dead T-shirt. He gazes directly into the camera. His gaze is riveting, voice clear and strong. The dying child star seems much more energized than in the previous four volumes. Clearly, he has been waiting for this moment for a long, long time . . .)

Steve Yslas was dead. Shot with his own .38 in the alley behind The Book Nook. He and Kip's young girlfriend, Choochie Ochoa, whose only crime was that maybe, just maybe, she could have identified the Bagley Bunch killer.

Steve was in Santa Monica that night because I'd asked him to be there. It was my fault that he was dead, and I was a wreck. I'd lost both of my on-screen sisters, Tina and Kelly. Lost my brother Kip. Now Steve, the man who'd been the closest thing I ever had to a dad.

A huge part of me wanted to escape from the horror. Head straight for the Pink Pussycat on the Strip. I knew a tasty dancer there named April September who always had open arms and a supply of terrific acid. I wanted to lose myself in a purple haze. But I couldn't – because I owed it to all of them to keep it real. And what lay ahead of me in Glendale didn't get more real.

It was the middle of the night by the time I pulled up at Steve's house. A police detail was parked out front. Two cop wives were seated there on the living-room sofa, drinking coffee. Elvia was nowhere to be seen, but I could hear her sobs coming from her bedroom.

'How is she?'

'You've got ears,' one of them answered me. 'How do you think?'

'You can leave now. I'll take care of her.'

They glanced at each other before one of them said, 'And who's going to take care of you?'

'We'll take care of each other, OK?'

That was the beginning for us. Not that we said a single

*word to each other. Not then. I just stretched out next to her
on the bed and held her. I was still holding her when the
phone rang many hours later.*

*It was Duane. 'We've lost another one, Tim,' he informed
me somberly. 'Darren Beck is dead. It happened at his place
in Brentwood.'*

Now four of the Bagleys were gone.

*'But it's all over, Tim. That's the good news. We got our
man.'*

Except Colin Gault claimed he hadn't done it. Any of it.

*'It wasn't me,' Colin insisted, seated there on Darren's sleek,
modern living-room sofa. Darren's muscular blond boyfriend
wore a lustrous purple kaftan. Before him on the coffee table
was a porcelain cup of tea. He reached for it and took a sip,
his hand rock steady. 'I didn't kill Darren. I didn't kill anyone.'*

*The kaftan Darren had been wearing was a lustrous aqua
– or it had been before his throat was slit open. Now it was
all covered with his blood. And America's favorite TV dad
lay dead on the polished slate floor of the master bedroom,
his bald head gleaming in the lamp light. Apparently, he'd
been getting ready for bed and had removed his toupee for
the night. The sight of Darren's hairless dome shocked me as
I stared at him from the doorway. How puny he looked, this
powerful sexual predator who'd passed me around to members
of the Velvet Underground like I was a new snack treat.*

*Duane had told me to meet him there. I guess he felt I
needed the closure. I've always been grateful to him for that.
We arrived just before the press corps did. Uniformed cops
were cordoning off the road.*

*Darren's modern glass show place clung to the side of a
steep slope high above Sunset at the top of Tigertail. He had
ocean views from his wrap-around deck, which was
cantilevered out over a narrow, scrubby ravine hundreds of
feet below. The living room, dining room and kitchen opened
out on to the deck. Darren's master bedroom suite and guest
rooms were downstairs at ground level. There was no backyard other than the hillside.*

*Four cops had been watching him at the time of his murder.
Two of them were posted in the street out front, one out on
the deck, one in the living room.*

'That "assistant" of his, Gault, keeps claiming someone

broke in,' reported the wheezy, pot-bellied cop who'd been stationed in the living room. 'But we've been right here the whole time, Lieutenant.'

'You guys didn't see or hear anything?'

'Not a thing. It had to be Gault. Doesn't play any other way.'

Duane sized up Colin from across the room. 'He's about the coolest customer I've ever seen. We've got him dead to rights for a half-dozen homicides and look at him – he isn't even fazed.'

For some reason, Colin kept shooting disagreeable looks my way. Beyond that, he did seem incredibly cool. Also clean. Not a drop of Darren's blood on him. I couldn't imagine he'd had time to wash it off or to change clothes. Not with cops in the house.

'Am I under arrest?' he asked. 'I'd like to talk to a lawyer if I am.'

'Not just yet,' Duane answered. 'If and when you are arrested I'll be sure to let you know. How long have you been planning this whole thing, Colin?'

Colin had an actor's strong jaw and sharp, straight nose. But not an actor's luminous, telling eyes. His were languid and uncurious. 'I didn't "plan" anything. I'm not the Bagley Bunch killer. You can't dump this on me.'

'Looks like you used a knife on Mr Beck. Want to tell me where it is?'

'I didn't kill him.'

'OK, then who did?'

'An intruder, like I already told those other cops five times.'

'Why don't you tell me?' Duane's voice was gentle and patient.

'I'd gone to my room for the night – as had Darren.' Colin's tone of voice indicated he hadn't been happy about the sleeping arrangement. But no way image-conscious Darren would have let him into his bed while cops were in the house. 'Shortly before eleven I heard Darren let out a cry. Then I heard a thud, as if he'd fallen. I went in and found him lying there dead. And I saw someone right outside of the window looking in.'

'Who, Colin?'

'I couldn't tell. It was . . . like someone's silhouette. Whoever

it was vanished in an instant. I called out to the police. They came rushing down the stairs, and that's all I know.'

'Did you take a look around outside?' Duane asked the pot-bellied cop.

He nodded wearily. 'That window's on the east side of the house. There's a narrow yard there. But the only way in is the front gate and we had that covered. Nobody went in or out.'

'There's no way in from the back?'

'There's no back, Lieutenant. Just a straight drop down to the bottom of the hill. Nobody could have climbed up and down that. Especially in the dark.'

'Someone did,' Colin insisted.

'Tell you what, Colin. We'll cordon it off and take a good look in daylight, OK?'

'Thank you,' he said softly.

'Did you often spend the night here with your . . . employer?'

'If we had a late shoot. Before we went back into production I was usually with him up at his winery in Napa Valley. Or at the beach house in Trancas. What'll happen to all of that now?'

'We're getting a little ahead of ourselves, Colin.'

Car doors slammed outside and in barged a pair of chesty gray-haired bosses. Duane went to fill them in. A uniformed cop kept an eye on Colin.

Colin took a Sherman from its flat red box, glancing around for a match. I lit a Chesterfield and tossed him my Zippo. He used it to light his Sherman, setting it down on the coffee table. 'Darren talked about you all of the time.'

'He did? I can't imagine why.'

'Can't you?' Colin lowered his voice so the cop wouldn't hear. 'He was still hung up on you. And it sounded pretty mutual, the way you two were always meeting for drinks, shopping for clothes together at Sy Devore.'

'We didn't do any of those things, Colin. Tina's funeral was the first time I'd seen Darren in years.'

'You wouldn't be bullshitting me, would you?'

'Call Sy Devore if you don't believe me. I've never been there in my life. There was nothing going on between Darren and me. He was strictly playing with your head.'

'Why, that nasty old queen,' Colin hissed between his even white teeth. 'He's lucky I didn't get wise to him, because

I would *have roughed him up. Only now . . .' He gazed around at Darren's glass house in bewilderment. 'Now I don't know what I'll do.'*

Duane returned and told Colin he'd have to be brought in for questioning. Colin climbed to his feet with a defeated sigh and was escorted out. Duane gave me a nod, which I took as my cue to split.

It hadn't cooled off outside like it usually did at night. The air was sultry, not a leaf stirring. Earthquake weather, LA old timers used to call it. A dozen or more police cars were stacked this way and that at the top of the hill. My babysitters, Crovitz and Thorson, waited for me in one of them.

I lingered on Darren's front porch as Colin was driven away, wondering if this nightmare that had ripped my life apart was at long last over. Had Colin Gault systematically slaughtered four members of my on-screen family? Murdered Steve? Murdered Choochie? I wasn't totally won over. Colin hadn't come off like a deranged killer to me. More like a self-absorbed leech whose host body had just left him homeless.

I moseyed over to the front gate and checked out that narrow side yard where Colin claimed he'd spotted someone through Darren's bedroom window. It really wasn't much more than a flagstone path – one that dropped right off the steep hillside into the black of night. Darren's bedroom windows were about four feet off the ground. The brightly lit room was casting light outside where I stood. Two medical examiner's men were hunched over the body, their backs to me. There were three windows in all. A fixed section of glass in the middle with sliders on either side. One of the sliders was securely locked from the inside. I tried the other one. It slid quietly open. So quietly the men inside didn't hear me. I stuck my hand in. No screen.

The window was unlocked and there was no screen.

Now I noticed a tiny glint of something on the ground at my feet. Reached down and picked it up and stared at it.

And then I was all done staring. I was running. Crovitz got out of his car and asked me what was up. I dashed right by him, jumped in my car and nosed my way through the police cordon, horn honking. Crovitz was still standing there as I tore my way down Tigertail and out of there. He and Thorson had zero chance. I left them in my dust.

I floored it out to Panorama City. Old Nate was on duty in his kiosk at the studio's main gate. He waved me on through. The lights were still on in a few production bungalows. Sitcom writers undertaking feverish late-night revisions. But the cavernous sound stages were dark. All except for Stage Four. A light was on over the stage door. I parked there and got out and went inside. Then I stood there in shock, taking it all in.

All of our old standing sets had been reassembled, right down to the smallest props, and laid out on the stage floor in their familiar horseshoe shape. The Bagley family living room, dining room and kitchen. The attic rumpus room. My old room that I shared with Kip, with its bunk beds and matching desks and the window that looked out over nowhere. I found it intensely surreal to look at the sets again. Because it was still 1959 in here. The Sixties had never happened. There'd been no Kennedy assassinations. No Martin Luther King. No riots. No Vietnam. No sex, drugs and rock 'n' roll. Absolutely nothing had changed.

Except it had. The whole goddamned world had.

I could hear muffled voices coming from the direction of the living-room set. I started across the vast sound stage toward them. A projector was rolling – the flickering images of a movie playing out on a home movie screen that had been set up in front of the fake fireplace. I stared at it in horror. Stared at those naked men joined together in twos or threes beside Darren's pool. Some of them were tanned and muscular, others paunchy and old. Some were famous, others complete unknowns whose faces I didn't remember. But I certainly recognized eager, floppy-haired young Gary. And an exultant Darren, his torso shiny with sweat as he stood over that pale, hairless young boy with the lifeless eyes – me.

Someone in a straight-backed dining chair was parked in front of the screen watching it. His back was to me but I recognized the frizzy hair and trademark Hawaiian shirt. When I spoke his name Herbie whipped his head around, eyes bulging as he strained helplessly against the ropes that bound him to the chair. His mouth had been taped shut with packing tape. He couldn't speak. All he could do was growl like a muzzled dog.

'Admit it, Tim, you're surprised!' a voice called to me from the darkness out beyond the projector.

'I'm surprised,' I acknowledged, my hand wrapped around the empty blue packet of Beeman's Black Jack gum that I'd found under Darren's bedroom window. Empty except for the scrawled note inside that read: "Stage Four – Prepare to be surprised."

'I shmeared a couple of guys from the crew to get everything out of storage. Thought it would be kind of cool. I hope you don't mind that we started the main feature without you. He kept it locked in his desk, in case you're wondering. It's amazing how much you can find out when you point a loaded gun at someone and . . . excuse me, but is that Paul Lynde? Who knew?'

'Please turn it off, Errol. I've seen enough.'

Herbie's real-life son flicked off the projector and strolled on to the set clutching that loaded gun – a snub-nosed .38. He wore a clean, pressed chambray work shirt and jeans. There wasn't any blood on him. Just a few scratches on his hands and fine-boned face. He didn't look the least bit desperate or crazed. In fact, Errol Landau seemed completely at ease as he stood there toking on a joint. 'Kip always had the best dope, didn't he?'

'Is that why you stole it?'

'I've never stolen anything in my life. I paid him honest bucks. Care for a hit?'

I shook my head as Herbie continued to snarl and strain against the ropes that held him in his chair. He had a big, red welt on his forehead. Errol must have knocked him out before he bound and gagged him.

'Pop was thoughtful enough to dismiss his police detail for the night, so we're all alone.' Errol flopped down in Walt Senior's leather chair, gesturing at the sofa with the gun. 'Have a seat.'

I sat directly across the coffee table from him. Herbie faced us both, quivering with rage.

'What took you so long, man? I was beginning to worry.'

'Lieutenant Larue had to question Colin before they took him in. I didn't have a chance to look around. How did you know I'd find your gum wrapper? How did you know I'd even be there?'

'I have faith in you,' Errol answered, the gun resting comfortably in his lap. 'I also knew you'd show up here without your

*own police detail. There aren't many people who I have faith
in, Tim. You should be flattered.'*

*'Darren had four cops watching his place. How did you
manage it?'*

*His joint had gone out. Errol put it down in an ashtray and
sat back, thumbing his strawberry blond hair behind his ears.
'There's an empty patch of land about a half-mile down
Tigertail from Darren's place. Some asshole developer will
probably shoehorn four houses on to it some day. Right now,
it's just weeds. I've done a lot of climbing. I know rough
terrain. A couple of days ago I bought myself a good, strong
climbing rope. Scrambled down to the bottom of the ravine
there and tromped through the brush until I was directly under
Darren's house. He wasn't home. Nobody was. It wasn't easy,
but I managed to scamper up that steep hill to the cement
posts that anchor his deck in place. I tied the rope around a
post, shoved it under the brush and used it to grapple back
down to the bottom. Then I left it there for whenever I needed
it – which happened to be tonight.' Errol's face darkened. 'I've
been watching them, Tim. Waiting for them to make a mistake.
Just one. And tonight they did.'*

'Who did, Errol?'

*'They need to be stopped. He needs to be stopped,' Errol
added, glancing over at his father.*

*Herbie had ceased his growling and straining. Just sat there
in miserable silence and listened.*

*'Tim, you're the only person I know who'll believe my story.
No one else will. Not the law for damned sure. And before I
say another word I want you to know how sorry I am about
what happened to Steve. When you're dealing with truly evil
people you should be ready for anything. And I wasn't. I never
saw that coming.'*

'By truly evil people you mean . . .?'

*'Pop and Mort and their whole gang of right-wing lunatics.
They don't love this country, Tim. They love money and power
– their own money and power. They'll have us by the balls
soon if we don't stop them right here and now. Every seat in
Congress will be filled by a hand-picked Christian crazy just
like Gary. There'll be no opposition, no dissent. Nothing but
lies. Just like the lies that got us into this immoral fucking
war and the lies that are keeping us there forever. Our whole*

future's at stake, man. And being a laugh monkey on the radio just wasn't enough for me any more. I couldn't sit around cracking jokes while Pop and his thugs hijack America. You can understand that, can't you?'

'I guess, except for one teeny-tiny detail. If this is about our future then why are all of my friends dead? What is it you want, Errol?'

'God, you really don't get it, do you?' Errol looked over at Herbie, whose googly eyes glowered back at him balefully. 'He adored you guys. You were special. You were perfect. But not me, never me. I was the one he had to keep hidden off-camera. Much too flawed and awkward and just plain pathetically real. All this man has ever done to me is-is . . .' Errol was no longer calm. His face had turned deep red. 'All he's done is ignore me or shit on me! And now I . . . what I want is a little fucking justice, OK? I want the world to know the truth! I want . . .' He could no longer get the words out. So he raised his gun instead and shot at the Bagley family photo gallery on the wall behind Herbie. The fake wedding pictures, fake baby pictures. He blew out one, missed the second. Took aim at the third . . .

Only to discover that Herbie was seated directly in his line of fire.

Errol's hand froze there in mid-air, the gun pointed right at his father. Herbie's eyes bulged, his face contorting with terror. Errol's hand tightened on the gun, his trigger finger shaking, whole hand shaking . . . Until with a shudder he sank back in the chair. 'I want him to get what's coming to him.'

All I could do was stare across the coffee table at Errol in shock. I'd only known the sweet and funny Errol. The impish prankster Errol. This Errol, the Errol who'd choked down so much bitterness and rage that it had made a monster of him, this Errol was a stranger to me.

'You were the lucky one,' I said to him finally. 'You had a normal life in New York with your mom. You've done incredibly well, Errol. Better than all of us combined. And you've done it despite Herbie.'

'I haven't done a fucking thing. Don't you get why I was at Darren's? Why I asked you here, any of it? You're totally blind, aren't you? That's the real tragedy here. Open your eyes, Tim.' He stared down at the gun in his hand. 'Because your moment of truth has finally arrived.'

I froze, absolutely certain Errol was going to shoot me dead at that very moment. He didn't. He reached around for something that was on the floor behind his chair. Taking his eyes off of me for a second. Not long. But it was all the time I needed – I dove across the coffee table for his gun.

'No, Tim . . .!' he cried out.

The two of us tumbled on to the floor, wrestling for it, both of us clutching on to that gun tightly until . . .

I got off a shot. One shot that Errol took directly in the forehead.

I lay right there next to him on the floor and watched him die. I felt no triumph in those final seconds of Errol Landau's life. No relief. Only tremendous sadness.

Then I got up and searched behind the chair. He'd been reaching for a clear plastic storage bag. Inside of it were bloodied overalls, a hunting knife – also bloodied – and a tightly coiled rope. I set the bag down on the coffee table before I yanked the packing tape from Herbie's mouth.

'He's . . . dead!' Herbie moaned, gulping down huge lung fills of air. 'My boy, my own boy . . .!'

I said nothing. Just stood there with Errol's gun in my hand.

'Untie me, will you?' he demanded, bucking back and forth in the chair.

'Tell me something, Herbie – is that the only print of the movie?'

'How can you ask me that now? My boy's dead!'

I pressed the still-hot gun against his temple. 'Is that the only print?'

He nodded his head up and down. 'It is, I swear.'

I set the gun down on the coffee table and went over to the projector and rewound Monty and Me. *I was putting it back in its tin when I heard the stage door open.*

Gary came rushing across the sound stage toward us, the Reverend Jeremiah trailing one step behind him. 'Old Nate at the front gate phoned my house. He said something was up and maybe I ought to . . .' Gary trailed off, his eyes widening at the sight of Errol dead there on the floor.

'Where's your police detail, Gary? Are they outside?'

'Maybe I ought to be asking the questions, Timmy,' he answered hoarsely, clearly shaken.

But not as shaken as I was when I got a closer look at

Jeremiah. The Reverend's face was all scratched up. So were his hands and veiny forearms. His hair was disheveled, his short-sleeved white smock filthy. He was a mess.

'It's all over, Gary,' sobbed Herbie, who was still tied to that chair. 'My boy's gone. Timmy saved me. He saved all of us.'

'I'll fetch the police,' I said, starting for the stage door.

'Not just yet, Timmy. Wait a minute, won't you, please?' Gary went over to Herbie and untied him. His hands were trembling. He seemed overcome by emotion. 'You're a hero, Timmy. I'll never, ever forget this.'

'We won't ever forget this,' echoed Jeremiah, nodding sagely.

I continued to stare at those scratches all over the TV evangelist's face and arms. They were fresh scratches, bloody. 'How did you get those?'

'That's none of your concern,' he answered dismissively as Gary finished freeing Herbie.

Herbie got up slowly from the chair, massaging the circulation back into his hands. 'Go ahead and tell the kid, Reverend.'

'I will not,' Jeremiah shot back, glaring at Herbie.

'I'm ordering you to tell him.' Herbie's own voice was low and threatening. 'You work for me now, remember?'

'I work for the Lord.'

'Is that a fact? Guess what, the Lord isn't syndicating your weekly telecast to a hundred and fifty outlets. I am. And Timmy's up to his eyeballs in this shit storm, so tell him. If you don't, I will.'

Neither Gary nor Jeremiah said a single word. They just gazed at each other. Then Jeremiah held his hand out to him. Gary took it and they stood there, hand in hand, glowing with love for each other.

I'd been shocked when I found out that Gary and Kelly were romantically involved. I shouldn't have been, but I was. I was shocked now to discover that Gary and Jeremiah were lovers, too. Again, I shouldn't have been. Gary had told me they'd grown close. I was well aware of Gary's bisexuality. Hell, I was living proof of it. And Jeremiah had spent a good-sized chunk of his youth in prison. Need I say more?

Like I said, I shouldn't have been shocked that night on Stage Four. But I was – so shocked that I almost couldn't breathe.

It was Herbie who did the talking after that, his voice drained of emotion. I can still remember what he said, word for word: 'It wasn't Errol, Timmy. Errol never killed anyone. He figured out what was going on and was trying to stop it. That's why he hog-tied me here on the set and summoned you. Errol wanted your help. He was going to ask you to talk to Larue.'

I looked over at Gary, who gazed back at me with a smile that was so beatific it gave me chills. As for Jeremiah, he just looked plain proud.

'Do you mean . . .?' Briefly, my voice failed me. 'Herbie, are you trying to tell me I just killed the wrong man?'

'That's exactly what I'm telling you.'

'Well, who's the right man?'

His googly eyes led me back to Gary. He was looking right at Gary.

'You murdered them?' I cried out. 'You did all of this? Why, Gary?'

'It's my mission,' he explained with that same angelic smile plastered on his face.

'Mission? What mission?'

'Our mission,' Jeremiah intoned, his voice soaring with religious fervor. 'By fulfilling it together we are unified. In body, mind and soul we are as one.'

'Cut the fag boy crap!' Herbie blustered at him. 'That's my boy lying dead over there. So just shut the fuck up about you two and your butt love!'

'Watch your filthy mouth!' snarled Jeremiah, pulling a .38 from the rear waistband of his slacks. Another gun. There were too many guns that night. He held it loosely in his big hand, not pointing it at anyone. 'I don't care for your kind, Herbie. I never have.'

'My kind? What kind is that?'

'I could shoot you right now and blame it on Tim.'

'Go ahead and do it, tough guy,' Herbie jeered at him. 'On Gates Avenue you wouldn't have made it to the nearest corner without getting the snot beat out of you.'

'Gary, this mission of yours,' I said slowly. 'What mission?'

'America faces a crisis of faith, Timmy. Our nation's being destroyed from within by its unholy worship of false idols.' Gary gazed around at these sets that we'd called home for

fourteen seasons. 'The Bagleys were evil. We were evil, all of us. Nothing more than fake television creations. In order to attain true spirituality, I must cleanse myself. We all must. That's the only way any of us can heal.'

'You're saying that Tina, Kelly, Kip, Darren . . . they're "healed" now?'

'Absolutely.'

'Without a doubt,' Jeremiah agreed.

'You two guys are out of your fucking minds.'

'No, Timmy, we see things very, very clearly,' Gary insisted, his voice throbbing with sincerity. 'I started with Tina. She was the first of us to go bad, after all. Couldn't keep your hands off of her, could you, Herbie?'

Herbie didn't respond. Just glowered at him.

'It seemed so fitting for Laurie Bagley, America's perfect blonde daughter, to be found with a needle stuck in her arm. Such an antidote to the falseness. So healing. Unfortunately, Tina wasn't using any more. I had to get her drunk first, which wasn't easy.'

'You held a gun to her head, didn't you?'

Gary looked at me in surprise. 'How did you know that?'

'Because I knew her. She was my sister, remember? Next you killed your precious Kelly. And you pointed her murder in my direction, same as you had Tina's. Why?'

'We wanted to get the public's attention,' Jeremiah said.

'You certainly did that. But you told me you loved her, Gary.'

'I did love her,' he acknowledged. 'And I always will. But my devotion to Jeremiah and our mission is something so much stronger. Kelly was my way of proving that to him. It sealed the bond between us. Ever since that night, we've acted as one. We've had to, since I've been under police protection.'

'You're the one who approached Choochie Ochoa,' I said to Jeremiah. 'Why did you?'

'She was around Kip's place a lot. I needed to know her schedule so I could work around her.'

'I understand why you left the bloody handwriting on Kip's wall – it got you even more attention. But why did you steal his dope?'

Jeremiah let out a harsh laugh. 'You would never understand.'

'Try me.'

'I grew up dirt poor, Tim. Scratching for every nickel, going to bed hungry night after night. I don't leave thousands of dollars worth of anything behind. I can't. Unfortunately, that spaced-out little airhead might have led the police to me. And this presented a problem – especially after you paid her a visit at The Book Nook.'

'You were watching me?'

'Watching her, actually. I had to go back later and take care of her. Them, I should say.'

'Steve was a pro. You shot him with his own gun. How?'

'He drew it when he heard me coming down the alley. But as soon as he realized that it was the leader of the Second Chance Ministry, he relaxed. I promptly kicked it out of his hand and shot them both.'

I turned back to Gary now. 'Veronica snuck out that night to be with Errol.'

'And he was welcome to her. Veronica goes her way, I go mine. I gave my police protection the slip tonight so that Jerry and I could see to Darren. But if anyone asks she'll swear I've been home in bed all night.'

'Even if she finds out what you've done?'

'Timmy, Veronica is the single most driven, amoral person I've ever known. She wants to be the governor's wife, period.'

'Tell me about tonight, Gary. Tell me about Darren.'

'We found an empty lot down Tigertail from Darren's house . . .' Gary then described scampering down the hillside several days ago much the same way Errol had. Tying a rope to a support post under Darren's deck. Concealing it in the brush for later use. Errol must have tailed them, I realized. Seen what they were up to and mimicked their behavior.

'When I bought the rope,' Jeremiah said, 'I also bought a hunting knife and overalls.'

I showed them the plastic bag that Errol had been reaching for. 'You mean this hunting knife and overalls?'

Jeremiah looked at it in surprise. 'I left that behind for the police to find. How did it get here?'

I put the bag back down on the coffee table. Briefly, my back was to them. When I turned around I had Errol's snub-nosed .38 in my hand. 'Just to even things up,' I said, pointing it at the two of them. 'You don't mind, do you?'

Jeremiah raised his own gun at me and said, 'Put that down, Tim. Right now.'

'Don't think so.'

'Let's not do anything crazy, guys,' Herbie cautioned us. 'Keep talking, OK? Just keep talking.'

'As you wish.' Jeremiah's eyes stayed fastened on my gun. 'I have considerable experience in rough country so I saw to Darren. Waited down there until he retired for the night. When his bedroom light came on I grappled up the hill, took care of him and got out fast. His boyfriend almost caught me going out the window. But by the time the authorities came running I was already back down that hill and gone.'

'So was Errol. He was bird-dogging you that whole time.' I gazed down at poor Errol, shaking my head, before I said, 'Gary, you've murdered six people between the two of you.'

'It's our mission,' Jeremiah stated emphatically. 'We're doing the Lord's work.'

'I'm not talking to you right now, Reverend, OK? I'm talking to my brother. Gary, I have to know this: do you feel anything?'

Gary beamed at me. 'Absolutely, Timmy. I feel reborn. I'm wiping away an entire lifetime of lies. No more pretending. No more holding back. I've never seen things so clearly. Or been so sure of what I'm doing. Believe me, we are making the world a better place.'

I looked at Herbie now and said, 'You knew about this. You watched your own people die, one by one, knowing who was responsible, and you didn't care. You don't care. You've even sacrificed your own son to protect Gary's future. Does the governor's mansion really mean that much to you?'

'Stop acting like some babe in the woods,' Herbie huffed at me. 'You know how the world really works. It doesn't matter who wins the election. All that matters is who puts him there. And that somebody's going to be me, damn it. And if you want to take that gun and shoot me, go right ahead. Just remember that whoever takes my place won't be any different than I am. Chances are he'll be worse. Oh, and one other thing – if you do decide to kill me then Jeremiah will shoot you right where you stand. Dead, probably. But if by some miracle you survive no one will believe a word of your cock-eyed story. They'll blame you for all of these deaths. You'll go down in history as the Bagley Bunch killer. Not Gary, not the reverend ...

you. It's not like you're so innocent yourself, you know. You just shot Errol in cold blood. He was a bright, talented kid and you murdered him.'

'You're right, I did – because I thought he was going to kill us both. I was wrong about that. He was trying to do the right thing. But don't paint me into your picture, Herbie. You could have turned these sick bastards in. You didn't. So it's your fault that Errol is lying there dead.'

'I think you'd better put down that gun, Tim.' Jeremiah's own .38 remained pointed right at me.

'Not a chance. The only way you'll get this gun out of my hand is by adding me to your list of the "healed". I'm certainly a prime candidate. Hell, I'm surprised you didn't "heal" me days ago. But if I go . . .' I aimed Errol's gun directly at Gary. 'I'm taking California's next governor with me.'

'Give our mission a chance, Timmy,' Gary pleaded. 'I'm convinced that you'll appreciate how right we are. And you'll definitely see the beauty.'

'There's no beauty here, Gary. All I see is a low-life con man who's made you into someone even more fucked-up than he is. You had an amazing life to look forward to. Now look at you. Why don't you just turn yourself in?'

'That's not possible. We still have so much to do.' Gary's gaze was fixed on the gun in my hand. 'And you can't stop us.'

'I have to stop you, Gary,' I said, my finger tightening around the trigger. 'I have no choice.'

'Yeah, you do,' Herbie spoke up. 'You can join the team.'

'He can do what?' demanded Jeremiah.

'Why not?' Herbie said, warming to the idea. His idea. 'Join us, Timmy. If you do, you'll be around to see tomorrow. If you don't then you die right here and now with Errol. You can choose life or you can choose death. Your call. But before you give us your answer consider this: it's not just your own life we're talking about.'

'Why, who else . . .?'

'Elvia will die, too. Sorry, kid. I know how you feel about her. She'd make a good wife for you. Steve always hoped it would work out that way.'

'You are nine million different kinds of evil, Herbie.'

'Don't be a dope. I'm trying to get you to say yes. I'll take *care of you, scout's honor. You want to act again? I'll give you Darren's show. He ain't using it no more. We'll make you Brock Junior. Hell, the network will love that.' Herbie waited for me to respond. When I didn't he kept talking. He always keeps talking. 'You don't want to act? Fine, take over Yslas Security. Build it into the biggest outfit in town. I'll back you all of the way.'*

My eyes remained locked on Gary. 'And what about the truth?'

'The truth stays right here on Stage Four,' Herbie replied. 'The Bagley Bunch killer met his tragic end here tonight. He's lying there dead on the floor. That's the official story. We're the only people who will ever know the real one. What do you say, Timmy?'

'I don't like this one bit,' Jeremiah said coldly. 'I don't trust him.'

'Well, I do, Reverend. And kindly shut the fuck up, will you? I'm doing the negotiating, not you. What's it going to be, Timmy, life or death?'

I glanced over at the film canister on the coffee table. 'I want that movie, Herbie. From now on it's mine.'

'Sure, whatever you say.'

'And that bag of evidence that Errol collected – as an insurance policy.'

'Fine, it's yours. Just drop your gun. You, too, Jeremiah. Put them on the floor right now. Both of you.'

Neither of us moved for a moment. Then, slowly, I put the gun down. I made a choice to put it down. I chose life. Jeremiah put his down, too. The stand-off was over.

I reached for the pack of Chesterfields in my T-shirt pocket and shook one loose.

'Give me one, too, will you?' begged Herbie, who'd been trying to quit for months.

I tossed him the pack. Fished around in my jeans for my Zippo lighter. But I'd left it on Darren's coffee table. Herbie had a lighter in the pocket of his baggy slacks. He lit his cigarette with it and tossed it my way. I held it in my hand, admiring it. In fact, I couldn't take my eyes off of it. It was shaped long and narrow, like a pocketknife. There was a painting of a pin-up girl on it, one of her breasts exposed.

He noticed me staring at it. 'You like that? I bought it in

Manila when I was in the service. It's been sitting in a dresser drawer for ages. Just had a guy on Pico recondition it. Keep it, it's yours.'

I lit my Chesterfield with Herbie's lighter and pocketed it, my chest tightening as I realized that when I shot Errol I had killed my own half-brother. Herbie was my father.

To this day, I'm convinced that's the only reason why I didn't die on Stage Four that sultry summer night in 1972. It's why Herbie gave me a choice. It's why he let me keep Monty and Me *and that bag of crime scene evidence. Because he wasn't prepared to sacrifice both of his sons to Gary's future. Not in the same night anyhow.*

I wasn't charged with any crime for killing the only real-life brother I'd ever had. I'd shot the Bagley Bunch killer in self-defense. Herbie and I both said so. Mostly, the police, the public, everyone was just relieved that this lunatic who'd been terrorizing Southern California for days was dead. The ordeal was over. We had survived.

Even though Errol was held responsible for it all, Herbie was embraced warmly by conservative Republican leaders. President Nixon, Governor Reagan and Mayor Yorty all expressed heartfelt condolences for this 'profound family tragedy'. The press portrayed Herbie as an innocent victim who'd very nearly lost his own life that night. No one blamed him for what Errol supposedly did.

Me, I was transformed overnight from Beanie Bagley, adorable boy, into Tim Ferris, daring action hero. Everyone wanted to interview me, congratulate me, be seen with me. I said no to it all. Spent my days and nights with Elvia, just us. Spent a lot of time staring at my reflection in the mirror in search of any resemblance to Herbie. All I saw was me.

California State Senator Gary Dixon and his lovely wife, Veronica, emerged after a period of 'somber spiritual reflection' to call on all decent Americans to renounce the wretched excesses of our 'Anything Goes' culture. 'We must restore the bedrock moral principles that made this the greatest nation in the history of the earth,' proclaimed Gary, who came up with a feel-goody name for his righteous new crusade: Family Values. He scored big with it, too. Especially after Reverend Jeremiah Staunton invoked it no less than seventeen times during his nationally televised sermon that Sunday.

And so, out of Errol's fictitious killing rampage, a new polit-ical movement was born.

Gary stayed far, far away from me after that. I did expect to hear from Veronica, begging me to keep quiet about her secret love affair with the madman. But Miss America didn't bother to reach out. She knew I was on the team.

Mother and I finally had it out a few evenings later at the house in Sepulveda. She lying there limply in bed, enfeebled by her stroke. Me perched there next to her, holding her frail, translucent hand.

'Herbie was a married man,' she confessed to me in a weak, halting voice. 'I was just some stupid girl in payroll who got knocked up by the studio playboy. When I got pregnant he wanted me to . . . there was a doctor. But I was afraid to, so I had you. He helped out financially and spent the night when he felt like it. Until he moved on to another girl. With Herbie, there was always another girl.'

'Is this why he cast me in the show?'

'No, son. In fact, he was dead set against it. Worried the press would look into your family background. But you were so perfect for it that he gave in – after I swore I'd keep my mouth shut. We stuck with the story that your dad died a war hero. Herbie didn't . . . he never wanted you to know the real truth.'

And so he'd worked with me day in and day out for four-teen long seasons – never once acknowledging to me that I was his own flesh and blood. Never lifting a finger to stop me from being devoured by the Velvet Underground. What kind of father could let that happen to his own son? What kind of father would use that awful smut movie against him? I had no father. I just knew this for sure now.

You know the rest. Herbie's empire grew and grew. Gary became governor of California, then a US senator. Now he plans to be our next president. Jeremiah Staunton is the single most influential religious leader in America. Veronica is a huge television star. Me, I took some $200,000 of Herbie's money and built Yslas Security into a huge operation. When Duane Larue retired from the LAPD two years after the Bagley Bunch spree he became my partner. By then, mother was gone and Elvia was pregnant with our beautiful daughter, Alicia.

I never told Elvia about the deal I struck that night on Stage

Four to save both of our lives. She never knew that Gary and Jeremiah were the ones responsible for Steve's death. Never knew that Herbie was my father. Never knew that he bankrolled the business. She thought the money came from Duane's retirement nest egg. I never told her any of this. I kept the awful truth buried deep down inside. I shouldn't have, because my complicity in the cover-up – my shame – ended up destroying us. I didn't blame Elvia when she divorced me. She deserved to know the truth. I realize that now. But I lacked the courage to tell her.

Every book on the subject states as fact that Errol Landau was the Bagley Bunch killer. Every book is wrong. Errol wasn't the villain. Just as I was never the hero – merely a recovering child star who killed the wrong man. I've never forgiven myself for shooting Errol. In my defense, I honestly believed I was saving Herbie and myself from certain death. Instead, it turned out that I was nothing more than an actor playing a role in another one of Herbie's fables. That's all I've ever been my whole life.

I made a conscious choice that night on Stage Four. I chose life. And participated in one of the biggest criminal cover-ups of the past fifty years. I've kept quiet until now. But not a day has gone by that I haven't been consumed by guilt. That's why, as I prepare to join Elvia and Errol and all of the others in death, I must now set the record straight:

Gary Dixon got away with murder.

The Reverend Jeremiah Staunton got away with murder.

And in case anyone cares, they've never cleaned up their act – merely exported it out south of the border to Jeremiah's beach house outside of Cabo San Lucas. If you're an enterprising reporter I urge you to talk to the locals down in Cabo. Seek out a man named Fernando Bacerro, the one who calls himself a tour guide. Ask Fernando how much they pay him for those innocent little boys he provides them with. Talk to the families whose boys have been hospitalized with unspeakable injuries after the man of God and his rich friend the Senator have visited. Find out how much hush money the families have been paid.

It's not too late for the truth. It's never too late.

Duane and I have had to be so careful preparing this memoir. We know it'll be destroyed if it falls into the wrong hands.

I've reached out to the distinguished American journalist Ernest Ludington Thayer. It's my hope, my prayer, that he'll manage to get my story out to you.

Lastly, a special word for my beloved daughter, Alicia. By the time you see this, my darling, I'll probably be dead. Goodbye, my sweet little girl. I'm sorry for everything I've put you through. I did my best. I meant well. But I'm not perfect. None of us is. Remember that I always loved you. And remember that the divine light in me will always see the divine light in you. That is forever.

Namaste.

(End Volume Five)

THIRTY

'My God, Herbie Landau's your *grandfather*.'

Annie didn't say anything to Hunt. She couldn't. The damned tears just wouldn't stop coming. And she'd been doing fine all along, too, keeping it together in spite of Hunt's frequent eruptions of shock and awe at the horrifying secrets her dad was revealing on the screen. It was when Dad started speaking those final words directly to her, begging her to forgive him, that the realization suddenly hit Annie. He wasn't a corrupt whore. Or a monster. Just a dying man who'd loved her. And then she fell apart.

'This explains why Herbie's been so obsessed with you,' Hunt chattered on. 'You're his flesh and blood, Annie. Not that family means a whole lot to the man. He's sacrificed both of his sons to put Dixon in the White House. What I don't get is why your father kept the truth from you until now. Do you get that?'

Hunt was waiting for a response out of her as they sat there together in Sharon's mobile home of streaming porn. But Annie couldn't respond. Couldn't even be there.

Blindly, she staggered past Sharon and Big Bob and out the door. Sat out there on the grass in the lotus position with her eyes closed, inhaling the natural fragrances of the dairy farm nearby. Annie breathed in and out as she gazed deep inside with her third eye, connecting to herself. The divine light inside of her reaching out across time and space to acknowledge her dad's divine light. Feeling it, feeling him. Releasing the anger she'd been holding on to for so long. Setting it aside as a judgmental and childish thing. Ready to move past it now. Start the healing process.

Annie held her palms together at her heart center and said, '*Namaste*.' Then she opened her eyes and went back inside.

Hunt was standing over little Sharon at a computer watching her upload Volume Five, her child-sized fingers flying over the keys. The two of them so absorbed in what they were doing they barely noticed her. Rudy came over and nudged her leg with his head.

Big Bob offered her a smile and said, 'I'm sorry about your dad, hon.'

'Thank you,' Annie said softly.

'There's a cold beer left. Want it?'

Annie shook her head. 'I'm fine.'

'We're all fine,' Sharon announced excitedly. 'All five volumes are now officially launched into cyberspace.'

'You've done it?' Hunt gulped at her. 'People can actually watch it?'

'Anyone and everyone in the world. All they have to do is click to play. Gary Dixon is done. We have just changed the course of American history. I can already see the headlines now: "*Outlaw Porn Skanks Save Free World.*" My folks would be so proud – if they weren't troglodyte Republicans. God, is this cool or what?'

'On your feet, biggie,' he ordered her. 'You are getting hugged.'

Sharon obliged him, practically disappearing in his muscular embrace.

'Now I have to ask you for another favor,' he said as he released Sharon.

'Just name it. I haven't had this much fun since I shut down the IRS for two days back when I was fourteen.'

'Wait, you did what?'

'On a bet. I won an ounce of killer weed, too. What is it you need?'

'To get my own statement out there, too. Can I do a live webcast from here with like a smart phone or something?'

'Yes, but no. They could trace it back to us.'

Hunt's face fell. 'Damn . . .'

'Hey, did I say it couldn't be done? I did not. See that little black square right at the top of my computer's monitor? That's a camera for video conferencing. All I have to do is link you up and you're in.'

'Sharon, you are awesome. Except, wait, there's more. Herbie has to know that I really do have *Monty and Me*. I totally understand your kiddie porn problem. But what if you, say, transferred it on to a DVD and then called it up on one of these monitors? Froze a frame for me that features Gary with other consenting adults. No under-aged Timmy.'

Sharon and Big Bob exchanged a guilty look. 'Being dirty

girls, we transferred it *and* watched it while you two were glued to Volume Five.'

'Strictly out of professional curiosity,' Big Bob explained. 'We had to find out if there was any way we can put it out there.'

'Can you?'

'Way not,' Sharon said, shaking her spiky head.

'But you would not *believe* some of the old stars who are on it,' Big Bob said. 'This thing ought to be in a national archive somewhere.'

'Hunt, I can absolutely freeze a frame for you. And position a monitor for everyone to see. Anything else you need?'

'Just a cigarette.'

'Wait, you smoke, too?' Annie demanded. The bubble gum was already bad enough.

'Only when the moment's right.'

Sharon tossed him her pack of Marlboros. He stuck one behind his ear while she called up *Monty and Me* on her computer screen. It was, Annie observed, just as her dad had described it. There were many, many bodies, some belonging to pale young boys.

Big Bob stepped in front of her and said, 'Take my word for it – you don't want to see this.'

Annie took his word for it.

There was a flurry of activity now as they shifted computers and chairs around to suit Hunt's purposes, shutting down the X-rated monitors that would be in the background. Annie stayed out of their way. Sat there petting Rudy while Hunt parked himself directly in front of the monitor's camera, the carton of evidence at his feet, a second monitor positioned next to his right shoulder. On it was the frozen black-and-white image of a college-aged Gary Dixon and his sitcom father, Darren Beck, sharing naked fun together.

Hunt cleared his throat, focusing himself. He had no notes of any kind, nothing written down. Yet he seemed not at all concerned or anxious. In fact, Annie had never seen anybody so *ready* in her life. It was positively Zen-like.

'OK, Scotty, beam me up,' he told Sharon.

She got busy at her keyboard, then gave him a thumbs-up sign.

And so he began. 'My name's Hunt Liebling. I'm a journalist. I'm guessing you've heard of me by now. They're calling

me the Unablogger. Ernest Ludington Thayer asked me to fly
out to Los Angeles last week in response to an urgent letter he'd
received from Tim Ferris. I'm also guessing – make that hoping
– that you've started watching the video memoir Tim prepared
shortly before he was murdered. I'm aware that I'm wanted by
the law for his murder, even though I'm completely innocent.
And I'm aware that Herbie Landau, the chief architect of the
Dixon for President campaign, will now employ his vast
Panorama Communications empire to brand Tim's memoir an
unsubstantiated smear job. Panorama-owned newspapers and
broadcasts will tell you to pay no attention to this dead man's
rantings. That none of his allegations can be proven. That not
one word of what he says is true.

'But it's all true. Here's one obvious way that you can tell it
is – just look at how hard they've fought to keep you from seeing
it. They killed Tim, killed his business partner, Duane Larue,
killed Lola and Tyrone Gilliam. And then they engineered a rush
to judgment based on disinformation and unsupportable "facts"
that make it look like I'm responsible for their deaths. It's been
widely reported, for example, that the murder weapon, a Glock
nine-millimeter semi-automatic, was registered to me by the
state of California. This is a complete fabrication. To buy a
handgun in that state you must present a valid California driver's
license *and* proof of residency. Plus California has a mandatory
ten-day waiting period. I was there for *two* days, have never
resided there, never held a California driver's license. So you
tell me, how did I buy it? Illegally? If so then it wouldn't be
registered to me, would it? And yet the news reports keep saying
it is. The Glock's not mine. That's nothing more than computer-
ized trickery. A story they invented and sold to you as news.
A lie.

'And the lies don't end there. You've been told that I boarded
a red-eye flight to New York City after I massacred everyone
at Tim's Topanga Canyon estate. My name, you've been told,
appears on the airline's passenger manifest. More trickery.
When that plane was in the air I was in Santa Barbara with
Flynn Leverett, the renowned breeder of Casey. Go ahead and
ask Flynn. She'll vouch for me. And she'll show you where
we hid Tyrone Gilliam's car. Check the airport security cams
for footage of me boarding that flight at LAX or deplaning
at JFK. You'll find no such footage. Show my picture to the

stewardesses. Show it to the passengers who I supposedly sat
next to. Not one of them will say they saw me. I wasn't there.
And yet my name's on the passenger manifest. How did it
get there? Computer hackers employed by Herbie Landau
implanted it there because they needed to place me in New
York City the next day.

'Why did they "send" me to New York? Because they'd hacked
into my emails and found out who knew I was out in LA
and why. They had to eliminate those people fast. They murdered
Ernest Ludington Thayer and his friend, Mike O'Brien. Don't
bother to look for Mike's computer. You won't find it. They
murdered my brother Brink and his wife Luze. Don't bother to
look for their computer either. Again, Herbie's people pointed
the finger of blame right at me. And told you that after I killed
these four people in New York I caught the Acela to Washington.
I wasn't on that train. They placed me on it because they needed
to eliminate my associate, a fine young journalist named Clarissa
Colette Reiter, and destroy any and every trace of the story that
might be in my apartment.

'The lies just keep on coming. The next one they tell you
will be about Tim's single most explosive allegation – that it
was Senator Gary Dixon and the Reverend Jeremiah Staunton
who were responsible for the Bagley Bunch killings, not Errol
Landau. There's no proof to back his story up, they'll say. I'm
here to tell you that there is . . .' Hunt reached into his shirt
pocket for the cigarette lighter. The one with the pin-up girl on
it. He lit Sharon's cigarette with it, holding the lighter up to
the camera for all to see. 'This lighter will look familiar to
Herbie Landau. It certainly held special significance for Tim,
who didn't realize until he saw it that night on Stage Four that
he was Herbie's biological son. Tim kept it. Now I'm holding
on to it. I want the American voters to know that. And I want
them to know that there's plenty more evidence . . .'

Hunt shifted over to his left so as to reveal the telling frame
of black-and-white film that was frozen on the monitor next
to him. 'What you're looking at is the underground X-rated
film that Tim refers to as *Monty and Me*. Child pornography
laws prohibit me from distributing it on the Internet. But
there it is. *Here* it is,' he added, carefully removing the brittle
reel of film from its canister. 'The public may not be able
to view this, but criminal investigators most certainly can.

And there's more. Here's the very bag of crime scene evidence that Tim confiscated that night on Stage Four – the coveralls and bloody knife and rope, just as he described it. I know what Herbie Landau will say to you next. That Tim could have concocted this so-called evidence last week in support of his bogus version of history. It's true, Tim could have. That's why a crime lab needs to authenticate it at once. An investigation should be launched.'

Hunt set the evidence aside and sat back in his chair. 'Tim Ferris wanted us to know that the history books are all wrong. Errol Landau was never the Bagley Bunch killer. The actual killers, Tim believed, are still among us. Since there's no statute of limitations on murder, the Los Angeles District Attorney may want to reopen that grisly rampage from the summer of seventy-two. And my journalistic colleagues may want to catch a flight for Los Cabos, just as Tim suggested. Find out what's been going on down there. Finally, the American voters may want to ask themselves if they know enough about Gary Dixon to elect him President of the United States on November Seventh. Tim has plenty to say in the memoir about the Dixon marriage. That it is, and always has been, a sham. That Veronica Dixon is, and always has been, the senator's compliant beard. I don't actually care whether Senator Dixon and Reverend Staunton have been secret lovers for all of these years. What matters to me is what they did or didn't do together in the summer of seventy-two. And what they are or aren't doing to under-age boys south of the border to this day. Is any of this true? We need to know. Have to know exactly who we're electing. History has taught us again and again that we can't afford to make a mistake. We must know the truth about Gary Dixon. No amount of campaign spin or countercharges can alter that simple reality. This will not go away. The truth never does.'

And with that Hunt ran a hand across his throat and Sharon shut down the webcast. A respectful hush fell over the trailer.

'I can't believe you did that whole thing without notes,' Annie said to him.

'No big, I wrote most of it in my head somewhere outside of Council Bluffs. I just didn't have my kicker. Not until I found you,' he explained, smiling at her. 'Big Bob, if Annie doesn't want that last beer I'll take it.'

THIRTY-ONE

It was out there now.

All five volumes of Timmy's incendiary memoir as well as that execrable blogger's live webcam statement. The highlights of Timmy's most damning charges had already gone viral on YouTube, which recorded so many millions of hits in the first two hours that the site briefly had to shut down. The liberal press was jumping all over it, naturally. Wall-to-wall coverage on the twenty-four-hour cable news channels. And a riotous mob of media lemmings were crowded outside of the mansion demanding a response, demanding answers, demanding . . .

I am toast, Gary realized as he sat behind the desk in his paneled study, tequila in hand, staring into the abyss of humiliation and shame that lay before him. *I am finished.*

Gary wasn't alone in the study. Herbie and Mort were seated there with him, as was Veronica, her lovely, unlined face drawing tight as she watched Gary throw back the shot of the tequila. His fifth. Or was it his sixth?

'You see, this is why I hate the fucking Internet,' Herbie fumed. 'You've got no controls, no safeguards. People can put anything out there.'

'Yes, like the truth, for instance.'

'Don't get down on yourself, sweetheart.'

'Yeah, don't go gloomy on us. I need you ready to go out there and fight.'

'Herbie, this is not just anything that Liebling has put out there,' Mort said quietly, grayish tongue darting over his thin, dry lips. 'He has the smut film and the crime scene evidence.'

'So what? He won't be delivering it to anyone. He'll be good and dead before he gets the chance.' Herbie shot a hard look at his fixer. 'Won't he?'

'That is certainly our hope,' Mort answered cautiously.

'It better be more than a hope, Mort. Joe Baer swore to you that a pair of major league hit men already have Liebling in their sights, correct? All they have to do now is nail the little pisher and destroy that evidence. No matter what Liebling says he's still the FBI's prime suspect. And he'll die their prime suspect. End of story. Roll closing credits. Goodnight, everybody.'

'Nonetheless,' Mort persisted, 'Tim's allegations about the senator's lifestyle will seriously compromise his standing among Christian conservatives.'

'We've all sinned,' Herbie said dismissively. 'We can all be renewed or reborn or whatever. Which reminds me, this Fernando person down in Cabo . . .'

'Don't give him another thought. He left port from Land's End two hours ago on a one-way cruise.'

'Good.' Herbie's googly eyes locked on to Gary's now. 'This probably doesn't need saying but here it comes. From now on you stay far away from your boy Jeremiah. You don't see him. You don't talk to him. Got it?'

'I don't even know where he is,' Gary said forlornly. 'I've been trying to reach him all day. He hasn't returned any of my calls.'

Mort's cell phone rang. He took the call, listened, then flicked it off. 'Senator, there's a good reason why you haven't been able to reach him. Jeremiah Staunton cleaned out his bank accounts this morning and fled the country on a direct flight to Seoul, South Korea.'

Gary drew in his breath. Briefly, he swore his heart stopped beating.

'Baer thinks Korea is just a jumping-off point – the reverend's on the run, God knows where.'

'I doubt whether God has any idea.' Herbie got up and began pacing around the carpet with his hands in his pockets, keys and coins jangling. 'Is this good or bad for us?'

'It doesn't have to be anything,' Mort said. 'The reverend's simply unavailable for comment. The public needn't know that he's taken off.'

'His parishioners will notice,' Veronica pointed out. 'Millions of them watch the Sunday broadcast.'

'We can substitute a rerun this week,' Herbie responded. 'Say he's gone into prayerful seclusion for a few days.'

'It wouldn't hurt if we did that ourselves,' Veronica said.

Herbie ran a hand over his frizzy white hair. 'Tomorrow we bury Timmy. And we *will* show up. And the senator *will* deliver the eulogy, head held high. After that, I agree with the princess. We'll find you two a new spiritual adviser. Someone old school and dignified. Can you think of anyone, Senator?'

Gary sat there in dazed silence, so devastated he barely heard what any of them were saying. His soul mate had left him. *Jeremiah is gone . . .*

'We just have to keep the public on our side,' Herbie went on. 'Keep reminding them that they've known and loved this guy since he was a kid. If we do that we'll be fine. I'll phone the DA myself, Mort. Make sure he understands that it wouldn't be in his family's best interest to reopen the Bagley Bunch investigation. Baer's got plenty of dirt on him and that local TV anchorwoman, hasn't he?'

'He has,' Mort affirmed.

'And we've got *tons* of it on Timmy. This guy was a mental case. By the time we're done with him no one will believe a word he had to say.'

'I won't trash Timmy,' Gary said softly.

'What's that, Senator?'

'He doesn't want to trash Timmy,' Veronica put in.

'Well, that's just too damned bad,' Herbie blustered. 'We'll do what we have to do – wrap it up and close it out, same as we did back in seventy-two. It worked then and it'll work now.'

'But it *didn't* work,' Gary said. 'It's blown up in our faces.'

'I don't agree. And I'm not giving up. We're in a fight for our political lives. We're not going to turn tail and run. And we're sure as hell not stepping aside for your total zero of a running mate. Tucker Mayne wouldn't stand a chance against Don Oakley.'

'I know someone who can beat Oakley,' Gary said.

'Oh, yeah, who?'

'You're looking at her.'

Veronica let out a gasp of astonishment, as if such a crazy thought had never occurred to her.

'Veronica's a figure of great public sympathy. The people are in her corner. And she'd make a terrific president.'

Herbie studied Gary closely. 'You're actually serious about this.'

'I most certainly am.'

'You feeling OK, Senator? You sound a little *meshuga*. Perfectly understandable given what's happened.'

'Perfectly,' echoed Mort.

Gary reached for the tequila bottle and poured himself another jolt. 'I'm fine. Never better.'

Herbie smiled at him encouragingly. 'Sure, you are. Just kick back and relax. Leave this kind of shit to us. It'll all work out fine, you'll see.'

He and Mort saw themselves out. Veronica stayed behind.

'That was very sweet of you,' she said, her eyes gleaming at him.

'I meant every word of it, old girl.'

'Why don't you come outside and hit some tennis balls with me?'

'I'm fine right here. I'll watch a little TV.'

She came around behind the desk, ran her fingers through his hair and kissed him on the cheek. Gary tried to remember the last time she'd done that. He couldn't. She left him there by himself, closing the door softly behind her.

He drank down the tequila, missing Jeremiah so much that his chest ached. The great love of his life was *gone*. Gary didn't just feel abandoned. He felt utterly lost – so lost that an overwhelming sense of terror now seized hold of him. His heart began to race faster and faster. Panic sweat poured off of him.

He raced over to the television and flicked on the DVD of Season Ten, searching the menu for his wedding episode. Walt Jr and Sandy's. One of the three highest-rated episodes of any series in network history. Walt Jr was late getting to the church and almost missed his own wedding – all because his irrepressible kid brother, Beanie, had insisted on driving him there in his beat-up jalopy. The kid had something important he wanted to say to him:

'You're the best brother a guy could ever ask for, Walt. Heck, you're more than my big brother. You're my idol. And if I turn out to be half the guy you are then I'll be awful darned proud of myself.'

'You're already pretty terrific, buddy.'

'Gee, do you really think so?'

'Heck, yeah. I'm the one who's proud. Don't you know that?'

'All I know is I'm real, real sorry.'

'Why is that, buddy?'

'Walt, I forgot to buy gas this morning.'

As the jalopy came sputtering to a stop miles from the church Gary reached for the remote and watched the scene over again, tears streaming down his face. Timmy was gone. Jeremiah was gone. *Everyone is gone. I have no one. I am no one.* Sobbing, he staggered into his study's small, private bathroom and flung open the medicine chest. Inside he found a three-month supply of Zoloft, the antidepressant he'd tried for a time. And Ambien, the sleep aid he'd been taking. Also a full bottle of Valium and another of that muscle relaxant, Skelaxin, the doctor had given him for his back pain. He dumped all of his meds out into the sink. Dozens and dozens of them. Hundreds. Then he closed the medicine chest and gazed at himself in mirror, hating the worthless fraud of a man who he saw before him. Positive he didn't want to look at him ever again.

Gary had never been so positive of anything in his life.

He gulped down all of the capsules and pills in huge, starved handfuls, washing them down with swigs of tequila straight from the bottle. Feeling nothing yet. Just a sensation of sourness in the pit of his stomach. It would take a few minutes. Fine, he could wait. He had time. He had all of the time in the world.

Senator Gary Dixon unzipped his pants and let them drop to the floor. Smiling, he sat down on the toilet and waited there to die – just like Elvis.

THIRTY-TWO

'What will you do now?' Annie asked him as she steered the pickup back to Balltown, Rudy sprawled on the seat between them.

There had been a long silence between them as they drove. Not an awkward one. Merely two people wrapped up in their own private emotions. They'd gone through a hell of an ordeal just now in Sharon Combs' trailer. Hunt felt exhausted yet exhilarated by the high-wire urgency of his live webcast. He felt exactly the way he used to after a bout in the ring. Annie? He couldn't even imagine what she was feeling.

'I've been taking things minute by minute since this started,' he told her, still keeping one eye out for that silver Crown Vic in the truck's side mirror. 'I have to write down every single detail of what's happened and post it on *huntandpeck.com*. I'll drive Flynn's van to Washington. I have friends there who'll help me.'

'Do you think you'll be cleared?'

'I have to be cleared. I'm innocent.'

'And what about after that?'

Hunt unwrapped a fresh piece of Bazooka and popped it into his mouth, his jaw working on it. 'After that I have family to bury.'

Annie turned on to Balltown Road and eased past Breitbach's. Flynn's van was still parked there in their lot. 'Hunt, you're welcome to crash here for a few days. I could get you a laptop in Dubuque like we talked about.'

He studied her, a strong, calm woman with huge brown eyes and glowing skin. 'I've already imposed on you enough, Annie. Plus I need to be where the action is.'

'This *is* where the action is. Haven't you noticed?'

As Annie drove around the bend to her farmhouse it occurred to Hunt that he might be the one doing her a favor if he stuck around. As soon as he left she'd be alone with her grief.

'Will you be OK?' he asked her, keeping both eyes open

for any sign of an FBI stake-out. He saw no one, nothing. All was quiet.

'I'm fine,' she assured him. 'My dad saying the things that he did . . . it feels like a huge weight's been lifted from me. I don't blame him for anything any more. And that's incredibly liberating. And I don't know – in answer to your other question, I mean.'

'What other question?'

'Why he never told me that Herbie was his father.' She pulled into her driveway and parked next to the pile of cedar shingles, lingering there behind the wheel. 'The only bad part is that I feel like an orphan now. I *am* an orphan. I have no one.'

'Same here.' Hunt looked at her. And looked at her some more.

Annie looked right back at him, her gaze open and aware. 'When will you go?'

'Now.' He snatched up the carton of evidence and climbed out.

'You really should wash those clothes first. And yourself.'

'OK, you talked me into it.'

They went in the house through her mud room around in back so she could grab him a pair of bib denim overalls and a John Deere T-shirt from the clothesline.

'These are huge on me. You can put them on until your own are dry. Just toss yours down the stairs after you peel them off.'

Hunt went up to the bathroom, stripped off everything he'd been wearing since he left Flynn Leverett's and wadded it up into a ripe-smelling ball. Naked, he tossed it down the stairs. Rudy, who was stretched out on the floor outside of the bathroom door, showed zero interest in chasing after it. Just lay there, stubby tail thumping happily.

Hunt closed the bathroom door, feeling himself relax a tiny bit for the first time in days. Tim's memoir was out there now, along with his own unfiltered version of what had gone down. He was definitely in a better place than he had been yesterday. Gazing at his haggard, stubbly face in the mirror, he noticed a change in those eyes that stared back at him. The wild and crazy look was gone. He saw more of his usual resolve again. He also saw profound weariness and pain, the face of someone who needed to heal. But there was no time for that yet.

Annie's old claw-footed tub was lined with an unbleached linen shower curtain that hung from the ceiling. Yawning mightily, Hunt yanked open the curtain, reached inside to turn on the water—

And one of the G-men from the silver Crown Vic was standing there in the tub with a SIG-Sauer pointed right at him. The white guy, the one with round glasses.

'Please don't make a sound, Mr Liebling,' he said in a soft, almost prissy voice as he stepped out of the tub. A pudgy little fellow in a tweed sport coat, striped necktie and gray flannel slacks. He wore white latex gloves on his hands. 'Do exactly as I say and this will be quick and painless. Give me any trouble at all and I promise you that you will die screaming.'

'Sure thing . . . right,' Hunt said as it dawned on him that this little man was no Fed. He'd been sent by Herbie to kill him. Kill them both no doubt. Hunt's initial response was to obey him, on account of the gun the guy was pointing at him.

Hunt's second reaction was to punch him in the nose with a huge right hand that caught the guy totally by surprise. His glasses flew off. Blood spurted from his nose and the gun clattered to the floor. Which gave Hunt an opening for a brief instant, and he drove through it. Pummeling the guy in the stomach with both fists, throwing every ounce of his weight behind the body blows. One blow after another . . .

Until the little guy gathered himself and fought back. With blindingly quick ferocity he chopped Hunt on the neck with the side of his hand, then kicked him in his bare ribs with a wing tip shoe, rocking Hunt back against the bathroom door with a thud.

And now he was all over Hunt, fists and feet flying, his eyes alert but expressionless. This was no bar-room brawler. This was a trained professional who probably knew eighteen different ways to kill Hunt with his bare hands.

Hunt threw another right but this time the little guy slipped it and drove the heel of his right hand hard up under Hunt's chin, pinning him helplessly to the door while his left hand took deadly aim at Hunt's kidneys. It took every ounce of strength Hunt possessed to wrench himself free. Panting for breath, he went into a defensive crouch now. They both did, facing off against each other in the confined space of Annie's bathroom, both of them sneaking peeks at that SIG on the floor under the sink. Hunt tagged him with a good left to the chin, but paid for it with a knee to his very exposed testicles that doubled him over, groaning, and then with a blow to the head that sent Hunt back against the door again. His knees buckling, Hunt groped around behind his back for the doorknob. He had to open that door, warn Annie. And he *did* get it open – just as a left foot connected with his chin and propelled him through the doorway and out into the upstairs hallway, the two of them grappling on the floor there with Hunt on the bottom and the little guy's hands wrapped around his throat.

Rudy just sat right there beside them with his head tilted cutely to one side and one paw over his ear. The damned TV ham.

'It doesn't have to be like this, Liebling.' The little killer tightened his grip around Hunt's windpipe. 'Just tell me where it is.'

'Where *what* is . . .?'

'The missing DVD, Volume Five. Tell me where it is and you'll save yourself a world of hurt.'

'You're . . . too late. It's *out* there. Has been for a–an hour. Check with your people. They'll . . . tell you.'

His gasping insistence caused the guy to ease off a bit, brow furrowing.

Hunt immediately kneed him in the groin – payback's a bitch – and drove his right fist into the bastard's left ear. Scrambled out from underneath him and pounded the guy twice in the face with everything he had.

But, Jesus, this little guy could fight. He took Hunt's best shots and came right back at him. Yanked Hunt by the arm, kicked his feet out from under him and sent him somersaulting down the steep, narrow stairs. Sent *both* of them down those stairs. Because Hunt wouldn't let go of him.

Together, they crashed to the wooden floor of the parlor.

And already the bastard was up on his feet again, circling Hunt, ready for more. Dazed, Hunt willed himself to get back up, too. And fight on.

Mostly, he was wondering how it was possible that Annie hadn't heard what the fuck was going on.

THIRTY-THREE

When Wally arrived back at the little farmhouse on Balltown Road he drove right on past and went around a bend until he reached an expanse of open pasture. He left the Crown Victoria parked there along the roadside and strolled the half-mile or so back to the house, latex-gloved hands in his pockets. Not a soul drove by as Wally walked along, his eyes taking in the neighboring farmhouses. None were particularly close to the target's house. But if a neighbor happened to glance out a window and notice him he'd be wise to go in through the front door. Sneaking around back would arouse immediate suspicion.

He didn't phone Mrs Pryor about Clover. It was neither necessary nor appropriate. Not in the middle of a job. That would be for later.

The enclosed glass front porch offered Wally fine protection from prying eyes. He found some power tools on the porch. He also found that she'd left her front door unlocked, same as Mabel used to when Wally was a little boy back in Inwood. Small-town people were incredibly trusting. It never ceased to amaze him.

Then again, after a quick look around Wally realized that there was nothing inside of the house to steal. He'd been planning to search her electronic devices for the missing DVD. She had none. No computer, no DVD player, not even a television. There was almost nothing of value in the whole place. Just a couple of old Nikon cameras and those power tools out on the porch.

Down in the cellar he found shelves laden with a helpful assortment of household accelerants. He lined these up in a row on the workbench, went back upstairs for some kitchen towels and tossed them down the cellar stairs.

There were two small bedrooms upstairs. One had an ironing board set up in it and a portable rack of lady's clothes. Nothing very alluring. Just plain, dark-colored business suits and slacks, a navy blue wool coat. The other room was where she slept.

She kept it tidy. No dirty clothes heaped around, no piles of papers or books. The bed was made, its patchwork quilt drawn taut and smooth.

Wally didn't find the DVD anywhere. Perhaps they'd taken it with them. Yes, that must be it. He'd simply have to wait for them to come back.

He was at the top of the stairs when he heard her truck pull into the driveway. He darted into the bathroom and climbed into the tub, closing the shower curtain around him. Whoever came in there first would get first crack at telling him where it was.

And then both of them would die.

It turned out to be the journalist. Perhaps Wally was taken aback by the sight of Liebling's naked, muscular body. Or maybe the Clover business had taken something out of him. But Wally was genuinely floored by how quick Liebling was. Quick enough to pop him in the nose, Wally's glasses flying one way, his weapon the other. After that he did not take the unclothed journalist lightly. He pinned him against the bathroom door and put a genuine hurt on him. But Liebling had boxed competitively at some point in his life. Wally could tell by the crispness of the combinations he threw, by the way he stayed up on the balls of his feet, moving, always moving. He could tell by the way Liebling absorbed punishment and kept on coming. He didn't go down, wouldn't go down.

Which was rather unfortunate. Wally had intended to obtain information from him. Instead he found himself locked in a death match that sent the two of them spilling out on to the hallway floor under the watchful gaze of that charcoal colored dog. It took Wally a full sixty seconds longer than it should have to put Liebling down on the floor, both hands wrapped around his throat. And *still* he could not get a straight answer out of him – Liebling merely kept babbling that Wally was too late. Wally's only option was to finish him off and move on to the girl.

Except the stubborn bastard wouldn't let go of him. He kept holding on, damn him. And so they went tumbling down those stairs together.

THIRTY-FOUR

O ut in the mud room, Annie stuffed Hunt's unbeliev-
ably stinky clothes in the washing machine, turned
it on long enough to fill it and then shut it off. The
old farmhouse didn't have enough water pressure to run the
washer and the shower at the same time. And Hunt's clothes
could stand the extra few minutes of soaking while he
showered.

Annie knew she was not going to be happy when Hunt left.
She wanted this man in her life right now. Wanted him so
badly she felt as dizzy as a blushing schoolgirl. Annie
wondered if she'd ever see Hunt again. If he'd think about
her at all after he took off. She decided, with a sigh of regret,
that the answer to both questions was a big, fat no. But Annie
was a big girl. She'd get over it. Return to the solitary routine
of her work and her photographs. An hour after Hunt Liebling
was gone it would be as if he'd never been here at all.

Sure it would.

She just needed to keep busy. Annie went out on the front
porch, loaded her Paslode nail gun with a fresh coil and flicked
on the compressor. As the compressor began to rumble she
headed outside, nailer in hand, and unrolled the fifty-foot hose
that connected them.

Shingling. The careful, methodical repetition would take
her mind off that gorgeous man with the smoldering eyes
who was upstairs in her bathroom right now without any
clothes on.

The Paslode model she'd chosen could shoot nails that were
up to an inch and three-quarters long. She was using inch and
one-quarter nails on her cedar shingles. It was a labor-intensive
process, but the air-powered gun was a whole lot faster and surer
than an old-school hammer. Admittedly, Annie had found it a
bit intimidating at first. But she was at ease with the nailer now.
Besides, it was built for safety. Couldn't, wouldn't shoot a nail
unless its carbide-tipped nose was depressed good and secure
against a flat surface.

She lugged two big armloads of fragrant cedar shingles over to where she was working, which was underneath the front parlor windows. After she'd trued up a blue chalk string line she set the adjustable shingle guide on her gun and started nailing. *Pop . . . Pop . . .* First one course of shingles, then a second . . . *Pop . . . Pop . . .* Carefully overlapping the second course so that all of the seams underneath were covered over . . . *Pop . . . Pop . . .* The nailer was quieter than a hammer, too, although the compressor's controlled bursts of air sounded just like the big bad wolf trying to huff and puff and blow her house down.

Annie worked, still seeing her dying dad's gaunt, jaundiced face before her eyes. Her mind was replaying not only what he'd said about that night on Stage Four but also the conversations she and Mom had about him back when Mom lay dying. How walled-off a man she'd told Annie he was. How moody and secretive. Maybe Annie could understand why now, at least a little. But she wanted to know more. As much as she could. She ought to buy a laptop in Dubuque so she could watch Volumes One through Four for herself. Find out what other secrets he'd been holding on to all of these years. After all, his video memoir was all that she had left of Tim Ferris now. She owed it to him to watch it, Annie decided, positioning one shingle snug against another and depressing the nose of her nailer . . . *Pop . . . Pop . . .*

She almost didn't hear the crash inside, but she *felt* it. The whole house shook. Annie's first thought was that the floor joists under the old bathtub had just given way and the tub had collapsed into the kitchen – with Hunt in it. She couldn't imagine what else it could be. Aghast, Annie raced for the front door, still clutching her nailer. When she got inside, Annie couldn't believe what she saw:

A naked Hunt Liebling and a pudgy little man in a tweed jacket and gray flannel slacks were beating the crap out of each other on her parlor floor. Or, more precisely, the pudgy little man was beating the crap out of Hunt. And now he was on top of Hunt with both hands wrapped around Hunt's throat, choking him. Hunt gagging, his eyes bulging, hands and bare feet flailing helplessly. Rudy, bless his heart, running circles around the two of them and yapping playfully as if it were some kind of a game.

But it was no game. This man was *murdering* Hunt Liebling right before Annie's eyes.

And she could not let that happen. If Hunt decided he needed to leave, fine, she could respect that. But no one was going to *take* him from her. No way. So Annie rushed right at this attacker who was crouched over Hunt, yanked down hard on his jacket collar and depressed the nailer's carbide tip against the back of his neck, shooting one, two, three, four of her inch and one-quarter shingling nails directly into his brain stem.

The man stiffened instantly, his torso upright. Then he flopped right over on top of Hunt, twitched once, then didn't move at all.

THIRTY-FIVE

'Well, this makes it official,' Hunt gasped as he lay there battered, bruised and naked underneath the dead man. 'As far as Herbie's concerned, you now qualify as family.'

Annie stood there gripping her nail gun, wide-eyed. 'Who is he?'

'One of the dudes in the Crown Vic that was dogging us. Except he's no G-man. Herbie hired him to kill us both. He's a real piece of work, your grandfather.'

'I wish you wouldn't call him that.'

'You can put that down now, you know.'

Annie seemed to have forgotten she was holding the nail gun. She set it down on the parlor floor, shaking. She'd just killed a man, after all.

'Listen to me, Annie, because we don't have a lot of time, OK? His partner's bound to be staked out somewhere nearby.' Hunt glanced over toward the parlor windows, which had no curtains over them. 'He may even be watching us right now through the scope of a sniper rifle – not that I'm trying to scare you.'

'And yet you're doing such a good job.'

'I'm telling you this place is no longer safe. We have to get out of here right away.'

'Hunt, I live here.'

'I can't help that, Annie. They've found you. Your new identity is blown, understand?'

'I understand,' she said reluctantly.

'Good. I need you to go up and get those clothes you loaned me. Hurry, OK? And you'd better bring down this bastard's gun and his glasses, too.'

Annie didn't hesitate. She went straight upstairs to the bathroom, Rudy on her heel. While she was up there Hunt searched the guy's pockets. Found a wallet with a California driver's license that identified him as John W. Norbis of Redondo Beach, age forty-two. In his tweed jacket Hunt found a cell phone.

Annie came back down the stairs with the things he'd asked for and turned around so that Hunt could scramble out from underneath the late John W. Norbis and throw on her over-sized T-shirt and overalls, which were shaped all wrong for him. He didn't care. He hadn't worn anything that fit him in days and days. SIG in hand, Hunt edged over to the front windows and sneaked a look outside. Annie's place was situated on high ground. Hunt couldn't see a natural vantage point from where someone might be watching them. Couldn't see anything or anyone.

But that didn't mean the other guy wasn't out there.

Hunt went down to the cellar and returned with a heavy mallet. 'He was planning to torch the place after he killed us,' he informed Annie as he used the mallet to smash Norbis' cell phone to pieces. 'There's a ton of flammable liquids all lined up and ready to go.'

She sank into one of her parlor chairs. 'God . . .'

Hunt sat down in the other and put on his sneakers, wincing from the sharp pain in his side. He hoped Norbis hadn't cracked any of his ribs. He had no time for that right now. 'We have to figure out what to do with him.'

'Why don't we just call the police? He did attack us.'

'Hello, I'm still a fugitive, remember?'

'So you can hide somewhere.'

'While you tell them what? That you stumbled upon a well-dressed man in your parlor and decided to test out your nail gun on his skull?' Hunt shook his head at her. 'No way, Annie. The law can't get mixed up in this. They'll ask too many questions, and they'll bring the media with them. I'm sorry, but you're caught up in my nightmare now. Our only option is to run like hell,' he said, waiting for her to grasp the urgent reality of their situation. He'd grown accustomed to this life. She was new to it. 'You can come to Washington with me. You'll be safe there. Pack a bag while I fetch the van from Breitbach's. I'll back it up to the front door so we can load him inside. We'll dump him on some deserted farm road after dark, minus his ID.'

Annie didn't respond. Didn't move. She just sat there looking at him with those huge dark eyes of hers.

He said it again. 'Pack a bag, Annie. We're leaving.'

'Sure, OK,' she agreed finally. 'Except I'm not going to Washington with you. You're dropping me off in Chicago at

O'Hare and I'm catching the first flight to Los Angeles. I have
to set that creepy old man straight about a few things. Because
he is *not* driving me from my home, do you hear me?'

'I hear you,' he said, grinning at her. Couldn't help himself.

She looked away, over at Rudy. 'Would you mind keeping
him?'

'We're good. Although he's *no* help in a fight.' Hunt climbed
to his feet, wincing, and started for the door with the SIG
stuffed inside the overalls. 'I'll be back for you guys in a
minute – unless I get shot.'

'Wait, should we come with you?'

'No, no. It's safer for you if we separate. Just be ready.'

Hunt darted out the front door and down the driveway,
moving fast and low, his eyes flicking around. He still saw
no one. And no silver Crown Vic. *Where is the dude?* Hunt's
thoughts were on Annie as he started up the road toward
Breitbach's, running hard. Tim's daughter was a gutty one.
Hadn't hesitated to blow Norbis away. And now she was ready
to take the fight right to Herbie. No doubt about it, Annie
Ferrarro, aka Alicia Ferris, was definitely someone who you
wanted on your side.

There was no sign of the Crown Vic in Breitbach's parking
lot. No police cars either. Panting hard, Hunt jumped in Flynn's
fan and started it up. The radio was still tuned to the all-news
station in Dubuque that he'd been listening to on his way here.

That's how Hunt found out that everything had changed
within the past half-hour. It was all over. Senator Gary Dixon
had just taken himself out of the presidential race.

He'd been found dead on a bathroom floor in his Pasadena
mansion. Panorama Radio Network was calling it 'a tragic acci-
dental overdose of medically prescribed drugs'. Virtually every
other radio news outlet was labeling it 'an apparent suicide'.
Hunt heard all about it as he drove home to Washington in the
dark of night, Rudy riding shotgun. The two amigos were on
the road again. Actually, Hunt felt as if he'd never left the road.
That he was staring at the same endless ribbon of highway he'd
stared at crossing Wyoming, Nebraska and Iowa. That Balltown
never happened. He'd never found Annie. Never met Sharon
and Big Bob. Never got thrown down that flight of stairs by
the late John W. Norbis. But it had all happened. And now

California Senator Gary Dixon, Herbie Landau's hand-picked protégé, the man who virtually every pollster considered a shoo-in to be America's next president, was a goner.

By midnight Hunt had cleared Indianapolis and was starting east on Highway 70, which would take him across Ohio through Dayton and Columbus, then into western Pennsylvania before it dipped south into Maryland at Hagerstown and led him home.

Hunt drove, surfing the all-news radio stations for every morsel of breaking news he could find. There was no shortage of it. The presidential election had just been thrown into total chaos. This was an unprecedented political meltdown. American history in the making. Who was going to take Gary Dixon's place at the top of the GOP presidential ticket? Was Don Oakley, Dixon's beleaguered Democratic rival, now the presumed front-runner? Would the election be held on November seventh or postponed? Nobody knew.

It was also a media shitstorm. Dixon didn't leave a suicide note – which left everyone in the world free to draw their own conclusions. And so they had. They concluded that the candidate had chosen to die rather than face up to the explosive charges Tim Ferris had made about him in his viral video memoir. Charges that the mainstream media was now reporting in eager, lurid detail. Herbie was all over the Panorama airwaves trying to salvage his precious candidate's legacy. Imploring the other twenty-four-hour news outlets to change their 'salacious' tone, to show the Dixon family some respect. But there was no respect. Only a feeding frenzy that even the great Herbie Landau was powerless to stop.

There was also no way to stop the creep of speculation that maybe, just maybe, there was some kernel of truth to what Hunt had said in his webcast: That this so-called Unablogger murder rampage was a calculated effort by Dixon campaign operatives to bury Tim's ruinous revelations and destroy anyone and everyone who might have knowledge of them. Not that Hunt was off the hook yet. Far from it. Officially, he was still a dangerous fugitive. Still sat atop the Most Wanted list. But the credibility of Herbie's skilfully crafted scenario was being called into question. Already, LA-based reporters had descended on the Cabo San Lucas home of Fernando Bacerro – and found it burned to the ground. The 'tour guide'

had disappeared. Was he dead, too? Again, nobody knew. But
people were demanding answers.

Hunt drove, wondering if he ought to feel personally
responsible for Dixon's suicide. Because he didn't. It was
Tim's story. He'd simply been the messenger. Besides, it
wasn't *his* so-called mission that had led to the Bagley Bunch
killings in the summer of seventy-two. That was on Dixon
and the Reverend Jeremiah. It was on Herbie Landau. Not
that anything would ever happen to him. Or had it? '*I have
a dream*,' he'd told Hunt that night on the beach. A lifelong
dream to mold a man from childhood and install him in the
White House. And now his dream lay dead on a bathroom
floor in Pasadena with his pants down around his ankles.
Herbie had come up empty. Maybe, Hunt reflected, that's the
best justice there is for a man like Herbie Landau. As good
as it gets.

Hunt drove, his thoughts returning to Annie. Both of them
sucked at the goodbye thing, it had turned out.

'Are you going to be OK?' he'd asked her as they sat there
double-parked in front of the airline terminal at O'Hare.

'Of course I am,' Annie answered, her huge dark eyes avoiding
his.

'Do you need any money?'

'I'm good.'

'I didn't ask you how you were. I asked if you needed any
money.'

'Hunt, I'm fine.' Annie reached over and squeezed his hand.
'Have yourself a nice life, OK?' Then she grabbed her shoulder
bag, jumped out of the van and darted through the glass doors
into the terminal.

Hunt felt an ache inside of his chest as he watched her go.

After that, it was just him and Rudy and the open road. Dawn
found them passing through Wheeling, West Virginia. By then
a Pittsburgh radio station was reporting that the fugitive Reverend
Jeremiah Staunton had hop-scotched his way from Seoul, South
Korea to a flight bound for Rio de Janeiro. Since the US had
no extradition treaty with Brazil it was presumed that the tele-
vangelist intended to remain in Rio. No doubt he'd start all over
again, Hunt figured. Set up a storefront mission to attend to the
spiritual needs of Rio's homeless teens. Many of them boys.
The reverend would land on his feet. Probably even thrive again.

Right up until one of those brutalized, pissed-off kids stuck a knife in his ribs.

Soon, dude. Not today. Not tomorrow. But soon.

It was late in the morning by the time Hunt made it to DC. He found it strange to be back home again. He *had* no home. His apartment was gone. Everything he owned was gone. All he had were the borrowed clothes on his back, Flynn's van and Rudy. But a blogosphere buddy offered him the finished basement of his house on 33rd Place near the National Cathedral. Also a spare laptop so that Hunt could revive *huntandpeck.com*. His first posting in more than a week was a detailed 20,000 word account of everything that had happened since he'd first landed out in LA. Everything he could share, that is.

After he'd banged that out Hunt retained the services of Mick Augenblick, the feistiest civil liberties lawyer he knew, and turned himself in to the FBI. Voluntarily sat down with a roomful of agents in a windowless third-floor interview room in the J. Edgar Hoover Building on Pennsylvania Avenue. He presented them with the carton of crime scene evidence that Duane had mailed to Annie for safe keeping – minus its address sticker, of course. And then politely answered their questions for four solid hours. The lead agent, a buttoned-down Ken doll named Swibold, did most of the asking. Hunt gave him everything he wanted. Within limits. He didn't volunteer a word about Balltown or Waukon. Nothing about Annie Ferrarro, Sharon Combs, Big Bob or the hired killer John W. Norbis. He would not reveal how he'd uploaded Tim's memoir or staged his live webcast. Merely cited a 'source close to the Ferris family,' same as he had in his posting. Otherwise, Hunt couldn't have been more candid.

Special Agent Swibold was reasonably candid, too – in his own stiff, guarded Bureau-speak way. 'I can inform you gentlemen at this time that certain key elements of the criminal case against Mr Liebling are less concrete than were previously believed,' he told Hunt and Mick Augenblick. 'Certain allegations that Mr Liebling leveled in his webcast were not without merit. There is no security camera footage of him boarding or deplaning that red-eye flight to New York City the night of the Saddle Peak killings. And Flynn Leverett does verify that he was with her in Goleta when that plane took off. She has led Santa Barbara County Sheriff's deputies to the remote locale where she and Mr Liebling hid Tyrone Gilliam's Buick Le Sabre. Crime scene investigators have found fingerprints inside the Buick's trunk.' Swibold glanced down at the open file folder before him on the table. 'Prints matching those of a Joseph Michael Gillis and a Steven Patrick Vanesian, both reputed San Fernando Valley mob enforcers. These men are now wanted for questioning in connection with the Saddle Peak slayings.'

'Does that mean I've been cleared?' Hunt cut in anxiously.

Swibold wouldn't say. That wasn't how the Bureau did things. 'As of this moment,' he continued, 'no evidence links either Gillis or Vanesian to the New York and DC homicides. In regard to those crimes, the Bureau is currently pursuing numerous lines of inquiry.' Translation: they had shit. Swibold shuffled through the file folder for a computer printout. 'Certain parties of interest came to our attention this morning. A pair of John Does who've been found ditched in two different locales situated within one hour's drive of Dubuque, Iowa. One is a black man in his forties, height six-feet three. The other a white man of below average height, also in his forties. The black man had been shot twice in the face from extremely close range. The white man killed from behind with . . . a nail gun. Mr Liebling, can you provide us with any information about these two men?'

'You're fishing with a mighty wide net, aren't you?' Mick Augenblick blustered at him. 'What possible connection would my client, a Pulitzer Prize-winning journalist, have with two dead yokels in the cornfields of Iowa?'

Swibold's eyes remained locked on Hunt. 'You drove here cross-country from Goleta, California, correct?'

'Correct,' Hunt said, his jaw working on a fresh piece of Bazooka.

'Did you, or did you not, pass through Iowa along the way?'

'I think I did, but it's all kind of a blur now. Iowa's one of those really, really flat places, isn't it?'

Swibold continued to stare at him, not yielding, not blinking. 'You can't positively identify these two victims?'

'No, sir.'

'Well, neither can the Iowa State Police. When they tried to run their fingerprints they hit a great big firewall.' Swibold paused before he added, 'Security clearance issues, apparently.'

Meaning they were spooks. John W. Norbis – doubtless not his real name – and his partner had been with the CIA or some other covert agency.

Swibold closed the file now, his face impassive. 'Mr Liebling, the criminal investigation into your connection with these deaths has been officially closed. You are no longer considered a suspect. On behalf of the Bureau, I want to thank you for your cooperation.'

Hunt was hoping for a bit more out of the starchy bastard. Like, say, an apology for any inconvenience that the Bureau might have caused him by placing him atop the Most Wanted list next to Osama bin Laden. But he didn't press his luck. The guy had just told him he was now a free man.

Hell, Hunt even read all about it two hours later on the home pages of *The Washington Post* and *The New York Times*. That meant it had to be true. He celebrated his freedom by using his credit cards to buy himself some clothes and a new laptop.

He'd missed Mike O'Brien's burial in Far Rockaway, Queens. But he visited Mike's grave and laid flowers there. And he did make it to the memorial service that was held for Thayer at Riverside Church. Every heavy hitter in the worlds of print and broadcast journalism showed up, as did two former US presidents and dozens of senators, cabinet officials and foreign dignitaries. As Hunt was filing out, Thayer's attorney gave him his card and asked him to stop by. Hunt promised he would just as soon as he took care of his family.

He arranged to have Brink and Luze transported up to Brattleboro so they could be buried next to his parents. Hunt was not alone at their funeral service. Luze's cousin from the Bronx made the trip. So did several of Luze's fellow teachers and a surprising number of her students. While he was in Brattleboro Hunt stopped off at his old high school to thank his journalism teacher, Mrs McKenna, for her support. She was so happy to see Hunt alive and well that she broke down and cried in his arms.

He was too late for C.C. Reiter's funeral in Radnor, Pennsylvania. And C.C.'s grief-stricken parents were not particularly pleased to see him when he showed up. But they told him where she was buried and he visited her grave and left flowers. The Reiters had already emptied out C.C.'s Georgetown apartment and driven her hot red Alfa Romeo home. It was sitting in their driveway. They were planning to sell it. Didn't want it around. Hunt asked them if they'd mind selling it to him. They didn't mind.

After that, he and Rudy hit the open road together again, top down, monster stereo blasting C.C.'s amazing mixes of Stax oldies by Otis Redding, Sam and Dave, and the incomparable Booker T and the MGs, whose 'Green Onions' he listened to at least ten times while he was crossing Ohio.

Hunt listened to the presidential campaign news, too. After frantic negotiations the leaders of the Republican and Democratic National Committees had agreed to push back Election Day by two weeks so that voters could make an informed choice about the GOP's new standard bearer. Gary Dixon's somewhat drab running mate, Governor Tucker Mayne of Indiana, now topped the ticket. The party had drafted a veteran Southern senator with a boatload of foreign policy experience as his running mate. Two nationally televised debates between Mayne and Don Oakley had been scheduled. Pollsters were calling the Mayne-Oakley contest dead even. Pundits were proclaiming it the most dramatic White House race ever.

Hunt listened, but he found himself no longer caring. He'd given everything he had to the campaign – and then some. He was over it.

She was up on a six-foot ladder when he got there, Paslode nailer in hand, shingling away ... *Pop* ... *Pop* ... Rudy jumped out of the car and ran to her, circling the ladder excitedly. Annie scrambled down and made a big fuss over him.

Hunt carefully tucked his wad of Bazooka in the Alfa's ashtray before he moseyed over to her.

'You shaved,' she observed, studying him with those big brown eyes of hers, so calm, so aware.

'Hey, I even showered, too. What do you think?'

'I think you still need to do something about your hair.' She climbed back up the ladder and resumed her shingling ... *Pop* ... *Pop* ...

'How was Los Angeles?'

'Pretty much as horrible as I remembered.'

'And Herbie?'

'I found out why my dad never told me he was my grandfather. It was shame, pure and simple. Dad *hated* that Herbie's
blood was inside of him. He didn't want me lugging around
the same awful burden. So he kept it a secret and begged
Herbie to go along. Which Herbie did even though he claims
it broke his heart. As if the old bastard has a heart. Get this,
he offered me a job. Wants to groom me for a really, really
important role in the Panorama corporate hierarchy. Can you
believe that?'

'What did you tell him?'

'To stay the hell out of my life. I told him if he or anyone
who works for him ever comes near me again I just might
tiptoe into his bedroom some night – with a fully loaded *nail
gun.*'

'And what did he say?'

'Not a word. His mouth was open but nothing came out. I
think he was actually speechless. Which has to be a first,'
Annie said proudly . . . *Pop* . . . *Pop* . . . 'So what brings you
back to the Midwest?'

'The little dude. I was thinking he'd be happier here with
you. Plus I never really . . . Would you please come down off
of that damned ladder so I can talk to you like a person?'

'Are you getting bossy with me?'

'I said please, didn't I?'

Grudgingly, she climbed back down. Her eyes fastened on
to his, waiting.

'I never really got a chance to thank you properly. I was
serious before about running that pipe down to the cellar for
your darkroom. I'd be happy to stick around for a couple of
days and do it for you.'

'That's really not necessary, Hunt. Besides, aren't you all
wrapped up in the election?'

'Funny you should mention that. I'm not, actually. Still
need to get a few things straight in my mind, I guess. I don't
have anywhere to live. And nothing more than some clothes,
a great collection of music and a new laptop, which I still
can't figure out how to work . . .'

'That's not a problem. I can school you.'

'Wait, there's more. I just found out from Thayer's attorney that the old man left ten million dollars to *huntandpeck.com*. I can expand my whole operation now. Hire full-time staff writers. I'll be totally independent.'

'That sounds like a dream come true, Hunt.'

'You'd think so, wouldn't you?'

'Well, yeah. That's who you are, isn't it?'

'It's who I *was*.'

'And who are you now?'

'That's what I have to work out. I guess I just need to slow down for a while. Which – I don't know if you noticed – isn't something I know how to do.'

'Again, not a problem. I can school you. Just remember to breathe. It's really not so . . .' She tilted her head at him curiously. 'Why are you staring at me that way?'

'I was just thinking about your mother.'

'What about my mother?'

'She must have been one hell of a good-looking woman.'

Annie slid neatly into his arms. She was a perfect fit. Somehow, he'd known she would be. They kissed, softly and tenderly. That part was pretty perfect, too.

She reached up and stroked his cheek. 'Every single time a car drove by the house I'd look to see if it was you. I never stopped hoping. Even though I had no real reason to.'

'Yeah, you did. You had every reason to.' Hunt gazed at her, losing himself in those huge brown eyes. 'But we'd better get something straight . . .'

'Is this about your bubble gum?'

'What *about* my bubble gum?'

'Nothing. My bad. You were saying . . .?'

'I don't have a very good track record. The sad truth is, these things never seem to work out.'

'Of course not. You hadn't met me yet. You won't have that problem any more.'

'You sound awfully sure.'

'Oh, I'm sure,' Annie told him.

Then she took Hunt Liebling by the hand, led him inside her little farmhouse and showed him just how sure she was.

LaVergne, TN USA
04 March 2010
175010LV00001B/2/P

C